Also by

Veil & Shadow Series
The Breaking
The Bleeding

(**Prequel** to *The Anavrin Series*- Stand Alone)
Little Red Rising

The Anavrin Series
A Kingdom Of Crowns And Malice
A Throne Of Chains And Fate

Eventide Series
Falling Even
Rising Tide

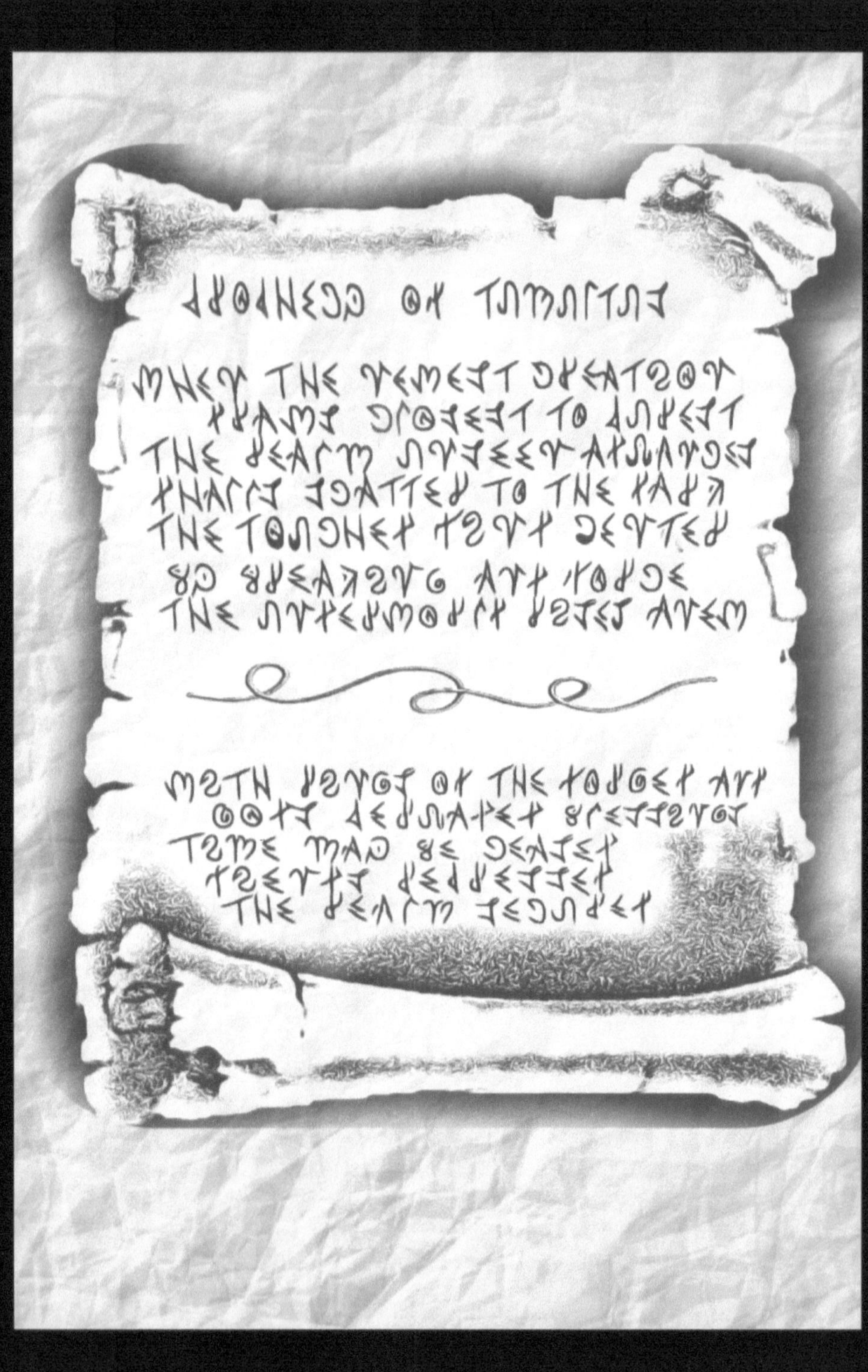

The Breaking

Anexa O.J Saphire

DOCHAIS
THE DEAD ZONE
MAXUM MANOR
UHDAN RIVER
SCOTTSDALE ESTATE
MANX RIVER
GHASTINGTON
LARNACH CITY
Pawn Shop
Kraigen's Diner
BRIE'S HOUSE
SKULLHEAD BASIN
ZANE'S PLACE
BÉAL BASIN
CRAVEVILLE
THE MAUSOLEUM

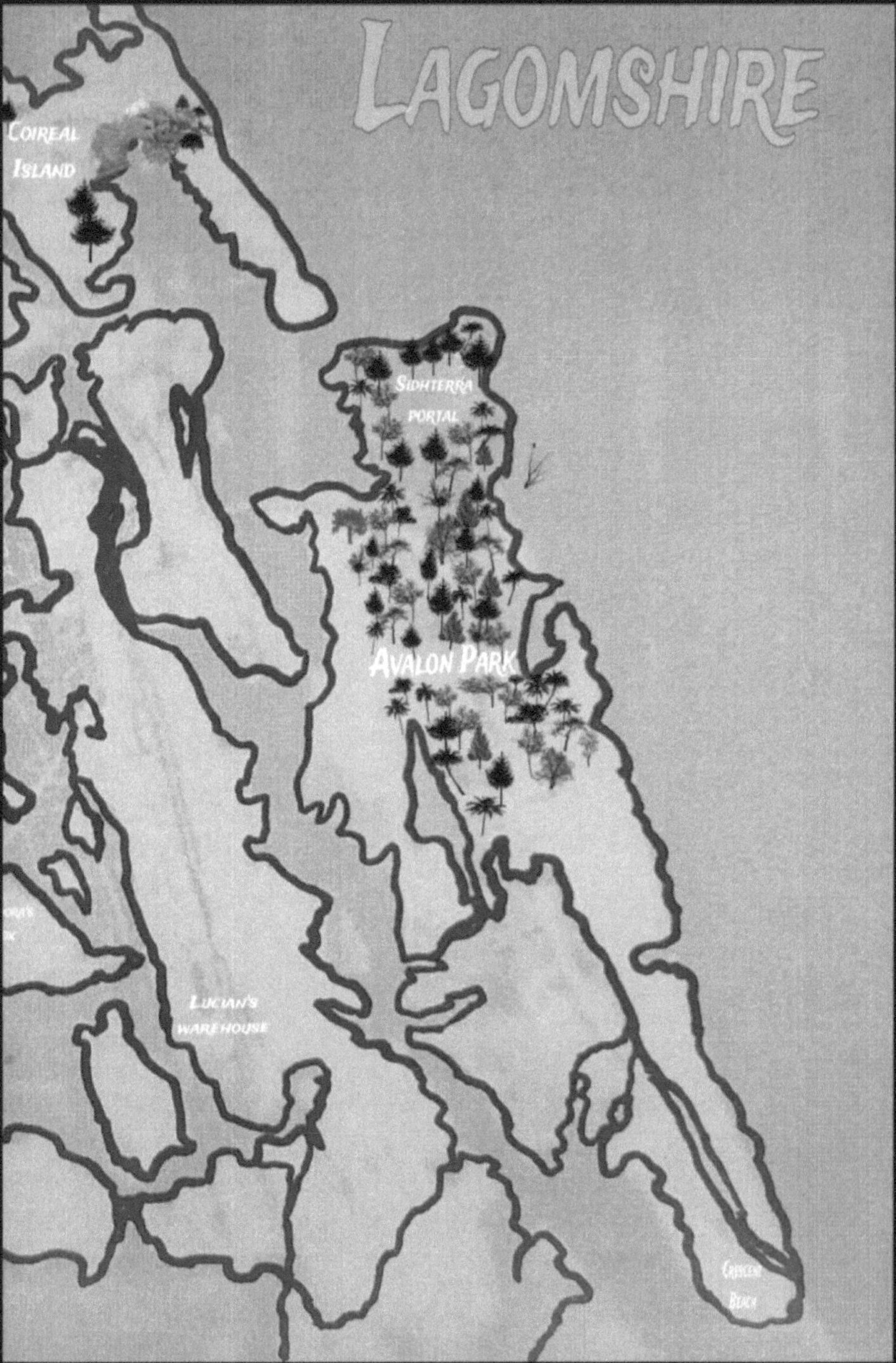

LAGOMSHIRE
COIREAL ISLAND
SIDHTERRA PORTAL
AVALON PARK
LUCIAN'S WAREHOUSE
CRESCENT BEACH

A*uthor's Note:*

Some Trigger Warnings

This book is a work of fiction. Any likeness to that of actual beings, living or deceased, is coincidental or embellished to tell a fictional tale.

It contains scenes that may be uncomfortable for some readers.

Including, but not limited to... violence, blood, explicit sex, alcohol abuse, and implied and/or unwanted sexual advances.

Some characters in this book are based off of real-world placement and classical works but do not strictly adhere to any one folklore.

The creative uses of such are fully fictional and not to be taken as fact.

Prologue

Hayden

There was a cold sweat on his forehead. Even as he ran, every muscle in his legs burning, every breath a struggle, he knew it was too late.

The life he had known would no longer exist.

If only he could push, just a little farther. One more task to finish.

He reached out, only just short. His dark eyes closed. He had failed.

I awoke with a start. The darkness all around me added to my disorientation. The dream had been so real.

They generally were when you were a foreshadower.

Trying to gather my bearings, I felt around for the light that sat on the corner of my nightstand.

Scrubbing at the crust gathered in the corner of my eyes, sleep threatened to pull me back under.

I grabbed the journal from the bedside table and attempted to write down exactly what I remembered.

In the quiet darkness of my room, it was still like trying to catch water in a spaghetti strainer.

I knew that not all I dreamt denoted future events, but foreshadowing's always had telltale signs.

The edges were sharper and more crisp rather than blurred. When I could feel the events rather than seeing them, that was a good indicator to pay attention to the details.

Honing a gift like foreshadowing took practice. I had practiced often enough to know this one needed extra effort put into recalling even the minute details.

The man in this dream was frantic.

Clutching my chest, the air felt heavy, and my heart hammered away. Anxiety twisting in the pit of my gut.

Gods, I was thirsty. Snatching a bottle of water off the nightstand, I took several long swigs until it came up empty.

Just breathe. There's no danger here.

A few minutes of deep breathing and concentration later, the panic attack was over.

Feeling other people's emotions when I was recalling a foreshadowing was a horrible drawback.

The man in my dream wasn't worried about himself. It was much bigger than that.

It unsettled me to my core.

I knew that this foreshadowing was of great significance, but had no idea why.

In the morning, it would be time to pay a visit to the seer.

Chapter One

Lara

I opened my shop, just like every other Tuesday morning.

Humid summer winds blew the briny scent of the Manxtas River inland, clearing out the last of the morning mist lingering in the air.

The sun lying just visible behind a scattering of clouds. It gave the start of the day a beautiful canvas upon which to paint.

My key to the shop was, of course, at the bottom of my suitcase of a purse. The smell of coffee and the fresh baked croissants I'd gotten before heading in today made my stomach grumble.

Hands full, I fished through discarded receipts and make-up that rarely got used before closing my fingers around the key ring.

Many trinkets had been attached over the years, but it only held three keys.

Home, the shop, and one of secrets.

The door creaked open, and the sound of a small bell chimed overhead.

Shelves lined the outer walls of the shop and books took up a third of my store. Pandora's Box was my life's devotion.

In an area in the back by the counter were the oldest and rarest books in my inventory. These were not for sale. I had collected them over the years for my personal library.

They smelled of must, vanilla, and of almond suffused with parchment. Undertones of floral scents wafted through the tiny space as dust moats fluttered around in the light coming from the large glass windows.

A street sweeper blew the door to the shop slightly ajar. The tinkling bell at the entrance made my eyes glaze as it triggered my "Sight".

"Hayden". A small gasp escaped me. Worry anchored the dread deep in my chest.

As quickly as it came on, it was gone. Shaking the feeling from my system, I focused on more pleasant things.

The smell of coffee beckoned to me.

Putting the cup to my lips, that first sip of the day was nirvana.

The butter from the flaky croissant produced a residue on my fingertips. It made opening the register's computer program nearly impossible.

Wiping one hand on the side of my dress, I popped the last piece of the delicious pastry into my mouth with my other hand.

Rising from my seat behind the counter, I strolled farther into the shop. I needed to get things ready for the day.

White sage bundles laid in a basket on a table with incense, crystals, and a few baubles. Picking up a bundle of the sage and lighting it to smudge the air, tranquility filled my senses.

Morning had always been my favorite time of day. I relished in the tidying up before any customers would arrive.

The crystals sang to me here in the quiet, peaceful time of reflection that was the start of a new day and possibilities.

That's what I needed at this moment. Peace from my thoughts.

Judging by the light coming through the window in that last vision, Hayden wouldn't be arriving for another half an hour.

The book I'd been reading on ancient prophecies laid on the table in the reading area. It was bound in leather, and the parchment was so old that it practically crumbled apart.

Gathering up my coffee and the book, I made myself comfortable settling down on one of the big purple puff chairs in the middle of the shop.

Sometimes, as a seer, it was the waiting for things to come about that was the most exasperating part. More so than the events themselves.

Opening the book to where I'd left off the day before would occupy time until my dear friend brought the news of whatever his foreshadowing gifts showed him that troubled him so.

I knew the bigger picture, but it wasn't for me to promulgate. Hayden's foreshadowing would help bring additional detailed pieces of the larger puzzle together.

The positive feeling from the white sage smoke permeated every corner of the small metaphysical shop.

Finishing the end of a chapter, I looked up to see Hayden's blue, worn out sneakers coming down the street. Faded brown dream journal in hand.

Brushing my long, auburn hair off my pale face, I glanced in the small mirror at the side of the shelves and shook my head. My hair had come free from the twisted I'd put it in this morning already. I never had any luck with my locks staying in place.

Oh well. Replacing the bookmark so I wouldn't lose my page, I set the frail book down on the counter.

As the door opened, the smell of garlic and onions from the pizzeria a few shops down came floating in. Heat reddening my face at a memory that came racing to my forethoughts.

Me and Hayden had gone on exactly one date in the past.

It was comfortable. It was pleasant. However, it wasn't a stomach full of butterflies' experience.

We even attempted a good night kiss.

It had been warm and wet and everything a kiss should be but still no spark of desire came from it... for me at least.

He could have done with a bit more kissing, but I wasn't interested in him that way after the chemistry didn't ripen.

Since then, it was often a bit of an inside joke between us.

If I were being honest, Hayden was a much better friend than a potential love interest.

I wasn't his type either, but I *got him* so well that he would often pine for something more.

"Good morning, Lar". His blue hazel eyes rose to meet my vibrant green ones, a seerer's trait. Mimicking his bright, impish smile with one of my own, I hovered near the counter. "I would ask if you're surprised to see me, but well..." he laughed. The sound suited him, "We both know you're not."

"Nope. I knew you were coming around today," Scanning his appearance, I noticed his shirt was half tucked in and the bags under his eyes... "What I don't understand is why you never come to see me for just a social visit?" Under my scrutiny, his shoulders drooped.

Turning my back to him, I rummaged through the papers cluttering the counter by the register. The mirror on the wall behind it revealed his guilty nervousness.

I had small mirrors all over the shop. Seer's couldn't "see" anything in regards to their own lives. It was only smart to make certain I could be aware of my surroundings.

He shuffled his feet and fidgeted with a piece of the leather binding on his dream journal. The stitching was frayed and his fingers twirled circles around the loose threads.

Finally looking up at me from beneath his long, smoldering eyelashes, he said, "You know I think the world of ya, don't you, Lar?"

In an intentionally slow move, I rotated to glare in his direction.

Glowering at him for another moment, just to make him sweat a bit, I couldn't hold out any longer.

A brilliant smile stretched my cheeks and made my face tight. Relief visibly washed through him.

"I am sorry, Lara. I promise to make a more valiant effort to come around and see you," he said. I grinned weakly. He noticed. "What is it?", he asked. Hesitantly looking up to meet his eyes, I said nothing. "Do you think... or know that I'm not going to?" he demanded. "What did you see, honey?"

"Hayden, it's about your latest foreshadowing." My voice was quiet but steady.

I could tell that his heart had skipped a few beats and then began to race as his eyes widened. We'd came to this point a lot quicker than usual and his body went rigid.

Usually, I liked to toy and play back and forth games a lot more before giving him the information he sought.

Hayden's eyes never left mine. I knew my emotions were written all over my face, but being a skilled Seer, I gave nothing away.

I was the universe in a human vessel.

He'd told me before that my skin always carried a faint smell of raspberries, burnt almonds and something he could never place.

The smell of the cosmos on my skin made me feel like I wasn't of this world the way other beings were.

Being a seer was not an easy thing. It gave the illusion of inclusion but trapped me on the outside of the looking glass.

Foreshadowing seemed like a parlor trick in comparison. Foreshadower's dreamt of the more solid future events, but Seer's, they Saw the many paths that came with each decision.

Like most Seers, I didn't interact very much with people. It was a terrible burden to "Know." Every little thing could be a choice that changed lives if I wasn't careful.

I had my shop in which a stray customer would come in from time to time.

They would ask for recommendations; which crystal would work best or book they should try, or which herbs would enhance an outcome?

Sometimes it was difficult for me to decide whether or not to give them the advice that would lead them in one direction or another. I felt it was too much like playing a part in fate.

Beyond the patrons of my small metaphysical shop, I liked my solitude... for the most part.

"Here", he thrust his dream journal into my hands, but my eyes were already unfocused and "Seeing" elsewhere.

The journal fell to the floor with a soft thud. I wobbled slightly and then collapsed forward into Hayden's arms.

"Lara", he prodded. "Lar, talk to me sweetie." Gently brushing the soft hair from my face, he placed his hands on either side of my cheeks. "Lar, come on honey", he repeated.

I could hear him just fine. Getting my mind to refocus on the present was a bit more difficult.

"Wake up, Miss Styne, or I will kiss you and you won't even get to enjoy it," he teased.

My eyes fluttered. Hayden's flirtatious quip pulled brought me back from the vision's grip.

"Oh my! Hayden", I breathed, barely above a whisper. "It's not good!" Unshed tears rimmed my eyes. "It's not good at all."

"We've had not good before", he chided with a weak smile.

I didn't return it. Grimacing, my gaze dropped to my hands.

"Never like this." My hands were absentmindedly playing with the ribbon on my understated green dress. Hayden waited patiently for me to continue. "We will need everyone we know... and possibly some who we've never met! The Breaking will be happening soon."

I knew he hadn't a clue of what I meant by that, but he sat quietly, waiting for me to continue.

Again, my eyes went unfocused, but this time I remained steady. "Hayden, we're about to meet more of the Shadowrealm than we ever knew existed."

Raising his left eyebrow nearly to meet his dark brown hair line, I felt his stared go through me, not really seeing me at all.

Assuming he was remembering his dream, it was the foreshadowing that ushered him to seek my counsel in the first place.

His color turned pale and chalky, and I hoped that his thoughts wouldn't bring his breakfast back up.

The mop that belonged in the shop had been thrown out last week and I hadn't gotten a new one yet.

Coming back to himself, he swiftly dashed over to the pitcher of water I had next to the coffee maker.

Pouring it into a cup with shaky hands, he spilled it all over the countertop and had to grab a few paper towels to clean it up.

After downing two glasses, he noticed I hadn't fully recovered yet myself and brought me a glass of water that I gratefully sipped, taking a moment or two to gather my wits about me.

Picking up a tiger's eye crystal from the table to help myself focus, it brought me a sense of calm.

After several brushes over the stone and a few steadying breaths, I looked back at Hayden with my knowing green eyes.

"There is a battle coming. The shadowrealm has reached its tipping point," I said with a rush of emotion.

This wasn't a vision. It was *the* vision. The one that had awoken my seeker abilities when I was just a child.

Now it contained more details and more possible outcomes, but it all meant one thing. An uprising.

Being a passive soul, I didn't like it when gifters and things in the shadowrealm clashed.

Hayden had known this about me for a while and his eyes filled with sorrow. Taking a step towards me, he placed a hand gently upon my shoulder.

"Are you sure?" he prodded, already guessing the answer.

"Well, with what you yourself have foreshadowed," I gave him a knowing glance, "and with what I have "Seen", I can only come to the point in the road at which those who make key choices choose. You know that."

Glancing at a small mirror hanging on the side of a shelf, tiny lines appeared on my forehead, around my eyes, and at the corners of my mouth.

The woe in my heart was engraved on my normally delicate features.

"Then I get different blurred scenarios." My vision was unfocused again.

My hands flew up to cover my mouth. "Oh my," I said after a few long seconds.

"What is it?" he asked.

I didn't suppose he really wanted to hear it, but he had to know.

"Well, you're not gonna like it", my lips pulled up on one side. "It's Bastian".

Hayden's whole body tensed. Jaw muscles locked. His fists began to clench.

I tried not to look up at him. Instead, I pushed forward with what I had to say.

"He's okay. He damaged a laboratory. The laboratory that, well..." I hesitated. "It's part of the reason we will be joining in on this battle of good and evil."

Completely stoic, he didn't speak.

Taking a slight step toward him, I laid my hand on his shoulder this time.

"He did a good thing, Hayden. The papers and experiments were mostly destroyed, but not all of them. And... well, he will be here in a few minutes."

Shocked reigned in his face. I knew his eyes searched mine for some sort of joke, but he wouldn't find one.

"I will let him tell you what is going on. I'll just fill in the gaps", I said, then walked swiftly away to locate a book.

He didn't say anything. Standing statue still for a minute or two, I could see the thoughts bouncing around his head.

He just stood there, mouth gaping and heart pounding in his ears, looking completely dumbfounded.

When I returned from the shelves, he'd opened his mouth to say something and closed it again audibly.

He needed to come to grips on his own terms with what I'd presented to him.

Opening his mouth a second time, he snapped it shut.

The large, leatherbound book I'd brought back with me was old. Covered in dust. And smelled of must and parchment.

Glancing through my lashes over the top of the book after a few minutes of silence, he'd finally found his voice on the third try.

"Do you mean to tell me," he said, spitting venom with each words, "that my stupid cousin and his need to prove himself better than Dhalls actually has something positive to add to a situation?"

Chapter Two

Briella

The alley was too dark for any Dhall to be comfortable there. Thick, heavy air filled it with a sense of danger that most shied away from.

The term, Dhall had been coined for the humans with no magics long ago. No one knew why.

Three figures stood cloaked in shadow, towering over a visibly shaking young woman.

I tried to suppress a grin as I inched stealthily upon the scene.

By rapidly approaching, letting them catch my scent, I knew the eager males mistook my proximity as a gift. They'd assumed I hadn't been paying attention to my surroundings.

Having the ability to feel the energies vibrating around me meant I was always acutely aware of what was happening within a fifty-foot radius.

I'd been counting on their miscalculations. It was almost too easy.

Closing in as quickly as a flash of lightning, I was fast upon them.

Up close, the girl's terror was a living thing. It nearly overcame my demon senses.

Humans could be so annoying. It was a wonder how they ever managed to survive.

Refocusing my thoughts, I tried to concentrate on the attackers.

The smell of garbage in the dark alley and the acrid smell of fear hung sharp in the night's air.

Fear always left a tangy scent in my nostrils. One that I could twist for aid or retribution. It just depended on my mood that day.

Turning away and facing the would-be killers, I had a better chance to look them over for weaknesses.

In the light of the full moon, I could see all three circling me now, closing ranks between them. Stupid fools.

Entranced by my Conservatrix demon's beauty, these unsuspecting males still hadn't realized they'd become the prey.

With a quick glance at each one, I weighed my options.

My empathic abilities, coupled with my training, told me that these hunters were still new to the game. They'd lack control and their hunger and lust would override their capabilities.

The pheromones I emanated were still working their magics. The Meathlu's seemed unknowingly powerless in her presence.

They were vessels for future demons to take root in this realm. It was my calling to end them before that ever happened.

Behind me, the young girl found her voice. A single word rang out... "STOP!"

It wasn't really a good time for it, but she had no clue about such things. Humans never did. Their emotions and fight or flight responses overrode anything that remotely resembled common sense.

The girl's ill-timed scream was enough to snap the Meathlu's from their trance.

A breeze fluttered in the humid night air, framing my flowing hair that cascaded around my beautiful face. It was all a trap. My looks were an alluring package filled with a deadly center.

I turned toward the girl for the briefest of glares. A moment that seemed endless.

My lungs filled with the humid air. Its suffocating presence was another sticky obstacle to overcome.

The Meathlu's shadows crept eerily in the light shining from the moon.

A loud scream from the girl ripped the night in two. Dreadfully useless.

With a quick lunge, I grabbed one of the Meathlu's by the neck and twisted him madly. I used his body as a springboard to jump towards the girl.

Finding my mark, I kicked the back of the second Meathlu's head to the ground. He rebounded upward, catching me across the face.

Blood trickled down my full lips as they curled into a slight smile. Snarling, the guttural, primal sound fed my rage.

My piercing hazel eyes stared directly into his as I sliced my razor-sharp nails across his throat, ending his horrible existence.

Quickly wielding around for the third, my eyes went wide as I caught him mid strike to the defenseless teen.

A vengeful fury awakened deep within me. Heat began to generate off my body in waves of power.

In a whirlwind of ultrafast dexterity, I snatched him from where he stood.

Burly as he was, I still outmatched him. Throwing him into the wall of a building first, I then slammed him hard onto the concrete road.

It was a game of cat and mouse, and I was a lioness.

He'd gotten past me, and I was mad at myself. His pain was my payback.

Lost to the vengefulness, the tiniest of whimpers came from behind me.

The small sound was all that was needed to help me refocus my priorities. It wasn't the poor girl's fault. I'd fucked up.

I did my best not to give in to the dark side of what I was. Mercy was where I always tried to live, not vengeance.

I liked to see things from every angle. Consider all outcomes and points of view.

Sometimes the demon in me overrode empathy but that was when I needed to rein myself in the most.

With a sharp blow to the head, the last Meathlu's life was extinguished.

Heedful of the girl's terror, I approached the wounded young woman cautiously.

What a sight this must have been for her. No one would ever believe her recount of the events, but she would never forget them... if she managed to survive.

Bending down cautiously, I swooped her up into my arms as though she weighed no more than a tabby cat.

Without haste, I ran swiftly to deposit her at the front entrance to the medical house around the block.

There would be no more I could do for her. That wasn't part of the job.

Thelzion would be rather upset about my little nighttime excursion this evening. He didn't like me hunting while he was away.

Funny really. I was quite capable of taking care of myself, but he was still a bit overprotective of me, his mate.

Thelzion was a Donnchadh. Some people might call him a vampire, but he was much higher up the demon chain of command than that.

As a true demon, his very purpose in this life was to seek out demon hunters like me and eliminate them before they could grow into their full demon hunter potential.

Donnchadh were the protectors of future "Evil". They were the police of the shadowrealm.

Meathlu, as they were often referred to, were demons born of humans. Some knew what they were destined to become, but most did not. They were the darker side of humanity.

Dhalls were regular humans without any gifts of magics, who knew nothing of the shadowrealm. They used the term Evil like they really understood what the word meant.

Meathlu's, even unknowing in their human form, tended to act out. They were your serial killers, your rapists, your murderers, just to name a few of the darker elements that the shadowrealm could unleash on the white picket fence, day-to-day, Dhalls.

They didn't have demonic powers yet though. Not in human form.

If they managed to die a natural human death, they would be resurrected with full demonic powers.

If a demon hunter, like a Conservatrix Demon, such as myself, could infect them, they were lost to the Underworld for eternity.

They didn't even have to die from it. A deep scratch from my nails would be all it took.

They could even live out a full life. In the end of their days, the infection's mark damned them forever.

The underworld was not what humans thought of as Hell. That was more of a fairy tale they told themselves to get others to be good and follow the rules of human society.

The real Underworld was much worse.

Lucky for them, most of humanity never even got a glimpse of it.

Humans slept better in their beds without knowing of all things that went bump in the night.

That's where all of the dangerous things lived. Out of sight. In the shadowrealm.

Chapter Three

Hayden

I sat seething in the corner of Lara's shop, a warm mug of coffee in hand, just thinking about all the asinine things my cousin had done since we were kids.

While I had always tried to be a good Scottsdale, my cousin, Bastian, was always dragging the family name through the mud. His gift was a nuisance when we were growing up.

Bastian was a deblocker. He could unlock or clear things.

It started off with him doing trivial things, like getting us out of the playpen or getting us cookies that our grandma had locked away.

As we grew older, Bastian became more mischievous. The police would end up bringing him home to the Manor after one of his antics had gone awry.

He wasn't that good at it back then and he would often break in somewhere and be unable to control his abilities long enough to get back out.

As it was with a lot of gifters, dhalls often bullied and made fun of him. He didn't take kindly to that and when push came to shove, it was usually the dhall who ended up on the losing side.

Bastian began to detest anyone who wasn't privy to the shadowrealm. He'd started using his gifts to his own advantage, never bothering with right or wrong or how it affected others.

My cousin and I hadn't spoken in nearly four years. The distance between us was of my own making and I wasn't really looking forward to it now. Especially in reference to my latest foreshadowing.

The tinkling bell above the door to the shop sounded. Lara went to the front of the store to greet the newcomer while I remained where I was.

Trying to rally my nerves enough, I wanted to face the situation head on.

I could hear them saying their hellos and knew I should probably get up to go meet my cousin at the door.

Setting my mug of coffee on the side table, I got to my feet. If I didn't man up now, how could I expect any better from him?

Ambling towards their voices, about to turn the corner, I stopped in my tracks.

It wasn't Lara I heard. It was another female's voice that had just spoken.

The sound was like the most beautiful musical notes I had ever heard. It had a dancing life of its own, even if nothing was being sung.

I didn't know Bastian was bringing anyone with him. It was strange that Lara hadn't mentioned it, though she must have known.

I turned the corner and saw the female whose voice enchanted my soul.

To say she was merely beautiful would have been an insult. Her face was demure and yet somehow fierce. There was a sheen to her pale skin that I couldn't place.

She and Bastian caught sight of me at the same time. Wonderful. Here we go.

"Here he is, Noella," Bastian said. "My cousin, Hayden, I have been telling you about."

She looked at me then. Her long eyelashes batted down once in a slow, seductive way.

I stood there, bewildered. I had seen this enchantress before. Only I hadn't been awake at the time.

Taking a step forward, Bastian extended his hand to me, but I couldn't help staring past him.

I stared at the girl with the beautiful face whose eyes danced like a candle flame.

I knew her. Felt drawn to her though I had never met her before. Her magiks were ensnaring.

It was then I caught the scent of her. A smell of Patchouli and earth and... Shadowrealm.

She was in my last foreshadowing. Had been a key part of it, but I couldn't remember exactly how.

Somehow, wherever she touched my vision, she blurred and spun away from my memory.

Sashaying over to us, she stood next to Bastian.

"Hello Hayden. I'm Noella," she said, extending her fingers.

Taking my hand in hers briefly, it was long enough for me to feel a current zap me back to my senses.

Lara stepped forward, placing herself between us with the air of a lion tamer. Everyone's eyes fixed on her, waiting silently for her direction.

"If you all would be so kind as to follow me to the sitting area," Lara said. "I will fill in the gaps where I can as you each tell your part of this tale.

Chapter Four

Briella

I had been lost in thought, thinking of my beloved's return.

I'd felt... fragmented in his absence. Not incomplete precisely, but just like some part of me was missing.

He was my Mate. The bond of a Mate was stronger than the heavens. When I could wrap my arms around Thelzion, I'd feel whole again.

We spoke often through a witch window, a small device made from black Obsidian. So long as our hearts remained connected, we could reach each other at any time.

I hadn't been able to reach him for a couple of days now and was beginning to worry.

This trip had taken him away from me for much longer than he'd ever been gone before. It was a necessary quest for information about Lucian's next move.

Thelzion and I had encountered a demon a few weeks back that had divulged to us a bigger storm was coming.

That the one called Lucian was orchestrating a huge demonic rise. The demon had succumbed to his injuries before we could get any more information from him though.

Thelzion and I knew the ways of Lucian all too well.

Lucian was a Donnchadh, like Thelzion, only he really enjoyed his work. He liked mayhem and relished in the creation of turmoil.

He was assigned a one hundred square mile radius to maintain by Saevus, a higher demon in the underworld.

Unlike most Donnchadh, Lucian didn't mind using or losing Meathlu to suit his own causes. Given an opportunity, he would use Full demons as well.

Far from being a protector to the Meathlu in his charge, Lucian only saw them as beings to further his own unsightly goals.

He was the truest essence of evil.

He was the thing that the Dhalls demon stories were made from.

Chapter Five

Hayden

We walked towards the back of the shop.

A bunch of odd, mismatched chairs and poofs sat in an informal semicircle in one corner of the room. The Nag Champa incense and white sage Lara had lit earlier lingered in the small, cozy space.

It was not as bright as the rest of the shop. A bluish glow lit the area in a soothing manner.

Picking a seat and settling in, we silently looked to one another to start, but no one seemed inclined to go first.

"Does anyone want to jump in here?" Lara asked.

No one said anything. The awkwardness of it was too much for us to find our voices.

"Okay, then", she said. Pointing one of her ivory pale fingers at Bastian, she began. "How about you tell us how you and Noella met?"

Bastian's eyes slid to mine. I sat with one leg casually propped up on my other, studiously fidgeting with the frayed hem of my worn-out blue jeans.

Taking a deep, steadying breath, he began. "I was being me", he said. "Stupid and ignorant of everyone and everything around me."

I raised my head from staring at my shoes, intrigue at the accountability my cousin had taken.

"I had deblocked my way into a rich Dhall's house one night" he continued. "I had been casing it for about a week."

Releasing a long and exaggerated breath, I shook my head in disappointment.

"I know, cuz. I was a jerk", he said. "WAS being the keyword." Opening my mouth to reply, I closed it again with a glare from Lara. "The truth is, I was lost. I had no direction, no purpose."

With a quick glance at Noella, her eyes steadily staring back at him, he continued. "She had been waiting for me, sitting in the dark kitchen of that house. I turned on the lights and nearly jumped out of my skin."

He turned back to her. "You really didn't need the theatrics", he said with a sly grin. "I would have done whatever a pretty girl like you would have asked me to." Lara bustled in her seat.

"Ahhh, yes", she said, "but how would I have known whether you'd follow through once I was no longer in your sight?" There was a little tinkling laugh in her voice. "I thought shock was the best way to get you to really hear me, to listen and consider what I was telling you."

It was me who spoke this time in a bit lighter tone. "And just why did you want to speak to this jackass? Why would you stalk him?" With a cunning gaze from Noella to Lara and back, I said, "I'm guessing that's how you knew where he'd be."

I gestured to Lara, looking for confirmation. She nodded, ever so slightly, but I saw it.

"Very perceptive, Hayden", Noella confirmed, a mild lament in her tone. "How much do you understand of the shadowrealm? Not just the humans with gifts, but the real shadows that inhabit this plane?"

I glanced away. Noella was burning a hole in the side of my face with her scrutiny.

A moment or two passed before I spoke. I needed a minute. Some time to wrap my head around a few of the odd occurrences from over the years.

"I've seen things", I said. "Things that really have no logical explanation."

Picking morosely at my jeans, I resisted the urge to look up at her.

To her credit, she waited patiently, and the awkwardness helped push me to continue.

"It'd be nice to be able to pretend they didn't have any validity. It sure would make it easier to sleep at night... But that isn't the case, is it?" From below my lashes, I peered up at her.

Noella smiled softly. Her Hazel eyes danced in the dim light of the shop.

She had a sapphire blue ring around those flaming eyes, and I let a small breath escape my lips when I'd noticed.

"Demons do exist, Hayden," she said. "And mixlings are more common than you would think."

Lara reached over and took my hand, giving it a gentle squeeze.

I searched her inscrutable face. Not for an explanation, but for some form of acknowledgement to an unasked question.

Bastian remained quiet; his eyes fixed on Noella with a sort of awed veneration.

It was both unnerving and mollifying. Did I really want to know anymore?

Taking a deep breath and letting it out slowly, as if stealing myself for whatever may come, I replied in barely more than a whisper.

"Okay. I have to know what I am dealing with if I have any hope of understanding my last foreshadowing. I'm ready. Tell me about the world we live in."

Bastian's head snapped up to stare at me, face astonished.

"I thought you just knew Hayden was going to be here," he said to Noella. "I didn't know he was here because... Well, he'd had an um" ... Bastian was stumbling for the words, trying not to accuse Noella but clearly letting the hurt show on his face, "well, foreknowledge that we would be needing him?" he finished. Clear hurt in his tone.

My cousin was an ass, but I was beginning to see him a new light.

There might be hope for him yet.

Chapter Six

Kalina

"Enter", the low, gravelly voice called from a dark corner of the room.

There was a strange, sizzling sound from somewhere inside the clandestine chamber.

"Did you find what I asked you for?" The smell of char and some peculiar incense permeated the air.

"I couldn't... locate it", I whispered in a remorseful tone. "Maybe if I backtrack to their last known whereabouts?"

My voice trailed off, shame coloring my tone. Dread loomed over me like a rock poised to crush the inhabitants below a cliff.

I knew how disappointed he would be.

The figure emerged from the dark shadows in the corner of the dilapidated room.

A small lantern cast the room in a sickly glow. The source of the sizzling sound was apparent.

In that same shadowed corner of the room, a gifter hung limp in chains suspended from the ceiling.

Quarter sized burns appeared all over his shirtless body. An old-fashioned cigarette lighter lay discarded a few feet away.

Whatever information had left his lips was long passed.

There was crimson blood dripping around demonic writing carved into his skin and sealed with some sort of ash.

"They will have destroyed what they thought to be of importance. I am much mistaken, however, if the mixling didn't hold on to the thing that we need most", he professed.

His words confused me. but then again, when had he ever divulged more than absolutely necessary?

He wasn't warm and friendly, or even kind to anyone. He was, however, the only father figure I had ever known. And his words felt prudent.

"You will get me what I desire, won't you Kalina?" he proclaimed the statement as a question but doubtlessly it was not.

"Of course, Lucian," I answered, without query.

I would do whatever he asked of me.

Chapter Seven

Briella

I was looking forward to a hot bath after the night's events. The fight had me wound up and blood from the scuffle was crusted in my long, dark hair.

It was April but the backwoods on the outskirts of Lagomshire still retained the heat from the midday sun.

Maybe I would enjoy a cool shower to wash away the evening instead. With the air this wet, it made it harder to think clearly.

As I approached the front door of my house, the smell of lemongrass in the air, I felt it. My empathic abilities usually overrode anything else that was going on.

It was a blessing and a curse for a Conservatrix demon.

Noticing my front door slightly ajar, I felt someone else's emotions coming from inside the house. Worry, excitement, anxiousness... it was all I could do to keep my own feelings in check.

Reaching for the light switch in the foyer and sniffing the air cautiously, I flicked it on.

Sitting in a chair, in what had been the dark, was a bloody, bruised figure.

"Thelzion!" I proclaimed. "I've been so worried."

Crossing the room to him in an instant, I dashed forward to embrace my mate.

He threw his hands up and I stopped dead in my tracks. This wasn't how I'd pictured our reunion.

Feeling hurt, I took in the sight of him. The cuts on his face and hands. The bruises along his jawbone. The puffiness of his right eye.

"Who did this to..." I started to say but he cut me off.

"What is my favorite part about being on this plane?" he demanded!

"What?" Confused but still grateful he was here, I stumbled over my answer.

"Please," he begged. "What is my favorite part about being on this plane of existence?"

Almost like a reflex, I searched hungrily for his eyes. My voice coming out scratchy, I replied "Getting to live in a world where I am in love with you, as much as you are in love with me."

That was what he had said to me the night before he'd left on his mission.

Thelzion dropped his hands and beckoned me to him.

I dropped to my knees beside him, throwing my arms around his middle and let out a breath I hadn't realized I'd been holding.

"I am sorry, my love," he whispered. "I had to be sure it was really you."

My head jerking up to his face searching for some possible meaning.

"I have a lot to fill you in on Brie," he said glumly. "It may be even worse than we first feared. We we'll need to contact the mixling witch as soon as possible!"

Chapter Eight

Kalina

It was dark in the warehouse office. Lucian had gone back to the comfort of Malum Manor.

I wanted another look around the room that had the tortured, dead gifter in it for some possible insight as to what my pseudo father wanted with the item the mixling took from the lab.

An acrid stench lingered in the humid air. He was still hanging from the rafters by his shackled arms.

A piece of paper laid discarded on the ground where Lucian had been seated earlier.

Picking it up, I flattened out the crumbled drawing. It was oddly familiar.

The ring had a design of some kind on it, dragon and snake maybe. It had a large gem in the center and a couple of smaller gems circling the larger center gem.

This was what I'd went to the lab for, but Lucian had never told me exactly.

I was to locate the facility, retrieve the research papers and an artifact the scientist would be guarding fiercely, but I'd been too late.

There were two words written on the paper under the ring, "Exolo Akasha".

I was so engrossed in what I'd found, I startled at the sound of movement in the room.

Staring up at the dangling body of the gifter, he moved and begged "Water... Water, please."

I ran to turn on the overhead lights.

The man who dangled from the chains, wrist bound by leather straps, squeezed his eyes shut. A moan of pain escaped his dry, blood crusted lips.

Cautiously approaching him with a glass of water I poured from the pitcher that Lucian had been drinking from, I put it to his mouth, and he gulped it down quickly.

A rasping heave ushered from his chest. He was choking.

Fetching the knife from the table and cutting him down, I turned him to his side.

Why had my father not made sure he was dead? And why did I feel the need to help this stranger?

Lucian had raised me to be a heartless demon, like him. Confliction was my wheelhouse. Why couldn't I just let him die?

Dimming the lights and giving him a few minutes, the coughing stopped.

His ribs were bruised. Big welts were forming all over his body.

Leaving would be in my best interest, but I convinced myself that he may hold some of the key pieces of information I was missing in the bigger picture.

I could wait and question him. Then I would let him die... or so I told myself.

"Has he gone?" the gifter mumbled through dry lips.

He looked at me now that his thirst had been quenched and the lights weren't so bright.

Stealing a quick glance around the room to make certain that there was no one else here with us, I nodded.

If I turned on the emotions I kept off, except when on missions, my empathic abilities would confirm it.

I didn't revel in the sensation of feeling things. Too messy.

Living beings put off energetic vibrations that gave away pain and angst and joy and a hundred more facets of their being.

My own sensibilities tended to conflict with what I was often called upon to do. It was one of the many things that made me feel like a failure to Lucian.

"There's no one here but you and me," I replied in a whispered hush.

Taking my word as a promise, he evidently decided I was telling the truth without question.

A great huff of air escaped his slacking form. A breath I hadn't realized he was holding in reserve.

"Good. I was done," the words came out in an unexpected rush. "I thought I was gone. I thought that it being dark, and the pain fading meant that I was already dead."

His eyes met mine for the first time. There was an earnestness in them that I didn't understand.

The quiet that followed that statement stretched on in its wake.

After a few more minutes with neither of us saying anything, he asked me an odd question... "I'm grateful, but how did you find me?"

Chapter Nine

Hayden

Noella took Bastian's hand in hers. "Bastian. I didn't want you to feel threatened by the situation."

She looked at him with an almost motherly longing to comfort his hurt.

"I'm fine. I don't need to be coddled Noella." Bastian turned to face Lara, directing his next accusation towards her. "Did you tell Hayden about Noella coming with me?"

Lara chose her words carefully. I could see the works of her mind churning.

I'd always been in a bit of awe at how she managed her seer's knowledge with a strong desire to not reveal more than absolutely necessary.

"No Bastian. I only gave Hayden a heads up to the fact that you were coming so that his emotions were a bit more rational by the time you arrived." Turning back to the group, she said, "Things in our world are not as they appear. Gifters and Dhalls are in more danger than they have ever been."

Her green eyes darkened like a forest in the night as she spoke.

As we watched, the candles flame that was burning on the coffee table between us rose higher and higher.

"We need to come together. Gifters, good demons, and ..." She looked intently into Noella's eyes, "Mixlings."

Noella broke her gaze from Lara and pivoted around to face us as a group.

The shop was strangely still as she began to speak. "Demons live amongst us", she said.

I gasped as I took in this information. I'd had my suspicions but hearing her confirm it brought a hollow pit to my stomach.

"They are not all bad. They are not what humans think of as demons." As beautiful as Noella was, what she said stirred a dour feeling deep in my gut.

Looking at Lara for some kind of answer and finding none, I stared opened mouthed at the room.

What was she saying? That she was a mixling?

Opening my mouth to speak, a wave of calm euphoria enveloped me, and I was no longer as concerned as I knew I had been a moment ago.

Noella sighed heavily.

"I am a mixling, Hayden," she said, "Do you understand what that means?"

Looking at her as if really seeing her for the first time, a cold shiver ran down my spine.

I'd dealt with just one other mixling in my past.

A ruthless one named Carnifax.

He would find people. Gifters mostly, but some dhalls. Someone who wouldn't really be missed by anyone. Those with not many friends or family to go looking for them.

He sold their whereabouts to nefarious gang leaders.

After that, the people who they'd been had completely changed. They were not the same at all, but I had no idea why.

I had assumed they were brainwashed or something.

These gangs were horrible. They were known for violence that was twisted and heinous.

Could she really be saying that she was part of that?

Noella began explaining when she realized that I wasn't going to speak up.

"Gifters are human descendants of a demigod, but they have one parent pure dhall. A mixling is a person who has one demigod or upper-level demon parent and one gifter parent. I am a witch, with abilities more powerful than most, but still, I stand firmly on the side of humanity."

Taking off one of the gloves she had been wearing, I noticed its strange coloring.

Her hand had an opalescent pale hue, as was the rest of her. As she moved it slowly through the air, a prism of colors seemed to ripple in its wake. You could no longer fathom a guess as to the complexion of her skin.

"I told you that demons exist. So do mixlings, with powers as unique and individual as gifters." Noella put her glove back on.

Sorrow reigned in her eyes. A burdensome air appeared to settle on her shoulders.

"I am told that you had the misfortune of meeting Carnifax. I take no more pleasure in his actions than you did in the knowledge of Bastian's." She paused, deciding whether or not to tell me more.

The light filtering through the shelves danced quietly around the sitting area. My whole being felt alert now. There wasn't anywhere else I needed to be, but damn, I wanted to get out of here.

Resignation colored her tone as she continued. "You know those people Carnifax sold information about? They didn't only appear to be different after they had been taken."

I started to protest but she pushed through. "They ARE different. Those are not gangs. They are covens of Valhess demons. The only way a Valhess demon can escape the underworld is to soul swap with a human."

My mouth fell open with an audible pop. I was at a loss for words. A first for me.

Sitting there, staring at each of the others in turn. I was hoping that this was all some sort of sick hoax.

With each passing moment, no one said anything. They were waiting for me to come to terms with the information they'd presented.

The realization that human souls were stuck in the underworld as demons possessed their former bodies forever was just too terrible to think about.

Bastian spoke first. "It's hard to take in, huh, cuz?" He lifted his eyes to meet my gaze. "I didn't want to believe it all at first either. I mean, really, the evil things that people do to each other is hard enough to swallow."

He looked poignantly over my head, staring out of the wide window onto the street beyond.

"And now, knowing that there are demons?" Bastian shook his head like he was trying to clear away a spider web of bad thoughts, "It's all I can do to keep from running and hiding in a cave somewhere."

Noella sighed and laughed a mirthless laugh. "Do you really want me to tell you what lurks in dark caves?"

Bastian and I both shuttered at her words.

Lara brought the focus back into the room. Standing over an anciently runed carved bowl, she held a liquid metal, all silvery and reflective, but somehow clear.

Dropping a small bit of herbs that gave off a purplish smoke, she asked us all to breathe in deeply.

Chapter Ten

Briella

"We need to find Noella as soon as possible," Thelzion declared. "We won't know what our next move will be until I know what she's got."

Looking down at his hands, they were all cut up and dried with blood.

I tried to follow what he was telling me, but he was muttering things under his breath. He wasn't coherent. His sentences were fragmented and some of the words he spoke didn't make sense.

With a sharp intake of breath, suddenly I realized the problem.

"When did you last feed, Zi?!?" I insisted!

He looked through me, like I was a ghost, sent to torment him.

Racing to the kitchen, I brought back a cup of dark liquid.

Thelzion was confused. He kept pushing me away, but I was a Conservatrix demon, and with that came strength.

Once the smell from inside of the cup hit his nose, his baser instincts took over. He sucked down the contents in a fit of overpowering hunger.

I was off to the kitchen for some more life-giving blood. On my way back into the room, I noticed something I hadn't before.

A torn piece of paper, covered in Thelzion's blood, lying on the floor.

The yellowing of the parchment and the curling, torn edges let me know that it came from an incredibly old book.

Seeing the mixling for answers was definitely what he'd meant. Once he was fed, he'd fill me in on everything I needed to know.

Now that I caught onto what was going on, we'd need to get a move on as soon as possible.

Only one thing took precedence over our missions... the need to take care of your mate.

With that thought in mind, I went to fetch more blood.

Chapter Eleven

Kalina

The gifter's words made no sense.

I wasn't sure why he thought he knew me. I had so many questions, but I never usually got any answers.

Nothing new for my way of life. My father kept me in the dark most of the time. He had the other demons at the Manor keep me in the dark as well.

I was intrigued by the idea of maybe finding out a few answers.

Who was he? And why did he think I would come for him?

Blood still trickled from his ear and the bruises on his body were becoming more prominent.

Moving a little closer, I asked, "Do you know me?"

Brushing my long, dark hair out of my eyes with a sweeping motion towards my ear, I played on my strengths.

My eyes were bright and alluring. My beauty had never been one of my questions, even if I sometimes felt that it was a hinderance.

"My name is Zane", he said.

A small grin appeared on his lips but faded quickly at the incredulous look I gave him.

"You still think I'm a gifter, don't you?"

"Why else would my father want to question you?" I said flustered.

I wasn't happy when I wasn't in the know.

My father had many secrets and often kept them close to the vest. It's been a point of contention for me.

"Do you know me?" I asked again, my voice raised in pitch.

Zane stared at me, not able to quite understand my anger or my line of questioning for some reason. I thought his brain might have been addled by Lucian's torture session.

Finally looking up at me, he spoke slowly. The words he knew would either kill him or set him free.

"He has you believing you are a villainous demon, doesn't he?"

What in all of the known hells was he talking about?

Chapter Twelve

Hayden

The purple smoke rose high in the air and spread like a mist throughout the shop. The strong smell of incense hung heavily around the room.

Scenes started to appear suspended on the mist, like a movie, only in flashes. The past was being laid out before us. Lara's voice came from all around.

"After the time of demons, a new dawn began. It was raw and meaningless. Humanity became the next chapter.

The gods each added something to the creation. They tried to be fair and balanced, but they had too many differing opinions to be just."

The next scene flashed into being and she continued.

"Time moved forward, and humanity grew in leaps and bounds.

With the demons banished to the underworld, there was no consternation, no reason for them to not believe themselves the greatest beings in the planet's hierarchy.

In the days of new, humans walk the earth like a plague. Consuming whatever suited them, unintentionally destroying all that stood in their way."

The scene shifted again. It went from older, caveman like days, to days in the past with wooden sailing ships and the introduction of more modern buildings and roads.

"They believed themselves to be all and superior. Those who came before them were made into myth and legend. Their sense of righteousness went unchecked." Lara paused.

She tossed another bundle of herbs into the runed bowl, and the smoke turned a bluish grey. *"That was, until the god, Aion, looked in on the newest of the gods creations."*

Lara looked at each of us briefly and then continued.

"Aion is the God of Eternity. He holds the wheel of time. He had foreseen a crack thousands of years after human creation. A breaking of the Deum Velum, or God's Veil.

It was the veil the gods placed over the world to hide the shadowrealm, the remnants of the time of demons and otherworldly occupation.

They believed that the jejune nature of humanity would be too fragile. It would be overly disturbed by what lurked in the shadows to be allowed to see all.

Humans would cause the breaking, but demons would use it as a catalyst to escape from the Underworld. The human events to come were not changeable but in his wisdom, he and a few of the other gods came together.

They created a means to aid in the balance."

She looked at Noella and gave a gentle nod before proceeding.

"They created mixlings and the first gifters came about soon after. Aion believed that humanity, whilst making leaps and bounds in evolving, would still be too infantile to stop the demons on their own."

I stood up and began to pace. This was a lot to take in. I was lost in my thoughts as they bounced around my skull, hitting on some points. Missing on others.

My eyes kept darting to my dream journal, lying discarded on the shop counter, and then back at the bowl that had shown us all our history.

One thought kept repeating over and over again in my mind.

Lara had told me that a battle was coming. I'd had a foreshadowing of someone being "Too Late".

Was the person in my dream too late to stop the battle... or the oncoming demon war?

Bastian got up slowly and clamped a hand on my shoulder. It was a few seconds before I was able to focus on him.

It was a kind gesture. One that Bastian had done many times in our childhood when I was lost to my thoughts, unable to break myself out of my mind's musings.

Lara's eyes glazed over momentarily. We all paused and waited.

When she opened them, she looked directly at Noella.

With a tilt of her head, she asked frankly, "There is a Donnchadh and a Conservatrix coming to see you soon." Noella looked mildly abashed. "Would you like to explain how you know these two demons and why they need your help?"

Chapter Thirteen

Kalina

"What on earth are you talking about?!" I demanded. "Of course, I am a demon. Why would Lucian take me in and raise me if I were anything but?"

A look of relief washed through him that I hadn't killed him as soon as he'd spoken the words.

He lifted his head and the dried blood on his face pulled his features taught.

"I can tell you what I know, but first I need a bit more water, maybe a few of those grapes from the table, and if you'd be so willing, help me to that chair," he said in a rushed breath.

I didn't know if I should be helping him or not.

The fact that Lucian had held him captive, tortured, and left for dead, should be all the information that was required of me to make a rational decision.

The fact was, he was still alive, even if that wasn't my father's intent. And he was willing to give me answers to questions that had nagged at me since puberty. It left me feeling that this was the only viable course of reasoning.

I'd become more restless lately, more agitated with all of the restrictions Lucian imposed on me and none of the other demons under his command. I needed answers to some of my questions more than I needed to *stay in line.*

Deciding to get the information I required and be done with him, I moved cautiously forward.

Needing to get my head sorted out in order to focus on the task that Lucian had assigned me, I made that my excuse. He'd be pissed if he found out, but I was a grown woman now, not some raging teenager.

Disappointing him again would not bode well for my longevity. He could be extremely violent when things weren't done to his liking.

He was a demon that didn't rely on one source and would replace anyone within the span of a heartbeat if it served his greater purpose. I was only as good to him as my usefulness served his agenda.

Even as a daughter figure, I knew he wouldn't hesitate in replacing me.

Walking over to Zane, I bent down and put my arms under his, heaving him up and into the chair.

A few of the grapes on the table were smashed or rotting but the rest remained edible.

After pouring another glass of water and thrusting it into Zane's waiting hands, I popped a grape directly into his mouth.

He winced as the juice from the grape brushed over his cracked lips.

I took him in fully for the first time since cutting his limp form down from the ceiling.

He was handsome, but not in the typical sort of way.

He had a lot of scars, one of them running from above his left eye to just below his nose. How he still had his eye intact was a mystery.

His lips, though swollen, seemed to have a natural fullness to them.

Zane had skin that was neither brown nor white. I supposed his heritage must be mixed.

He really was a ruggedly beautiful man, even covered in blood and bruises.

There was something in the set of his eyes that drew me in. They were a silver grey that complimented his short, black hair perfectly.

When I realized I was staring and that he was smirking at me, I dropped my gaze and started fidgeting with the piece of paper that I'd found.

He ate a few more grapes and downed the glass of water, seeming to be waiting for me to push him for information.

I didn't know how to begin this particular interrogation, being more than a little anxious about what he would tell me.

Opening my mouth to ask him what he knew about me, what came out was much different.

"You're too good looking to be a gifter," I blurted out.

Without thinking, my hands flew to cover my mouth.

Mortified at my own bluntness, cheeks heating and surely turning red, I turned away as a sardonic smile lit up his face.

"Well, that was unexpected," he said. "I've never known a Trixie to be so forthcoming with their feelings." The twinkle in his eyes danced in the dim lighting.

Glaring in his direction, feeling like a silly little girl right now, I wasn't trying to give him the satisfaction of knowing it.

Instead, I turned around to fully face him. Crossing my arms over my rather full chest gave me the air of an annoyed hen.

I'd let him imagine me pecking his eyes right out.

"Sorry, I'm still more than a bit groggy," he said. "I wouldn't mock you if I was in my right mind."

The corner of his mouth pulled up on one side. That little motion had my stomach fluttering for some weird reason.

Leaning against the table casually but cautiously, I thought over what I wanted to say.

What answers did I want the most?

If I was to complete Lucian's mission, those should be the kinds of answers I tried to obtain.

The look on Zane's face was enough to make my choice for me.

"What did you mean before, about me being a Trixie? What would make you think that?" The words tumbled from my mouth.

For a long time now, I'd wanted out from under Lucian's constant thumb.

It was time I found out how much had been kept from me "for your own good", as he would say.

Then I'd be better prepared to make decisions about my life for myself.

"Gods, he really has gone too far. You poor girl."

His words pissed me off. Pity wasn't what I wanted. I hated being mollycoddled. It's why I'd agreed to questioning him instead of letting him die in the first place.

"I'm a grown woman, you asshole! Give me one reason I shouldn't slit your throat and be done with this conversation?"

Breathing hard, my chest heaved as I tried to rein in my emotions.

"I'll give you two. One, you're better than he is. And two, I have the answers you desire more than the air you breathe."

It was a fair point. Game set.

Chapter Fourteen

Quinn

"Enter," Lucian's droll voice called out.

I opened the door to the sitting room to find him perusing an old leather-bound book.

The dim light coming from an oil lamp in the corner threw the contents of the room into shadow.

Approaching the highbacked chair he was reading in, I mindfully sauntered over to him.

Standing only a few feet away, I waited for him to address me before speaking.

Lucian was the epitome of dangerous. I had worked with him for over one hundred and seventy years.

Even I sometimes found his casual violence disturbing as a demon myself.

We may share a bed from time to time, but I never confused our sexual exploits with him having feelings for me.

At least, not any more feelings than he did for any of his valued inner circle.

We all knew his caring for us only extended as far as his need for what we could do for him.

I was thinking of the information I had recently gathered for Lucian when my eye caught on an entry in the book.

It was similar but slightly different than the one from my mission.

The ring, with strange gems, appeared to be almost the same but the inscription was different. It read "Reverto Akasha."

On this one, the Latin word was for Return, but the Sanskrit word was the same. It meant Primary Substance out of which all things are formed.

The information that I had gathered for him was in reference to "Exolo Akasha".

That was the Latin word for exile. This information would make an enormous difference in our mission.

Lucian had seen me looking for just a moment too long.

His secrets were always held close to the cuff. He trusted no one more than their need for the protection he was supposed to provide them.

So basically, he trusted no one enough to let them close.

I looked away but made it seem like I just happened to be staring in the general direction of his work.

Setting the book aside, he stood up and walked over to the whiskey decanter sitting on the desk. Picking up two glasses and pouring a finger of whiskey in each, he handed one to me.

It was a small act, but it made the tension diminish just as quickly as it had come on. Drinking his down in one long pull, he raised his glass for me to do the same.

I only did so as to not draw his turbulent emotions.

As smooth and smokey as the aged liquor had been, I knew that the moment of camaraderie would be short lived.

I hadn't found any new information on the artifact's whereabouts. He would either overreact or not react at all. Both were unnerving.

Lucian took in the sight of my face. He knew my tells after all these years. He knew it would not be the outcome that he'd hoped for.

Schooling his facial features to be less severe, he tried to smirk at me sending a shiver down my spine. "You failed," he said.

It wasn't a question. Picking up an object from the desk and turning it over in his hand, he directed his faded blue eyes at the blood stains on my shirt. "It would seem that you had some fun at least."

I looked up through my lashes to see him as he smiled down at me. I knew that look.

He was disappointed in the outcome but not in me. That was a mild relief.

There must have been more to the story than he was willing to share but at least I wasn't on the wrong end of his ire. For now.

Trying to smile back, it fell short of real mirth.

Having the bigger picture would help me to put together the right team for the mission he'd put me on.

It would also help me figure out exactly what the grand scheme Lucian had planned. The right demons with the right skills could be essential in accomplishing our end goal.

Only I didn't have all the pieces I needed to see the whole puzzle. It was like being in a band where each person with a different musical instrument practiced separately and not together.

We all know the song but playing it as a group in the finale would be hit or miss.

Persuading Lucian to let more of his circle in on the finer details, at least those who resided at Malum Manor with him, hadn't worked.

It had been a touchy few minutes for me after I'd brought it up. With hands folded behind his back, and his mood already disagreeable, I'd waited on bated breath.

Choosing to not thrash me, he grumbled and sent me to deal with a problem concerning a Valhess/ Meathlu dispute. Stupid busy work to deal with the demons in his district. Point taken.

I hadn't gotten a direct answer from him, but the dismissal was answer enough that time.

He'd noticed my lack of enthusiasm. "What seems to be the problem?" he asked me, not really caring about what my response would be.

Pretending to have concern for his subjects let them feel he cared, even if it was just a fraction of a bit.

Occasionally, they would drone on or whine about their feelings. Blah blah blah. It was tedious. And meaningless.

However, doing it sometimes gave them the renewed enthusiasm to further his goals. As much as he loathed this part of the job, he attempted to listen without lashing out.

I made to reply but the words got lost on the way out. Instead, I laid my hand on his arm and gave a gentle squeeze.

Grooming my face into that come hither look that usually brought about a toss in the sheets. I smiled up at him from under my lashes this time, batting them seductively.

Now was not the time to bring on his wrath. He hadn't flown off the handle about the mission and I wanted nothing more than another chance to bring home the artifact and solidify a place at his side as his second in command.

Sex wasn't the way to reach that goal but fighting about things certainly wouldn't make him give me the team I wanted to assemble either.

He took the bait and pulled me close, biting my neck and tracing his strong fingers down my arm.

A trickle of blood leaked down to my collarbone and Lucian wasted no time in lapping it up.

I sometimes felt more than lust for him, but I knew that after as many years as we had been each other's release, he would never feel more for me than a means to an end.

Nevertheless, I shuttered as the wet longing between my legs had me leaning in to his touch.

"To the Boudoir then" he said, placing his hand at the small of my back and guiding me towards the door.

Chapter Fifteen

Briella

I went to fetch Thelzion his third cup of blood. I simply couldn't believe that he would let himself get to this state. It hurt my heart to know how much he struggled with what he was.

Not all demons were bad but the Donnchadh demons, by nature, were not known for being good.

Thelzion loved me. We were Mates. I knew he made the conscious decision every day to be the best person he could be to feel worthy of my love for him.

Not only was he not bad, but he also strived to go above and beyond, to actually be good... to make the world a better place.

He wasn't always good. He'd done many horrible things for a few hundred years before we'd met.

The century or so before I was born, he was like every other Donnchadh.

He did his job policing the dark side of the shadow world and keeping young Meathlu safe and out of the hands of the mortal police.

He made sure that full demons were not drawing attention to themselves and that their black practices were going under the radar of the gods.

Thelzion felt like he was doing his duty and was good at it... But it was beginning to grow tiresome. The same thing, day after day, decade after decade.

He'd told me the story of how one hot afternoon, in the middle of August, in a small town called Dochais, there was an assignment.

He and a Donnchadh named Lucian were to go to a hospital where underworld higher ups were reporting a good demon birth... A Conservatrix birth.

The indecorous powers that be usually didn't send two Donnchadh's on assignment together. It was unusual, but not unheard of.

He and Lucian had worked together on occasion before. Thelzion wasn't fond of him though.

Lucian had little to no reverence for human life. He barely had tolerance for other demons.

They were sent to dispatch the parents and dispose of the newborn after performing a ritual to ensure it wouldn't rise again.

Conservatrix demons posed a threat to Meathlu and full demons alike. It was the Trixie's job to ensure that Meathlu never made it to full demon and to keep humans from being victims of demons in any stage.

Conservatrix demons were the polar opposite of a Donnchadh.

Their births were not that common. Only a dozen or so per continent existed and when one was born, they grew like a normal human until they reached puberty.

However, their minds distorted most of their adolescence.

The way it worked had puzzled demonkind since the first one came to be. It was believed that this happened to ensure their formative years were with humans and goodness was cemented in their subconsciousness before puberty.

Puberty did not start until between nineteen to twenty-four years old. Their human parents just thought them to be late bloomers. A Trixie's mind would convince them it started in their teens.

And the pheromones they emitted would convince their human parents of the same thing.

As they developed, they would begin noticing more of the shadowrealm around them. Glimpses here and there were all they had until that point. A fifty year-old Trixie only looked between twenty-four to twenty-eight years old.

They were not immortal, but their growth was so slow that they generally lived between eight hundred to a thousand years. At the end of their days, they would still only appear to be the age of a sixty-five year-old human.

The more good demons that came to be, the harder it was for Donnchadh vampires to do their job.

So once the higher ups learned of a Conservatrix eminent birth, they would dispatch a Donnchadh to take care of the future problem.

It hadn't raised any alarms in Thelzion's mind.

He'd told me that when he'd gotten there, Lucian was the one who made his intuition flare up. Something nefarious was brewing and Lucian was at the helm of it. That he could feel it in his bones.

I returned with another cup of blood. When he looked up at me, there was a tension around his eyes that caused my heart to ache for him.

"You were there", he said. "You were at the lab, just after Noella and the gifter smashed everything and grabbed the artifact!"

He glared at me. An incredulous look was clearly etched upon my demonly enchanting face. I knew it.

He muttered "Only, it wasn't you, was it?"

I gawked at him. My mouth dropping open with an audible pop.

I'd thought about his reaction when I'd came in the door. Realization settling in, my heart constricted.

He'd thought I had done this to him. It made no sense.

I began to tell him it wasn't me, but he was mumbling under his breath.

Finally seeing me, really seeing me this time, he fell to his knees, wrapping his arms around my waist.

"Oh Brie!" He exclaimed. "We need to talk honey... About the past."

Knowing how much he hated to think about his old self, it must have been something genuinely bad if he was willing to bring up that period in time.

"Okay Thelzion," I encouraged him. "Whatever it is, you and I can get through it together, my love."

The look of pain and sorrow on his face made me hurt deep inside.

Thelzion hung his head and let out a deep breath. His sad eyes met mine, nothing but love and understanding in them.

"You may hate me after this," he whispered, knowing my enhanced ears would hear him. "I haven't thought about it for a long time, and I don't even know if I'm putting it all together right now, but I have to tell you more about the night you were born."

Chapter Sixteen

Hayden

Noella glanced around the shop.

Getting up and retrieving my dream journal, she came back to the sitting area and took a clear quartz crystal from her pocket.

"I need to start at the beginning of my personal history," she said. "It's not a pleasant tale but to not know the antecedents of my past would do you all a great injustice".

She proceeded to remove her glove once again.

Waving a hand over the crystal and reciting a phrase in Latin, she placed the crystal inside of the runed bowl. Though there was no incense added this time, it blazed to life once more.

Lara looked to me and I acknowledged her with a quick dip of my chin.

"Have you ever heard of the LHCS?", Noella began.

Bastian and I shook our heads no, but Lara didn't show any expression at all.

She wasn't giving away anything that her seer's sight had shown her.

Noella continued. "They are the Scientist that created one of the Large Hadron Colliders."

I arched an eyebrow. The incredulity I'd felt must have been written on my face.

Seeing my disbelief, her scrutiny left me feeling like an ignorant child. "Yes, that's plural. There is a secret one. The entire lab is highly classified."

Turning to Bastian, she gave a little smile. He reciprocated the gesture.

"It is located in one of the most remote parts of the Saltu jungle. You would have to follow the Fadaglais River north for many days on foot just to get to the border of the Forbidden Zone. Any new deliveries or personnel are taken in by helicopter".

With a wave of her hand, the image appeared before all of us. Looking back at Bastian now, she asked, "How old do you think I am?"

Bastian's eyebrow rose in contemplation. It was almost comical the way he was assessing her. Scrunching up his nose like it was a trick question.

I would have guessed from her appearance that she was around twenty-four, maybe twenty-five years old.

Her demeaner and the cadence of her voice were more like someone who spoke from a place of wisdom that comes with age.

I'd thought that she must be older than she appeared, so I just remained silent, waiting for her answer.

"I was born in the year 1556 post demon. I am four hundred sixty-seven years old," she batted her eyes and the tinkling laugh that followed was so amusing that Lara let out a bark of laughter.

Bastian did a double take. Apparently, I was not the only one taken aback.

The first to speak was Bastian. "How?" was all he managed to get out.

He and I were both utterly dumbfounded. How was it possible? It was crazy to think this beautiful female was over five times as old as our grandmother.

"I am a mixling, but my mother was a demon, and my father is a demigod," she said modestly.

The shop fell still. Both of us trying to make our minds catch up to the reality of the situation.

She was telling us that she was old. That she was powerful. And that she was not human at all.

I took a breath. Reclaiming my voice, I asked "Your mother *was* a demon?" Noella grimaced.

The look was so at odds with her beauty, it seemed almost comical.

I knew it could be no such thing. That look was something of heartache, of a remembered pain.

"She is lost to the underworld," she pronounced. "I will never be able to see her again, even after I leave this plane." The lament in her voice was anguish.

Bastian hung his head, but I studied her face, needing to understand the full story.

Lara stood and lit three candles. Walking over to the counter, she retrieved a bottle and brought us all a glass of elderberry wine.

Noella took hers and gave Lara a weak smile. Lara smiled back, an acknowledgement of her grief. Three candles for the triple moon goddess and elderberry wine to honor ancestors.

We all raised ouir glasses and Lara toasted, "To those who came before us. To those who stand beside us. And to those whom we shall never meet again."

Drinking in silence, when the last of the wine had been polished off, Lara cleared away the glasses and returned to her seat.

Giving a slight bow of her head, she smiled towards Noella. The tiny gesture was that of encouragement to divulge the rest of her story.

"Maybe I should clarify", Noella said. "My biological mother's body was a gifter. A powerful telekinetic. A Valhess coven cornered her and forced the soul swap. She didn't go down without a fight. She managed to kill two of them and wound a third. There were another two who were uninjured that completed the ritual."

Bastian's mouth hung open. I sat in stunned silence. Lara's eyes gave nothing away but sadness for her friend.

"The swap had been made. She was gone. A demon took up residence in her body. It wasn't until a few weeks later that it realized the gifter had been pregnant."

She waved her hand over the rune bowl once again.

"Demons do not give birth. They come to be from a gathering of negative energies and form a mass. It's not a soul exactly but close enough that swapping is admissible."

A dark shadow of thousands of particles swam in the bowl and began gathering to form one large mass. As we watched the shadows, several sparks of bright light danced in their midst.

"Demons are made from the dark, but the light always manages to sneak a bit into the mix. The more light, or positive energies, which are cross weaved into the formation, the greater the chance of the demon having the ability to be good."

My emotions were on a roller coaster of vicissitudes. Waves of nausea churned the fermented berry wine in my stomach.

I hadn't even heard the rest of her story yet and was already so sickened that I didn't know if I wanted to learn any more.

Breathing through my nose, I took several deep breaths and tried to remember that this beautiful female in front of me was safe and whole.

Peering up at her dancing eyes, I found them staring back at me.

Gathering myself together I muttered, "Please... continue".

The shadows that foregathered in the bowl transformed into a face.

"This was my mother," Noella resumed. "Not just my gifter mother's body, but the demon that lived within. Her name was Solene. I loved her a great deal."

She lowered her head and sighed. A ripple of sadness going through the room hung heavy in the already still air.

Lara cleared her throat. It brought Noella back from her sorrow.

"My father loved my gifter mother very much. His name is Draxus. He is the son of Hecate and a mortal man. Hecate is the goddess of magics and keeper of the realms. My father is a demigod with sorcerer's powers that are nearly unmatched," she stated with a hint of pride in her eyes.

The scent of vanilla, patchouli, and leather coming off her skin was practically intoxicating.

"When he found out what had happened to his beloved, he went looking for the Valhess demons that did it. In the five months it took him to find them, he killed every Valhess he came across. One night, on such a hunt, he located the responsible coven in the warehouse district of the same town he had begun searching for them all those previous months ago. He didn't know what made him go back to this town. He said it felt like a tug from deep inside his heart. Coming face to face with these monsters that had taken her from him, his rage was so fierce that it was over in mere seconds."

As she recalled the events, they appeared in the smoky mist above the rune bowl.

A blast of white lights materialized as kinetic energy and ripped the remembered room and the demons to shreds.

We were not only hearing her story, but we were also watching it unfold before us.

Her father had been brutal with his vengeance. Blood and body parts flew in all directions.

A few breaths of silence followed before she found her voice again.

"My mother was hiding in a large crate cast in darkness in the back of the warehouse. My father ripped the crate open preparing to end the demon that possessed his love's body. He recalled the golden color of his skin turning chalky white. He realized that she was pregnant with me. At six months pregnant he could smell me, his child." One side of her mouth drew up.

"He could have very well killed us both, but he knew that I was in there. A child of his and his love's. And my mother was trying desperately to protect me." The smile faded at some memory that entered her mind. "The minute he ripped her out of her hiding spot, my mother set about hurling objects at him from around the room."

Bastian opened his mouth to speak but she launched back into the story.

"There is a reason that Valhess demons prefer to swap with gifters. They maintain any of the abilities that the gifter possessed before they swapped. And as I recounted to you earlier, Draxus' beloved was exceptionally gifted," she said with a wink.

I'd felt better than I had a few minutes ago but still didn't feel great.

It was a lot to take in. Demons and mixlings. Gods and gifters. A veil that covered the human realm so they couldn't see the shadowrealm.

As a gifter myself, I could see glimpses of the shadowrealm but had no idea of its true nature. Finding out that demons could actually be somewhat good, it was all more than a little bewildering.

My brain was reeling from all the new information, and we had not even gotten to the meat of the story, much less the motivation behind this meeting.

Bastian glanced over at me and offered a perfunctory grin.

Lara's eyes glazed over briefly and when she recomposed herself, a look of vexation donned her gentle face.

It was so perturbing that I sprang to my feet and was across the small space in half a bound. I took her hands in mine gently but adamantly. Lara gave them a quick squeeze.

"We had better finish this up hastily. Our company will be here rather sooner than last expected. And Noella," she turned to look her full in the face, "Thelzion will have told Briella everything he knows about her past by the time they arrive."

Lara leered at Noella for a moment longer, then turned to me.

Keeping personal knowledge and seer knowledge separate had to be distressing.

"I promise this will make more sense soon, but you will have to be patient." With that, she let go of my large, calloused hands and returned to her seat, gesturing for us all to do the same.

Chapter Seventeen

Zane

I was popping a few grapes into my mouth when I noticed just how girlish Kali looked. More the innocence of a young woman rather than the confidence of a full grown Trixie.

I hadn't thought before I'd made my pitying comment.

She was fully grown but her demeaner was that of a refractory late teen.

Confidence and poise didn't lend themselves to this Trixie the way they should.

A Conservatrix demon naturally felt self-assured, at times even arrogant.

Wondering why she was so insecure; I ventured a guess. "Do you know what a Conservatrix is?"

Defiance was shining through her hazel eyes. Lifting her chin, she gave a textbook answer.

"It's a good demon. It poses a threat to Meathlu and full demons. They're objective in life is to ensure demons return to the Underworld forever." She smiled, clearly proud of her retained knowledge.

Taking a slow drink of water, I lowered the cup and simply stared at her face. I was quiet for so long, she began to fidget. Trixie's didn't fidget.

It was beginning to feel like I really may have died, and this was some sort of afterlife hell.

Not wanting to believe that maybe I was wrong about her, I started asking questions rather than giving answers to hers.

"How did you come to be in Lucian's circle?" I pushed her with the conviction of someone in authority.

If I had the measure of her right, she'd want to tell me. Feeling the need for approval was what I'd picked up from the tidbits she'd said to me already.

Rocking on the balls of her feet, nervous energy escaped from every pore. The room filled with the scent of bonfire, sweet blood, and tangy citrus.

The pheromones of a Trixie were seductive and entrancing to demons but still alluring to everyone else. She tried to snag me on her hook, but I wasn't biting. Even if it took all my waning strength to fight it.

"There's no need to be defensive," I said. "I wasn't trying to get you to hand over his secrets." Raising one eyebrow speculatively, she put her hands on her hips and glared. "Really, I wasn't. I was merely trying to figure out how to give you the answers you seek."

Her position relaxed as perhaps it dawned on her that maybe Lucian was so secretive because the less she knew, the less she would question.

"Okay. Say I give you my backstory. How does that help me?"

That sassy attitude was adorable. I wanted to give her whatever she wanted because of it.

I wouldn't.... but I wanted to. There was just something about her that played with my resolve to immediately give in.

"It helps you because then I know where to start from."

A grin crinkled the corners of my eyes. Hers responded to the small bit of information.

"It helps because if I start from what you should already know of things and it doesn't make any sense to you, then I have to go back over that too."

I was mildly enjoying myself now, watching her bottom lip jut out in a semi-pout.

"It helps because if I can understand why you haven't a clue about your own personal history, I think I could ultimately be of service to you, and you would spare my life."

Now I was just being a playful rascal. I knew how to play into people's insecurities and use them to my advantage, but I found that I didn't want to take advantage her. I wanted to help her.

That didn't mean I was going to change my charming asshole personality anytime soon.

Fidgeting some more, her fingers twirled around a strand of her raven black hair. It was clear that she was pondering where to start.

"I have known Lucian all of my life. He says that I was an insufferably whiney baby when he found me." My lips curled upward, and Kali grinned. "I have no idea about why my birth parents abandoned me. Lucian speculates it was because of my high-pitched crying, but I don't know if he's serious or poking fun at me."

Pacing the small space, she was clearly trying to calm herself before she spoke again.

"Whenever I try to recall my childhood, it blurs. It's like trying to chase focus on your peripheral line of sight. I can almost catch it, but it always eludes me."

Sliding my eyes over her from head to toe, my abilities were subtle. I was able to scan a being and see their true self; human, demon, gifter or whatever else they may be.

I could also see their energy, like using an MRI, and see if anything ailed them. It was good in a fight to be able to know where your opponent's weak spots were. It didn't provide much in the way of physical defense though.

I had some other gifts too, but I had to train extra hard and keep my muscles well primed for conflict.

Now I knew for sure that she was a Conservatrix. It was written all over her energy field.

The confidence she lacked must be a mental block, conditioning of some sort.

She spoke with a bit more animation in her gestures now.

"I have been a burden on Lucian from the start. He had nursemaids quit after a week. He says that I cried and wailed relentlessly."

She grimaced at something she remembered but did not vocalize it, instead refocusing on her childhood.

"I ran around the manor like a hellcat when I was younger. I would see all sorts of beings coming and going. He told me they were demons and his guests would not like me, the particular type of demon that I was, and that I was not to antagonize them."

Scrunching up her face like a rebellious teenager, she went on. "As I entered my teens, he taught me how to fight and how to avoid entangling with other demons. I surpassed all of his trainers quickly and Lucian decided to put me to use working for him right around the time puberty hit."

Looking at her feet and fidgeting some more with the piece of paper in her hand, Kali's face flushed.

She might have been half a century old, but she was no more an adult than a senior fresh out of high school thought themselves to be.

All this time, I hadn't spoken. With her ramblings, I was trying to understand the root of the problem and was sure I knew what it was now.

Looking up from below her lashes at me, like any other Trixie would do during a round of questioning, I felt her seductive energy push against my skin.

It was a good thing my shields were up. I wasn't even sure if she knew she was doing it.

A demon, of any sort, untrained in their own abilities, was a danger.

Kali didn't know she was a Trixie so how would she master her full potential?

Lucian had her trapped in her own mind, wanting her to feel small. He wouldn't be able to use a Trixie to do his bidding if he couldn't control them. She could quite literally damn him before he took two steps.

What was his end game?

"Is he a good father figure?" I needed to poke the bear. It would prove essential in calculating whether she could be rehabilitated.

Letting her come to terms with what she was and turning her against Lucian were two vastly different things.

Had Lucian been good to her, it may not matter that he was lying by omission.

On the other hand, if she came to grips with the fact that he was trying to keep her in her place, Kali may want to play a big part in the upcoming conflict against him.

She hadn't responded so pushing the issue farther might make her snap. "Does he make you feel important?"

Standing up and pacing the room again, her eyes were brimming with unfallen tears. Clenching her fists and taking an exaggerated breath, she gave voice to her pain.

"Important? No one has ever made me feel important!" She stopped pacing and faced me. "I am a low demon. I am not meant to be valued or endeared." She spit the words like she was reciting a pledge.

She glared at me, then hung her head and walked towards the grimy window along the far wall.

Peering out at the night sky, Kali turned her body halfway around to see what my expression would be.

Stupefied! There was no other way to describe the incredulous look that held my mind suspended in torment.

It took me a few minutes before I recovered enough to speak. "You can't possibly mean that!"

Scrutinizing every facet of her face, the entire truth laid itself out before me.

She had never known kindness or been appreciated. She had no idea of who she was or the full capabilities she had at her fingertips. Worst of all, she had never known any kind of love.

It made me irrationally angry. I wanted to find him and beat the ever-loving shit out of him. I wanted to seek out every weakness in his good for nothing body and exploit each and every sore spot.

There was no good reason for my reaction. She was a stranger. A stranger who'd saved my life, but still. She was simply a stranger to me.

The formative years for a Conservatrix demon were meant to be spent with human parents. Love was to be ingrained in their being to help them navigate their future.

This Trixie was truly lost, but she did feel it. Kali knew deep down that something didn't sit right.

She was here, asking me questions, wanting to connect, even if she didn't realize that it had been what she was doing.

My mouth had gone dry again. A laborious breath issued from a fathomless pit that had opened inside me. My heart was still and pounding at the same time.

Wrapping my mind around the severity of the situation took longer than I thought it would. The way I groundlessly felt I needed to be protective of her disquieted me.

After many numberless minutes of silence, I realized that she was still staring at me, waiting for some sort of response that would fill the void inside her.

A whispered proclamation ushered from her lips. It broke me to hear it fall from those full lips.

"I don't need anyone. I stay with Lucian because he raised me. I'm fine being unimportant."

She let a few tears spill over the bottom lids of her eyes and down her cheeks without wiping at them.

The last vestiges of my self-control crumbled, as did the wall around my heart. A shield I'd put into place many years ago to keep from feeling anything too deeply ever again.

There was no explanation to why her pain called to me to be soothed. I didn't even know her but there was a beast beginning to rear its head from deep within. And it wanted out!

"You are of the utmost importance!" I declared. "You have been played for a fool, Kalina." She looked up at me from beneath her wet lashes. "You are a Conservatrix demon with all the bells and whistles that come with it!"

My breathing became rapid as I tried to let her know she mattered.

I couldn't speak the truth into being quick enough. All I wanted was to take away her hurt.

She didn't realize that her sadness emanated from her body, that her emotions could be used as a weapon or a relief. And right now, my shields were starting to fail under their weight.

Taking a steadying breath, I refocused. "Do you want to know one of my abilities?"

She wiped at her moist cheek and gave a teeny nod.

"I can see energy. I know... not guess, what any being is. I am not new to my abilities. Practice has made perfect," I said with a wry grin.

She grinned back. The heavy sadness in the room lifted slightly.

"I know for a fact that you are a Trixie, even if you doubt it yourself."

She was rolling my words over in her mind, that much I could tell. Her silence meant she was trying to figure out if I was highly skilled at deceit and wanted to draw information about Lucian out of her by gaining her trust... or if just maybe everything she had been feeling for years was valid.

Watching her face as all the little tells started to fall into place for her, my heart gave an involuntarily hard beat. Every nuance of a job that her mind and body perceived as foreboding but had been the intuition of her nature. It was all there, laid out in front of her, waiting to be acknowledged.

Lucian didn't treat her as a father should. I'd make sure he got was coming to him one day soon.

My torture at his hands had only lasted a few days. Hers had been on going over her entire lifetime.

Power must have been persistently itching at her core, to unleash, to destroy other demons. Lucian brainwashed her and made it clear that she was to do no such thing.

Whenever she lashed out at one or became too focused on a circumstance he laid before her, he must have shut her down and sent her on a meaningless mission.

"How do I know you are telling the truth?" skepticism written all over her face.

The way the light shown with hope behind her eyes was enough to tell me that she wanted so badly to believe me, it hurt. I wanted her to grasp that hope with both hands and accept it as the truth.

"You told me what a Trixie is. Do you know what their abilities are?" I waited patiently for her to remember the studies Lucian made her do.

"They are strong and agile. They use their seductive beauty and pheromones to entrance their opponent." She glanced down at her own physique when my eyes trailed down her body.

Her full breast and toned body certainly fit the bill. Her face, with a set of full lips, a perfect nose, and gleaming hazel eyes were befitting a Trixie.

"What else?" I urged, with a little eagerness.

Looking up from her musings, she finally answered with what she knew I was getting at. "They are empaths."

I was having trouble keeping my own emotions out of the equations. She needed someone on her side. And damn it! For all intents and purposes, I wanted to be that someone for who knew whatever reason.

"Not only are they empaths. With the right training and practice, they can push their emotions out from their bodies to the room or to an individual person."

I popped another warm grape into my mouth and let the tart juice roll over my tongue, relishing its taste and the way it felt going down my aching throat, making sure every emotion I had clung to the surface of my being.

As Kali watched my every move, every emotion. I knew she *felt* it. Relinquishing her own emotions, she experienced mine.

She'd probably had felt things on missions that didn't match her own emotions but dismissed them as nerves or adrenaline.

A Trixie could only dim their abilities. They could never truly shut them off.

"What you are feeling right now, hold on to it. Concentrate." I got up and moved closer to her. "Feel what I am feeling. Ask me again if I am telling the truth and reach out with your senses."

Doing what I told her, she asked again. "Am I a Conservatrix demon?"

Taking her hand in both of mine, I looked deep her in the eyes. "You Are a Conservatrix demon, Kalina. And you are not only important. You are a coveted being."

Chapter Eighteen

Quinn

I picked up my shirt from off the chair where I discarded it when we'd come in the room.

Lucian smiled over at me. One of his rare grins. They only came about from bouts of debauchery or devastation.

My body was satisfied but my mind still had found no repose.

"On your way down to the kitchen," he said as he buttoned up his shirt, "Get Jax and Parker to come to my office in twenty minutes.

I finished attaching my knives to my thigh holster and pulled on my boots. I never felt more naked than when they weren't on.

"Why do you assume I'm going to the kitchen?"

With a raised eyebrow, he purred "Because I know how much energy I made you burn."

"Cocky much?" My eyes didn't match the smile on my face. It faltered after a few seconds. "Shouldn't I be attending this meeting with them?"

"I don't think that will be necessary. Not everyone should be privy to the same information." Lucian rubbed his chin with his forefinger and thumb. "I had business in the warehouse office earlier today. See to it for me that things are in order, won't you?"

I understood that this was my dismissal. Typical asshole male in power. Got what they wanted and then... *don't let the door hit you on the ass on your way out.*

Heading out the door and towards the stairs I got a ping of satisfaction. My intuitive abilities only worked in close proximity to a subject, so it must have come from Lucian.

The corner of my mouth pulled up against my will and I bounded down the steps two at a time, drawn by a need for a post coitus snack.

Upon reaching the outer door of the kitchen, I heard hushed voices talking adamantly.

Stopping by the entry to the kitchen, just out of sight, I tried to pick up what they were saying.

Jax and Parker were discussing their latest feeding and wondered if the carnage left in their wake was worth cleaning up.

Smart demons knew to keep the secret of being on this plane from the notice of the gods but something in their tone made me wonder if there was more to it than that.

Were they on a mission, and feeding just seemed the natural course of action after they completed it? Or was this something else?

Lucian never let us all know the same things, but it was apparent that he had these two doing a lot of jobs together lately.

If they discussed it with me, and Lucian found out, he would not be pleased.

And Lucian not being pleased was just another way to say violent.

After another few minutes of listening to see if I could hear anything worth knowing, I decided they wouldn't be so bold as to discuss anything in the Manor.

As noiselessly as I could manage, I sidled into view at the end of the island.

Jax grinned but Parker was startled. My ability to sneak up on him was just another reason he hadn't warmed to me after more than a century of working together.

"What's the haps, boys?" I asked cheerfully.

The kitchen was bright and white. Large enough for a double stove but small enough to not feel overly exuberant. I did enjoy the fact that there was a double sized, restaurant style refrigerator and freezer. It was always packed with all the best yummy foods a gal could ask for.

Jax hopped off his stool and offered it to me. I knew he had a small crush on me, and I really didn't mind using that to my advantage from time to time.

"Nothing new," he said. "Just the same old secretive bullshit as always."

He threw me a sideways glance that let me know he thought it was crap but didn't want to chance Lucian's wrath.

"And how are you doing Parker?" I smirked. "Anything exciting to get you riled up lately?"

Parker grimaced in my direction. "I know you're not asking about any missions we might have been on."

The death glare that came my way was almost comical. He had always been a huge pain in the ass and I there was nothing I loved more than pushing all of his buttons.

"Of course not!" I exclaimed mockingly, swishing my shiny brown hair over my shoulder with an exaggerated motion. "I was asking about your personal life."

Strolling to the freezer, I grabbed a pint of ice cream. Plenty of flavors in there to choose from but I tended to stick to my favor. It had bits of toffee in a vanilla ice cream with a gooey caramel core and chocolate sauce swirled around the sides.

Jax burst out laughing. Boisterous and bass, it was a great sound whenever he graced us with an actual laugh.

Parker didn't find it all that funny. Taking a bite of the apple in his hand, he challenged, "After sex snack, Huh?"

That stopped Jaxson's laughing cold. I flushed. Asshole! Parker took another bite of the apple with a smug smirk plastered on his face.

Retrieving a spoon from the drawer and returning to my stool, I smiled to myself.

"When you're through doing whatever this is, Lucian said to tell you both he wants to see you in his office."

Popping the top and spooning a hearty helping of ice cream into my mouth, I let the sweetness melt on my tongue before I continued.

"He said twenty minutes but that was fifteen minutes ago." They'd have to run all the way across the manor. If they made it on time, it'd be a miracle.

Jax jumped to his feet like he'd been electrocuted.

Parker, on the other hand, rose slowly and scowled at me.

They both left without another word.

I *felt* a ping of hatred from Parker, but it was the ping of distress from Jax that had me feeling guilty.

The ice cream wasn't hitting as good after that.

Chapter Nineteen

Thelzion

I tried to steel myself for what I was about to tell Brie.

Nausea roiled through my insides and my head began to pound. I knew I should have told her about her past long ago.

Loving her with every cell in my body and the thought of losing her made me put it off for way too long.

Looking up into her encouraging eyes was torture.

I had to tell her now. The next part of our mission against Lucian depended on her knowing the whole truth.

"You know that I wasn't good in my past." Nodding affirmatively, Brie kept quiet so I would continue. "As you already know, I was sent to," I hesitated on the word, "...dispatch you and your parents upon your birth."

It wasn't a pleasant memory for Brie, the one where I told her I had been sent to kill her parents. Parents she had never and would never know.

The thought sometimes brought a lump to her throat that I felt on her behalf. Demon or not, anything that might hurt her was too high of a price.

It was my job to protect her. Even from the likes of me.

She'd had a decent childhood with a wonderful foster family. She'd never wanted for anything.

They didn't treat her like a daughter but more like a favorite visiting cousin. The rules that applied to their other children were often dismissed for her.

She'd found out later that I had used my mind pushing abilities and arranged this but during the time, she said she was glad she didn't know.

She'd felt safe, loved, and cherished. That was what a Conservatrix demon needed in childhood to thrive as an adult.

"Go on, Zi. It's okay. I need to know, don't I?" Her hand rested on my lap. Picking it up, I put it to my lips.

"I killed your father," I said, hanging my head.

She reached up with two fingers to lift my chin. Her eyes were fierce, but no tears welled in them. I could never deserve this woman. Working to that goal every single day was why I existed now. For her love.

"Lucian said he would take care of your mother. You had been born already, and your father had taken you down the hall to the waiting room. Your grandparents and aunt were waiting to see you."

My searched eyes her for any sign of vacillation. Brie's steadiness gave me the courage to go on.

"On his way back to your mother's room, I pushed him into a janitorial closet. You were in his arms." Tears welled in my eyes, but I wouldn't let them spill over.

I thought it would be her that broke, but it was my heart that was betraying me. If anyone other than Briella ever saw this side of me, I'd killed them without a second thought.

"It was quick. He didn't even know he was dying until he was already dead." I took a slight comfort in the way I'd extinguished her father's life.

Had he been her kin, her flesh and blood, and I'd taken him from her before she'd ever gotten to know him. That part still weighed on me.

I wanted her to comfort me and knew how ludicrous that was. She shouldn't want to even be near me, but she was still here, listening to my side of her story.

"When he fell, he fell backwards, cradling you to his chest. I thought for sure you would begin to wail and give away our position." I looked at her with such veneration. "You didn't make a peep. In fact, when I picked you up, all pink and puffy, you grinned. Your little smile reached all the way to your enormous eyes. I was mesmerized and I knew I couldn't do it."

Brie stroked the back of my hand with her other hand. "What happened next? I'm here. So, I know you didn't complete your mission." She gave me an encouraging smile. "What did you tell Lucian?"

"That's the thing, Lucian was still in the room with your mother. He'd killed her and I was worried that he would insist on doing the ritual over your lifeless body with me. I hadn't brought you back to the room and I was afraid that he wasn't going to take my word for it when I told him that I ... killed you."

I took a sip of the blood that was left in the cup I had set on the table.

"He was preoccupied though. He held a bundle in his arms, but it wasn't moving." I looked at Briella to see if she understood what I was telling her.

Her mouth was slack and the constant fire in her eyes dulled to a mere spark. She stood and crossed the room.

The absence of her warm hand left me feeling frozen but simultaneously the heat in the room rose to an uncomfortable level. I knew it was coming from her.

"I should have told you. It was so wrong of me not to." I pleaded for her understanding. I'd never meant to keep it from her.

As she grew, safe and happy, I'd convinced myself that her knowing would only cause her heartache. That the knowledge of her twin sister could do nothing but hinder her development.

I'd planned on telling her when she was older, but when I'd become more entangled with her in her puberty years, I'd convinced myself that telling her would make her think I was trying to coerce her into being who I wanted her to be.

Then I'd fallen in love with her. Her, Briella.

She wasn't just some Trixie I had overseen since birth.

She was smart and charming and made me feel things that an upper-level vampire should not feel. She awakened a light in me. A goodness that I wasn't used to.

It led me down a path of demon ruin but brought me to a paved road of redemption.

"I am going to ask you this just one time, Thelzion." She was pacing back and forth and stopped in front of me as she asked, "Did you see Lucian perform the ritual on the stillborn?"

"No. He held fast to the babe. I was too preoccupied, thinking about you, alone with your dead father in that closet. I was worried that you would begin to cry, and someone would come to investigate." Standing, I crossed the short distance to her.

Stopping inches away, I held my hands up in front of me in surrender. As powerful as she was, I didn't want my baser instincts to kick in and hurt her if she lashed out. I'd sooner kill myself than let that happen.

"I know I should have thought more about it, Brie. I should have been all over it. I knew Lucian was a ruthless demon. He would never have cradled a baby the way he was. I just wasn't in my right mind. All I could think of was getting back to you and setting you on the path you were meant to be on. I am so sorry."

Our small house was dimly lit. The smell of dust and the humid air crept up my nose as I waited for her verdict.

"I suppose I understand that" she said. "Why haven't you told me all of this before now?" Watching her closely, she considered me for a moment.

The way I'd been overprotective of her in more than just a Mated way. The way I tended to put her needs before my own. The way I would become frenzied if I felt she was in danger.

And putting it all together, I could tell she was realizing the way the first time we allowed ourselves to open up about the love we were feeling. How it made me feel ashamed.

I'd felt like a guardian to her. I'd crossed a line falling in love with her and my cold heart didn't know how to reconcile the two halves of what I'd felt.

Now that we were lovers, I was even more terrified of losing her love than ever. She was the nucleus in which my moral compass tried to hold to the side of good.

After taking a few minutes to collect herself, she reached over and took my hand in hers again. Her eyes bade me to continue.

I'd do anything she wanted. Be anybody she needed me to be, but in this moment, it was difficult to keep telling her story... but I'd do it anyway. For her.

"I don't even remember making the decision to save you," I said. "I had been feeling lost for a long time. When your big doe eyes looked into mine and you didn't make a peep, something in me took over. I knew I had to go meet Lucian head on. I didn't want him anywhere near you. And when I found another baby in his arms, I was in a daze," I finished lamely.

Brie gave my hand a gentle squeeze. I responded by letting tears spill over my bottom lids, running freely down my cheeks. She deserved my pain. It was hers to use or throw in my face or whatever she decided to do with it.

"So, after you saved me?" she mildly nudged me onward. Her scent was like home. It soothed my cracks and filled the spots in my soul that had bled for hundreds of years in her absence.

Coming out of a far-off train of thought, I picked up where I'd left off.

"Yes, I saved you... from me. I didn't know what to do with a baby. I knew that you needed human parents to bring you up and I couldn't let that task fall to just anyone."

Smiling wryly in her direction, her eyes lit with that love she held deep inside. Completely stunning.

"Trixie's tended to be mischievous and get into all kinds of trouble in their formative years. I found a very nice family in a semi-rural town with a few kids of their own. I watched for about three weeks, to make certain that they were patient and loving parents."

My eyes grew bright as I recalled a distant memory. Taking care of children had been well out of my realm of expertise.

"Taking care of you and your needs just for those few weeks was well out of my comfort zone. It was hard and easy, all at the same time. It felt ... right."

Swallowing hard, I cleared my throat. "Well, I knew that you needed human interaction, and I wasn't the best at it at that time. I knocked on the door of this family's house when I knew they'd all be gathering for dinner. I compelled them with my mind pushing to accept you as a foster child that they had wanted for a long time but that would be treated extra special."

A light rain sounded on the rooftop and the smell of fresh petrichor ushered its way into our tiny bubble of recollection.

"Did you check in on me? On them?" she asked. "I don't remember you at all before puberty."

Pulling her close, she plopped down on my lap in the reclining chair. The top of her head laid against my chest, just over my dead heart.

"I did. I made sure they had everything they needed and if they had felt overwhelmed, I took that fear and angst from them too. I would observe you every couple of months."

She certainly had been a handful back then. I'd overcompensated the foster family I'd left her with because of the guilt I had felt at leaving them to deal with what should have been my responsibility.

"You used to run around and terrorize your siblings," I barked a laugh. "You'd try to get them to do all of the daredevil stunts you could do."

Grimacing a little, I proceeded to give her an example of her mischievous ways. Some of those times had been gods awful. Other were simply amusing... well, only from a demon standpoint I supposed.

"I had to intervene when you convinced all three of them to climb to the top of that ravine with the waterfall. You wanted them all to jump, even though the water in the reservoir wasn't deep enough for a human to be safe."

Taking a thoughtful sip of blood from the cup with my free hand, I stroked her hair with the other.

"It's a good thing I was there that day. They would never have survived the plunge."

Briella looked up at me, shocked. I knew she recalled the instance but wouldn't remember me being there at all.

Donnchadh's could compel nearly any other being. Demigods, mixlings and Trixie were the exception. Other Donnchadh's couldn't be compelled either, only ordinary vampires.

With the puzzled look on her face, I quickly explained.

"I stayed in the shadows and moved at ultra-speed. And, as you are well aware, your childhood memories blur when you attempt to recount them. It's a ruse of the mind for all Conservatrix. I have come to believe it's meant to help spare them most of the sorrow that comes with watching their human families grow old and pass on. It blurs to re-enforce their humanity while carrying onward with their duties."

Brie batted her eyelashes and tempted me with a sly smile. If it were any other time, I'd snatch her up and run to the bedroom. Little vixen.

"When did you make the decision to interact with me? Was it my alluring pheromones that drew you in?" she said playfully.

I blanched, struck by a feeling of guilt and shame. She hadn't meant it in a bad way, but I knew she could sense from my reaction that this was exactly what I feared she'd believe of me.

"I didn't mean that!" she exclaimed. "I wasn't suggesting that was your whole intent, Zi. I was simply wondering why you had decided to be more direct with me."

My heart started beating again after its brief stop. Assembling my scattered thoughts, I pushed my guilt to the back of my mind.

"I'm a demon, Brie. I was a bad guy for four and a half centuries before you were born. Being close to you was never supposed to be the plan." I swallowed hard. For a different reason this time.

The past wasn't a good place for me to revisit. It was filled with senseless violence and emotionless death.

"After your foster dad died, I saw you. The heartache that you felt was evident anywhere within a twenty-five-foot radius of you. I hadn't known heartache, not really. I wasn't used to the sensation of longing or loss... or love. You exuded that from your every cell. I knew you didn't know you were doing it, and I assured myself that I was staying close to make certain you could get a grip on your emotions. The car accident had been such an unexpected event, and you were only nineteen years old. And being not quite at puberty yet but still so powerful, it gave me reason to be concerned."

Her foster father's death had come out of nowhere. It was a bombshell that had ripped her family's heart apart.

She could probably remember the pain and the love she'd felt for him but wouldn't feel its presence. The experience would be wholly separate from her now.

"I made trips more often to see you. I was beginning to be negligent in my Donnchadh duties. The blood thirst of the demons and meathlu in my care was wearing on me. Seeing you, naturally practicing the art of fighting and gracefully going about your day-to-day life, it felt like a balm to my aching soulless soul." I smiled and Brie grinned back.

"When your foster mom died, I was there, hiding in the shadows. I didn't want you to be alone with your grief, even if I didn't know how to help. The illness had run its course, and your foster siblings felt like you were an outsider because of your unnatural youth. You were twenty-six years old and still looked eighteen to them. I had to take them in turns when they would leave the room. Compel them so you appeared aged when they looked at you. After that, they gathered with you in their mutual sorrow rather than huddled away from you. You were sad, but you found solace in her passing."

My eyes brightened. I smiled from ear to ear. "I was performing my duties and cleaning up after an overzealous vampire who'd gotten sloppy. You came around the corner to investigate the scene."

Brie raised her eyebrow at me but I continued. "I hid."

She looked at me with doubt written all over her face. She was so easy to read. That cute expression of her would be my undoing one of these days.

"You were only about twenty-seven. Puberty was over but your skills weren't honed yet. And believe it or not, at nearly five hundred years old, I'm pretty good at what I do." I winked at her. "I scaled the building and watched from the rooftop."

"Why would you do that? Why not stay and confront me?" she asked.

"I didn't want to fight you. Young and skilled as you were, I'm an old vampire. As you know, instinct tends to be in the driver's seat when our primal selves are engaged. Hurting you was the last thing I wanted to do. And as young as you were and new to the game, your mind wouldn't accept me or whatever I might have to say."

Incredulity written on her beautiful face, she took a moment or two before I knew that she conceded I was probably correct in that assumption.

Waving her hand in a gesture to proceed, I smiled. Her ability to think through every rationale quickly and accept her conclusions wholly was just one more thing I loved about her.

"As I watched you, I couldn't tell if you were mad at yourself for not being able to intervene. Or if the anger coming off you was a projection of rage towards the demon that caused the carnage. Your empathic abilities most definitely were not under control yet."

She started to protest but I booped her nose and pushed forward, luxuriating in the feel of her in my arms.

"The way you scrunched up your face made me laugh. Your concentration was solely on the scene in front of you. And that made me scared. I don't think I had ever been scared before. It wasn't something demons felt. Nervous, anxious, or excitable, sure. This was something new to me. I had lived many centuries with nothing new. It reminded me of when you looked at me as a newborn. I felt hollow deep inside. The fact that you weren't aware of your perimeter made me want to jump down and scold you. It made me want to scoop you up in my arms and protect you. It was such an irrational feeling. It confused the seven circles of hell out of me."

Sitting back in the chair, I pulled her close to me. Our faces were inches apart. Brushing a soft kiss over her plump lips, I picked up where I'd left off.

"I didn't want to let you out of my sight. Following you home proved more frustrating than I thought it would. I watched you dispatch several meathlu and demons, all supposed to be under my protection. I was scared that you'd get hurt. I was nervous that one of the demons would see me and call out for my assistance. I was floundering in a sea of emotions that I was having trouble coming to grips with."

Brie leaned back against my chest again, nuzzling her nose in the crook of my neck. Her light breath had me hardening beneath her.

"You changed me. From the moment I laid eyes on you. You changed me." I had been asphyxiating in a stagnant life, and she had been a breath of the most refreshing air I'd ever experienced.

Scraping my fangs over her skin, the smell of her blood stirred my desire, but I pushed it aside.

"I didn't know if fate was a real thing or just something humans made up, but I felt like you were born to be mine and that I searched for nearly half a millennium not knowing what it was I was searching for."

"Please, get to the good part," she said with a wink. "When did you decide that the night we met was going to happen?"

Her coy smile did things to my insides still, after all these years. With a gentle sigh, I stroked her arm in a circular pattern.

"So impatient, Hellfire" I said, kissing the top of her head. "Okay, okay," I proclaimed after she pulled back to glare at me. "I had been following you for nearly a year."

"What!?" Brie exclaimed! "A year? And I never even knew you were there?" She hung her head.

My poor, sweet fallen angel. If she only knew how I'd fretted every time she'd gone out hunting. I'd followed her most of the time. From a safe distance, of course.

"You were getting better all the time, honey," I reassured her. "I'm old, and again, I'm good at what I do."

The one side of my mouth tugged up. Her mood didn't improve. She was sulking and I could feel it.

"You may want to reign that in, sweetheart. It gives away so much more than you think."

With a sideways look at me, she locked it down. Still upset with herself but under control, she remained quiet so I could finish the story.

"As I said, I had been following you for nearly a year. Every night. You had acclimated to the sleeping patterns of those you hunted quicker than most of the trixies I'd ever met."

A wry smile fell upon her lips and the hand she placed mockingly over her heart patted her chest.

"You are insufferable." I kissed the top of her head again and continued. "I heard the commotion of the would be mugging from a quarter mile out. You took off running in that direction. I got there before you, of course, and waited until you were in view so you could see the scene clearly before I intervened and stopped the robbery with heroic, but human looking, effort."

I'd never forget the look on the faces of those meathlu's. They'd been a couple of my charges. Their sense of betrayal nearly stymied my hand, but I reasoned that Brie would end them anyway.

At least with me doing it, she'd stop to hear me out without a fight first.

She chuckled. "You looked like a Greek god fumbling for a hold on them." She played with a stray piece of my hair and my stomach twisted in knots at her touch. "It was still convincing enough to give me pause and let you introduce yourself."

That had been the plan a few times before that night, but I'd never worked up the nerve to follow through.

"The rest is history. You were enthralled with my wit and helpless to my charm," I ribbed, rubbing my fingertips up and down her arm.

Goosebumps rose to the surface. A soft moan escaped her throat. The scent of her arousal nearly threw me off course, but she recovered quickly.

"You said we had to find the mixling witch soon. What does Noella have to do with any of this?"

Her quick mind was one of my favorite things about my mate. I gave her a second. She'd get there before I'd open my mouth anyway.

"You told me about the past for a specific reason, didn't you? The still born, my twin. That was the point of this talk, wasn't it?"

Bingo.

Not so still born after all.

Chapter Twenty

Lucian

A knock came on the large oak door. Perusing a book from behind my work area, I looked up lazily and bid my company to enter.

Parker strode in and sat at one of the low chairs, meant to make the visitor feel inferior, across from the oversized desk. Jax sauntered in after but remained standing.

Jax was a typical length demon. Stubborn and strong with a rapidly calculating mind. The human body he wore was honed with rippling muscles and his dark skin shimmered with a light sheen.

When Jax was present, I was more careful about the secrets I kept than I had to be with any other demon I dealt with. There was a time when I trusted Jax completely. It had been many years ago now since my old friend was wholly himself.

Quinn was not privy to the information I would need from Parker and Jax, but they were in on the last failed mission I'd sent her on.

"Won't you have a seat, Jax?" I asked casually but Jax knew it wasn't a request. "We have business to discuss, and I'd like your insight."

The length demon took a seat in the other unoccupied low chair.

A wry grin spread a crossed Parker's face. He was an asshole, but that didn't mean he wasn't good at what he did.

The flare that always came with them working together was worth the extra hassle.

"How did the mission go?" I was angled towards Jax, but Parker spoke up instead.

"We found the mixling witch. We didn't engage, like you requested. There was no vantage point to tell if she had the ring or not. And we overheard her tell the deblocker that they would be traveling to see a Seer." Parker was pleased with his report, but I wasn't satisfied with it.

"Anything to add, Jax?" I asked.

The burly man reached into his pocket and pulled out a ring.

My eyes widen incredulously. I knew it wasn't the ring I'd sent them to locate but I recognized it.

Taking it from him, I examined it at length. It was silver and had two hands reaching together and clasping around a clear gemstone.

"The Fainne Todhchai," I said in a reverent whisper. I looked over at Jax who raised his eyebrows nearly to his hairline, not understanding the language or the longing my voice held. "The ring of foretelling. I haven't seen this in over three hundred years."

Parker peeked around Jax elbow to get a better look. His expression told me that Jax did his job well. Parker had no clue what the ring was. Or where or when Jax had procured it.

I thumped my fist lightly on Jax shoulder for a job well done. I hadn't sent him for this but asked, in passing, weeks ago if he had any ideas on where he might begin his search.

The ring had set me on this path. I was done with playing keeper to the meathlus. It was time for me take my rightful place as a king amongst demons.

The future had been shown to me, and I knew what I must do to ensure it.

My only regret in my long life was that I had to kill the only other person on this plane that I'd had a connection with.

If I were being honest with myself, it was love. The one time I'd allowed anyone close enough to my heart, I had to forsake it.

Caylum had made it clear that he was going to work against the uprising. He was passionate and head strong and alluring. He was a witch with drive and the heart of a griffon.

I wanted us to be together for eternity but ultimately, Caylum stood in the way of my dreams of domination.

Parker cleared his throat, bringing me out of my reverie. I clutched Caylum's ring to my chest for just a moment longer.

I knew Parker found the sentiment uncomfortable as he rose to leave but I motioned for him to retake his seat.

"I thank you, Jax" I patted the pocket of my jacket that the ring now resided in. "I will have to find a gifter who is from Caylum's bloodline to see if it can be used for our purposes." I turned my attention to Parker. "Did you succeed in finding out the next location of the witch's travel plans?"

Parker's color went from golden bronze to green in the fraction of a heartbeat that it took me to ask the question.

"We could only find out the general area of the shop she was heading to." He hung his head and waited for the wrath that usually followed.

It didn't come. Even I was surprised with my reaction. I unconsciously patted the ring in my pocket and gazed off into the distance.

Both Jax and Parker sat quietly, waiting for me to come back to the present.

After another quiet moment, I finally met their faces with a hard look.

"You know that won't do. Go there and scout her out. Find me something I can use," I finished with a flourish of my hand.

The lackies got up and walked towards the door but I called after them in a quiet whisper. It felt more deadly somehow.

Shifting my eyes to theirs, I said, "Boys, do not disappoint me."

Chapter Twenty-One

Hayden

Lara had gone to the back of the shop, near the coffee maker and mini fridge.

I bustled around the counter and offered my help gathering the refreshments. A quick peck on the cheek made her blush. Smiling down at her slight frame, she smiled back.

"Thank you," I said. She didn't pretend to be puzzled or act coy.

"I knew you needed to see him. You have for a while now, but..." she hesitated, entertaining her own amusement. "Well, you're stubborn."

I knew he couldn't argue with that. My obstinate attitude regarding my cousin had always been a trivial point of contention with her.

No matter how she might broach the topic, I'd always shut her down. She'd been right not to give me all of the information and just tell me Bastian was coming. I wouldn't have believed her without seeing the change in him myself.

Lara prepared the finger sandwiches and iced tea and set them onto a tray. Grabbing a few glasses from inside the cabinet, we'd need some napkins from next to the coffee maker too.

With one more shared smile, we walked back to the sitting area where Noella and Bastian sat in casual conversation.

We'd all decided not to discuss things in further detail until after we'd filled our bellies.

The makeshift luncheon was winding to a close when Noella's phone rang.

Excusing herself, she walked a few aisles away to take the call.

Lara's pursed lips were all the indication that I needed to tell me this was the call we'd been waiting for.

Noella came back into view and Bastian stood to receive her.

Thinking of who Bastian had been growing up, and the contrast to the young gentleman I saw in front of me now, the difference was astonishing.

Again, I thought of the few times in the past couple of months Lara had nudged the conversation in Bastian's direction. I'd been so hung up on our youthful rebellions that I'd forgotten people could grow.

"Thelzion and Briella are on their way here. They are only about 20 minutes out." She looked to Lara for an answer to an unspoken question.

"I think we should wait until they're here to go on any farther," Lara said. "We should also maybe review what's already been stated in order to make sure you've got a handle on it."

She looked to me and Bastian. The lunch we'd just eaten churned slightly in my stomach at the realization we were about to meet two demons. Real, live demons.

"Do you understand the things we've told you? Your histories and the way the gifters came about?"

It was Bastian who spoke up. "So, if I'm getting this right, gifters are descendants of humans and demons or demigods. And Demigods are descendants of the gods who helped Aion to put in a loophole for an event in human history that hasn't come about yet but can't be changed?"

Noella nodded in affirmation and Bastian continued. "And mixlings are the offspring of a demigod directly and a gifter."

It wasn't a question. He looked at Noella's face. "You are basically a goddess twice removed."

The burst of laughter that followed from the rest of us was enough to fill the space with a bit of levity.

Bastian's face went red, but his smile was dazzling. With his golden hair tied back in a ponytail, the blue ring around his grey eyes shined bright.

Noella's opalescent skin appeared to shimmer next to his rich bronze coloring.

Bastian took her gloved hand and brought it to his mouth, brushing it ever so lightly with his closed lips. Noella sighed and glanced over at Lara from the corner of her eye with a look that I didn't miss.

Lara made herself busy with picking up the dishes and left the area. When she came back, I posed the next line of questioning.

"Is that everything we should know? This realm, the Godly realm, and the Underworld are all there are, right?"

"I'm afraid not. There is also Sidhterra. It's where the fae reside." Lara said.

Her face gave nothing away, but I knew her too well. She wouldn't be telling us about it unless she knew it would be useful later on.

It made me wondered just how often and how much she kept to herself. The burden of knowledge must have been exceedingly heavy.

My foreshadowing's weren't always life and death. They could be mere decisions to help a day along. Coffee over alcohol. Cross the main bridge rather than taking the back alley.

I had to make hard choices when it came to telling others about a foreshadowing involving their lives. I couldn't choose for them, only present them with the fork in the decision. It was stressful enough.

My endless veneration of Lara's concinnity left me feeling like a child for the gifts I had compared to hers.

"Sidhterra is another realm?" Bastian asked. "The fae are here in this realm. I've seen and interacted with quite a few."

Puzzlement at why or how presented me with an old bitterness but I didn't voice it. Bastian looked to me and answered the unspoken question anyway.

"I fancied a pretty girl I met at a dice game with some other gifters. And before you ask, yes. They weren't a reputable lot." He gave me a wistful look. "I didn't realize that she was fae until after we were involved. I guess I should have been upset that she hadn't been more forthcoming, but I really liked the attention she showed me. It was great... until it wasn't."

"What does that mean?" Arching my brow, I'd really had no idea about anything fae related, never having known they existed.

"Faeries can be tricksters. Some of them are a bit malicious. Not all of them, but they get a reputation for the way they tie your words into deals that benefit them. They can have a nasty side. They don't even see it as bad. They aren't malevolent but don't ever trust one completely!" Bastian stared off into the distance, as if remembering something foul from his past.

I could tell that Bastian was still thinking on some unvoiced memory. "Okay, I have a question. Why do different gifters have different abilities. How does that work?"

"Great question, Bastian," Noella said. "The fact is, every gifter is a descendant of a particular god or goddess. It doesn't matter how far down the line they are. Their gifts will manifest as some diluted version of that particular deity."

"Hayden and I are cousins, so how come we have such different gifts?"

I'd thought this was a shrewd observation from my formerly bumbling family member.

"Ah yes," she said. "Well, the gifter gene is carried on the maternal side. If I'm not mistaken, you and Hayden are cousins via your father's side."

The answer was simple enough, but it did make me wonder just how many potential gifters there were and how many were yet to be born. If my father and Bastian's father both found a woman with the ovum of the gods, was it coincidence or destiny brought about?

Turning back to Lara, I asked "So, if Sidhterra isn't another realm. What is it then?"

"Technically, it is another realm, another dimension. It's as if a piece of tracing paper has been laid overtop a map of our world. That's the best way that I can describe it."

"How do they enter our plane? Can we go to theirs?" My head was beginning to spin slightly.

All the information I'd gotten today and now this. I could feel a headache forming from the tension in my neck.

Noella touched Lara's shoulder as she passed. Then she answered for her. "There are entryways hidden all throughout Lagomshire presenting in many different forms, usually in a natural setting. The closest one to here is in Avalon Park, off the Ancient Dunes Nature Trail. They have access to Larnach City quickly from that spot."

My back stiffened as I sat up straighter in my chair. This tidbit of knowledge made my heart thump loudly and brain swim with nervous energy.

Pushing up off the chair more forcefully than I'd meant to, it crashed over sideways and broke the leg.

"Oh Lar, I'm sorry," I sputtered out. "I want to be doing something. This information has my teeth itching. I want to go and explore and..."

She cut me off with a hand to my chest. "You can't go to Sidhterra!"

There was a severeness to her voice that I'd never heard before. A tension around her eyes that held me fast.

"I'm begging you, Hayden. Don't do anything reckless. You know nothing of the ways of Faery, and it isn't going to help us if you are made to dance or sing yourself to death. Or whatever other deals they persuade of you. The food & drink alone could keep you trapped for years. Time in Sidhterra doesn't work the same as it does here," she finished, a bit winded from the longest speech I'd ever heard her give.

The sun dipped to the level of the trees across the river casting shadows here and there around the room through the large front window to the shop.

"Okay. honey," I said. "You don't have to worry. I won't do anything that doesn't need to be done."

Gently touching both sides of her face, I gave her a withering look before swiveling around to glance at the runed bowl.

Asking the room in general, I stammered out what I really wanted to know. "How many fae bed and have children with unknowing humans?"

Noella shared a glance with Lara. It frustrated me to be left in the dark. I knew they weren't telling me everything but that was going to change.

"I want to know what in the Damning Stars you're not telling us, Noella." And glancing back to Lara, I said, "You too, Lara. I don't want to be in the dark anymore!"

The tinkling of the front door broke the sudden tension.

Sashaying into the shop, a tall man and a stunningly beautiful woman monitored the scene before them.

The man, having heard my declaration before even opening the door, said mildly, "Then by all means, have a seat and we'll get on with it."

Chapter Twenty-Two

Zane

A smile lit Kali's face from ear to ear.

I could tell that she had *felt* the words and emotions I'd spoken to her. Watching her face, I could see the roller coaster of emotions roll through her.

A part of her was absolutely thrilled at the new realizations but I knew a part of her hurt deep within.

If all that I had told her was true, and she could feel that it was through my own emotions, then Lucian had lied her entire life.

Surveying my word's effect, I could see the rage beginning to fill her. The emotions she'd harbored broke free of the damn in her mind.

The room was thick with the angst, anger, and self-doubt she'd kept penned up. It pressed down on me like a thick blanket.

I had unwittingly given her permission to feel all of her suppressed feelings.

Raising my hand as if against a rushing storm, I reached for her. It was all I could think to do.

Kali couldn't get herself under control. The dirt and debris that accumulated in the corners of the room flew in all directions. A cyclone of thick air met my face as I laid my hands on her shoulders.

"Breathe!" I said urgently over the whooshing sound in my ears. "Kali!... Kali!... Kalina!"

Shouting her name over and over. Gently but firmly placing a hand on either side of her face, I stared into her eyes. The touch began to bring her back to the present.

The things floating about the room began to drop one by one. Dust settled back to the surfaces. The light that had danced in a frantic pattern of sparks and shimmers went dark.

"Kalina" I tried again to help her focus. Her warm face wet by tears of rage and sorrow glistened in the now dim light.

Without warning, she reached down around my back and pulled me close to her. Her strength mixed with my current weakened state made my mind reel at the surprise attack.

Our lips met with bruising force, splitting my bottom lip back open. The sting was nothing compared to the sweet taste of her lips.

I tried to let go of her face but that just made her hold tighter to me. If she didn't stop soon, I didn't know if I would be able to stay honorable against her assault.

It would be like taking advantage of a drunk person and that wasn't who I was, but she made me feel so damn alive for the first time in decades.

Realizing that she needed to feel something good, anything, I allowed myself to give in, parting my lips allowing her access to the warmth of my mouth.

Our tongues tangled in a match of wills as I attempted for tenderness, and she went for primal lust.

A zing of electricity swept through my system. The taste of my own blood mixed with the sweetness of her honey trap mouth. It was intoxicating.

After a few minutes of this aggressive kissing on her part, she slowed.

Duplicating my technique with effort I could feel her exuding, she lost herself to the passion I was trying to show her. It didn't feel right to be this close to her and not show her what caring could be like.

My one hand found the small of her back while the other made its way to cradling the back of her head.

After a few more seconds, she pushed away from me as abruptly as she'd drawn me close. Embarrassment coloring her cheeks. Her fingers began twirling the ends of her hair again. Adorable.

"Well, that's one way to get control of yourself," I said with a broad smirk.

She really was the most adorable thing I'd ever seen. The thought made my heart stutter.

"I... it all just... I don't know." The words tumbled incoherently from her swollen lips. "I'm sorry." Sheepishly, her eyes met mine.

I knew that if I made her feel rejected in any way, she would run right back to that shitshow of a life with Lucian and never have the opportunity to blossom into the powerfully beautiful Trixie she should be.

Kissing her was unexpected, but it was thrilling. I didn't want her to feel obligated to me, but I would love the possibility to do it again.

The fact that I was the first person to show interest in her, to tell her she mattered, couldn't be the only reason we came together though. It wouldn't be right.

"There's no reason to apologize. It was an effective way to regain your control."

Not knowing what else to say, I picked up the cup of water and brought it to my lips to bide some time and get myself under control. Her gazed stayed fixed on me with every swallow.

I'd honestly believe she'd never kissed anyone like that before. The sensation had left her body reeling. With my gifts, I could see all of the little lit up spaces along her body.

It made my cock twitch to see my effect on her. The little vixen would be the death of me.

Her eyes trailed from the opening of my shirt to the blood crusted at the nape of my neck, to my plump red lips. Her tongue found her bottom lip and slowly, her top teeth pulled at its puffy edge, making my hard on even more uncomfortable.

It wasn't an anxious gesture. It was more lustful, a yearning I saw there in her face. It matched my own and damn it. I wanted to take it for face value.

If I didn't nip this in the bud now, I would become helpless against my own drive. She deserved better than a romp in the hay simply because I gave her a compliment or made the most minimal amount of effort in caring about her well being.

A sound from the warehouse below snapped us out of the silent tension. Kali moved quicker than I'd thought she was capable.

"You're supposed to be dead, remember?" she said as she pushed me towards the window.

"Can I see you again? We still have a lot to discuss." It killed me to leave her here. My brain rejected the idea even as I allowed her to corral me.

Carefully climbing onto the ledge, panic set in that I may never again get this close to her. The humid early evening air clung to me the instant I was outside of the building, muddling my thoughts.

The angst I felt leaving her here was akin to physical pain. Reaching back to touch her face once more, I wouldn't go until I could be sure she'd see me again.

"Crescent Beach. Around 3am. Come alone or I will *know*." Her hand pushed at my shoulder, and I nodded and smiled widely.

Giving me a wistful look before closing the window and the curtain, she'd stepped away from the sill just seconds before I'd heard the door to the room banged open.

Kalina

"Hello Kali", the female said as she slid into view.

"Hello Quinn." My nose prickled at the scent of Lucian on her. "What brings you out to the slums?"

A wry glance beyond the door frame confirmed that she came alone.

The scent must be mingled in her sweat. The thought made me nauseated.

Quinn made me feel small at every chance she'd gotten over the years. My father's lacky and sometimes lover took great pleasure in belittling me at every turn.

Minor incidents seemed to feel more significant in light of the new information that Zane provided. It was now all clicking into place with every memory that came to the surface.

Lucian never cared enough to stop Quinn's verbal denigration of me whenever he was privy to it.

Through new eyes, I could recall his smirks and amusement at my maltreatment.

Biting back the bile that had risen in the back of my throat, I continued with mine and Quinn's usual dance.

"Has he sent you to clean up after him again?" I took a small bit of pleasure picking at the sore spot in her carefully donned armor. I could always tell she'd wanted more from Lucian than he was willing to give.

"No. I was here to see if Lucian still needed me, but he wasn't here when I arrived. I was just on my way back out," she lied. Jealousy of me I'd never understood until this afternoon. Quinn hated me and at least now I knew why.

I headed towards the door for a prompt exit while Quinn inched around the room, taking in even the smallest of details.

In a blink, she was in my path with a hand on my chest, blocking the exit.

"Where is the prisoner?" she said with unconcealed venom saturating the dripping hate in her voice.

"What?" I replied, feigning ignorance. "There was nobody here when I arrived. Did you lose someone... again?"

The little dig felt good. I so rarely got to unleash my enmity for this seidre demon with Lucian around.

"I am on my way back to the manor. Would you like me to ask the boss if he took care of the matter?"

Cruelty at Quinn's expense seemed better than confronting Lucian at the moment. A wry smirk crinkled in my eyes. If that kept up, I was going to get wrinkles from all the smiling I'd done today.

"That won't be necessary. I will handle the situation," she said. "As I always do."

With a flip of her hair, she turned her back to me and began studying the room intently.

The feeling of despair that came from Quinn was much easier to pick up on now.

Zane had led me to the water, and I was prepared to drink as much as possible.

With a bit of practice, controlling my gifts wouldn't be so hard. I sincerely hoped.

Other people's emotions were as screwy as mine so I knew it wouldn't be a walk in the park, but I would get better eventually.

I knew what my abilities were supposed to be now. Gaining access to them would be my top priority.

"If there's nothing else, I'll be going." Before Quinn could respond, I swept out the door and to the stairs at the end of the corridor.

Without so much as a glance back, I made for the exit.

Maylum manor and Lucian would be the next stop and if things went as I suspected they would, meeting up with Zane would be the start of a new destiny.

Chapter Twenty-Three

Hayden

Noella pushed forward and extended her hand to the woman.

With both of hers, the woman took it and kissed Noella's knuckles.

"It is so good to see you again, Brie," Noella said. "It has been ages."

"Hayden, Bastian, this is Briella." She motioned to the woman. "And this... is Thelzion."

I remained seated but Bastian came forward to shake his hand.

Thelzion looked uncomfortable but extended his to meet the gesture.

"Lara love," Noella said and immediately blushed. Recovering quickly, she pushed through, "Could you please get the dream journal from the counter?"

I was mildly taken aback. I could now clearly see something I'd missed earlier.

The surprise of Noella showing up with Bastian in her initial vision and being caught off guard wasn't because of the premonition.

It was Noella herself coming that caused her trepidation.

Bastian had eyes for Noella, but looking at the situation now, I could see it wasn't in a romantic way. It was in a reverent sort of way. A relationship between an adoring acolyte and their mentor.

Coming back to the present, I stood up and bridged the gap, extending my hand to Thelzion as well.

"Nice to meet you." Walking back to I seat, I looked to Lara and our eyes met.

She gave me an unsure, weak smile that I instantly reciprocated. If she was happy, I was happy for her.

Noella waved her hand through the air and two more puff chairs came from the reading nook on the other side of the shop, arranging themselves beside the four we had been sitting at.

Lara motioned for all of us to take a seat.

"Is everyone up to speed?" Thelzion directed his question to Noella, but it was Lara who spoke.

"We have filled them in on the histories of the magical world. The ways they are connected and how things came about. They know of Aion's discovery and how we became the loophole."

Lara's words were simple enough but there was definitely a protective edge to her voice.

"We were waiting for your arrival before discussing the mission that Noella and Bastian went on or the reason you are here."

Pursing her lips, she turned to me. "Thelzion is a Donnchadh, but he has forsaken their cause. Briella has been his new path since she was born. She is his mate."

I had no idea what she meant by that, but I trusted her judgement and her Seer's ability without question. If she saw danger from them, she would tell me straight away.

"It's nice to meet you both," Bastian said. "I think I remember you from the lab?"

He posed it as a question, but I was sure it wasn't. It was a recollection.

"That night is hazy at best. I still have bad dreams about it." He glanced over to Noella with a meek smirk.

Turning back to the group, he said, "It was my first mission doing something good and I was a bit flummoxed the whole time."

He gave a slight chuckle and stopped talking altogether. Bastian's bronze face flushed with shades of pink.

Thelzion didn't seem the type to care for another males feelings being worn on their sleeve.

"So, tell us about why you went to the lab in the first place, Noella," Lara intervened on Bastian's behalf, sensing the same thing I had.

"Aion had seen that stopping the humans progress would not be beneficial. Even though their scientist will bring about the Breaking, he deemed it must be allowed."

She thought for a moment before elaborating on the matter. I could see the clockworks of her mind in full grinding mode.

"Evolution is a tricky game. He didn't want to throw off the course of natural selection either. Going farther down the loop of time, he saw the fork. If the Breaking wasn't allowed, there were more substantial consequences than if he added a loophole."

I was still lost. The fact that the gods could see what was happening, when they cared to look in on humanity, and still were unwilling to correct problems themselves, left my heart feeling heavy.

Noella went on, "He gave the demigods a prophecy to that end. If the prophecy was tended to and the actions of the handful of gods he gathered to his cause fulfilled, then humanity would have a shot at beating the demon uprising."

"I found Bastian through Lara," Noella said timidly.

Glancing up from under her lashes, the curve of her lips gave a hidden insight to my wonderings about how my cousin became involved.

Lara returned the look, mildly abashed.

Brie spoke next. "Noella, why didn't you tell me what you and Thelzion were up to? I thought we were friends."

The slight hurt in the accusation shown on Thelzion's face and had him swiveling in his seat to face her.

"It's not like that, Hellfire. The fact that you'd think I'd keep it from you pains me."

Briella hung her head and Thelzion gripped her chin with his forefinger and thumb, raising her face to meet his.

"I was on a mission to find out more about Lucian, remember?"

A look of understanding brightening in her eyes. Calculating. Smart.

She was radiantly shining from within. There was no other way to describe how she glowed under Thelzion's staring eyes. Love like none I'd ever experienced. That must have been what it was to be mated.

"I had no idea it would lead me to the same mission Noella was destined for. It seems the gods have had this well planned out for many centuries."

As the sun began to dip below the copse of trees, Lara turned the lights on over our sitting area. The coffee had been long gone, and I was feeling like I might need another cup before long.

"Brie, you know I would never keep you out of the loop intentionally." Noella reached over and gave her friend's hand a gentle squeeze.

A long inhale and quick exhale later, Brie shook her head and smiled back all of us.

"I'm sorry. I'm a bit out of sorts." She looked to Noella again as she spoke. "Did you know about the circumstances of my birth? About my twin?"

Noella shifted uncomfortably in her seat. There was a pregnant pause. If it was awkward for me, then I could only imagine how it was to be Noella right now.

Lara broke the tension. "Knowledge is not always your friend. It can cause more problems before their time. Wisdom should come first."

She gave a poignant look into Briella's eyes, and I'd been shocked that the woman absorbed the meaning so quickly.

"Thank you, Lara. I will take that into advisement as I sort through my feelings." The sentiment was sincere.

The fact that this woman, this demon, could adjust so quickly to new information made me feel like an admiring child.

That kind of emotional intelligence was what I associated with age and wisdom. Seeing it portrayed on someone who looked so young was emboldening.

Thelzion began the story again from his perspective. His gruff voice was another reminder that he was a demon. I couldn't think too hard on it or I'd probably turn and run for the hills.

"I had infiltrated the building from the south side when I heard a small explosion, and all of the armed personnel went running in that direction." He smiled at Noella and Bastian. "I set off towards the lab at breakneck speed. I thought that I was getting a lucky break. Turns out, I was just slower on the uptake than the witch."

It wasn't said in a mean way. In fact, Noella returned his smile broadly.

"I didn't even know what I was there to look for. I only knew that it was where Lucian had sent his top lackies and their mission had an air of urgency to it. I had no idea that I'd be vecting into the heart of a heavily guarded lab."

Bastian raised his hand like he was in school. Thelzion didn't acknowledge it but Lara did. "Do you want to add something, Bastian?" authority ringing in her tone.

"I have a question," the quaver in his voice making his nervousness about Thelzion evident. "What is vecting? And who in the Damning Stars is Lucian?"

Brie let out a little laugh and turned to Thelzion. "You need to remember that most gifters have a blind spot to most of the shadowrealm. You can't expect them to understand everything your ancient ass takes for granted as commonplace."

She brushed a stray strand of his silver blonde hair behind his ear and leaned in close. The adoration they had for one another had been something I'd longed for my whole life. It was mesmerizing.

"I know you're out of your comfort zone but do try to behave civilly." Her beaming smile had Thelzion's posture relaxing a bit more.

She turned to face Bastian and myself. Apparently, Noella and even Lara knew of all the shadowrealm stuff already.

It made me feel downright naive for things I didn't know before today. Even Bastian had known about faeries. I was the odd man out in this group.

"Vecting is how full demons can go from one place to another in the blink of an eye. The more powerful they are, the farther they can go in one shot. Otherwise, they have to pop in and out of existence until they reach their destination." There was no condescension in her voice.

Her explanation was thorough and didn't leave me feeling belittled. Simply facts.

I was really beginning to like Brie. My initial anxiety of meeting with full demons was only ignorance. Opening my mind was becoming easier with every word she spoke.

With a hand now resting on Brie's for support, Thelzion continued. "Lucian is another Donnchadh. He is vile and works only to his own ends. The human stories of vampires ripping people to shreds before draining their bodies originated with him."

Disgust was painted on every inch of his face. It reminded me of the first time I'd tried blue cheese. Lips curled up. Eyes squinting in discomfort.

"I am not innocent, by any means." Thelzion sounded tortured by something. I couldn't say what though.

Brie reached up and ran her hand down his face in a loving way.

He continued. "I'm not. I was never the monster he was though. I needed to drink blood to live, like we all do, but there's no need for us to take pleasure in the traumatizing of humans. It can be done quick and nearly painlessly."

Noella seized this moment to speak. "Lucian is not as hands on as he once was. With the evolution of medicine and the easier access to blood banks, he has evolved as well. While he'll gladly tear a person apart for sport, in the privacy of his own home, he prefers a clean and sophisticated tumbler of blood."

Thelzion didn't have anything to add to that. His face was impassive.

"Why were you there, Noella? I need to understand the part you all are playing in this" he said, a forced calmness to his voice.

Lara rose to her feet, gathering herself to her full height, and pushed herself through an unseen obstacle. "I sent her there."

Shock ran in ripples over each of our faces. This meant that she'd *seen* something months ago. It also meant that... oh... ohh.

With a piercing look at Noella, she took a deep breath and continued. "We have been... exploring a relationship for the last several months."

Shifting from one foot to the other and rubbing one hand over the top of the opposite arm, she fidgeted, as if divulging a damnable heresy.

The smile Noella had just moments before wavered in the wake of Lara's self judgement.

"So, you saw a need to send her there through a vision?" Brie asked. There was no perdition. No defamatory thoughts directed towards her friend or new acquaintance. A simple question posed at an awkward time to alleviate the tension.

I was truly awestruck with Brie's demeanor. Everything about her was inspiring. Even the love she exuded for Thelzion. It showed from every facet of her being.

"I did," Lara recovered but Noella's mouth was still turned down at the corners. Her eyes had lost a bit of their sparkle.

With a glance to me, Lara pushed on. "We were discussing her father and the vision hit with brute force. I managed to relay all I could to her instantly and we put some small pieces together over the next few days."

Bastian opened his mouth to speak and closed it again. Discombobulated thoughts must have left his nerves too frayed to utter anything.

After I had my own in check, I proceeded to air my own feelings. I'd had a feeling this was the case. It wasn't like I'd ever thought Lara and I would be an item after that initial date. It was just weird that she hadn't mentioned anyone new in her life while we did our little dance still.

"I think it's great, Lar. Why didn't you tell me?"

She just gave me a coy smile that I understood only too fully. She wasn't used to the idea yet and valued our flirtatious repertoire. She had worried how I would react.

"Aww, Lara. Do you not know me at all?" I laughed quietly and leveled my eyes at her, "For a great seer, you sure can be rather obtuse."

"Speaking of Draxus, have you heard from him lately?" Thelzion was more intent on sticking with the meeting's purpose than caring for all of the touchy-feely aspects of those gathered. "Would he be willing to help us against the uprising?"

Noella shifted in her seat. Light bounced off her skin as if she couldn't contain all of the magics inside her for a moment or two.

"My father has no interest in anything but his own drunken and drug induced ways anymore." The pursed set of her lips told me that she wasn't thrilled with him.

It wasn't up for discussion, but Thelzion didn't pick up on the cues.

"He could prove to be beneficial. It should be a no brainer for him to want to help!" Thelzion seethed.

Briella touched him on his arm, drawing his attention to her. A slight nod of her head was the only communication that past between them. A dip of his chin was his only response.

Raising his hand with a flourished wave, he gestured for her to continue.

A mollifying breath later, she did. "As Lara said, we were discussing my father when she'd had a vision. I had just finished filling her in on my personal histories. The vision took us in a new direction."

Chancing a glance in Lara's direction, I could tell she wished she hadn't. The seer was studiously ignoring her gaze. The hurt welling up inside of Lara had me unconsciously reaching out to comfort her. Noella looked away before continuing.

"Aion had enlisted the help of a few other gods. They were to procreate with humans to create demigods, who, in turn, would mate with humans to create gifters." We all nodded in understanding. "He also wrote the Prophecy of Tumultus. It was handed down to Draxus. Aion trusted Draxus. As the son of Hecate, he felt the sorceress' son would be the most inclined to fulfill it."

"Is that what you were after at the lab?" I couldn't help myself from asking. I was on the edge of my seat, enthralled with the story.

Thelzion sat up straighter. He too, wanted to get to the crux of the matter. Bastian spoke instead.

"We were after a ring. An old ring that the prophecy spoke of. We don't know how the scientist came to have it." He scrutinized Noella's face.

Trying to see if she had deceived him in other ways too? Her relationship with Lara was a blow my cousin wasn't prepared for and certainly wasn't handling well.

"There was a photocopy of a small portion of the prophecy in the lab too." Noella produced a torn piece of paper from her pocket.

"What is it they do in that lab?" Brie asked the room in general. "Do we know if it's what will cause the breaking?"

Thelzion's eyes shot to hers. It was apparent that he hadn't even thought of that when he was there.

"They do something with particles. Matter smashing or something like that. I don't know the technical aspects of it. Aion's prophecy was clear. The humans must be allowed to cause the Breaking. Even if we don't agree, we can't see all that he can see through the wheel of time." Lara gave Thelzion a pointed look.

Noella continued the story before Lara could bore a hole in the side of Thelzion's head with her glare.

"We got the ring and needed to get out. I heard the armed guards heading back to the lab and used a strong barrier spell to keep them at bay when I saw Thelzion enter from a door in the back." Noella looked to Thelzion to tell his side from that point.

"I came in, just in time to see her throw up the barrier. I had no idea what she was doing there but I was grateful to see her. That was when I saw Lucian's forces coming in from a door that ran into another containment area. I shouted to Noella to run. I'd try and hold them off." He trailed off towards the end of his recounting.

A far-off look gripped him tightly. Briella brushed a hand up and down his arm, recalling him to the present.

"I saw Lucian's second, Quinn, come barreling towards me. She shouted to Jax and Parker... they're the two closest demons next in his hierarchy of lackeys, even if he won't validate any of their positions. They were to look for the artifact. That's the only info I got about their mission." He ran a hand through his hair and over his face. "I had no clue what artifact they were talking about. Quinn was on me in an instant. I was holding my own but then Brie walked in." His face went slack.

We all stared at Brie as she raised her hands in surrender. He still wasn't fully back in the present, but he continued where he'd left them hanging.

"It wasn't her. She didn't even glance in my direction. She searched along with Parker and Jax, turning the lab upside down. They never bothered to pursue Noella and Bastian."

Shaking the cobwebs from his thoughts, he brought Brie's hand up and brushed a kiss over her knuckles.

"I should have realized that it wasn't you sooner. I didn't feel the tug. Nothing. Honestly, the fact that I didn't make the connection that our Mating bond was missing makes me feel stupid."

Lara gave Noella a knowing glance which she quietly ignored. Magics hummed in her aura. The doubt Lara expressed earlier hurt Noella more than she originally let on.

Bastian chimed in, as only Bastian could.

"You made us invisible, didn't you?" A corner of his mouthed pulled up on one side despite himself.

"We couldn't be seen by them. It would have meant more ruin than you know. If Lucian had been there, it wouldn't have worked. He'd have smelled us." She turned to Thelzion. "I should have stayed to make sure you were okay. I'm so sorry, old friend." She touched him on the knee and then sat back in her seat. "What happened next?"

Thelzion seemed lost. A man stuck in the turmoil of a thunderous mind. Briella answered for him.

"He was captured." Noella gasped and her hand flew to cover her mouth. "It wasn't me there. It only looked like me. It would appear, my twin is alive and in the employ of Lucian.

Chapter Twenty-Four

Kalina

I arrived at the manor full to the brim with questions. I knew I should see Lucian before heading out to rendezvous with Zane.

My composure was tenuous at best. Anger at Lucian, pride in myself for never totally falling in line, excitement to fully learn my abilities, and a confused elation from kissing Zane drove me to tip toe through the halls.

I'd had trysts before. Many, in fact. They were all simply for release. No one ever made me feel drawn to them or in need of something more substantial than just sex.

This kiss with Zane was different. All I wanted was fifteen minutes to sort through all of my feelings.

If I could make it to my room unnoticed, my mind could untangle some of the garbled thoughts that were flying around.

Almost to the door, hearing chatter, I stopped in the shadow of one of the Three Fates statues there in the hall.

Lucian rounded the corner with a demon I'd seen here before. The female was short and lithe, her ears coming to points. The blouse she wore had a small bulge in the back, like a hump.

An errant thought pushed its way to the forefront of my mind. What if the bulge was hiding something? Maybe she wasn't a demon after all.

I couldn't help but to eavesdrop. The weight of what Zane had told me prodded me on in a quest for truths that I'd been in the dark about. And I was done with that. No more *Must Play Nice.*

I pushed out with my keen sense of hearing, listening for anything that might be useful.

"To what do I owe the honor of your company?" Lucian's voice was strained with false flattery.

I knew him too well to believe he actually cared for the company of this woman.

"I have a message from Her Majesty. I have to bring it to you because no other courtiers are willing to meet with a ruthless liar, such as yourself." There was something malicious in what she said but the words were harmless enough.

I wondered if she might be a Fae from Sidhterra. They could be nice and evil, all in the same breath.

I hadn't realized Lucian knew any Faeries. It was odd that she would disguise herself.

I shelved my thoughts for a moment to listen more attentively.

"And what, pray tell, is this message, Skylar? The importance of it would have to be great if she sent her favorite devotee."

I could practically hear the smirk in his voice.

"Queen Talisin asks that If you are successful after the Breaking, the mortals with any fae lineage be spared from the carnage unleashed once you become king of this plane," Skylar said casually.

I had to cover my mouth for fear of gasping too loud. King? What was she talking about? Why would mortals have any Fae blood? I must have heard wrong.

"Does that mean that Queen Talisin is willing to hold up her end of our bargain?" A moment passed in silence. Skylar didn't make any noise. No loud breathing.

I couldn't even detect any variation in her fluttery heartbeat. I was sure that Skylar was fae now. Faeries couldn't lie but they were all skilled in half-truths and lies by omission.

Inching forward just a little, fingers pressed tight against my lips, I tried to get a look at the female fae.

Tension hung heavy in the air. Lucian's back was to me, but I could just make out Skylar's face in profile. Unease shown in the set of her mouth and her eyes were locked with inner conflict.

"If Her Majesty expects me to look after her wayward subjects, she must give me something in return." Lucian's droll voice grated on my raw nerves.

I'd never thought about it before. Now that I knew what he'd been keeping from me, everything about him grated on my nerves.

Skylar's eyes darkened and her mouth became a hard line.

Lucian was a man of few words. Moreover, he was a demon of violent outbursts. It made his civil façade all the more menacing. "I will need the prophecy to be translated in full. No more of these cryptic half meanings."

"Anexian Script is the oldest writing of the gods. Not all are privy to its inner workings. I shall relay your wishes to the Queen at once." A ripping sounded along with her words.

I heard a whooshing sound just before I saw the movement.

Translucent wings shot out through the back of the blouse the Faery was wearing.

Lucian let out a snarl of displeasure. "You know the rules of my house! You are to blend in as a demon!" he growled.

"If you want us not to be cryptic, then deceitful is off of the table too!" With that, the faery flew to the end of the hall and out the open window into the night breeze.

Lucian stormed off in the opposite direction and I heard him slam the door to the study with a loud bang.

After what I'd just witnessed, I couldn't doubt that Zane had been telling the truth.

It was time to pack a bag, go meet up with him, and decide my next move.

Chapter Twenty-Five

Quinn

There had to be something left behind. Lucian would be pissed if I went back to him and said the prisoner had escaped. He was supposed to be near death or long past it.

Lucian had begun the torturous interrogation several hours before he'd sent me to spy on Riedyn, the Commander of the Fae Elite Unit and his former lover.

He didn't trust the Faeries to give him all the information needed. What he expected was for them to betray him if given the chance.

I sifted through the ashes of the paper that was left burnt on the floor.

There was a big enough piece with a small bit of smudged writing on it. Nothing really useful. A few Latin words. Out of place they would do no good.

Spotting a few drops of blood leading to the chair and a few more at the table, I looked harder at the footprints that had been made because of the ash and dust in the room.

Four different sets were there. A large set of male size shoes trailed from the chair to the door. The steps were clear and concise. One foot lifting and then the other. Those must have been Lucian's.

Another set circled the room. They were more feminine in size. They made the circumference and rested with her.

Looking to where the prisoner had been hanging by the chains, I saw his footprints in more of a gliding motion, like he was dragging. Too exhausted and hurting to pick up his feet, he pulled himself to the chair... but there was another set of prints next to him.

They were feminine and possibly supporting the majority of his weight.

"Kali! Ugh...That bitch helped him."

All I could do was shake my head in disgust. I'd hated Lucian's pet project and knew it wouldn't be long before the Trixie figured out the things that were being hidden from her.

It was the main reason Lucian didn't want Faeries coming and going from the manor in their true form.

He needed the fae to decipher the old scrolls but Fae work to their own ends. "Damn it!"

Tracking the prints of the prisoner, I walked over to the window. Fresh blood speckled the sill, and the disturbed dust showed her all I needed to know.

Lucian must be told but his violence would be wall shaking.

If he suspected Kalina of helping the prisoner, he'd make the connection. She would know most, if not all, that he has been keeping from her.

With his plans for her already more than half a century in the making, his reaction would be nothing but pure wrath.

At least I would catch a glimpse of his true intent. That was something, I guessed. Better than the normal nothing.

If he showed the emotions of losing her like a daughter rather than a project, my answer about his capability to love would be answered.

If he could love and didn't love me now, he never would. Shocker.

I still had no proof. Suspecting Kali and proving it were two different things. I'd never known her to be anything but smart, regardless of how I felt about the bitch.

I couldn't believe the way she'd eat up all of the lies and omissions Lucian fed her. Perhaps that's why he kept her busy most of the time. Not giving her time to think too hard on any one thing.

If I told him and I was wrong, the punishment would be painfully horrible.

If I didn't tell him and I was correct that the little bitch was involved, he would kill me for not informing him right away.

I knew I should sleep on it at least but my dislike for Kali ran deep. She'd grated on my nerves since he'd first brought her back to the manor as a wrinkled, whiny baby and didn't let us make a meal of her.

Snapping a few photos of the area on my phone and grabbing the glass off the table, I made the decision to go to the Manor and tell him. He'd either hurt me or kill me, but at least he'd know I did my job to serve him.

Self-doubt had never been part of my physiological make up and I wouldn't give in to it now.

I just hoped, for my sake, that I was right.

Chapter Twenty-Six

Hayden

Noella had no idea how to respond to that news.

Thelzion looked at Brie's face before he began again. A grimace on his lips, he said, "I thought that I was in my own private hell. I thought that Lucian had been working behind my back to turn Brie against me."

"You know that would never happen," Briella said softly but her eyes didn't meet her wry smile. "Together, forevermore. That's our vow."

With a wince of some unseen pain, Thelzion continued his dismal recounting of his tale.

"I saw her at the lab, and she ignored me. I hadn't had any blood in days, so I was already not in a good headspace."

I couldn't take my eyes off of Brie as she watched Thelzion so protectively. It was the kind of love I'd always wished for. The kind of love that was so rare in this day and age.

Thelzion must have felt my stare because his lips pulled back and he snarled menacingly in my direction. I averted my eyes as Brie rubbed soothing circles onto his forearm.

Lara clicked her tongue and Bastian shifted closer to me in solidarity, and I had never appreciated my cousin more.

After a few tense seconds, he took a breath and continued his tale.

"Quinn, Jax, & Parker bested me and took me to a tent somewhere in the jungle, probably fifty miles or so from the lab. They only jumped twice through vecting. I knew we couldn't have gone farther than that."

His breathing started to catch. Brie put her hand on his face, soothing the memory. I couldn't help but to glance at the two of them from under my downturned lashes.

"I don't know why they didn't just attempt to kill me. Beating and emotionally torturing me was all that seemed to be their aim."

Picking up the glass of tea in front of him, he finished it off before jumping back into his tale.

"The fake Brie would come into my blurry line of sight occasionally. She wouldn't look at me. She didn't help me. I wanted to call out to her but after a few hours, I felt she was my punishment too."

He looked to Noella. "They figured out through the guard's cameras that you were there."

"He got away the morning after they abandoned him chained in the tent," Brie finished for him.

My head was pounding. Bastian sat there. I could tell that my cousin's idea of their mission and the violence that could have occurred just now catching up to him. That much was written on his face.

"Did you know any of this happened?" Noella asked Lara.

She wasn't as upset with her as she was before, but the question was marred with unease.

"I didn't. There are way too many players in this game for me to be able to know everything," Lara said, pursing her lips.

It didn't sit well with her. I knew her too well to not see the signs of her frustration. She wasn't used to being caught unawares.

Her eyes fell to Noella. I could only guess at her thoughts. She'd been my friend for quite some time but right now, all of this was so new, I couldn't begin to understand where her head was.

The safety of her friends was one thing she'd always thought her sight would gift her. Now maybe, she wasn't so sure. It had me reaching for her hand instinctively, but Noella got there first.

Thelzion wasn't part of her close friends list but the fact that his path was known to cross ours in this mission... her fears were a living thing, donned in the lines on her face.

Apparently, Noella felt it was her turn in this play. "We got the ring."

I wasn't the only one left in puzzlement at her words. Thelzion and Briella looked bemused as well.

"One of the Rings of Potentia from the Prophecy of Tumultus. The Exolo Akasha."

Thelzion and Brie appeared to understand right away. Bastian and I still had no idea what they were talking about.

"What is that? Is the ring that important?" Bastian asked before I had the opportunity to.

"This is one of the three rings that Hephaestus forged at Aion's request. It is the ring of Exile." Noella pulled a piece of black velvet from her pocket.

Slowly she pulled back each of the four sides covering an ancient-looking metal.

The ring had a black obsidian stone in the center and a circle of smaller deep red painite gemstones around it. There was a dragon on one side and two intertwined snakes on the other.

It wasn't necessarily pretty but it did draw your eye. A power still radiated from it. It didn't glow or shine, but it pulsed inside me.

Leaning in for a closer look, Lara snatched my arm, dragging me back.

Thelzion angled his body away from the thing all together.

Noella covered it back up with the black cloth and put it back in her pocket.

It wasn't until it was safely away that Thelzion relaxed his position.

"You could feel it, couldn't you?" Noella directed her question to Thelzion.

The lantern light flickering across his face sent a chill down my spine. He wasn't doing anything threatening and yet he still looked... well, eerily evil.

"It felt like death and suppression and a pull that I can't explain."

The fear in his eyes made me want to hide myself away. If a big, bad vampire leader was afraid of this thing, I should probably high tail it out of here.

"The ring of exile damned the demons to the underworld. As a demon yourself, you don't belong on this plane."

Thelzion hung his head and let out a defeated sigh. Brie rubbed his arm in comfort, but his eyes were far away.

"You will feel a heavy weight. If you were to touch it, it could possibly cause your body to dissolve and your demon essence to be forced back to the underworld."

I didn't know what to think. I had to ask the questions that were rushing through my mind. If I didn't, I would probably never sleep soundly again.

"Would Brie be sucked back too? And why can you touch it? You're a Tri-mixling. You have demon in you as well." The words swirled over my tongue with an odd sensation.

Briella waited on bated breath for Noella's answer, blood welling in spots where her nails dug into her palms. Thelzion looked down at the blood and gently brushed his fingers against her wrist until she relaxed a bit.

Honestly, I'd thought he would lick the blood right off her hand. My closed mindedness about demons was getting a true education today.

"I didn't touch it. I don't know what would happen." Lara nudged Noella's shoulder with her own. "I do think that my godly blood would protect me but I'm not willing to take the chance."

She thought for a moment about the Trixie. I didn't know much about her, but Noella seemed the type to side with logic. Crazy, seeing as how see was the epitome of magics.

"The gods that Aion conspired with to make the loophole also had a hand in the creation of Conservatrix demons. It's hard to say if it would affect Brie but I'd advise not tempting fate."

Brie nodded. It was all the conformation she needed. Noella's assessment. I found it foreign to me to trust someone that completely.

Lara would never let any harm come to me and yet I still thought that if something as serious as this was presented, I'd have at least some small doubts in the matter.

"If you have the Exolo Akasha," Brie whispered, as if not wanting to know the answer, "where is the Reverto Akasha?" Breathing deeply, looking to Lara, she continued. "Do we know if Lucian has located the Fainne Todhchai?"

I wasn't the only one confused. Bastian looked totally lost too. His face had never been one good for playing cards.

Bastian demanded "Can we all get on the same page here?!" I had to nod my agreement. "How about starting with filling us in on this Prophecy."

He glanced over at Noella, apparently still hurt. Poor guy.

"Then we can work up to these rings and their importance. I think I should know why risking our lives for jewelry is a good idea."

He'd raised an eyebrow, trying to look menacing but it was so non-imposing that I let out a bark of laughter.

Bastian turned four shades of red and sat down in a huff. I thumped my fist on his shoulder, not meaning to humiliate him. He was just so damn ... Bastian.

Lara went and retrieved a browning piece of parchment from the safe under the counter by the register. The lock clicked and her keys clanged together as she threw them back onto the counter.

I'd always wondered where that third key went. Mystery solved now I supposed.

There was a brief smell of ethereal discharge when the enchantments around the safe had been disengaged. It dissipated quickly but the closer she got to us, a faint scent of fiery smoke and sweet ambrosia clung to the parchment, permeating our nostrils, wrapping around our senses.

Lara laid the paper in the center of the coffee table before us. It was written in a script that none of us, but Noella could read.

"It's in Anexian Script, the writing of the gods." Noella took off the glove on her left hand and waved it over the parchment.

Nothing happened.

Brie's beautiful face looked radiant as one corner of her mouth pulled up in a smirk.

"It appears you've lost your touch, Noella." Poking the sorceress didn't seem wise but she laughed it off.

"I can read it, but it's transcribed by the gods themselves. Lara saw it, plain as day, through a vision a few months ago. The powers that be must think it's nearly game time. That is when she contacted me." With a wry smile, she gazed over her shoulder to Lara and a blush crept into Lara's cheeks.

"Have you heard anything more from your father?" Brie asked.

I'd thought we'd already broached this subject enough. If Brie was pushing it again, there must be a good reason.

"No. He has been getting worse over the last couple of centuries." Her face was stern but concern shown in her eyes. "I don't think Draxus will be much help to us in his self-pitying, blizzunken state."

Clenching her fists and pursing her lips, she tried to reign in her power. The rune bowl on the table began smoking again.

Lara came and put a reassuring hand on the small of Noella's back.

"It's not me, love. I'm not doing it." she said with a bemused twitch from the side of her mouth.

Chapter Twenty-Seven

Hayden

Thelzion stood and half blocked Brie from the bowl. That had me and Bastian on our feet, quickly casting our eyes into the shadows, glancing around for the danger.

The purple smoke filled the space around the coffee table completely. A figure appeared, rising and rotating in the bowl to the waist.

A voice rang out. It was beautiful and horrible and diapason.

It was godly.

"Noella. Blood of my blood. Daughter of my heir on this Mortal plane. I beseech an audience with you and your court," the voice thundered throughout the small space.

Noella dropped to her knees, bowed her head, and extended her arms in front of her on the floor.

Thelzion and Brie followed suit. Me, Lara, and Bastian were a bit slow on the uptake but, after a quick glance at each other, we did the same.

From her face down position on the floor, Noella trembled. Her whispered response barely registering in our ears.

"Great Hecate. Blood of my blood. Mother of all sorcery. I humbly accept your audience."

"Rise child. It is not necessary for you to bow to your grandmother." The goddess's form materialized in the purple mist.

After what appeared to be a moment of uncertainty, Noella got to her feet.

With her ungloved hand, she swirled the air around. A sense of understanding came over us to remain noses to the floor until told otherwise.

"To what do I owe the honor of this meeting, Grandmother?" The only sign of her discomfort was a slight shake to her voice.

"I have come to you on behalf of Aion and those of us who created the way forward. It is nearly time. The Breaking will occur within a fortnight. Are you prepared to mend and maintain the damage it shall cause?" As the goddess spoke, an array of colors floated around the room with each word.

"We have the Exolo Akasha, My Goddess." Hanging her head so low that her chin touched her chest, she confessed, "We haven't located the Reverto Akasha yet."

The silence that followed was deafening. The purple smoke turned dark.

I noticed the cold seeping in and wanted to look up but didn't chance it. Pressing my forehead to the floor with enormous effort, I grabbed the front of my shirt with both hands in order to not be tempted.

"And what of our family ring? What has become of the Fainne Todhchai?" We couldn't see her, but we felt Hecate's sweeping glance graze each of our backs.

"I had gotten word this morning that the demon, Lucian, has obtained it. One of his commanders killed the entire coven in whom Draxus entrusted it after Caylum's demise." Noella pulled her shoulders tight against her body as I watched from my peripheral vision on the floor.

Her hands worked in small circles. Sparkling dust motes landed on and around each of us as we felt an unpleasant, invisible force pressing in on our bowed bodies.

I'd realized Noella was protecting us from the brunt of Hecate's unintentional assault. It made me wonder how much of the goddess's power she felt herself.

"Draxus will have my next audience." The chill in the room lifted and the deep purple smoke became lavender. "My son needs to be reminded of his duty to the gods."

Hecate looked at us all, still bowed with our heads to the floor. I could still feel her eyes on my back through Noella's protective magics.

"It is not my place to say, Granddaughter," her voice lighter, "but your court may rise if you see them fit to do so."

A flurry of shifting sparkles and flourish of fabric as her skirt swished and swayed occurred as Noella allowed us to unbend our backs. She'd worked her magics to still kept us guarded from the goddess's beaming aura and I found myself once again in awe of her. Lara was a lucky gal, for sure.

"Oh, yes. Sorry." Noella was not expecting us to see her as our leader. We all knew that. It still stung a little to hear it.

I suspected that she knew Hecate would see us as nothing but her followers though. She wouldn't correct her because it would just be more hassle than she wanted at the moment.

"Please, rise friends." Her protective energy left our backs to be able to fully stand now, and I straightened without thinking.

I hadn't meant to lift my chin high to a goddess. I could only hope she wouldn't smite me where I stood. Bastian had done the same.

The goddess seemed to note Noella's use of the word *friends* rather than simply telling us to rise. Hecate gave her granddaughter a wry smile.

Bastian was the first to open his mouth at the sight of the goddess. "Woah. You're ..."

Words failed him. The idiot spoke directly to her. Geesh.

Thelzion, I observed, never brought his eyes to look directly at her. Briella even had trouble looking at the figure in the swirling smoke too.

"You keep unusual company, Noella," Hecate's chin lifted to Thelzion and Briella. Then to the rest of us. "And... Am I sensing your heart's desire amongst these gifters?"

Lara's face became the same shade as the pink roses in the vase on the counter. On her pale skin, the blush was prominent. Adorable.

"Ah yes. The great Seer." The goddess dipped her chin in approbation. Speaking directly to Lara, Hecate said "You are a wise match for the talents of my granddaughter. My line is strong."

Turning back to Noella, she became serious once again, bidding her granddaughter a warning.

"Know this, blood of my blood. If the three rings are not recovered, the ripped fabric of time and space won't be able to be mended. The gateway to the underworld shall allow those below to walk above once more. The mere mortals will perish quickly, for they haven't any gifts to help them avoid the demons."

No pressure. We only needed to find some jewelry. Meet up with a vicious vampire lord. Stop the spread of evil. And save the fucking world. Good gods!

"We will keep the dhalls safe, Goddess. May I ask, why is the Fainne Todhchai important to retrieve? I mean, I understand that our family ring has great power in seeing events, but why must it be recovered to mend the rip?" Noella pressed Hecate for an answer, not just a cryptic tid bit of partial information. "Does it play a role in joining the Akasha rings?"

Hecates figure began to spin and shimmer in the rune bowl. The smoke clouded the air as it rotated. I held in a cough as the sweet smoke shoved its way into my nose.

"In due time, all shall be revealed, Granddaughter. For now, set forth the task of your court to obtain the Reverto Akasha *and* the Fainne Todhchai." The figure in the smoke boomed out, "The time is upon you. Set your triumph in motion, blood of my blood."

With that, the figure vanished, and the smoke dissipated completely. The rune bowl went clear once more.

Chapter Twenty-Eight

Kalina

I was just arriving at Crescent Beach when it dawned on me that I had nowhere to go after this meeting with Zane.

For the first time in my life, I was on my own. I could do whatever I wanted and didn't have to account for every minute of my day to anyone.

It was an intoxicating feeling. It felt right. I hadn't felt this kind of excited joy in... well, ever.

I knew I should have some sense of loss but all I felt was elated. Free. Hopeful for the first time in my life.

Rounding the corner of the dunes, I saw him. It'd only been a few hours, and I'd already missed his stupidly handsome face. Weird was an understatement since I didn't even know him.

Speed crept into my movement of its own accord. My heart beat faster. The thundering of blood filled my ears, and my skin felt tight the closer I got.

The need to move towards him filled me with a rush of trepidation that I had no reason to feel.

It was unnerving and invigorating at the same time.

The briny air washed over my face, wet and sticky, the closer I got to the shore. At this time in the morning, a blanket of quiet framed the sound of the waves crashing along the shore.

As he came into clear focus, the moonlight lit his face and the scar that marred his otherwise perfect features shown in sharp contrast.

His smile beamed back at me as I approached. Never in my life had I felt so... content? I didn't know if that was the right word.

It was the oddest sensation I'd ever experienced. There was no rhyme or reason to it.

We'd met once. Kissed. And now what? I was smitten? Way to be so naive, Kali. Good gods.

That didn't seem it though. There was more to why I felt drawn to him. There had to be. I just couldn't place what it was, but it wasn't unpleasant.

Leaving Lucian had been the biggest step I'd ever taken in my life. It was a blessed freedom.

No restraints. I could kill all the demons I wanted to. Being a Trixie was amazingly freeing.

Free to make my own decisions. Free to explore the world around me. Free to be myself for the first time... Only I didn't know who I was. That part was kind of terrifying.

Zane motioned to me as I approached. He'd shown up where we'd planned to meet.

I'd fully expected to come to the beach and find it empty but for the crabs that crawled along the shore and the birds resting in the dunes.

No one counted me as important enough to show up for. No one saw me as significant.

Yet here he was. Waiting for my arrival. Making himself vulnerable to recapture just to show up where I'd asked him to.

Sprinting down the beach, I made a beeline towards him. Towards my newfound freedom.

Chapter Twenty-Nine

Zane

I took in the sight of her and breathed a sigh of relief. I hadn't been certain she'd actually show up.

Worse, if she didn't believe me, she'd show up with Lucian or his lackies in tow. I'd have been dead for sure.

The time crawled as I'd waited on the beach. The crashing waves drowned out the thoughts in my head enough for me to briefly sleep under the stars.

It was still hot. Humid. The breeze coming of the water helped enough to take some of the stagnant air away. It was one of the reasons I loved this beach.

If you walked down to the channel and around the corner, the ocean was just on the other side of the bridge with a beach all its own.

If I was to die tonight, I would be glad this was the place she'd chosen for my demise.

"You're here!" Kali exclaimed. "I know I told you to meet me here, but I wasn't sure you would."

Aww. The little vixen missed me. How lucky was I? Sweet, innocent thing.

"I told you I'd help you. My word is my bond." I stood up and brushed the sand from my blood-stained jeans. I looked a mess. Days of torture would do that to you.

The swelling in my eye had gone down a bit and I could see more clearly out of it now. It still stung though.

My cracked lips were parched. Blood kept welling up every time I'd accidentally move them the wrong way.

I may have a cracked rib or two as well. Hard to say. My healing was fast but not nearly fast enough to save me the hours in pain it needed to make me whole again.

The light from the moon illuminated the beach around us, but the darkness of the night was comforting. Stars danced out here away from the city lantern lights.

She seemed to be thinking along those same lines. That girlish smile did funny things to my insides.

"I left." Her declaration held a hint of sorrow, but the excitement in her tone overshadowed it.

My eyes went to the bag she had thrown over her shoulder.

"Did you confront Lucian?" Unconsciously, I checked her over for any signs of injury.

If he'd hurt her, I'd take my time carving him up before I killed him. The bastard had it coming anyway.

Scrunching up her brows and nose, her beautiful face took on a new kind of adorable look. "No. He was in an argument with a Faery."

I closed my eyes and swore. I'd gotten wind that Lucian had made a bargain with the Fae Queen, but I hadn't had any conformation if it were true or not. It appears it wasn't a rumor after all.

"Did anyone see you?"

That was my main concern. I should be more concerned about my mission... or, oh I don't know, my life.

It wasn't like I had many people I'd count as allies. A few, but I hadn't spoken to any of them in some time. My constant go go go ways didn't really leave time for socializing.

For her though, I'd make time. No idea why. It was all kinds of frustrating, but it was true none the less.

"No. I didn't want to be seen." She smiled. "I'm stealthy like that."

Grinning wide, her eyes lit up. The stars appeared to twinkle brightly in acknowledgement of her newfound joy.

"I guess we should start with the basics." I motioned for her to pop a squat next to me on the beach towel I'd laid out that I'd found abandoned when I'd arrived.

She sat, crisscrossing her legs and handed me a bottle of water from her bag. I hadn't expected the kindness. It took me a little by surprise that she'd thought about it enough to bring me a small comfort when her life was crumbling away around her.

"Thank you." Opening the bottle and downing half of it in one long gulp, I hadn't realized how thirsty I'd been. "That was very thoughtful of you."

"I figured you'd probably need it. Torture takes a lot out of a person," she said with a smirk.

Was she flirting with me? Cheeky vixen.

The draw to her was intense. I'd been alive a long time and I'd never felt anything like it in my life.

She was a Trixie and could seduce a person easily. This felt different.

It wasn't just lust and desire. This felt like a connection. A locked door with a key in it, wiggling, testing the mechanisms of the tumblers to see if it'd open.

The sun was creeping its violet glow into the early morning black sky. Stars were beginning their dance of in and out as the darkness turned a lighter shade ever so subtly.

"What do you know about the Prophecy of Tumultus?" I figured it didn't hurt to ask. See what she knew, if anything.

Who knew how much she'd glimpsed when Lucian didn't think she was paying attention?

Kali fidgeted with her hair. I could tell she didn't like not knowing things. Embarrassment colored her face.

"It's fine," I said. "Not a lot of people have even heard of the prophecy."

Relaxing back on her arms, she gave me a smile that lit up my world with colors I'd never knew existed. Stunning.

"I only got to learn basics. Lucian told me lesser demons weren't privy to all of the workings of things." Her chin dipped, eyes staring at nothing but the sand.

Again, that anger on her behalf reared its ugly head from deep in my chest. I think I might have actually growled a little bit. Geesh.

"You're not lesser, Kali! The simple fact that he wanted you to feel that way should infuriate you." Seething, I took a few deep breaths to calm myself.

Reaching over, her fingers gave my shoulder a gentle squeeze. The sensation sent a zap of electricity straight to my heart.

That was definitely not a Trixie trait. What the fuck?

"What was that?" she said. "It felt like a small bolt of lightning. Is that one of your gifts, like, for protection?"

So, she had felt it to. I didn't know what to make of it. This zing through my system hadn't been just in my head.

"I don't know what that was," I said honestly. "I've never had it happen before."

Those beautiful eyes of hers stared over at me. I couldn't be sure, but it felt like she was looking passed my features, straight into my soul.

"Can I touch your face?" A mild pinkness rose in her cheeks under the light of the moon. "I don't want to presume I have the right to put my hands on you."

Her lack of confidence and the fact that Lucian had made her insecure had my blood boiling. I was all for consent, but this went farther than that. I could tell.

"Sure", was all he managed to say.

Reaching up, her fingers ran along the side of my cheek. Leaning into her touch, I sighed.

It felt like home. There really was no other way to describe how her presence made me feel.

"How did you get this scar?" Her hand ran lightly over the white edges of my ragged skin.

I sat back slightly. The sensation of touch to my scar wasn't something I ever got used to. It didn't hurt, per se, but it wasn't pleasant either.

"It's a long, personal story." Not sure whether this minor rebuff would upset her, but now wasn't the time to divulge my past.

We'd just met. No matter what this strange attraction was to her, I certainly wasn't ready to bare my soul.

"It has character, you know." Kali brushed her fingertips over my scar again, not giving me the leave to back away. Her fingers ran from above my eye, trailing down to rest on my lips.

Not knowing what to make of the look in her eyes, I reached up gently but firmly to remove her hand.

"We're here to discuss you, remember?" Twisting around and grabbing a sword I'd retrieved from one of my caches on the way to the beach, her body shift to a defensive mode. "I'm not going to try and hurt you. I want to see how trained you are... if you don't mind," I added as an afterthought.

With a smile that lit up the night, she unsheathed her own sword.

"Okay, but maybe I should take it easy on you. You wouldn't want a matching scar," she teased, biting her lip the moment it left her mouth.

There was no nervousness about sparring. Her anxiety came from not knowing if her last statement had been callous, but I'd long since passed the point that my scar bothered me.

Smirking now myself, I raised my sword to parry her stance.

"I think you'll find I'm not so easily bested."

With that, I brought it down without pulling any punches. She was a trained demon. One with upper level demon strength. I simply wanted to see what she was capable of.

The metals clanged together, and I was glad for the loudly crashing waves. Her sword met mine blow for blow.

Twisting and lunging, spinning and twirling. Clash after clash.

Her moves were fluid, carefree even. She looked at home with a sword in her hand.

Watching her evade and counter strike each thrust gracefully like a well-practiced dancer, it took my breath away.

In a quick spin move, she threw her leg out in a sweeping motion, landing me on my back.

My sword now laying a few feet away in the sand, she stood over me, sword to my chest, smiling broadly.

"Did I pass?" Her words were breathless and confident. It was the most confidence I'd seen from her.

Now I had a starting point. A kernel of ground to build her up. It was a good foundation.

Before I could answer, she bent down and planted a quick kiss on my surprised lips and then flicked the tip of my nose.

Again, that zap of exciting electricity. Laughing, she rolled over to my side and grabbed the water bottle.

"I see you know your way around in a fight." My smile was tentative. I had the urge to grab her and never let her go.

Why though? It made no sense.

No one had ever brought on the emotions she had. The longing. The protectiveness. The anger on her behalf.

"I've always been good at that stuff. It's the reason Lucian sent me on so many missions." A contemplative look crossed her face. "Now I'm thinking that maybe he just didn't want me near all those demons I could damn to the underworld."

"I bet you would have demolished all of his lackies." My smile grew wide as her eyes brightened.

Praise was for sure something new to her. It only took the slightest bit for her to beam with pride.

Clearing my throat, I stood and walked toward the water. The tide was going out now and small crabs were scattering to get back into the sand at the shoreline.

"I don't know what I'm supposed to be feeling," she said. "I feel like maybe I should be sad at losing all that I've known."

She unconsciously fiddled with a piece of seagrass that had washed up with the last tide.

"I don't though. I feel... I don't know." Looking out at the water and me, standing at its edge, she said. "I feel set free."

Lowering my head, I was happy for her. I wanted to go to her and hug her, kiss her even. It just didn't seem right though.

Not when she'd never had any other choices. I couldn't be sure that she wouldn't do whatever I asked just for a little praise.

Taking advantage of vulnerable females was not who I was.

"What is it you would like to do now, Kali?"

"I could do with some more kissing." She smiled up at me, pink flushing her cheeks.

This little vixen. How was I ever going to keep my integrity with her around?

"I'm flattered... but I was referring to next, as in life." A light huff of a laugh was stifled by my concern.

Resting her arms behind her to remain propped up, I could see her mind working restlessly. Elation and fear crossed her face in even measure.

"I'm honestly not sure. I have nowhere to go." She sat up and wrapped her arms around her knees. "Don't get me wrong... I am glad to finally know the truth and be out from under Lucian's thumb. I just never thought it through past there."

Considering her for a moment, there was no other choice really. I'd offer her a place to stay and a part to play in the upcoming mission.

The question was, was I getting her involved more for her or for myself?

The thought of her out on her own, no allies, not understanding her abilities, made my chest ache.

"Listen, I have a place just outside of Larnach City. It's not much. Just a place to crash during down time." I was a little embarrassed at the thought of her in my bare essential, not so nice, atypical bachelor pad.

I was sure that there were dirty dishes still in the sink and the gods only knew when the last time the bathroom had been cleaned.

Cringing internally at the thought of this beautiful goddess seeing my slovenly ways, the thought still wasn't unpleasant.

"You're welcome to crash there too. I mean, until you figure some stuff out."

Walking towards her, I hesitated for a moment, then sat down beside her on the towel.

She seemed so small, curled in on herself, unsure.

The chasm in my chest grew bigger with each of her timorous breaths. It felt like physical pain to watch her emotionally suffer.

Reaching out my hand, I splayed my large, calloused fingers over hers. It wasn't a sensual touch. Just a reassuring gesture.

"I can ride the couch for a bit. No biggie." Finally looking up at me, her tear-filled eyes went wide.

"You don't want to sleep with me?" The question was so pregnant, it was almost to full gestation.

"You are very beautiful, Kalina, but what I want is for you to feel safe and free." I paused for half a second. "That's not to say that I don't want you. Gods, I don't want to lie to you about that."

Reaching up to brush the back of my fingers along the side of her face, sweeping a piece of stray hair behind her ear.

That zing went careening through my system again.

"First though, I want you to know who *You* are, without influence from someone else. What I want is for you to feel important."

Her eyes welled up again. A single tear spilled over the bottom lid and ran down her cheek. The side of her mouth pulled up on one side.

"Alright," she said. "I'm in. Let's go see this bachelor pad of yours."

Chapter Thirty

Parker

"It's fucking pitch in here," I bitched, moving through the dense woods at a snail's speed. "The moon is full. Why in the sevens is there no light?"

Jax grunted from behind me. The sound of large leafed branches smacking into each other was the only other sound. If there were any forest animals nearby, they weren't making a peep.

"What happen to all that bravado you were throwing around before we got here?" Thwack! Another branch swung back, hitting Jax square in the chest. I huffed a laugh.

"I didn't say I was scared, asshole. I said it was dark." Pushing through the underbrush, we moved towards the entrance portal to Sidhterra.

"I guess not every demon is lucky enough to be blessed with good looks and great night vision." Jaxson laughed again.

We walked on for another ten minutes, with me grumbling under my breath the whole time. If I could get out of doing this menial surveillance crap, I would.

Lucian was an even bigger prick than me though. Couldn't push my luck too far with that twisted fuck. He'd find all kinds of new and inventive ways to make my life hell.

Moonlight began filtering in through the woods. Jax snatched me by the back of my jacket, and I started to holler until I saw the warning on his face.

Quickly realizing the danger, we ducked behind a cluster of trees, just in time to see four fae warriors emerge from the base of a huge Cypress tree.

One minute, it was just us, trudging around the wet forest. The next, we were there. At the portal to another realm.

How Jax had sensed it before it opened, I had no a clue. It must have been yet another one of those length demon abilities that he kept secretive.

The air shimmered around the trees and bushes that camouflaged the entrance for another few seconds, until the warriors stepped away and it went back to looking like any of the other trees and undergrowth in the area.

"Queen Talisin wants Lucian followed," the apparent leader said. "Do not let him be aware that you are there. His ignorance is of the utmost importance."

The three other fae nodded to the commander. Each Faery was armed with an obsidian knife.

Their looks ranged from rusty reds and brownish orange like autumn leaves, to greys and browns like the trees, to green like the underbrush.

Blending into the forest was surely no problem but the cities and town in Lagomshire would pose a bigger hinderance. That's where we'd have the advantage.

Me and Jax had been sent to spy on the fae queen, but it seemed that she was already making her move too.

We'd need to get back to the Manor and inform him before the fae could take up their positions.

The stealth of demons was great, but the fae were in their own element and would notice if the trees whispered their secrets.

Restless energy itching for me to move made it difficult to stay put, but I trusted Jaxson with knowing when it would be safe.

Working together for a while now, we'd realized that even though we might not always like each other, trust was an unspoken thing for survival as partners on missions.

The warm breeze that blew through the woods was unnatural. Humid air was the norm in Lagomshire most of the year, but this sudden gust held none of the usual sticky demon's balls heat to it.

The Faeries moved out swiftly after it past. Dancing over the grounds through the forest and out of sight in a blink of blurred movement. Blending in with the surroundings.

Jaxson used hand signals to motion to wait another five minutes before we were to leave the area. I didn't want to give them too much of a head start, but he was right.

Fae hearing was notoriously fine. Certain demons had amazing hearing, but it was nothing in comparison to theirs. And their sense of smell was beyond unreal. Creepy even.

The all-clear motion from Jax had me up and instantaneously ready for flight. We would have the advantage once we got out of the woods.

Lucian was going to be livid, but for now it wouldn't be directed at us. As long as we made it back before anything could be leaked, he'd play out his frustrations on some poor, undeserving meathlu.

If the demons he was supposed to protect objected, he'd simply kill them.

That was probably one of the best perks about being an upper level demon in this realm. Lucian couldn't dispose of us with the higher ups taking notice.

That didn't mean he couldn't make our lives on this plane hell. If anything, he often gave us all a good reminder of why he was the boss.

And seven hells, I admired the bastard for it.

Chapter Thirty-One

Hayden

Thelzion stood quickly and grabbed Brie by the hand the second Hecate vanished from the rune bowl. He didn't seem to want to be in this room anymore.

The goddess's proximity to him had the demon frantic to get away. Demons weren't meant to be in the presence of the Heavens. Even I knew that.

The urge to flee had his fangs slipping their housing and a snarl was tearing up from the back of his throat. I may have a little shadowrealm in me, but I was never going to be enough prepared to fight a vampire.

Briella was partially behind him. Every time she tried to step around him, his defensive stance took half a step to block her from view.

"Breathe Zi," she was saying. "There's no danger, love." Her voice didn't reassure him the way it had over the last few hours.

If this was what true love looked like, maybe I'd take a pass.

Making a move to block Lara and Noella from Thelzion's glare, hadn't been the correct thing to do but also felt right.

It sent the Donnchadh vampire into a full-on growl and half crouch. If any of us were to breathe wrong at the moment, I was positive Thelzion would rip us to shreds.

Brie tried again to calm him through her touch and soothing words. Fangs fully extended; he took a half step toward our group.

Noella glanced quickly at Brie a second before a wave of power flew and knocked Thelzion across the room. Seeing her magics used for defense was unnerving. She could surely take care of herself and level the place if she'd wanted.

He landed in another crouch, fingers digging in and slowing his backward roll. Then launched forward again. The idiot was going to get himself killed if Noella thought he might get to Lara.

Briella's graceful pounce a split second before she tackled her Mate to the ground looked more like a violent dance. Her hair swooshed across her face and arms extended to get a good hold of him.

Grabbing Briella and knocking her to the rug, his fangs inches above her neck, Thelzion must have caught her scent. He'd gone somewhere else in his head apparently, but he was back in the driver's seat now.

Jumping hastily to the opposite side of the shop, Thelzion put as much distance as he could between himself and the rest of us.

Bastian made to grab anything he could as a weapon to defend against the vampire's attack.

I put a hand on his arm, silently telling my cousin to just wait, but I refused to step out from in front of Lara. I was no fighter, but I'd go down before I let anything happen to her.

Eyes blown wide, nostrils flaring, Thelzion's rational mind must have been slowly catching up with his primal actions. At what he'd done.

His breathing started to level out and his fangs slipped back into their sheaths.

He had only eyes for Briella. The pleading in them was brash, in a remorseful way. His pain seeped into all of us. Brie must have felt it and wasn't reining in her gifts as well as she usually did.

"Thelzion," Brie said, walking in an inchmeal pace, her hands up as in surrender. "It's okay, love. I knew you wouldn't hurt me."

Glancing around the room at the group and then back at Brie, Thelzion relaxed his defensive posture, face impassive.

The tension that had filled the shop began to settle back down. It was dark outside. Moonlight bathed the street in an uncanny glow.

Without another word, Thelzion turned on his heels and fled the shop, disappearing into nothingness as soon as he'd crossed the threshold.

Noella and Lara both stepped forward to somehow comfort Brie, but she was already picking her keys up off the table to follow him.

"I'm sorry. I have to catch him before he does something rash." She took two steps before pivoting around. "We are heading to a meeting with a friend tomorrow about the prophecy. I will text you if we find out more." With that, she was gone.

Bastian flopped down in one of the puff chairs and breathed out a jittery exhale. His skin was ashen, and sickly sweat covered his face. In true to Bastian fashion, he proclaimed...

"Well, I don't think I like vampires much."

Me, Noella, and Lara all burst out in a fit of relieved laughter.

Chapter Thirty-Two

Quinn

I'd arrived back at the manor before Jax and Parker. I still didn't know how to broach the subject of Kali's betrayal.

We all knew what the Trixie was, but I could never understand why Lucian decided to raise her instead of just killing her.

The vibe of the Manor had changed a lot in the last fifty years.

There used to be lots of demons with violence and mayhem encouraged to go unchecked. Debauchery and violent acts played out in most of the estate as naturally as breathing.

Now it was a shadow of its former self. The fun we'd had being our demon selves was brought to an abrupt end when he took in the babe.

I remembered the day Lucian brought home that screaming bundle of pink flesh.

At first, I'd thought that he'd kept the infant alive so he could enjoy its blood fresh.

He'd called me into his study and asked me to have a seat. I'd known he was dispatched to take care of a new Conservatrix de-mon.

With his invitation to join him that evening, I'd thought that maybe he was going to share a taste of that powerful, sweet blood.

"I am going to need you to find a wet nurse." I'd given him an incredulous look at the command. "You are also going to need to purchase everything an infant may need for a nursery."

He never explained. Blind obedience was expected. No information before its time ever left his lips.

Fifty years later and I still had no clue what the end game was for this particular pet project.

The manor was quiet as I walked the halls, looking for any sign that Kali might have come back.

Approaching the outside of her room, no lights were on. No sounds came from under the door.

My hand rested on the doorknob for a few seconds before I found my nerve, turned and silently pushed it open.

It was dark. Even with the moonlight shining in from the open curtained window it couldn't fill the cavernous room.

Kali's scent hovered on every surface. It dripped from the walls. It clung to the bedding. Sweet and alluring. And it plain pissed me off.

Jealousy slipped into the back of my mind, as it often did when it came to the Trixie, at the size room Lucian had gifted her.

Making out the shape of the king sized, four poster bed across from the ornate fireplace with walk in firebox, I approached with caution.

Lots of pillows and girly bedding covered the enormous monstrosity. Feeling for signs of life and finding none, I pushed all the bedding to the floor.

The light on the nightstand turned on with the brush of my skin against its base. Lucian had gifted his *daughter* with it. It held fae magics in its housing that allowed it to be lit with flame.

Overindulgence at its finest. I had to roll my eyes. After a moment of seething, I started examining the room at large.

Nothing seemed out of place but that didn't mean the Trixie hadn't come back after setting the prisoner free.

Her closet was so large and filled with so many clothes and pairs of shoes that it would be impossible to know if there were any missing. Even if there was a week's worth missing, you'd be hard pressed to realize it.

The painting on the wall was slightly crooked. Crossing the dimly lit area and moving it aside. Ah-ha! A safe.

It was locked but did that mean it hadn't been recently accessed? I couldn't be sure.

Kali's weapons armoire was ajar. If there was one thing I knew about her, it was her obsession for her weapons.

Bingo! The little bitch took her favorite sword and several daggers. I bet she took money from the safe and clothes too, but was I willing to bet my life on it?

Yes. I was. If I presented the information to Lucian and I was wrong, my life would be the price. He'd see it as my betrayal, not hers.

I wasn't wrong though. I could feel it in my bones. Ding dong, the bitch was gone.

It was time to hang my head, put on a show of concern, and tell Lucian that his pet was off the chain.

Chapter Thirty-Three

Briella

I couldn't catch Thelzion before he vected away. Getting in the car, I drove quickly home.

The twenty-minute drive took me only twelve minutes. By the time I'd reached the front door, my anxiety was through the roof.

I knew he'd be beating himself up about the whole situation. Mostly, I knew that he would be upset at attacking me.

The primal state for a demon was near feral.

It wasn't often that the feelings of protection for your Mate were put to the test.

Not one Mated couple I'd ever met was able to separate the irrational jealous feelings or the need to peacock. The "mine" factor crept in at inconvenient times as well as the justified ones.

Thelzion had gone fully overprotective vampire and, if I were being honest, I'd thought it was rather hot.

The fact that my powerful partner would burn the world to cinders to keep me safe had the sweet spot between my legs aching.

Opening the door and strolling inside, I spotted him in the same chair I'd found him in the other night. His head hung in self-loathing.

Sauntering into the front room, he looked up at my arrival. The pout on his lips and the haunted look in his eyes told me that he was mentally torturing himself.

My lips curled up in a broad grin. Confusion overtook his features but then he scented me... my arousal. It was a living thing that filled the space between us.

Thelzion raised an eyebrow, and I licked my lips. He never could understand how deeply I longed for him. He'd never allowed himself to feel worthy.

I, on the other hand, was more than happy to remind him at every chance I could of how much he turned me on. Of how intertwined our souls were. He could never wrap his head around the fact that, if we shared a soul, we were more alike than he could fathom.

"I could have ripped out your throat," he grimaced as he spoke. "I wanted to protect you, and I ended up being what you needed protection from."

Putting my fingers to his lips to stop the self damning words, I hitched my stiletto boot up to rest on the arm of the chair, angling my sex towards him.

My skirt had slits on either side. You never knew when you'd need flexibility to fight. Now, it provided easy access to the bundle of throbbing nerve endings between my legs.

Thelzion's breath caught as my eased a hand up his thigh. Strong muscles lined his legs. His cock hardening instantly, making me crave the feel of him.

Breath hitching as my hand grazed him from over his pants, he shook slightly. "Brie, I want to talk about this. I want you to know how sorry I am."

"I have a better idea," I said. "How about you let me enjoy the sight of my Mate, remembering his protective stance in front of me, knowing he'd rip all of Lagomshire to shreds to keep me safe."

Panties soaked; they were nearly dripping with my desire. To avoid further arguing, I bent down and kissed him.

Placing my hand on the throbbing length of him under his pants, I brushed my tongue over his bottom lip.

Thelzion stood instantly, all conscious thought gone. Sweeping me up into his arms, I giggled as he hurried towards the bedroom opening the door with a kick of his foot.

Our bed was soft and full of pillows that he couldn't get rid of fast enough. Our mingled scents permeated the sheets, the blanket, pillows. It was home.

The rising moonlight shone through the window illuminated the muscles of his chest through his thin, white t-shirt. I made quick work of ripping it off his chest. It hung in shreds, clinging to his muscular arms.

My appetite for him was ravenous. Barely containing my need, I whispered into the shell of his ear, sending visible shutters along his skin.

"Taste me, Thelzion" I didn't waste time taking off my boots. The panties he groped at snapped at the tiny strings securing them and he cupped my swollen mound. "I need you... Now!"

He wanted to savor me, gentle and lovingly but I wanted to be taken. Claimed with the desire of his primal side.

I was his and he was mine. It didn't matter if the rest of the world turned to ash. It was us. Together. Forevermore.

Spreading my legs and staring at exposed sex with awed veneration, he slid a calloused hand up my inner thigh, his thumb resting on my pulsing clit.

Working light circular movements over the heated nerve bundle, he bent forward, sucking it between his teeth and lightly flicking his tongue.

"Taste me, Zi!" His head between my legs, I squeezed his ears with my thighs. "Damn it, Thelzion! You are such a tease!"

He knew what I wanted and was hesitant to give it to me after his earlier display, but I was going to crush him if he didn't do it soon.

Slipping a finger inside me, I let out a small gasp. His fangs slipped their sheaths and inched along my inner upper thigh.

"Please, Thelzion! You're driving me mad." His little caresses were all and good, but I needed a more.

Working my erect pearl with his thumb, he slipped a second finger inside unexpectedly. Ahhh. It was blissful.

Squirming with pleasure, I rocked against his hold, driving his fingers in farther. He knew my body better than I knew my own, but he also knew how insatiable I could become in his presence.

Every movement of his hands found their mark with expert precision. My inside muscles begin their revolutions of contraction. The pressure built quickly under his careful ministrations.

"Oh, fuck! By the gods! Zi!" I cried out, just as the first orgasm hit. Waves of ecstasy washed over my entire body. Hot liquid coated my inner thighs, running down towards my backside.

Working his fingers inside me in a flittering movement, he found that perfect spot again in record time. I squirted this time. The sweet honey, sticky and hot, covered his face in a glistening sheen.

It ran down the inside of my trembling legs even more as he dragged his fangs along my inner thigh, sinking in like little needles of pain and pleasure.

My juices mixing with the blood created what he'd described as an ambrosia of the gods. He lapped it up. All of it.

Laying back, I panted for dear life. The glint in his eyes told me that we were far from done. My breath hitched at the sight of his need.

Inching up my body with his tongue, he ripped my shirt open, buttons flying in every direction. The black lacey bra I'd worn was his next target.

Gently but firmly, he unhitched the front closure, exposing my overly sensitive nipples to the humid evening air. Fresh off of double orgasms, they stung for a brief moment.

Our eyes met but no words were needed. The way he looked at me, my mind conjured up a blind man seeing a rainbow for the first time.

He was mine and I was his. No one and nothing could ever take that away from us.

"You're so damn beautiful, Brie."

His mouth came down around one of my erect nipples. With his teeth rolling the sensitive flesh lightly, his tongue flicked the tip, and then all around that central point of pleasure.

Tearing his mouth away and inching his way up, he placed delicate kisses along my collarbone, the nape of my neck, just below my ear, and around to the back of my shoulder.

Goosebumps raised all over my body. The fan in the corner of the room blew a breeze over my exposed skin, making my nipples so hard, they felt pinched.

His soft, supple mouth found mine with loving expertise. There was a gentleness back in his touch now that he'd given me what I'd asked for.

Zi always tasted like spearmint and smelled like the earth after the rain. I couldn't get enough of him. I never would.

The bulge in his pants nudged along the top of my swollen clitoris. I knew he needed release as much as I yearned to give it to him.

It was never enough. We could do this for hours and it would never be enough. The thought sometimes drove me to near insanity. A thousand years would still be too short of a time to relish in each other's souls.

The room now smelled of sex and sweat. Of his scent and mine. It was intoxicating.

Reaching down with both hands, I freed the monster from its cloth prison. The veins along his shaft pulsed with desire.

Thelzion shimmied the rest of the way out of his pants and tossed them to the floor and made to settle himself between my legs, but I was having none of that.

At least, not yet.

The hunger in my eyes had him swallowing audibly. Comical really. Big, bad vampire scared of little old me?

Good. He should be. I aimed to claim what was mine... with force, if necessary. Not that he'd ever not give me whatever I wanted.

Using my demon strength to my advantage, I flipped him to his back. A quick gasp escaped his lips, but he chuckled. And then his eyes widened.

I brought both hands around his hard cock and devoured the tip. I knew, with his girth and length, I'd never be able to fit the entire thing down my throat. That didn't stop me from trying.

Thelzion let out a moan of pleasure that egged me on. His gasping and whimpering heightened my arousal, and his head and shaft slid into my throat farther than they ever had before.

He moaned deeply and his hand found its way to pulling my hair. Damn it, if it didn't make me want to cum again.

Working the pleasure from my Mate drove me on, to lick and suck what was mine for all it was worth. Slurping noises filled our room, alongside his moans which grew louder and louder with each pull of my cheeks.

A warning tap came to my shoulder, but I was going to have his seed. He couldn't stop me if he tried. This cock was mine and I would claim it with everything I had.

A few more long pulls and he exploded deep in the back of my throat. I sucked and slurped and consumed every bit of him, as he'd done to me. Turn about being fair play and all.

Thelzion laid there, out of breath and panting like a marathon runner. This was only the first leg of the race though. I knew he'd never let me have the last power play. That was hot, in and of itself.

Grabbing a couple of waters from the mini fridge beside the bed for both of us, I gulped mine down in one long pull. The spring water was so much better than the sediment filled crap that came from the tap.

The old well on the property needed cleaning out but we'd never gotten around to doing it. There was always one thing or another that needed done around the house.

That was tomorrow's problem as we usually said. You never knew how many more of those you'd get though. Oh well.

My hair had come loose of its tie and hung down over both of my breasts. The real sex was about to begin but I needed a few minutes to recover.

Seeing it as an opportunity, he pounced. With his fast hands grabbing my ankles, giving a quick yank, I fell to my back on the bed.

Water spilled down my front and I giggled. If he wasn't the most devilish demon I'd ever encountered, I'd think I'd slipped into the afterlife and was granted a boon.

"What do you have in store for me, paramour?" A gleam in Thelzion's eye told me that he wanted to ride but he was beyond words.

Instead of saying anything, he flipped me over on all fours. Reaching forward, he wrapped one hand firmly around my throat. It wasn't painful. I could still breathe just fine.

"You're going to be a good girl for me, aren't you, Hellfire?" he exclaimed.

Releasing my throat, he ran his fingers down both sides of my back, making them tingle in the most delicious of ways. They came to rest on my bare ass.

Reaching his hand between my legs, his fingers roamed all the way to my preciously erect jewel, slowly rubbing my swollen sex. A groan escaped his lips as I dripped with sweet honey again.

One finger grazed my entrance from behind; his hand covered in my wetness.

A sudden, unexpected smack had my ass stinging, but my nub and insides ached for more. My nipples tightened from the surprised pleasure.

I could hear him behind me, that skin slapping skin sound, and knew he was readying his tool for the ride.

Reaching forward again, Thelzion placed his hand under my chin, swiveling my head to look him in the eyes.

"Do you want my cock, baby?" He didn't let go. He wanted me facing away from him but looking at him as he hardened again.

The sight nearly undid me. I pushed myself back, trying to gain contact.

"Fuck me, Thelzion! Fuck me like I'm yours and yours alone!"

That did it. His hardened length slammed into me from behind in one swift motion. His length and girth filled me completely. Almost painful, this side of pleasure, riding the edge like a poised knife.

Bringing both hands to rest on my hips, he pounded all the way to my brink. It was heaven. It was pain. It was ecstasy.

He rode and claimed and existed only for me.

The sound, smell, and feel of him thrusting into me brought gasps and moans easily to my lips. His cock hardened even more with his build up and mine built with it. We were seconds away from rapture.

I screamed my approval, begged witness of the gods, and called out his name in cherishment.

Just before we both reached our climax, he withdrew. The sudden loss of fullness left me wanting. Aching fiercely.

Looking back in time to see his hands as he flipped me over in one swift motion, he rammed his full length deep inside me once again, this time from between my legs.

Our eyes locked onto one another as passion climbed within us both.

One, two pumps, three. Slow and agonizing. My insides longed for release. It was torture and ecstasy in a well-rehearsed dance.

Thelzion's dark grey eyes stared into mine. His hands found both of my hips, and while still buried balls deep inside me, he flipped to his back.

I was now on top, riding that over long shaft to the hilt. My eyes rolled back in my head, and it was then that I understood the slow technique was meant to get me ready to straddle his monstrous cock.

"I love you, Hellfire!" It was simple and sweet, and I felt the swell of my own sex bulging in just the right way at his exclamation.

"I love you too, Zi." It was all the words we'd ever need.

Starting to grind back and forth, rubbing my painfully bulging nub on his mound as I went, my muscles began contracting around his girth.

As I began to increase my speed, my swollen clit, aching and erect, released first, sending chills and tingling into my extremities.

His moans grew with each ripple of my own. His orgasm hit just as my g-spot released its own onslaught of pleasure.

We rode the waves of bliss together into the night.

Chapter Thirty-Four

Hayden

The shop was relatively quiet after Noella and Bastian headed out into the night to find Draxus.

I'd stayed behind wanting to talk to Lara alone. She had to know that I'd always be there for her? I couldn't understand why she hadn't told me about something so intricate to her life.

Instead of acknowledging my presence, her tiny frame fluttered about the shop without rhyme or reason. It had been a long day and night. How did she still have so much energy?

She'd busied herself with tidying up the already neat area. That was my first clue that she knew something and didn't want to reveal a possible future to me yet. That had been her way in the past.

Sitting down and waiting quietly for her to realize that I wasn't going anywhere, I picked up a book and thumbed through it.

The unfamiliar text was fluid and staccato all at the same time. The tome tried and failed to explain Anexian Script. The letters matched symbols to the common tongue alphabet well enough.

It was in looking at the Tumultus Prophecy that I'd understood the problems for translating. The words vibrated and symbols switched places.

When I looked away and glanced back quickly, the Prophecy was back to its original orientation. Magics like that were one thing to know about in the abstract... but seeing them first-hand? Bizarre wasn't a strong enough word.

No matter how fast I studied the translating book, trying to glimpse the Prophecy's true form was no use.

Lara gave up stalling and walked to the seating area. A big sigh left her lungs as she plopped down preparing to hear me out.

"Okay, Lar. Spill it." With a pointed look, I sat up on the end of the puff. At least I tried to. "What's the prophecy say? And why didn't you tell me about Noella?

Pursing her lips, I could see the hurt in her eyes. Did she think I was going to judge her for finding happiness?

"Noella is my business!"

Her words came out curt, but her eyes softened after seeing the grimace on my face.

"I just wasn't ready, Hayden. It's only been a few months, and I've never been attracted to a female before."

With my mouth curled up on one side, I took her hand in mine. When she saw my smirk, she smacked me sheepishly with her other hand. A small smile appeared in her eyes more so than her lips.

"Honey, you shouldn't feel awkward or ashamed of loving someone's heart and soul. No matter what or who they are, love is a grand thing."

I'd never understood why some people felt it was their business to have an opinion on something that had little to nothing to do with them.

As far as I was concerned, it didn't matter if it was opposite sexes, same sexes, or inter species. What happened in between friendship and finding a true connection to another being was a wonderful thing.

Love was love. The world needed more of that.

She smiled with her lips this time.

"Besides," I said. "If the Goddess approves of you for her grand-daughter, who else's opinion could possibly matter?"

Color bloomed across her cheeks giving her the glow of an infatuated schoolgirl. It did my heart good to see it there.

"Well, when you put it that way..." a true laugh in her voice. "As for the prophecy, Noella wrote it down for me."

"The translation is confusing, but she worked it out before she came to me a few months ago." A far away gleam twinkled in her eyes. It wasn't a vision. Just a normal, run of the mill recollection.

I had to clear my throat to bring the attention back to the present.

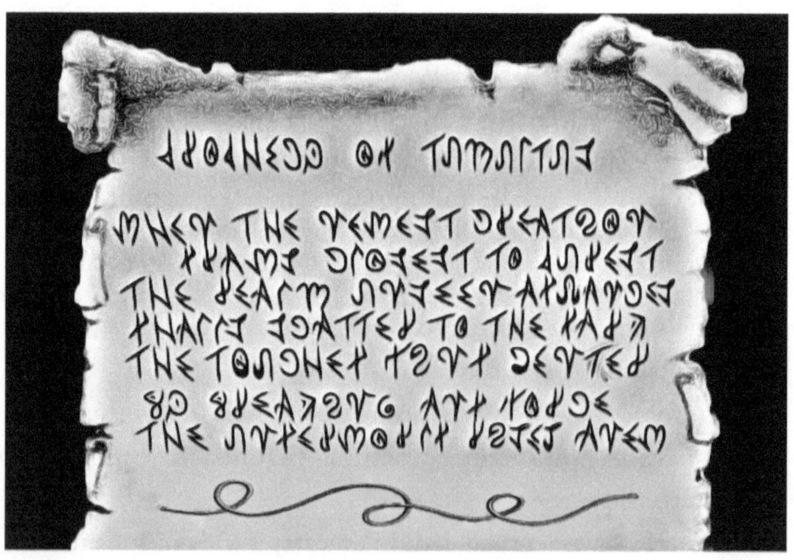

When the new creation draws closest to purus

The realm unseen advances
Dhall's scatter to the dark
The touched find center
By breaking and force
The Underworld rises anew

"Noella said there is an appendage at the bottom of the scroll, too."

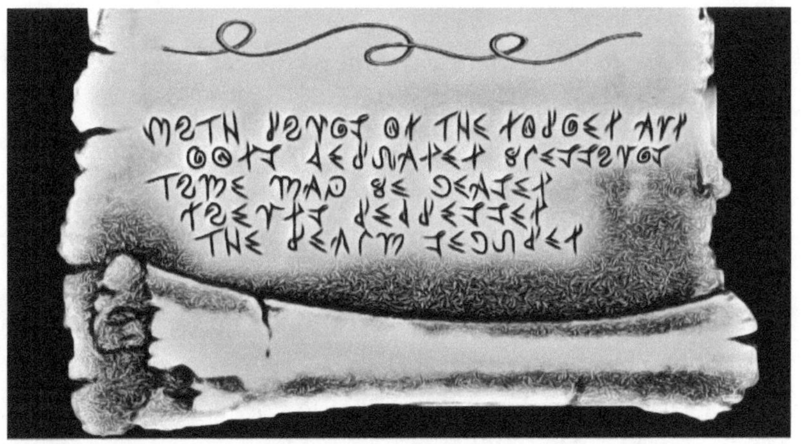

With rings of the forged & God's pervaded blessings
Time may be ceased, Fiends repressed, the realm secured

My hands scrubbed at my face. She'd known it was vague at best.

"Hayden?" Lara raised her hand to my head and swept a piece of run-away hair from my eyes. "I need to tell you something. I'm not sure if I should or not, but you are my friend and honestly, I don't want to have this information as my burden anymore."

"What is it?" Leaning so far forward, about to fall out of the puff chair, I fixed my eyes on her face.

"After the breaking, you're going to meet someone." That wasn't anything I'd expected her to say. "Please don't go to Sidhterra. I can't see past multiple forks but none of them are good for you." She was wringing her hands. "The girl you meet, she is good but will drag you into that place to help her and I worry... I don't know why, but I do."

Making promises to her without all the information wasn't something I'd ever do. She knew that.

"I can't make any promises, Lar, but I will keep your words in mind." It made me wonder what the universe had in store for me in the way of love.

It was good to know there was some prospect on the horizon. At least I wouldn't be so lonely for much longer.

Pushing out of the chair, I wrapped my arms around her.

"Looks like we both might not be alone, huh?"

Her hair smelled of raspberries and I couldn't help to inhale deeply.

"I really do like Noella. Do you think I messed up too bad today?" Her head hung.

My charming angel seer didn't realize how appealing she was. Noella should call herself blessed that Lara was with her.

"If she has your heart, I don't think a tiff will be the end of the world."

She smiled up at me, and I gave her that dimpled half smile she loved so much. She'd felt like family for a while now. The sister I never thought I'd want, if I were being honest.

Secretly, I was glad it hadn't worked out romantically between us. If anything were to have happened and we'd went our separate ways, my life wouldn't be as bright as it was with her in it.

With that in mind, I had to give her a bit of brotherly advice.

"And just in case, I've found that women really like getting flowers," I said with a wink.

Her burst of laughter tinkled like the sound of windchimes with each giggle.

Precious little siter vibes, indeed.

Chapter Thirty-Five

Parker

"Parker!" Jax exclaimed in a hushed whisper.

We approached the tree line with buildings in sight. The fae warriors had breezed through the forest like a wind carried over a field of wheat.

Now, it was our turn to blow by unseen. I gave Jax that devilish smile and shot forward. Partnered on this mission or not, we were always in competition.

Always wanting to get a leg up on other demons in Lucian's employ, I knew it made me reckless and impulsive to the point of being a danger to some of our missions. A demon's got to demon though, right?

Jax had gotten used to working with me well enough but that didn't mean that he appreciated my antics.

"Don't be such a buzz kill. I can handle myself," I teased.

This Jax was a far more subdued one than he'd been a century ago. The old Jax was ruthless, cruel even. I missed that fucking bastard.

This miserable excuse was a poor imitation. Always so level-headed. Goody fucking two shoes. It was rather annoying.

"Look asshole, I don't want to end up gutted because you need to prove something!" The langth demon hardly ever lost his cool, but by the seven hells, I enjoyed pushing it.

It was refreshing to know he was as vulnerable as the rest of us sometimes.

"You're so uptight sometimes. You need to let your *inner* demon come out and play." I knew that'd eat under his skin. Good. I wanted it to trip him up enough for me to get to Lucian first.

Peering around the last set of trees by the road, I gave Jax a thumbs up. The fae had disappeared into the early morning shadows.

Heads down, we moved swiftly towards the parked cars on the side street where we emerged from the woods.

Light from the full moon still shone bright over the area enough to see things in full detail. The predawn haze was beginning to burn off some, but it clung to the surface streets like a blanket.

Jax made the call. "Let's split up. We need to get to the manor before they see us. It'll take two or three vects to make it from here and they can detect the magics. It's better to be safe, than sorry."

Without another word, he darted around the side of the closest building to the north. Thanks for the heads up, asshole.

Setting off for the south route, I planned to get there faster. We couldn't vect in because of the wards. I'd have to make a few jumps to get there anyway.

When I rounded the corner of the alley, one of the fae warriors was ready and waiting for me.

A lovely treat to start my morning off right. Just great.

Chapter Thirty-Six

Zane

Upon reaching the apartment, I finally sighed a breath of relief.

Under the mat was my spare key. Lucian had taken everything I'd had on me when me hung him up to be tortured.

My fears were alleviated some when I realized that the door was still locked and the wards hadn't been triggered.

Turning the knob and pushing it open cautiously, I swiped the switch on the wall and the gas light chased away all of my lingering trepidation. Nothing waited to pounce. No one had invaded my sanctuary.

"It's not much, but it's home." If it hadn't been for the fact that I was exhausted, hungry, and completely wrung out, I would have probably been a touch more embarrassed by the state of my place.

Glancing around as Kali noticed some of the miscellaneous objects tossed haphazardly about the living room, I cringed internally.

"It's small but I like it." She walked through the open space, obviously noticing it's lack of finery but cozy homeyness. "Is there someplace I can wash up?"

Images of her in my shower jumped to the forefront of my mind before I could chase them away.

"Down the hall and to the left. You'll find some extra towels and soaps in the closet across from the bathroom." I glanced down at her bag with its lavish exterior and back to her face. "I don't have anything posh. Sorry. It's just simple soaps and shampoos."

Gods, what she must think of my messy nest.

"It's fine. I'm not picky," she lied to spare my feelings. Cute.

My eyebrow arched but I didn't make any further comment on it. If she could overlook my lack of finery, who was I to push the issue.

My stomach gave a loud rumble. I didn't remember what I had in the pantry, but anything was better than this gods awful gnawing. Other than those grapes she'd fed me, it'd been at least three days since I'd last eaten.

"I'll see what there is and make us something to eat while you wash up."

Her grin lit up my heart as well as the room.

"That would be great. Thank you." Running her hand over the back of the couch, she paused. "No one has ever cooked for me. Not me specifically anyway." Red tinted her cheeks with the most adorable blush I'd ever seen.

My mouth agape, I couldn't take my eyes off her as she walked down the hall, bag in hand.

After another few seconds, I turned towards the kitchen. If my mind didn't rein in these thoughts, I was screwed.

Now that I'd had the option of food so close, hunger dug its claws in deep and that bottle of water she'd brought me aside, I was extremely thirsty.

Grabbing a bottle of spring water out of the pack I'd left on the counter, I went to the fridge to see what could be made quick and easily. I'd gone to the market for a couple of things the day I'd been taken, so at least the house wasn't completely void of groceries.

Finding some ground beef, I decided to brown it up and use the bakery bread before it was wasted. My mouth watered at the idea.

Lucian held me prisoner for less time than I'd thought. What felt like weeks under the torture had only been a couple of days. Kali filled me in on what day it was on the way here.

Making a quick sauce for pasta was as easy as peeling the garlic, chopping the tomatoes and herbs, and letting it all simmer for a bit while she showered.

The bread was a bit hard on the outside already, so garlic bread would be a perfect addition to the meal. With no time to roast the garlic like I usually would, I threw it in a pan with a lid to heat a bit before I'd spread it on the bread.

Not quite as good, but at this point, I'd eat my own arm if I didn't get something in me soon.

Searching for a big enough pot to boil the water for the noodles, I noticed the receipt from the market. There was a handwritten note on it I didn't see the day I'd come home with my meager staples.

It was just a number. There was no name or any idea of what they wanted. The handwriting was familiar though I couldn't place it.

Walking over to pick up his phone off the coffee table and hearing the shower still going, I dialed the number. One ring, two, three rings.

"Hello?" A rough, deep voice answered.

"Yeah, hi. I found this number on a receipt from the market that I got a few days ago. I just now saw it. So, what can I do for you?" I asked.

There was a moment of quiet before he responded.

"I think it's time I called in that favor," said the deep voice on the other end of the line.

"And what favor would that be?" I'd given out several over the last decade or so. Some a little longer ago though.

"You owe me a life debt."

My mouth went dry. I hadn't heard that voice in over fifty years. "Thelzion?"

My hand automatically went to the scar on my face, rubbing it unconsciously.

With a quiet chuckle, he replied, "It's been a long time old friend. We have much to discuss."

Well shit.

Chapter Thirty-Seven

Lucian

It was dark in the study. The only light was coming from the large windows, where the full moon illuminated everything it touched in the early morning, before the sun rose. The sky a deep purple.

Sitting in my chair behind the desk, I found myself staring fondly at the ring in my hand. I hadn't seen it in over the three centuries since it was stolen from my possession.

Not since I was left hollowed out by killing the male I loved. I allowed a single tear to roll down my cheek.

Living in my memories, I startled at the knock on the door, not having heard anyone approach.

Wiping the tear away, the ring was tucked back into the ornate lockbox and shoved hastily into the drawer within seconds.

"Come in." My voice sounded melancholy in my own ears. A weakness I couldn't afford.

Clearing away the cobwebs of memory, I tried to get a hold of myself. It was my fault he was dead. No good could come from dwelling in the past.

"Lucian?" Quinn inched into the dimly lit room.

My patience had been wearing thin for weeks now. Stupid questions racked on my nerves tenfold.

"Who else did you expect to find in here?"

Her trepidation amused me. Thrilled me. Fear was a potent aphrodisiac.

"Can I turn on the lights? I need to talk to you."

After making sure I looked the part of vicious, brooding vampire again, I motioned for her to go ahead.

"The prisoner was gone when I arrived at the warehouse." She hesitated for a moment, steeling herself for the next part. It made me harden instantly. "It appears that Kalina helped him escape."

Not what I expected. Blowing out one long exhale, I sat quietly fuming.

Too still. The stillness of a predator sizing up its prey.

"There's more... I checked her room. She's taken some of her things. I don't think she's coming back."

Exploding from the quietness in the room, I leapt from behind my desk, pouncing on her without saying a word.

Chapter Thirty-Eight

Kalina

Showering the grime of the day away, I allowed myself to settle into the idea of being out from under Lucian's thumb. The feeling was thrilling and scary all at once.

I believed everything Zane had told me. It wasn't easy to just accept that my whole life had been a lie, but I had always felt that there was something missing.

Lots of questions sprung to mind over the last several hours. Maybe he could help answer them. He didn't owe me anything, but I hoped he would help me anyway.

Dressing quickly, I opened the door to the hallway. The luscious smells of our supper wafted through the apartment, drawing my legs forward before my mind caught up to the fact that I was moving.

"It smells wonderful." I stopped at the look on Zane's face. I knew that look. It was one I'd mirrored myself on many occasions. Incertitude.

It was my default setting. He looked worried and confused, and it put me on edge.

"I just got off the phone with an old acquaintance. After we eat, we need to take a ride," he said.

That didn't sound too bad, but what did I know? The world could have been crashing around me. Lucian kept me in the dark so often, I wouldn't know the signs.

Maybe it was nothing, but his hesitancy caused my heart to race.

Motioning for me to sit at the little table in the dining nook, I took the seat across from him. If there was something to be read on his face, I needed to see it full on.

My empath gifts would let me feel my way around, but I'd been second guessing them for a lifetime. Now was the time to observe them. Hone them while I could match up the feelings to the tells.

Grabbing two water bottles from a case on the counter, he sat down and handed me one. There was an anxiousness coming off him in waves.

Nervousness. Amusement. Dread. They all bounced around his aura and feeling them all, I needed to learn quickly how to read them without them overwhelming my own emotions.

"Who are we going to meet?" Thinking it was a trap had been my first instinct, but branching out further with my abilities, that didn't line up with what he was feeling.

All I could feel was a fierce protectiveness towards me. It wasn't what I'd expected at all.

Heat crept into my cheeks. I averted my eyes downward once I realized I'd been blushing like some silly teenager at the thought of a man caring for me.

"Thelzion and Briella. He's a Donnchadh... and she's a Trixie, like you."

His words didn't match his expression though. If Lucian hadn't shackled my mind with so much doubt in myself, maybe I could be sure about Zane's intent, but I had an ill at ease feeling gripping my gut.

There was something he wasn't telling me, and it made me irrationally angry.

I jumped immediately to my feet. The heat in the room began rising and the air became stifling. I was aware of it, and still, it didn't make it any easier to get myself under control.

"Woah... easy there, Kali." He threw his hands up in surrender. True concern tugged at the corners of his mouth. I didn't feel fear from him though. Only concern for me.

Seeing him like that snapped me out of my own emotions. Zane had been nothing but helpful to me. I owed him a chance to explain.

"I'm sorry. I just.... It feels like there's more to it than what you're telling me," I confessed. "I am tired of always being left in the dark."

One heartbeat. Two. Three went by before I looked up from the floor to his eyes.

"I am keeping something from you." The moment the words left his mouth, the fire inside me ignited.

Heart splintering, it twinged from an ache that began deep inside long ago. Now I could feel the fissure starting to crack into a spiderweb of hurt.

Zane tried to reassure me. His voice came from far away, even though he hadn't moved an inch. "I want to tell you absolutely everything. I really do, but it's not my story to tell."

Taking a deep breath at his words, air returned to the depleted supply in my lungs. He wanted to tell me everything. Those words rang a bell in my chest that sailed through my defenses.

Thinking now, instead of just reacting, the realization that he was up front about not disclosing everything settled like a comforting blanket.

"Okay. Then tell me the basics. Why do we need to meet with these demons?"

The one side of his lips drew up in a sheepish grin. The way his eyes crinkled laid the rest of my doubts to rest, melting the icy feelings of mistrust away from the tense moment.

"Zi saved my life about half a century ago. I owe him a life debt."

My eyes went wide in shock. Fifty years ago? He only appeared to be in his late twenties to early thirties.

Gifters lived a slightly extended life; one hundred thirty years was the average.

How could he owe a life debt from so long ago? And to a Donnchadh? Lucian never mentioned another lead vampire in the area.

"How? I mean... how?" I couldn't wrap my mind around it. I was in my fifties. He was older than me? That was crazy.

Misunderstanding what I was asking him, he answered a different question.

"It's a long story. I will tell you all about it sometime," he motioned for me to sit so we could eat.

I'd hopped out of my seat when in ire before hearing him out and I'd nearly knocked the meal to the floor. It smelled divine. It would have been a shame to waste this food because I couldn't control my temper tantrums.

"What I can tell you right now is that we have to meet them so they can explain to you about your past."

Our eyes met. It was an effort to not let my emotions take control of my abilities. What the hell could all of these strangers know about me that I didn't know about myself?

Everything. The clear answer was everything and anything because the truth of the matter had always been my lack of understanding the essence of who I was.

"They gave me the gist of it on the phone, Kali. I've realized that all of our fates were intertwined but their part in this is not my story to tell."

Picking up his fork, he began to eat, motioning for me to do the same. Too quickly. He hadn't eaten in days, and he'd wolfed down the first half of his plate before I'd even taken my first bite.

"I wouldn't be able to get it all right anyway. It's better to hear it first-hand," he said as he swigged down the entire bottle of water in one go. It made me fearful that he'd choke.

Picking up my fork, I'd made to eat quickly, but the meal he'd made us was delicious.

The garlic and tomatoes washed over my tongue in a well married dance of flavors. Now that I'd open myself to all of my emotions, eating felt almost orgasmic.

A grin stretched across my cheeks. His care for me not only helped me escape Lucian, but it seemed to extend to me in everything he did.

If there was one word that I'd allow myself to feel in that knowledge, it was... contentment. Not something I'd ever consider having the ability to feel before.

Damn. If I didn't know any better, I'd almost think I was capable of being... happy... some day.

"Then let's hurry up here. I want to know who I am."

Chapter Thirty-Nine

Parker

The fae warrior stood perfectly still with a hand resting on his sheathed sword. I could just make out the outline of his face.

Shadows swallowed up the majority of light in the alley. A voice like running water met my ears through the otherwise quiet morning.

"Following in stealth isn't your strong suit," the fae chuckled.

Relief washed over me, but I didn't let my guard down. My hands relaxed only slightly. I knew how quickly the faery scum could move.

"Riedyn." I acknowledged the male with mild annoyance.

Stepping from beyond the shadows into the full moon light, his pointed ears stood out. Broad chest rippling with power, the male encroached the space between us. If it wasn't for the fact that I lived to egg on my enemies, I'd have vected away before he'd moved out of the shadows.

"It's been a while. I'm sure my brother will be pleased to know you're on the opposing side of our mission." A sneer spread wide across the male's face.

We were always on *opposing sides*, but Lucian had once made it clear that we were to play nice and keep up the ruse of our deceptions.

"Just as Lucian will be glad to know that you are sneaking into his territory and working against him. Tell me, it's been a hot minute. How long since your feelings got stomped on because you thought he favored you?" I knew the dig would cut Riedyn hard.

Nothing gave me greater pleasure than being the natural born asshole that I was.

The question was pointed. A redirection of my current circumstances in an effort to be able to slip away by tripping him up.

My desire to pick Riedyn apart warred with the fact that I needed to get back to the manor and make Lucian aware that Queen Talisin sent warriors, not just spies.

And I didn't want to lose the upper hand to Jax. That bastard had won the last three out of four times we'd made bets.

"Where'd your other friends go?" I said casually. "Surely, they didn't already abandon you. I know you're not likeable, but this has to be a record."

I couldn't help my nature. I'd always been a prick. It felt good to scrape against this arrogant fae's pride.

"They know their duties. I don't need to babysit *my* warriors." Touche. That comment was pointed as well.

Living long lives, with even longer memories, became tedious at times.

It had been decades since I'd had that romp with Riedyn's sister-in-law. Not happy about his wife's infidelities, I was run out of Sidhterra by Riedyn's brother, the general of the queen's army.

Faeries were notorious for their free loving ways but apparently, General Ashwood took offense to his wife having a demon lover.

He gave one nod to his personal guard and that was it. They didn't need any further instruction before trying to flay me alive.

"Yeah, I remember how well trained the fae dogs are."

The fae warrior's back stiffened, pointed ears straightening. Good boy.

Quick as a strike of lightning, he shot forward. His hands coming up empty in the night air in the same instance that I vected away.

Chapter Forty

Thelzion

"They'll be here shortly love. Are you ready for this?" If I could spare her even a second's worry, I would.

The fact that we were having this meeting at all was a miracle. Fates knew, I'd never could have imagined the incredible stroke of luck of finder her twin so readily.

If the higher powers that be hadn't planned Zane's attack to lead me to him owing me a life debt, we'd never have gotten to this point so quickly.

He'd given me a run down on the phone after I'd told him I was calling it in. I'd wanted his help tracking down the Trixie in Lucian's care.

Everything the Fates set in motion fit together like a puzzle. Each piece separated, but once put together, the picture was growing clearer by the minute.

Reaching over, I took her hand in mine. Brie's pupils dilated a fraction. With every breath, her heart grew more unsteady. It was so rare to see her confidence shaken.

I wanted to lash out at the cause of her trepidation... only, I was the reason for this. If I'd made sure the babe was stillborn instead of trusting Lucian in the first place, Brie could have spent the last fifty years with her sister.

My failings had caused her pain. This was my damned fault. The least I could do would be to see to it she gets as much time with her family as possible.

"I have to be," she said. "I don't know what I'll do when we're finally face to face... but she's my sister. I want to know her."

Shutting my eyes, the inner turmoil roiling off my body was a living thing. Perfectly still, I didn't shift or fidget. A vampire trait that suited me in times like these.

The fact was that the twin of my Mate, the one that I hadn't given a second thought to before a few weeks ago, was on her way to us. Alive, well, and fresh away from Lucian. It was surreal.

I truly hadn't expected her to be with Zane. I'd written the number on the receipt days ago, wanting to have a bit of help with this whole prophecy business.

Then, when he'd called me back, my first thought wasn't of saving the world. I'd let it burn if it meant bring Brie happiness.

When I'd heard his voice, I knew what I'd ask of him to call in my chip; Brie's sister's whereabouts. I'd charge him with finding her and task him with luring her here, away from the bastard that had stolen her right out from under my nose.

After our first few clipped words on the phone, imagine my surprise realizing that destiny had planned things well. He and I agreed that the next step was to meet up.

Selfishly, I'd thought it'd be easier if Lucian had killed the infant. The thought was there and gone in the flash, but it reminded me all too well that I was still a bad demon to my core.

Brain working in circles, the self-loathing coiled like a noose around my neck. I didn't deserve Briella. She should hate me.

I'd killed her father and robbed her of a sister she'd never known existed. Truly selfish and evil, that's what I was.

Picking up on my feelings, Brie wrapped her arms around me. Soft and smelling of home. Nuzzling her nose into the crook of my neck, she breathed against the shell of my ear.

"I love you, Zi. You are a good man."

It was too much. That earnestness in her voice tugged at my heartstrings in an uncomfortable way. A way that screamed at me *she deserves better.*

Shifting in her grip, I pulled back to stare at her face, then hung my head in shame.

"Hear me! I. Love. You!" she said more forcefully. "It's you and me. Together, forevermore!"

She was gently reminding me of my promise to her from the first time we'd consummated the Mating bond. It was subtle but effective.

I had to be strong. I had to live, not just exist. I'd made her a promise. Keeping it was all that mattered.

"I love you back, Hellfire. With everything I have and everything I strive to be. For you."

Leaning up and into her embrace, my lips brushed softly against hers. A promise sealed.

The second kiss was more heated. Our passions beginning to rise. Kissing her was a gift, one I never took for granted.

Sleep hadn't helped after our long night. If anything, once I'd gotten Zane's call, sleep was impossible.

Waking her to tell her had caused all kinds of emotions I wasn't prepared to deal with, but I tried my best to be what she needed.

A knock on the front door quelled the sudden heat rising between us. Jumping to my feet, I had to shift my hardened member to the side to make walking easier as I answered the door.

Her little giggle from behind me set butterflies lose in my tightened chest, easing some of the tension for the moment.

"It's been a long time," Zane said from the front porch. Reaching up, he started to go in for a handshake but, at the last second, he brought his hand to the scruff on his chin and rubbed it thoughtfully.

I wasn't one for physical contact. Other than Brie, no one usually got close enough anyway. Those gifters at Pandora's box fell to the customs of their species and I'd made an exception to help Noella ease them into meeting a couple of demons for the first time.

Standing in the door frame, looking into the shadows, I spotted her. Briella's *identical* twin. The sun was fully risen in the morning sky. Heat and humidity clogged the air.

Zane motioned for Kali to come forward into the light and my eyes went wide, frozen in consternation.

"Hi. I'm Kali." She reached out to shake my hand and mine went up to meet hers without a thought. "I take it you're Thelzion."

"I... umm, yeah," I said, finally getting a hold of myself a bit. "Come in." Not the smoothest introduction. I'd been thrown for a loop for some reason. Twins, I'd been prepared for, but identical hadn't crossed my mind once.

Zane and Kali walked into the main living area. The lights were dim. Brie was sitting in the reading chair, half hidden in shadow.

Turning on the light beside the chair, she leaned forward but didn't get up. I knew her well. She was using the chair for emotional support.

"Well, isn't this the damnedest thing?" Slowly she stood, coming to stand next to me, staring incredulously at the woman in front of her.

I could sense her curiosity, joy, and anxiety though the bond, but she gave nothing away on the outside.

"Uncanny," Kali whispered, looking back to Zane for a brief second. Almost like a child wanting reassurance.

Zane and I were just bystanders to this reunion but neither of us had any words to add anyway. Both of our mouths gaped in the same astonishment. The women were a near mirror of each other.

"Hello Kali. I am Briella. I would tell you that we are sisters but that point seems obvious," she said with a small smile tugging up one side of her mouth.

My heart gave a hard thrum of delight. My mate was... happy.

"Hi. I'm Kalina." She paused, unsure of what she wanted to say next.

She was so un-Trixie like, it gave me pause. After a few seconds of awkwardness, her lips grinned wide, dimples beaming.

Then in a big sigh she asked, "So, am I your big sister or the baby?"

We couldn't help it. Me, Zane, and Brie all burst out laughing. Kali's smile spread from ear to ear.

Chapter Forty-One

Hayden

Gathering my jacket and dream journal up to leave, Lara had a book ready for me, along with a few words of encouragement.

"I know you know this already but with everything going on, I think it's important to say it out loud... You are dear to me, and I love you."

"Aww, honey. I love you too." I gave her my best sheepish grin. "I knew we didn't have a romantic connection. I just like having you in my life."

She sashayed over to me, putting some extra swing in her hips. Reaching up to take both sides of my face in her delicate hands and looking into my eyes, her words sincere, "You will always be in my life. I love you like family."

She was that to me. Had been for years. Our gifts had brought us to meet but our friendship carried the weight of a soul circle.

"You are my family too, Lar." It felt good to say it aloud. Like somehow, that solidified it.

She smiled and dropped her hands. Taking another step towards the door, she called after me again.

"One more thing. You know your abilities are still growing. They're advancing in ways you know and in ways that you haven't even guessed at yet." She smiled.

I waited, knowing there had to be more. She wouldn't mention it if there wasn't.

"Out with it, Lar," I said, arching an eyebrow after she stalled again.

"Well, I just wanted you to be aware I guess." Her hands started that familiar wringing in front of her. "I didn't want it to take you by surprise."

That was new. Usually, she didn't give me much to go on about things she'd seen.

Hesitating, she added... "After the Breaking, things will advance quickly. Gifters' abilities will grow stronger and more pronounced. It's going to take a lot of them off guard. I just wanted you to be prepared."

Worryingly biting on her bottom lip, I waited for her to say more, but nothing else came.

"Okay, honey. I'll pay attention." Winking playfully, I stepped out into the humid morning air. Darkness gone, a few stars and the full moon lingered high up in the sky.

My next plan to tackle the day would be to go home and settle in with the book she gave me so sleep could come faster.

They were relying on my next foreshadowing to tell us in which direction to look for the rings. No pressure or anything. Just have to dream about the ways to save the world. Good gods.

Noella and Bastian would be letting us know how it went with Draxus in the next day or two. The Breaking was less than two weeks away.

Yesterday morning, I'd had no idea of what to expect. Now, I had no idea where the future would lead.

It left an exciting tingle in my chest. My nerve endings dance with the possibilities.

Scary, yes... but exciting just the same.

Knowing Lara was with someone, I realized that it made me happy for her, more than I'd thought it would have.

She'd given me hope too. I'd begun to think that didn't exist for me anymore. Telling me I would be meeting someone soon had been the best gift I could have gotten.

If love was waiting out there somewhere, I'd fight all that much harder to preserve our way of life. We all needed a reason to go on. To keep getting up day after tedious day.

Maybe she'd sensed how much I'd been struggling lately. I didn't want to worry her. And gods, I didn't want to pull her into my darkness through her visions.

Whatever reason she'd decided to tell me, I was grateful.

Grinning to myself, the world could quite literally turn to hell in the next couple of weeks, but now I had hope to fight against the rising odds.

Chapter Forty-Two

Jaxson

Hitting the manor stairs in a run, I arrived at Lucian's study moments later. Not even bothering to knock, I threw the door open in my haste to beat Parker back to the study.

"What in the seven circles of fucking hell is going on!?" I exclaimed when I took in the room.

Lucian was crouched over Quinn, blood dripping from her neck. She gasped for air when he sat up abruptly at my arrival. I knew I'd overstepped, but fuck! She looked seconds away from death.

Lucian lazily made his way off of her and to his chair, dripping blood all over the otherwise clean floor. With a swipe of his large hand to wipe his mouth, he set his gaze leveled at me.

"Quinn was just donating some blood dues," he said with a cold smirk.

Quinn pressed her hand against the side of her still bleeding neck. It would stop and be healed within the hour, but the loathing look she cast at Lucian told me all I needed to know.

"Mmm hmm. Is that so?" The disdain that made it into my voice was barely muted, but I wasn't willing to fight with him about it. Not now at least.

I'd done worse in the past. My inner demon fought for control most of my waking hours, but I had him locked down. Behind a cage so thick, he'd be hard pressed to ever manage to surface again.

"Why have you foolishly come barging into my study?" he asked casually, a fake calm brimming with a sea of turmoil under the surface that we all knew way too well. "And without knocking?"

Straightening my back, I puffed out my chest, trying to reclaim my composure.

I had to remind myself that Quinn isn't mine, no matter how much I desired her.

That she's never even shown any interest in me whatsoever, no matter how much I'd pined over her throughout the years.

"There are four Fae warriors on their way to take up spying spots around the manor. Parker and I split up to get you the message as fast as possible."

Footsteps rushed up the hall and a few seconds later, Parker came bounding in. The glance he threw my way before turning to Lucian made it clear that he was hoping to be here to report before me.

His eyes landed on Quinn's neck and the blood that stained the front of Lucian's shirt. The bastard smirked. Fucking asshole.

"Was there a party I missed?" he said, clearly taken aback by the mood in the room after a few seconds passed in tense silence.

"Jax has just informed me of the Faeries coming to the manor." His hands raised in front of him, steepled in thought. "Is Commander Riedyn among them?"

Of course, that's where his mind would go. For an evil overlord, he thought with his dick more than anyone I knew.

"I couldn't make out their faces before I raced to the manor," I said.

"Yes." Parker looked towards me for just a second before speaking again. "Riedyn stopped me in an alley. We had a little tiff before I vected away."

Quinn slinked towards the door, hoping to go unnoticed. Lucian's eyes met hers just before she got there, halting her in place.

"I want the three of you to find out everything you can about why the Fae queen sent warriors to spy."

Odd that he hadn't mentioned the Trixie. She was usually the one he'd task with dangerous, but menial work.

"What about Kali?" I asked.

Quinn's eyes grew wide, warning. Parker just cocked his head, trying to suss out all he'd missed. Lucian's tone was quiet but deadly.

"She has left us. I want no more discussion on the matter. You lot have your orders. You're dismissed."

We walked in relative silence until we reached the kitchens. Quinn grabbed a rag, filled it with ice, and pressed it to her neck. I sat on one of the chairs at the end of the island.

If there was one thing I knew about Parker, it was how he instantly irritated the shit out of every person he came in contact with. The fae were no different.

"You and Riedyn at each other's throats again, huh?" I pushed.

The blood seeping from Quinn's neck made it hard to concentrate. I wanted a taste so bad, my dick twitched. My demon rattled his cage before I'd pushed him farther into the recesses of my mind.

"That bastard's never going to let it go. You'd think he'd be happy that someone finally satisfied his sister-in-law." Parker said, grabbing a bottle of beer from the fridge and taking the seat next to me.

I huffed out a laugh, but Quinn was still grimacing. There'd be bruising under her skin for a day or two, even after the wound healed itself closed.

"What happened with Kali, Quinn?" I prodded as gently as I could but it still came out more of a demand.

Going into the cabinet and grabbing down a bottle of whiskey and three glasses, she brought them back and set them on the island in front of us. A two finger pour for us each in the cups, she handed me and Parker a drink.

"She's gone. And we're gonna need something stronger than beer to get through his coming wrath."

That didn't sound ominous or anything. Fucking Lucian.

Chapter Forty-Three

Noella

I had advised Bastian to stay behind me, but he wouldn't hear of it.

Locating my father in a mostly empty tavern on the impoverished side of Dochais, the smell of alcohol wafting off him was enough to knock me back when I'd first approached.

We'd been there for over an hour, sitting in a booth, trying to convince him to stop drinking enough to get him out of the place.

"Hecate said she was going to find you. I spoke to her earlier today father." Try as I might to remain stoic, pity took up root in my heart, as it always did when dealing with Draxus.

Drinking and power like his were a deadly combination. It never ended well for those around him once he hit the *one too many* mark.

"My mother saw me already. Why do you think that I am here, drowning my sorrows?" He hiccupped and the smell of stale beer and musty clothes shoved its way up my nose. His beautiful features were slackened by alcohol, and it hurt my heart to see him this way.

Bastian hadn't said anything since we'd first arrived. He just sat there, a constant presence for me. Really, what was he supposed to do?

"You know what you are supposed to be doing. Draxus! Act like the demigod that you were always meant to be!" I yelled as I hovered over him. "We will need your help. I will need your help." Pleading with his paternal side, I laid my gloved hand on his shoulder. "I know you're in there somewhere. That rage you had after Solene had stolen your beloved's body, find it. Please!"

He looked up at me again. Sorrow in his eyes. I knew it was a low blow, but desperate times called for desperate measures.

"You look like her, you know." His hand came to rest on the side of my face. "So beautiful... it's a torment to look at you," he pushed my face to the side before dropping back down to the table.

Bastian cleared his throat, finally having something to say. Picking up his glass of wine, he made a toast.

"To those we have loved. To those who've been taken. To those who we can never claim again." With that, he downed the whole glass.

Incredulously, I gawked at him. By the gods, what was he thinking? We were trying to get Draxus to stop drinking, not plow him with more.

"Well said, young man," my father cried out.

"My name is Bastian. I am a friend of your amazingly brave daughter, sir."

Draxus peered at Bastian through blurry eyes but tried to take the measure of him all the same.

"I'm sure you'd be proud to hear of her efforts towards The Prophecy of Tumultus so far," he said with a wink in my direction.

"The way she infiltrated a lab and stole one of the rings right out from under them."

The drunk sat up straighter, staring at me. Heat spread in my face as a blush spread across my cheeks at my father's gaze.

"She was unstoppable," Bastian continued. "I didn't even realize that she'd used her magiks to protect us until earlier today. That's how good she is."

Draxus looked over at him and then back to me. He hadn't paid much attention to the man at my side in the last hour, but he was paying attention now.

"You seem quite enamored with her," he said, sizing him up.

His eyes were beginning to focus a bit more and the drunken stupor was lessening enough for me to glimpse the male I loved underneath.

"You bet I am. She is one of the most amazing people I've ever met," another wink in my direction. "I can't imagine being in such good graces with her that I wouldn't jump at the opportunity to help her."

The alcohol that was constantly needed to keep my father's demigod body from healing itself back to sober was going untouched. I smiled over at Bastian, catching on to his game. I knew he was distracting him, dangerous as that game was, so he'd be less inebriated and more willing to discuss the matter at hand.

"Are you giving me sass, boy?!" Draxus half shouted, but it still came out a bit slurred.

"Not at all, Sir. I was simply pointing out how wonderful your daughter is."

Looking at Bastian now, he was the craftiest being I'd ever seen. Wording trap after trap. Pushing Draxus' buttons without being disrespectful.

It was an art form. He'd come a long way in the last few weeks. He most certainly wasn't lost or floundering anymore.

Eyes clearer, Draxus' voice was becoming more sobered by the minute.

"Oh, well...yeah. She is wonderful." He hesitated for a moment. "She thinks on her feet, like her mother."

At that, I stiffened. He didn't usually like talking about my biological mother. It brought about the drinking and drug bouts. I'd never heard him voluntarily divulge anything about his beloved.

"Her name was Ephiny." I froze. Referring to his beloved's name only a hand full of times in my four hundred plus years, this declaration was highly unusual. "She shined brighter than any diamond or star in the sky," he hiccupped.

"She sounds like she was as unique as her beautiful daughter," Bastian offered.

Bastian bowing slightly at the waist, my father inclined his chin deeply in response. Lara wasn't going to believe it when I told her later.

"By the Goddess, yes," a smile plastered itself across Draxus' face. "And her sassy personality? That mouth always gave me a run for my money," a chuckle leaving his ragged throat.

Bastian leaned in across the table, elbows resting in front of him. His eyebrows both raised in consideration.

"No offense sir, but how do you think Ephiny would feel, knowing the daughter you two made, was doing dangerous work to save the world while you sat around drinking?"

My hands flew to cover my mouth. Was he crazy? Of course, Bastian had never seen his power, but surely, he'd heard of his wrath.

Draxus had a far off look in his eyes, his hands resting on the table. After a few minutes of silence he said, "Son, I don't think I'd ever like to find out."

With that, he pushed the remaining alcohol to the end of the table, stood and walked to the bar, then brought back a few bottles of water.

"I like you, Bastian. You cut through all my bullshit." He took a long swig from one of the water bottles. "Not many people can say the same."

Turning on his heels, without another word, headed towards the door.

I called after him. "Where are you going, Father?"

He turned but kept walking. Steadier with each step.

"I'm going to see a man about a horse." The waggle of his brows caught me right in the heart.

It was perplexing. His words. His attitude.

He grinned, waggling his eyebrows again. "I'm going to do what my mother asked of me."

With a final parting grin in my direction, he was out the door.

Getting up from the table, Bastian followed me out. Words escaped me for a time.

Once we were back in the carriage, I finally found my voice again.

"That was brilliant. How you worked him into that, it was brilliant."

He smiled. The clockworks in his brain didn't even need tweaking. It wasn't his wit really.

"I don't think it was, actually." My quizzical expression encouraged him to continue. "I just saw the answer to unblocking him."

I saw where his line of thinking was at and it impressed me.

"You think it was an extension of your Deblocker gift?"

"I don't know how else to explain it. I got that same buzz under my skin and itching in my teeth that I get when I'm trying to Deblock something." His face lit up. "I think my abilities are advancing again."

I grinned from ear to ear, beaming at him. "I'd say. And it happened at the absolute perfect time."

Bastian's lips matched my smile. He was proud at how much he'd been able to ground himself in the past few weeks.

Hayden had been right to think he was an ass, but I knew he could now prove himself worthy of redemption once he got out of his own way.

Chapter Forty-Four

Queen Talisin

Revelers were making merry; dancing, eating, and showing off their various talents, all in hopes of catching my eye. Pity they'd think they matter to me on an individual level.

The brightly lit space shined not from the stars and moon, but from the glow of thousands of fireflies captured in lanterns.

Night dew touched the surface of everything in the courtyard here in Sidhterra. An audience with ancient fae gods, under the full sky, was the reason I had built my throne room more like a garden courtyard.

The forest surrounded a crumbling stone wall. The open ceiling allowed for the drifting smells of soil and rain and rotting wood to fill up the space pleasantly.

My most cherished messenger was edging around the bacchanal fae, heading towards my throne. I'd sent her to the Lagomshire realm to deliver a message to that horrible Donnchadh vampire lord.

It eased my mind, if only in the slightest, to see her safe return.

"What word have you from Lucian?" I asked Skylar the moment she was in front of the dais. Patience was not something I'd ever been gifted.

"The Donnchadh proved himself unworthy of Your Majesty's favor. He may be their leader, but he is no more a king than a common skitter bug." Averting her eyes downward after her little outburst she added, "My Queen," with a small curtsy.

My lips pressed together in a hard line. The spark that usually took up residence in my eyes turned to a blazing fire I could feel simmering in the warmth under my skin. That demon was more trouble than he was worth.

Nevertheless, I could not let the surrounding fae see my disquieted disposition. Faeries didn't play well with others. Especially those with whom they perceived as weak. And strong emotions were something they'd delight in as my weakness to lead.

"Pity. I was hoping to keep his alliance intact, at least for a while more."

Skylar nodded. Trust wasn't something freely given in Sidhterra. It was earned and then maintained through careful cultivation.

My favored messenger, my general, and his commander brother were the only three I would trust with my life and court affairs. I knew their loyalty was never in question.

"I may have been a bit flippant with the demon after he was less than commending of my queen," Skylar deviously smirked and dipped her chin. I'd dare say she was proud of herself.

The raging fire in my heart dimmed a small bit. The corners of my mouth pulling up slightly.

Odd. I hadn't given my face leave to do so.

"Will he give his word to protect our kin once the demons make the breech?" That was the only thing that mattered. I may not care for my subjects individually, but I cherished them as a whole.

The faery picked at a spot on her wispy short skirt. Lifting her gaze level to mine a moment later. A brazen act for sure.

"He set conditions, Your Grace. He will only give his word when he has the full interpretation of the prophecy."

I stewed for a brief moment. He couldn't read the script at all. If I gave him the full translation, he wouldn't need my alliance anymore.

The bastard was crafty. I'd give him that. So crafty in fact, I would almost believe him to be fae.

Lucian was the worst type of frenemy. He had vision and long term planning as his wheelhouse. He was also conniving and secretive, even within his own ranks.

It was something we'd had in common, but demons were a plague upon the realms.

"I've sent Commander Riedyn and three of his most trusted elite warriors to watch the goings on. I'm certain he'll have everything in hand," I told her without pause.

She could be headstrong, but Skylar was fiercely loyal to me. Any information I passed along would go no farther. Of that, I was certain.

She'd only fidgeted for a moment but didn't say anything. That act annoyed me. Weakness, indeed.

"Well, spit it out dear."

"It's just... I don't want to overstep my bounds, Your Majesty. It isn't my place to question your decisions."

I waited, letting the faery gather her thoughts and squirm for my own amusement. I did so wickedly delight in the small things.

After a heavy sigh that fell from my closed lips, Skylar pushed through her apprehensions.

"Commander Riedyn may not be the best choice to have sent. His history with the vampire lord clouds his thoughts."

Steepling my hands in front of me, I contemplated her words. After all, my trusted three were the only advisors I had, though their titles were never that.

As much as I valued their opinions, ultimately, it was my decision to make any calls. I wouldn't second guess the commander of my elite unit. At least, not in front of anyone else.

"Riedyn is loyal to me, Sky. He would never do anything to lose my favor." After a brief pause, I said, "Thank you for your concerns, my dear. I know you always have my best interest at heart." I smiled down at her, enjoying her mild discomfort at being dismissed. "You may rise. Go and enjoy the merriment."

"Yes, my Queen. Thank you."

Watching her flitter away, weaving in and out of the crowd, I was reminded of my daughter. The way she had been so carefree and enjoyed everything that the Fae lands had to offer.

A pang of heartache resonated in my chest. Sky wasn't a replacement for Griane but she did help me not always feel like a childless mother every minute of every day.

With one more glance at the revelers, I stood from my throne, and my guards followed me in formation out of the courtyard.

Lucian would have to be dealt with, but for now, all I could do was wait for Commander Riedyn to report back.

The protection of my kingdom and kin was all that mattered. Scheming and tricksters that the Fae could be, they were my responsibility.

I would never let the fate of my people be tied with that of Lagomshire.

Chapter Forty-Five

Lucian

I headed out the front door of the manor dressed fully in black. Stealth in the night was something that demons did well.

Glancing around the bushes by the columns of the front porch, I noticed the pointed toed footsteps in the soft soil.

"Tsk, tsk, tsk. You should know better than that," I smirked as I stated the obvious.

Riedyn sauntered into view. His lean-muscled chest shown fully beneath his fae uniform. The colors were meant to blend into the forest, not the city. It was an array of greens and browns that clung to his muscular form, leaving little to the imagination.

"Leaving so soon? I was hoping we could... reminisce," Riedyn said with one corner of his mouth pulled up in that cute, dimpled way that I'd liked so much. He'd always been less stoic with me than anyone else.

"I have business in Larnach city. Care to walk with me for a bit?"

Looking down at the ground, the fae warrior shuffled his feet. His eyes squinched up, face tight, he nodded without saying a word.

Sometimes, I missed his company more than I'd cared to admit. It would do me no good to live in the past though. If I'd learned anything from the situation with Caylum, it was to not get attached to anyone I cared for.

"What does the Queen want to know? Maybe I can help you stay in her good graces." It was a small taunt, but it brought me a measure of satisfaction to see his face faulter.

I had respect for the fae in a lot of ways. It was another realm and with the right steps in place, another grasp of power. Knowing what it was that Queen Talisin wanted would be useful.

We walked through the grounds, passing trees and gardens of fragrant bushes. The air was sickly sweet with the nectar of the flowering azaleas and climbing jasmine. Moonlight made the grounds relatively bright for a nighttime stroll.

The strong male at my side was the personification of a warrior. Strong hands, muscular physique, and a lean, agile body made Riedyn the perfect killing machine, even without his gifts.

The chiseled angle of his jaw was magnificent. And those pointed ears?

Purring internally, this walk had become more difficult. I'd forgotten the intoxicating scent wafting off his tawny skin. The memory of how he'd tasted of honeysuckle and boysenberries drifted through the recollection itching at my skull.

Adjusting my hardening member, I stopped to face the fae warrior. Riedyn stayed at arm's length away from me.

"My Queen's agenda is not any information that I would betray to you, Lucian." His eyes held cold indignation. His chest rising and falling in an agitated manner told me he was cut to the quick by the perceived disloyalty.

Taking a step forward, filling in the empty space between us, I rested a hand on Riedyn's chest. The warrior didn't bat me away, but he didn't relax his posture either.

He remained a statue, stoic in his emotions. I was half a foot shorter than my former fae lover. It didn't matter to me in the slightest, but my whispered breath was only tall enough to reach along his ear and caress his neck.

"Your absence in my bed has been dreadful," I said, broaching the topic. Leaning my body into him, I let the stiffness in my pants brush along the commander's thigh.

Riedyn shuddered as my hand came up to cup his jaw. He leaned into my touch before his hand shot up to firmly grab my wrist.

"I won't fall for your deceits again vampire!" Breathing heavily, he dropped my arm and turned to walk away. That wouldn't do at all.

I was upon his back in a blink, fangs at the top of his neck. A hard bite just below his ear, the tiniest pinprick of blood bubbled to the surface.

Mmmm. That had been the taste I'd been craving.

Riedyn swung around, hands and legs in a defensive stance. With his eyes wide, he stared at me. If there was ever any doubt that he still felt something for me, it melted away with that look.

Smirking broadly, my hands going up in surrender.

"It was just a taste, for old times' sake."

Riedyn stared incredulously at me. Tension still in every limb. Quick as a flash, he closed the small gap between us.

A hand going up to cup my jaw while the other tangled roughly in my hair. Our lips smashed together in a brutal sense of urgency.

Leaning into the kiss, my lips parted, allowing him access. Our tongues danced and tasted each other for several long minutes. Neither one of us willing to come up for air.

Realizing what he was doing, the enemy with whom he was fraternizing, Riedyn pulled away. The sudden loss of his body heat sent a shiver along my spine.

Stepping back and breathing hard, he straightened, turned, and walk swiftly in the opposite direction without another word.

Such a waste of a hard on. We could have at least made the most of it before he walked away from me again.

Smirking shamelessly, I called out to him in barely more than a normal conversational tone, but I knew his fae ears would hear it.

"Shall we pick this up again later then?" My smugness was just the right balm for my bruised ego.

Now wasn't the time to engage in pleasures of the flesh anyway. It was still nice to know that I could affect my former lover like that. Keeping him off his game was an added bonus.

The stable house was a short few minutes walk across the sprawling estate grounds. The automated carriage was already waiting and ready to go.

A humid midmorning breeze in the air blew the smell of hay and horse up my nose in a pungent tug of war with the sweet flowers. It was nauseating.

This realm had been the perfect atmosphere for demons. No brimstone or fire. Simply hot as one of the seven circles and humid enough to help them adjust easier to the contrast.

Getting into the carriage and shutting out the world beyond, I again smiled to myself. Riedyn still tasted of honeysuckle and boysenberries. And his fae blood still gave me that same high after all these years.

The carriage started down the long drive to the road from the manor. Glancing out of my window, I spied the fae warrior standing in the shadows, leaning up against a tree.

The poor bastard seemed conflicted. And that's exactly how I needed him to be. The commander would be less effective at his job if his feelings leaked into his mission.

The Queen always played games herself. And this wasn't checkers, it was chess.

Riedyn wasn't a pawn, but knights were still used to the advantage of Queens... and of Kings.

Chapter Forty-Six

Kalina

Zane and I got back to his apartment around 2am. Brie was everything I would have wished for in a sister if only I had known to want one.

I came in, headed right for the bathroom and took another shower. Sweat covered my body, and I couldn't wait to feel clean again.

When I'd finished up, I went into Zane's room to lay down.

True to his word, he made up the sofa and was sleeping before I'd even finished my shower. The poor guy had been tortured for days and still went with me for support when I'd needed him.

It had been an extremely long day. This wasn't the first time I'd slept somewhere other than the manor. Missions sometimes took me away for a few weeks even. This *felt* different though.

The bed wasn't a hard ground or a hole in some cave. My belly wasn't rumbling, and my senses weren't heightened, waiting for an ambush.

The bedding was comfortable. Not just in the way the pillows cradled my head and the blanket wrapped around my curves.

In his bed, with his scent all around me, I was comfortable in my own skin for the first time in my life.

The knowledge of things that had eluded me for so long had taken up residence, not only in my mind, but in my very soul.

When I closed my eyes tonight, it would be the first time in my long life that I'd felt whole. Zane had given that to me.

We'd known each other for only two days but he'd already been more of a friend to me than any other being in my past.

Sure, we had a dangerous mission ahead of us. I was now beginning to see how evil Lucian truly was with every new piece of information presented to me.

He'd raised me. He'd kept me fed, sheltered, and given me purpose. The thought of him not being there when I'd needed someone the most was all the proof that I needed for myself once I'd realized how easily Zane, Briella, and Thelzion accepted me for exactly who I was.

Did it hurt to know that I'd meant so little to him? Absolutely!

Remembering every little snide comment and how his other lackies were allowed to make me feel worthless but I wasn't supposed to speak up against them.

Remembering every time my true Trixie self would rear its head, and he'd shut me down and send me away on menial missions instead of addressing my concerns.

I didn't feel regret for leaving him. I was never meant to be with him in the first place.

Thelzion had told me everything about my parents, about what happened with Brie, about Lucian. He also trusted me immediately with the knowledge of their mission.

His open honesty was so in contrast to the secretive ways of my foster father. He didn't even know me and yet, he accepted me without any thought because my sister was his mate.

Technically, until tonight, I'd have been the enemy, but he'd placed his trust in me with one shared glance to Brie. They shared a subtle nod and then he spilled all of the details without censoring anything at all.

Brie had been such an unexpected shock. We were definitely identical twins. She carried herself better. She exuded confidence and had a natural charisma about her.

The only way to describe Briella's demeanor was sage. It reminded me of how much I still had to learn. If her smoothness was all a trixie trait, I couldn't wait to find out. I had a sneaking suspicion that it wasn't all about *what* she was, but simply a Briella thing.

She'd been patient and kind. She'd also seemed at odds in letting me come home with Zane. Not that she would ever have stopped me. It was more like a familial pull to want me close.

In the morning, we'd be heading to Dochais to look for a ring. Then we were to meet up with others in a group that I hadn't met yet who were on the same mission. Everyone was on the same page. Lucian would have never allowed that at all.

As refreshing as it was, it was also a bit overwhelming to think about.

Maybe I should feel nervous or anxious but all I felt was excited. It was my first adventure doing my own thing, not because of orders. I was doing a mission because I chose to. It was my first taste of true freedom.

Brie and Zane both assured me that if I didn't want to be a part of any of this, I was free to not be. I could sit this one out and they wouldn't hold it against me at all.

Lucian had been a father figure to me for my entire life, and they had taken that into consideration.

The beginnings of tears welled in my eyes. I wouldn't release them.

Happy tears for all I'd gained or sad tears for all I'd lost and never had. It made no difference. I wouldn't let them spill.

These people whom I'd just met cared more about my mental wellbeing in the short time they'd known me than anyone who was supposedly close to me.

I'd do this mission. It was a realm saving mission. It wasn't for personal gain for any of them. It felt right. It felt like the path I was meant to be on.

Besides that, I wanted to get to know my sister. Family. I had actual family, and I felt nearly whole.

With that thought in mind, I closed my eyes and swiftly fell into a dreamless sleep.

Chapter Forty-Seven

Hayden

I hadn't been asleep for more than a few hours when I woke with a start for the second time in the last couple of days.

Grabbing my dream journal, I jotted down what I could remember. It wasn't much but it was better than nothing.

The feeling of a bottomless pit was still open in my gut. It wasn't quite hopelessness, but it was a chasm of despair that was dark and endless. The feeling that we would fail overwhelmed me.

With sweat dewing on my forehead, my mouth was as parched as the desert. Why was it so gods forsaken hot already?

Stubble itched along my unshaven chin. Standing and feeling my way in the dark to the bathroom, I flicked on the switch to the gas light. The sudden brightness had my eyes squinting in protest.

It was almost dawn, so I figured I'd shave and shower before heading to the diner for breakfast.

Noella and Bastian sent me a message through the witch windows she'd handed out before I'd turned in for the night. We'd decided to meet everyone at the diner around 8am instead of giving details over the mirror.

After my shower, I dressed and headed out. Our meeting was still several hours off but the walk through the city in the early morning always soothed me after a hard foreshadowing.

The smells of petrichor as the dew evaporated from the grass and bread freshly made from the bakery's oven enveloped my senses and brought with it a calming atmosphere to settle my frayed nerves.

A few blocks over was Lara's shop, Pandora's Box, and the waterfront. The smell of brininess from here on Main Street permeated the sticky air.

It wasn't cool outside by any means, but it certainly wasn't yet as hot as the day was destined to be.

I'd arrived at the diner just as the owner, Kraigen, was un-locking the door. The middle-aged man nodded a silent hello.

As a regular here, I enjoyed the privileges of being let in and coming to sit at my favorite table while Kraigen did the morning prep.

The diner didn't open until 7am but I'd often found myself awake, unable to get back to sleep, after a Foreshadowing.

Kraigen wasn't the most talkative or friendliest of people, but he was always willing to let me in, bring me a cup of coffee and allow me to skim over my journal or quietly read a book before opening.

The light from the coming dawn peaked over the buildings along the Manxtas River. The diner was bathed in sunshine as it broke through the front picture windows.

Kraigen was in the kitchen, pots and pans banging around, the sound of sizzling coming from the grill. The smell of bacon and eggs and various other foods permeated around the smell of the strong coffee already in the air.

With the clinking of the front doorbell, customers began coming in and sitting at booths, tables, and a few at the stools up by the counter. I hadn't realized how much time had passed while my nose was face down in my book.

Kraigen took their orders, fixed their food, and wiped up after they'd finished and left. Day in and day out, this was what the man did.

I'd often wondered why anyone would want to live the same day on repeat, but I was grateful to the diner owner for a place to come regularly. It had become a sort of refuge to me. Next to Lara's shop, it was the only other place that had a homey, welcoming feeling.

It was nearly 8am now. My cousin and Noella should be here at any time.

Out of the corner of my eye, I caught a glimpse of what looked to be Brie. I waved but apparently, she didn't see me.

Standing from my table in the back, I walked over to hers. She looked at me in puzzlement. If I didn't know any better, I'd have sworn she'd forgotten who I was in the last few days.

"Hi," I said awkwardly. "I didn't expect to see you until tomorrow. Are you here to meet with Bastian and Noella too?" She started to reply when a tall man walked over, coming from the bathroom.

"Can we help you?" He sat down across from her.

The scar across his face gave him a menacing aura. Where was Thelzion? This guy would be in for a world of hurt if the vampire saw him alone with his mate.

"I was, uh, just coming over to see if Brie was here to meet up with us. My table is right over there." I'd stumbled over the words. Something wasn't right.

The bemused expression turned into a full-blown smile reaching all the way to his now amused eyes.

The woman smiled up at me. Confusion played with my nerves. Thelzion was nowhere in sight, and something didn't feel right. Ugh. I needed the others here now!

"I'm sorry. I don't know you," she said. Still her smile widened. "I'm guessing you think I'm someone else... My sister perhaps."

That brought me up short. The clanging of dishes and voices faded away into the background.

Her grin was dimpled in her cheeks. She was beautiful, like Brie, but she definitely had more of a girlish way about her.

"Really? I would have sworn you were her." Briella had an identical twin sister and here she sat. Well shit.

"I'm Zane," the man said. "And this... is Kalina."

Shaking Zane's hand, I then turned back to her. With the smile still on her face, she extended her hand to me.

"You can call me Kali. Did you say we're having a meeting?" The lightness of her hand grasping mine felt weighted. Not in a bad way. It was strong but soft and the handshake went on a little too long.

I cleared my throat and then dropped her hand, trying not to offend the guy she was with.

"I thought you were Brie. My cousin, Bastian, and a woman named Noella are supposed to meet me here this morning."

Sure enough, just as the words were out of my mouth, the bell to the diner rang again. In walked Noella with Bastian a few steps behind her.

The Mixling looked cautiously in Kali's direction. Eyeing the man, she stepped forward to make her hello's. When Noella looked at Brie's twin again, it was steady and sure.

"Hello Kalina," she said. Kali's cheeks pinkened. "Ahhh, perhaps you do not remember me. We met a long time ago, you were a little girl. Lucian had you tucked away in his manor."

The air in the diner grew colder. It became thick with tension... but also a pressing weight.

Zane stood up and was at Kali's side in an instant. His hands went to her face while he told her to breathe. Slowly, the air returned to normal as she stared into his eyes.

Looking up at the witch, Zane spit his next words.

"Real nice, Noella!" he said. "Did you mention him on purpose to piss her off?"

Bastian and I didn't know what to make of the exchange. Zane took his hands away from Kali's face and walked over to Noella.

I braced myself. I didn't know how effective I would be, but I wasn't going to let this big, scar faced guy hurt her.

Noella threw her hands up as he reached her. Instead of magics, they'd went around his waist, and she nuzzled into him as he embraced her back.

Sharing a look with Bastian, he had been as confused me.

Kali growled. She actually growled. The sound was guttural and feral.

Zane released Noella quickly and was at Kali's side again. His touch seemed to calm her, but her eyes were still staring daggers at the witch.

"Kali, I'd like to introduce you to Noella... My cousin." Her face went from tense to relaxed in a blink. Her eyes shot to Noella's. Noella smiled and she smiled back at her.

I'd felt foolish for not knowing she wasn't Briella. She was so different. Her looks were the only thing the same as the Trixie I'd met.

Remembering that fact, that this woman was a demon, I took a casual step back. Bastian noticed and did the same.

Zane said that he was Noella's cousin. I'd almost glossed over that fact in the moment.

"You're a Mixling then?" Bastian asked Zane.

He nodded. Kali's eyes looked at him for conformation.

"I am. I'm not a Gifter." He spoke to everyone but looked only to the Trixie.

"Why didn't you tell me?" she said. The hurt was written all over her face.

Bending down slightly to look into her eyes, there was tenderness there that I hadn't expected from someone who appeared so fight weathered.

"When you found me and made that assumption, I didn't get a chance to correct you." He took her hands in his. "I was not keeping it from you, I swear. We just had a lot going on and I honestly forgot that I hadn't told you until Noella walked in." He hung his head. "I'm sorry, sweety. Truly. I promise, I wasn't planning to keep Anything from you... Ever!"

She wore her emotions on her sleeve. Unlike Brie who seemed so confident and put together, there was something broken about Kali.

Filing that away for future inquiry, right now, I had a different question.

"Did Thelzion and Brie send you or are you working for Lucian?" I demanded to know.

The words came out a lot braver than I'd felt on the inside but Bastian and Noella both stepped to my side, solidifying my resolve.

Anger flashed across Kali's face, but she let it fall away quickly.

"Lucian raised me, but Zane has shown me who I am. I will never work on his behalf again!" She took a step towards our little group. "Brie and Thelzion filled me in on the mission and I am 100% in."

After a few tense seconds, we all relaxed a bit. Zane smiled at his cousin, and she smiled back.

Taking a step towards the table, I brought my hand up to scrub at my face. Kraigen glanced over at me from behind the counter with a questioning nod. I gave him a reassuring nod back that said *all good here*.

Lara hadn't come. She'd rarely left the shop in years for more than groceries or the post office. Personally, I was glad. Her safety meant the world to me.

"Let's have some breakfast. We have a lot to discuss." I'd walked over to pull out a chair for Noella before I took my seat. Pulling out the witch window, Bastian nodded his approval in my direction. "I'll call Thelzion and Brie. We have a ring to find and a realm to save."

Chapter Forty-Eight

Quinn

I went back to my room and pulled off the ice pack I'd held to my neck. The swelling had already gone down. The holes in my throat were just faint pink pinholes now.

The only sign that still remained was the blood that had run down onto my blouse and stained one of my favorite shirts.

Unbuttoning it all the way down, I swore. "FUCK!"

He had attacked me, again!

I'd given him information that was imperative and still I'd taken the brunt of his anger. If Jax hadn't come in when he did, I might not have survived his wrath this time.

When would I learn? He wasn't ever going to be good to me.

He was the worst kind of demon. I knew all of this and yet for years, Years! ... I'd told myself that it was just sex. That I was still his right hand. That his feelings for me didn't matter.

None of that mattered. Lucian was a self-serving narcissist.

Taking sex off the table would be the logical way to help me move past him but I'd never seemed able to stick to my guns when it came to him.

For all of his brutish ways, his charisma and sex appeal kept dragging me back to his bed.

It was time for a change. One that would leave me reeling but might possibly save my wretched life in the long run.

No sleep could be claimed last night but the bed looked comforting now in the morning light.

I would rest today and tonight; and tomorrow I would prove myself worthy of the title of his second.

No more feelings. No more trying to gain his attention in any other way than the mission in front of me.

It was time to be the heartless demon I was meant to be.

Chapter Forty-Nine

Hayden

Briella and Thelzion came into the diner around 8:45am. Brie ordered a couple of coffees and a muffin.

I'd thought it was odd that she didn't order her Mate any food. Then it hit me, blood was the vampire's nourishment of choice. It made nausea roil in my stomach.

It would take some getting used to the fact that demons existed. That they weren't Gifters. Worse yet, that the things that sustained them were things that were best left unthought about.

"What help can we expect from Draxus?" Thelzion asked.

The diner was full of patrons and the sounds of clanking dishes and idle chatter filled in around us.

No one looked at our little group, but I couldn't help looking around, making sure we weren't being watched. It was odd, sitting in a diner full of people, talking about the world ending with no one bothering to look sideways at us.

"He didn't say," Noella told him. "Bastian got him out of his stupor and when he left, he said he had to see a man about a horse."

Thelzion looked at Noella, face scrunched up in concentration.

I, however, was looking at Bastian. A grin lit up my cousin's face and he waggled his eyebrows.

"I think it was an advancement of my Deblocker gift. He seemed stuck, ya know, like on repeat in his own head." Bastian wiggled his fingers. "It was the same feeling I get when I need to unlock a door or move an obstacle. So, I just applied the same principles with my words. And voila," he snapped his fingers. "He came through the other side of his mental block."

"You really have grown, cuz," I said with a smirk. Bastian grinned back.

Glancing around at the rest of them, I'd put my hands on the table and opened my journal. Everyone's attention was now on me. It was nerve wracking.

"What did you Foresee?" Brie asked.

With a look from Brie to Kali, I clamped down my buzzing nerves and turned the open journal to face them all.

"We aren't going to have both of the rings when we need them." My voice was shaky, but I continued. "It's not set in stone, and we should definitely keep looking, but according to my latest foreshadowing," hesitating for a second, I delivered the bad news, "well, we won't possess both of the rings when the Breaking occurs."

"Is that all you can tell us?" Zane asked. Looking at my hung head to see if there was anything to add. "There's more to it. What's up?"

I lifted my eyes to meet Zane and Thelzion's. Speaking to them was easier than looking at Brie or Kali. Noella shifted in her chair beside me.

"I just met Kali, so I didn't know what I was looking at in my Foreshadowing. I can see now that the perspective was off because of the twins," I said.

"Spit it out, Hayden!" Thelzion demanded.

Now the worse news... quick like a bandage.

"One of the Trixie's will be in danger, but I can't tell which one. It was confusing when I was dreaming it because I couldn't understand Brie being in two places at once." I gave her a small grimace, and she nodded for me to go on. "I can't tell which one of the twins it is but as it stands, it was a death Foreshadowing."

Dropping my head again, I always felt as if I was the one responsible for what I foresaw.

Guilt sat on my chest after a death dream. I had no control over them but voicing them made me feel like I had brought the death about.

"Can we change the circumstances? Maybe switch up the places that we look with each other?" Bastian asked but realization donned the expression on his face. "Or is it the place that's the reason? Somebody is going to die because we have to get the ring to save the realm."

It wasn't a question. Bastian had known me his entire life. He already knew the answer.

"Nothing is set in stone," I repeated for good measure. I wasn't so sure of it this time, but I wasn't going to give in to fear. "We just have to find the rings because the alternative is a faster seepage of more and more demons. And they will all flock to Lucian for protection."

"We'll do what we have to do because we can't let that happen," Brie said. "Keeping Lagomshire safe for those we love is the most important thing."

Zane's mouth turned down at the edges, but his resolve was written in his hard eyes. I didn't know what Kali was to him, but I'd seen that look from Thelzion the day Hecate had appeared in the rune bowl. It was the same look he wore now.

I knew the look. I'd seen it in my dream. Keeping my stare as blank as possible, I addressed the group.

"Okay then, we have to discuss who's looking where? Then we can meet back at Pandora's Box in a few days."

Glancing around the table, no one hoped for a better outcome. Resolve sat heavy on every chest. Their minds filled with what they were willing to do to secure the world's survival themselves.

"I guess I'd better live a little in the next few days, ya know, just in case," Kali said. She smiled at us. "Anybody know where the nearest playground is? I want to go down a slide."

Brie grinned at her sister. "You know what, I do too," she said. "We can take an hour or two and have some quality fun time. Living a little sounds perfect."

Our rag-tag group might lose a member in week from now, but we weren't going to live in fear when all of Lagomshire needed us.

I, for one, was grateful to be playing an active role rather than a mere bystander.

Bastian winked at me. "After we save the world, we're taking a holiday and getting laid."

If it wasn't so Bastian, I'd have baulked at the callousness.

Kali reached over an squeezed his hand. "If I die, get laid for me too," she smirked.

We all chuckled. Time wasn't our friend, but our friends were worth our fight.

Demons, mixlings, and gifters. Fighting side by side.

To whatever end.

Chapter Fifty

Lucian

The last of the morning fog drifted across the cemetery grounds, swirling around the headstones and tombs. It brought with it the briny scent of the Manxtas River.

Sunlight crept eerily through the sleeping place of the dead. The light filtering in through the large trees and hanging moss illuminated every name and date etched onto the aging stones.

The air was fresh but breathing around the lump that lodged itself in my throat, I realized that even after three hundred years, I still missed Caylum.

The guilt of killing him was a heavy price to pay. I didn't regret it though. Caylum would have tried to stop me.

Ruling on this plane was my dream and no one was going to stand in my way.

Approaching the mausoleum anxiously, I looked around for any sensors or traps. It was the little annoyances I hadn't been able to rid myself of over the years.

When Draxus and Noella had come and claimed Caylum's body, it was a fight I hadn't won.

Draxus was a demigod and with Noella's heritage, her power was even more than she's allowed herself to realize.

Being alive nearly half a millennia still had not granted her the knowledge of her full potential. Good plays by rules and that's why evil always had the advantage.

I couldn't blame them for wanting the body. I could understand it even.

Caylum was their kin, and I'd killed my lover in cold blood. That kind of grief built rage, on both sides.

Losing graciously wasn't in my repertoire, but I'd fled from the fight after being magically beaten into a bloody mess. I had a bigger goal.

It wasn't until after returning to the manor and searching every inch that I'd realized Caylum's ring of knowing, the Fainne Todhchai, wasn't there.

Our last weeks together had been strained. Caylum had found out that I'd been making plans behind his back.

Being Draxus' first born son, he was the one who'd been entrusted with one of the god forged rings and knowledge of the Prophecy of Tumulus.

It was from his own soft lips that I'd first heard about The Breaking and what potential it held for demons. For me.

Caylum had begun to suspect my thoughts. We'd been together for a very long time. It was one of the reasons Caylum had finally confided what the prophecy meant.

He didn't trust me fully with it though. That was apparent after our first confrontation on the matter.

I had started meeting secretly with various demons. They'd come to the manor and discuss things behind the locked study door.

My lover was the only one who'd ever wormed his way into my heart. And therefore, we had been a team. No secrets from each other and no lies.

In hindsight, that was where I'd fucked up.

After Caylum told his most treasured secret, our dynamic changed. He was more suspicious of every off encounter. He wasn't as talkative or affectionate.

I could feel him pulling away and knew I couldn't allow him to spoil my plans.

What I didn't know was that there was an addendum to the Prophecy.

It was all in Anexian Script and not knowing of what it could possibly say had eaten at me for over three centuries.

With The Breaking in less than two weeks, my time was running out. The fae queen wanted to demand something from me in exchange for the translation.

That was not how I planned to rule, being tied to promises and having strings attached.

If there was anything left in Caylum's final resting place, now would be the time to uncover it.

Jax had procured the Fainne Todhchai and this Hephaetus forged ring was the only shot I had at making it past any barriers Draxus and Noella may have bestowed upon the crypt.

On the outside of the door was a symbol; a full moon at the center with a waxing moon before it and a waning moon to the opposite of it.

I didn't dare put the ring on or even touch it with my bare hands. The gods would have imbued it with some form of divine power.

Demons couldn't touch that power without severe consequences.

Instead, I held it in my gloved hand and placed the circular stone against the center moon on the symbol.

A puff of dust and debris bellowed up as the sealed concrete door cracked open.

Grabbing a lantern from the nearby wall, I made my way inside.

Chapter Fifty-One

Lara

Feeling restless, I opened the shop as the light of dawn was barely an hour old. No one usually came in at this time of day, but this was my happy place.

Having some things I wanted to check on, Noella was supposed to stop by around 10am. I couldn't shake this eerie feeling of impending disaster since waking up.

My visions hadn't shown me anything, which meant it must be directly related to my own well-being.

The universe was a fickle mistress about allowing Seerer's glimpses of their own lives.

Grabbing a bundle of sage, pine, and bay leaf, I lit the end and walked around the room, smudging the air as I went. The calming herbs helped clear away the negative thoughts and dispel unwanted energies.

With the rising sun creeping it's way higher in the sky, the big front windows allowed for light to fill every nook and cranny. Dust motes flittered through the air, floating along the wispy smoke still hanging there.

Coffee was an essential part of my morning ritual. It wasn't just the taste that set my day in the right direction. The act of brewing it was a segment of the practice.

Adding fresh whole beans to the maker, it ground them to semi fine granules. The smell was rich and dark and absolutely delicious. Smells so often triggered *Sight* that coffee was my safe space.

Even when I had troubling visions, the scent of the roasted beans was a balm to my nerves.

As the pot was brewing, I picked up a feather duster and dusted the nearby surfaces, fluffed up the pillows on the bench seat, and straightened the magazines on the end table.

There was no thought to it. A simple morning process to begin the day. Those were the best kinds of tasks. They gave me a sense of normalcy in my overly magical life as of late.

The coffee finished brewing and I went over to retrieve a cup before snatching up the book of translations I'd wanted to check on when I'd gotten up this morning.

The tinkling of the bell at the front door perked my ears up. Looking up from the book, I hadn't known how late in the morning it had become. Noella should be here soon.

A female's voice drifted to me over my wandering thoughts. It was strange that I wasn't shown anyone who would come in today. My visions often helped to aid me in assisting the patrons of the shop.

A whiff of Underworld hit my nose at the same time the woman came around the corner. Her dark brown hair was drawn up in a short ponytail. The woman's dark eyes and severe features of her face presented her desires before she'd even opened her mouth.

This was definitely a demon.

"How can I help you?" I asked, already sensing the answer.

Unease skittered beneath my skin, crawling into my stomach. Not *seeing* was worse than *knowing* in this instance.

"I need a book on translations," she said casually. She glanced at my hand. "I believe it's the book you're holding actually." Her voice didn't raise or fluctuate but there was a menacing undertone in it.

"I'm sorry. This is a personal book. It's not for the use of the public or to purchase."

The woman took a step closer. Whirls of dark energy swirled around her body. Leaning in, she lowered her voice to a mere whisper.

"Maybe I wasn't clear. I need that book and I will have it." The one side of her mouth tilted upward and a dimple appeared on her cheek. It didn't sit right on her beautiful face. It made her look dangerous.

Leaning away, I took a step backwards, tripping over the corner of the end table as I went. Pain seared at my temple.

My hand flew to the side of my head. Hot liquid seeped through my fingers.

Blood. It covered my hand as it leaked down onto my palm as the female approached.

"My name is Quinn. Running a shop like this, I'm sure you've heard of my boss, Lucian." She arched her brow and bent down.

Her hand extending, I thought, just for a second, she was offering it to help me up. It had been a foolish hope.

She grabbed the book instead and swept the room with a glance. "I know that there are artifacts and books in your collection that could prove especially useful for my purposes. You're going to help me."

"And if I don't?" I said, not feeling half as brave as I sounded. "What happens then?"

The sickly sweet smell of oleander wafted from her skin. Another reminder of her deadly nature.

"I think you'll find that I can be very persuasive." Quinn pushed her two fingers into the cut just to the side of my eye with bruising force.

A whimper of pain escaped my lips before I could clamp it down. I didn't want to give this demon the satisfaction of my screams.

Reaching down quickly, she pulled me up by my arm. The room in front of me was spinning and I thought that I might actually throw up. I needed to clamp that down too.

Yanking me to the counter, Quinn pointed at the computer. A silent demand.

"What is it you're looking for?" I said innocently.

The pain in my head was becoming a hard thumping. I couldn't see the screen through the tears filling my eyes.

After getting to the shop search page, the demon roughly pushed me to the side. My light frame was no match for Quinn's strength. The shove sent me flying.

Tumbling over a box that had been left to be unloaded from yesterday's deliveries, I slammed into the shelf behind me.

The contents came crashing down on and around my head. When a large book fell and whacked me in the back of the head, I stumbled forward and landed in a heap on the hard floor.

"You poor dear," she tsk'd, smiling down at me in a purely predatory way.

The blood still leaking from my cut, I'd realized I was about to be the demons latest meal.

She crouched slowly... then she pounced.

Chapter Fifty-Two

Riedyn

Lucian had thrown me off my game. It was time to meet up with my other elite fae warriors in the woods around Avalon Park, but I needed to get my head on right.

Coming around the last building, I shook the bastard from my mind. What was it about him that drew me in time and again?

The others stood swaying within the line of trees. Their uniforms adding to their body's camouflaging.

The entrance to Sidhterra was a fifteen-minute run from the outer edges of where we were gathered. The leaves rustled in the trees as the songbirds took flight all along the forest.

With the dawn had come more risk of being spotted out and about the city. My unit was good at stealth. That didn't worry me.

One of us was going to have to go purchase ordinary clothes from a shop down by the riverside to stay on top of this mission. We would need to glamour some leaves to use as currency and decide who was to go.

"I think it should be our mighty and all powerful Commander," said the tall female fae.

She was the only female in the unit, and it rubbed some faeries in the court wrong that she'd been allowed in.

"Shut up, Willow." I gave her a small grin, and she smiled back.

It hadn't always been this easy with her. Her spirit had practically shut down at one point.

"Willow should go pick out the clothes. She'd dress us better anyway," said the dark-skinned male to my left.

He was well built but not overly bulky. The black hair around his pointed ears was long while in the back of his head it was cut close to his neck.

"When I want your opinion, Oaken, I'll ask for it," I replied.

"You did ask for it. Two minutes ago."

The smartass was about as subtle as a snake perched in a robin's nest.

"I asked who we should send. Not commentary on fashion sense." Shaking my head, I didn't need more male ego to deal with at the moment.

Oaken refocused his thoughts before replying. "Well, I think she would be better at interacting with the locals. She has that charming way about her," he said.

The smirk on his face was enough to bring a booming laugh out of the fae warrior to his right.

"Strategic and funny. I agree with that assessment Commander." The golden fae lifted his arm and held out a handful of whole leaves that I took carefully so as not to damage them.

"Sorry, Willow. It looks like Oaken and Borias have made you our personal shopper." My upturned lips did nothing to hide my mild amusement at their logic. "Just size us as close as possible and come right back. We have a job to do."

Willow took the now glamoured leaves and left with a huff. Turning back to the other two warriors, I shook my head. They had the good sense not to open their mouths.

"When are you guys going to stop looking at her as just another female and start seeing her as a fellow warrior?" My tone was firm, but they heard the hurt underneath. "It's been ten years since she passed the last of the trials and was granted a spot on her Majesty's Elite Unit by the Queen herself."

"Aww, come on Commander. It's not like that," Oaken said. Both my eyebrows sat in my hairline. "Really, it isn't. Don't you remember how long it was before the Unit stopped razzing you?"

Well fuck. I hadn't thought about that actually. Maybe they had accepted her. The newest recruit was always razzed until the next recruit joined.

Damn. Maybe I was the problem? I'd let my caring for her blindingly lead me to a conclusion that wasn't there.

"I hadn't thought of it that way." I raised my hand to rub at the scruff on my chin, resigning myself to the notion. "It was when you joined up, Borias. That's when the others stopped making me the lacky and brunt of their jokes."

Oaken clapped me on the back. "See, it has nothing to do with her being female." He pointed to his head. "It's all about the hazing," he said with a wink.

Borias chimed in his thoughts on the matter too. "There's nothing personal to it at all. In fact, I rather like having her around. She smells better than the rest of you lot."

Both me and Oaken laughed and I decided to leave it at that. I knew it was me who was a bit touchy over Willow. I'd found her to be a great friend over the years.

She'd been like a sister to the Queen's daughter when we were growing up.

When Griane disappeared, it nearly broke Willow. Her spirit and the essence of who she was shifted.

Queen Talisin never fully believed that she didn't know any-thing about why Griane left.

It was after the months that turned into years that Willow spent grieving and wasn't getting any better that the Queen finally saw through her own grief to the fae in front of her.

She'd realized that Willow was barely enduring living and knew that there was no way she'd had any information about what had happened to the Princess.

Her Majesty was able to break through to her and get her to agree to start the training for the Elite Unit. Willow was already a trained soldier for the Queen's guard, but the EU was a lot more advanced. A specialized unit.

It gave Willow something to channel her angst and hurt towards. It made her into a female who had more focus than most of the other warriors in Her Majesty's royal army.

She became a weapon. Her gift was one of growth, plants, shadows, and water. Whatever she touched her power with had that purpose. Her stealth and fighting skills came to outshine her natural gifts after a time. She was a true warrior.

Spotting the color of a few bags swinging in and out of view, Borias called over the chirping of the birds, drawing me out of my recollections.

"That was fast wee one." He smiled.

Her nose scrunched up. The points of her ears turning red.

"I hate it when you call me that." She didn't sound severe, just annoyed. "I did the best I could. The three shops that had any clothes in them had little to choose from."

The sun was almost over head. Somehow, the morning had slipped away faster than fresh dew on a field.

Taking the bag closest to me, I peeked inside. The fabric was bright and unnatural. Some had shiny bits and others had zippers and snaps. The shoes looked constricting and were no doubt uncomfortable.

After all these years interacting with them, I still couldn't understand how the Dhalls wore this stuff every day.

"Hey, this is not what I had in mind!" Oaken said. "Why is it so... flourished?"

She chuckled. "If you aren't satisfied with what I got, go get something different yourself."

Clever girl. The spot on way she'd put it to him brought a grin to my face.

"Oh, I see your game." His smile reached all the way to his eyes. "Do it badly and we won't make you do it anymore?"

"Smart little bird you are." That was high praise from Borias.

This meeting was getting nowhere fast. Time to wrangle these characters in.

"Will you lot focus!" I knew they were just having a little fun, but the Queen had sent of few of her EU to do a job that she considered to be of the utmost importance. It was time to get back to it. "Get dressed and we'll split up. Oaken and Willow, you find out what Jax and Parker are up to. Borias, you take point with Lucian."

They all snapped their attention to me.

I wasn't proud of myself for my lack of control around the Donnchadh. I knew where my loyalties sat, but that also meant delegating responsibility to the person who could handle the situation the best.

"Why wouldn't you be taking lead on Lucian?" Borias asked.

Just because I knew what needed to be done, didn't mean I wanted to lay myself bare in front of my warriors. No lies, but half truths were the faery way.

"I want to find Quinn and see why his second left before dawn this morning."

No one said anything. They knew of my past with Lucian.

We'd been lovers for a time. I'd thought I'd meant something more to him, but he cast me aside one day without any explanation.

He'd broken my heart. He'd nearly broken my spirit. Over the years since, he'd occasionally lure me back only to push me aside all over again. I couldn't seem to quit him properly.

All of their faces held confusion and understanding in equal measure. None of them thought I'd give up the post so easily or entrust it to anyone else.

It was then I knew they'd all seen my composure when I came back.

Fuck. I'd thought I'd hidden it better.

"Okay. Well, if that's all, let's get on with it." If I was a braver male, I'd lean on them for support.

With a nod and a fist thump to each of their shoulders, I signaled our break. It was the EU way.

Without another word or a backward glance, we all slinked off in opposite directions.

Chapter Fifty-Three

Thelzion

The humid air clung to our skin even now, before noon. Briella and Kalina were perched on the swings chatting and getting to know one another while me and Zane stood in the shadow of a large oak tree.

The laughter of a few children rang out through the playground and into the small field beside the parking lot.

Two horses remained hitched to a post close by an automated carriage that sat unattended in the lot.

"I'm not going to let anything happen to Kali, Thelzion. I don't know what the Foreshadower thought he was doing telling them that one of them was going to die, but I can't let that happen"

Zane's tone made it clear that this wasn't a discussion. Just a statement of his truth.

Shifting from one foot to the other, I crossed my arms in front of me and glared at him. Brie was my world.

If one of the twins was to die, I wouldn't let it be her. I'd prefer neither of them to die.

My mate had only just found her sister. Ripping her away would cause Brie heartache I couldn't bear.

"What makes you think I'd let anything happen to Brie?" I demanded. "She is my Mate! I think that makes me a little more inclined to save her life at all costs, don't you?" I didn't raise my voice but the tone was more vicious than if I was. "I can't let anything happen to Kali either. Brie just found her sister, and it would tear out her heart to lose her again."

If we agreed on anything, it would be this. I knew he'd have my back.

"I see your point," Zane said. "I didn't think of it that way but you're right." He clapped a hand on my arm, swiftly removing it when I glanced down at the spot. "We need to protect them both, but we can't make them feel useless either. They are fierce warriors and won't take kindly to being mollycoddled."

Contemplating Zane's assessment for a moment, an odd thing occurred to me. My eyes zeroed in on the vein at the side of his throat.

Pushing out my Donnchadh hearing, I listened to the tempo of his heart. An underlying double beat thrummed under his skin. Barely there, but most definitely present.

"You two just met recently. You never got to tell me that story," I continued listening to Zane's heart. "Why are you so vested in Kali's well-being all of a sudden?"

Zane chose his words carefully, but his pulse would give me the information anyway.

"Lucian had been holding me captive," Zane said. My stomach roiled slightly. I knew Lucian's ways all too well. "He left me for dead. I think he thought that I was a Gifter so it never occurred to him to take the more necessary measures to kill a Mixling." He grinned. "I have always played that card close to the chest."

A respectful smirk perched itself on my lips. I'd saved his life fifty-seven years ago from a group of demons under my command.

It was the first in a string of many things that led me to save Brie as an infant. I was in no way good at that time, but I'd been realizing that life needed to be more than blood and violence.

A squeal from Kali had both our heads snapping up. Laughter fell from Brie's lips as she wiggled her feet and showed her sister how to swing high over the top bar.

After a few moments of shared contentment, he took up his tale again.

"I thought that I was already dead. Kali came in and saved me." Zane dropped his chin to his chest. "I don't know how to explain this right... but I felt something when she kissed me."

With an arched eyebrow, I waited for him to continue. Saving him and kissing him were not the same thing. Suddenly, I felt a bit overprotective of my mate's newly found sibling.

"It was like an electrical shock, but it didn't hurt. It felt right, possessive even." He shook his head, his chest puffing out.

The more he spoke of her, the louder the double thrum in his chest became. More pronounced.

"I don't know man. It seemed surreal at the time, but I couldn't make myself leave her side. It still feels like a tether, a pull towards her wherever she is."

It was my turn to clap him on the arm. I looked over to where the sisters were swinging and then back to Zane. I knew that feeling. That pull. More importantly, I was certain of what that double beat meant.

"She's your Mate." A rare real smile tugged my face taut, but Zane's mouth fell open with an audible pop and I chuckled.

"How do you know? I mean... how?" he said, tripping over his words.

"I've felt it before. What you just described to me, that was exactly how it felt with Brie." My grip on his arm tightened slightly. "Besides that, there's a dual beat to your heart. The more you speak about her, the harder it thrums... I guess this makes us brothers now."

Zane was struggling for words. His world was being turned upside down at the revelation. He shook his head to try and dispel my assessment.

I wasn't so sure he saw it as a good thing. That perplexed me greatly.

When I'd figured out Brie was my mate, when everything fell into place and the stars aligned our destinies, it had made me the happiest I'd ever been.

Zane fidgeted with a leaf he'd ripped off a nearby tree. "Look, I don't want her to have another decision taken out of her own hands. She's lived her whole life like that. Lucian was always in control of her actions." He began pacing in front of the tree and I didn't know how to help him through what he was feeling. "Do you know that she didn't even know she was a Trixie?"

That pumped my brakes. "What?! How in the Sevens is that even possible?" I exclaimed. "Does she even have any training?"

"Physically, yes. Her abilities as a Conservatrix, nope." Disgust was written on his face, and I was sure it was mirrored on my own. "I've had to calm her down from her emotions pushing out her abilities a few times in the last couple of days."

One thing was clear, with their irrational reactions to a practical stranger, there could be no doubt in my mind they were each other's other half.

"That should tell you right there that you are Mates, Zane. Trixie's aren't meant to be calmed. It usually only riles them up more. The fact that you were able to get through to her when she was in that state makes sense only if you have a soul connection." I clapped him on the back, harder this time. "Welcome to the family bro."

Zane's hand went to his head, running his fingers back through his hair. His eyes crinkled and the sides of his mouth drew up into a wide, but troubled, grin.

"She growled at Noella when she hugged me this morning. It felt protective, jealous even." The troubled look on his face fell away. "I pulled back when she kissed me on the beach. I really don't want to make her choices for her. If destiny has other plans, how am I supposed to fight my inner instincts to be with her or protect her or hell, how am I supposed to not fall in love with her?"

My nose scrunched up on my face up but didn't say anything. I had no words of advice.

Brie had been my world from the moment I saw her as a pink bundle of wrinkles wrapped in her dead father's arms. The mating bond hadn't kicked in until decades later. When it did, I was helpless against it.

"I'm actually asking you, man. I don't want to take anything away from her, but this pull seems determined not to give us any choice in the matter."

"Sorry dude, I don't know how to help you with that. Brie had me wrapped around her finger from the time she was born. I didn't know we were Mated until she unexpectedly kissed me during one of our training sessions. After that, we were tied to one another and I've never regretted a minute of it."

Zane peered over to where the girls were getting off the swings to head our way.

"Ya know, I've been alive a long time. I deserve to be happy... don't I?" Zane said.

"I still don't feel like I deserve Brie, but I'll tell you one thing, let a mother fucker try to take her from me. I will rip this world apart to get her back!"

My emotions seeped into my words without my consent. I didn't wear them on my sleeve. Briella brought out the light in my darkness and sometimes it felt overwhelming to be in her presence.

Honestly, without her, my life had no meaning. I watch the world burn if it meant keeping her safe.

Quietly, I said, "She's your Mate. She growled in your defense. Even if you give her choices, trust me, she is always going to choose you." A small smile lifted the corners of my lips as Brie and Kali approached us. "You have to tell her, man. It wouldn't be fair to her otherwise."

Kali approached Zane's side. Their eyes met and I turned my head to smirk.

"Tell me what?" Kali asked.

Zane threw me a hard look. "Thanks traitor."

"Anytime, *brother*."

Chapter Fifty-Four

Jaxson

Me and Parker rounded the corner at the same moment as the pawn shop owner swung the door open.

We quickly made our way past the front entrance and bypassed the security measures that were in place by pushing through seconds after him. He turned around to look and saw two demons behind him. Poor guy.

He was a squat little man with wrinkled tanned skin and spectacles that took up his whole face. His body had a strong smell of cheese and procured meat. His short stature made him have to crane his neck to look us in the face.

"Hello Fhail. How are you this fine morning?" I asked. It seemed the polite thing to do.

Parker rolled his eyes and picked up a funny looking metal bowl off of the closes shelf.

"Jaxson," he said, giving a little nod. "Why are you here?"

Parker turned around, dropping the bowl on the ground with a loud clang, and addressed the shop keeper.

There was no fear in him. No scent of it tainted my nose. The male was a peculiar little thing.

"Lucian seems to think that you might have some information on where to find an object that he needs," Parker said.

He ran his fingers over the dust on the shelf. Letting another object fall to the floor. Broken pieces of artifacts and gadgets littered the aisles as he went.

"Where can we find one of the Rings of Potentia? The Rever-to Akasha, to be exact. And something called the Gregarious?" Parker was nothing, if not a determined asshole.

He lifted his hand to the shelf once again and toppled over a jar with a deathly looking powder inside. It crashed to the floor and broke, sending the powder and bits of light floating out of the shards.

"Knock it off, Parker," I said. "Give the guy a chance to answer." Turning back to the shop keeper, he was staring down at the broken jar with shock and outrage. "Look Fhail, we just need to know what you know. My associate here is a little overzealous. You can see my dilemma, can't you?"

Fhail squinted through his thick, dirty glasses at me. They were so thick, they had to be heavy to haul around on such a small framed face.

He leaned in and quietly spoke only to me, like we shared a secret friendship or something.

I may be on the chain, but I was still a demon. One who worked for a ruthless boss.

"I have a book that I can check in later tonight. It's not here right now but I will contact you after I find out whatever I can," he finished whispering and stood back.

Standing back up just as Parker knocked another relic off the shelf with a thunderous crash, I shook my head.

"Oops. So sorry. I will have to insist that you get the book and look it up for us right now," Parker walked up to tower over the shop keeper, but I stepped forward, cutting him off.

"Why can't you get the book now, Fhail?" he said.

He restlessly took off his glasses and attempted to clean them with a soiled rag he pulled from his pocket. It only made them worse. Streaks of whatever had been on the rag now ran across them directly over the center of one of the lenses.

Replacing them onto his face, it didn't sit quite right with me that he was this calm. Something about him screamed *not right*, but I couldn't place it.

"Another person has it at the moment. I will get a message to them and have them return it post haste. I swear," the little man said.

Beads of sweat formed on his forehead, and he wrung his hands in front of him, finally exhibiting the fear he should have had all along.

Fear had an acrid smell. It also gave the blood a richer taste. I threw out my arm to block the shop keeper just as Parker launched himself at him.

"Check yourself, asshole!" I hollered at Parker. "We can't translate anything from the book, even if he did have it here."

"Get your fucking hands off me!" Parker snarled at me.

We'd come to blows before, but we both knew Lucian would hand us our asses if our tasks weren't met to his standards before we tore each other apart.

Dropping my arm from the other demon's chest, I ran a hand over the freshly shaven area of my face.

"Look, Fhail is under Lucian's protection rule. If you haven't figured it out by now, our boss is a maim first, ask questions later kind of guy. But by all means," I gestured to the shop keeper with a wave of my hand. "Be my guest."

Parker looked over at the squat little man and back to me. Throwing his hands up in the air in surrender, he strode back down the aisle and out the front door.

"Would the person who has this book happen to be a Mixling woman?" I asked as casually as I could muster.

"Oh, no. Just a friend from one of the shops in town. I'm sure she'll send it back over as soon as she receives my message. And I swear, I will get right on it," he said. "If there's anything to be found on the rings location in there, I will find it and send word to the manor."

Taking a deep breath, I gathered my resolve. His blood did smell delicious. Parker wasn't wrong about that.

"For your sake, I hope you do find what Lucian wants." I tapped my fist on the little man's shoulder and headed towards the door.

Looking back one last time, I reached into my pocket and pulled out a handful of coins and placed them on the shelf closes to him, dipping my chin to the shop keeper before exiting.

Chapter Fifty-Five

Noella

The door crashed opened and a flash of blinding light illuminated the entire space.

The sight before me was paused in mid-action. The female demon was just inches away from Lara's neck with drool dripping from her sharp teeth.

In actuality, I couldn't stop time. My mind just worked super-fast to assess and catalog real-time events when I sensed danger.

The fact that my lover was about to be devoured meant that my senses were working overtime.

Throwing out my hand, a wave of pure power crashed into the Seidre demon with the force of a stampeding horse.

The female flew across the room and slammed into a shelf that contained jars of herbs and other ingredients. The book she'd been holding fell to the floor. Glass rained down on her crumpled body, covering her with different liquids and various other bits that stuck to her skin.

She lifted her head and stared at me. The blood lust trance was broken with the force of the blow to the shelf.

"Noella," the demon acknowledged as she slowly stood.

"Quinn," I said, staring daggers at the demon.

My chest heaved in anger and the sight of Lara still on the ground, blood dripping down the side of her face was making it difficult to contain the magics that wanted free reign.

Reaching a hand down to help Lara up, I never took my eyes off Quinn.

"I was here for something Lucian needed," she smirked. "I thought I'd grab a bite to eat before I left."

My hand raised on instinct to accost the female again.

In an unexpected jolt forward, Quinn dashed towards us and I had to re-adjust to block Lara from another attack.

Quinn quickly diverted her path and sprinted to the door. It opened from the outside and a tall, dark figure stood in its frame.

She seized the opportunity to dash around the male and out the door without a backward glance.

Damn it! Lara reached around my middle and embraced me, but I was still in protection mode. My hands were steady, but my breathing and heartbeat were erratic.

Somewhere in my mind, I assessed the newcomer and realized that the threat had left the area. Calm down and breathe. Simple, right?

"What are you doing here, Riedyn?" My tone none to kindly.

I hadn't mean to be so harsh but the fact that he'd unintentionally made it easier for the threat to Lara's life to get away had me irrationally vexed at his presence.

"I'd been checking around for Lucian's second's whereabouts in the area and heard a ruckus from down the street. I came to see what it was. Are you okay?" He directed the latter towards Lara, his eyes lingering on her bloody shirt.

"I think so," she said. "I don't know what happened. One minute she was asking about something and the next, I was hurt and, and... I don't...," she trailed off, not knowing how to finish.

Turning into her embrace, I wrapped one arm around her. Bringing the other up to the side of Lara's head, gently as I could, I wiped away the blood to see the damage.

It wasn't too bad. Just bad luck that it was in a spot that bled so much.

Riedyn looked between the two of us. Realizing that this was more than just friendship, he walked over to peruse a nearby item from a shelf to give us some semblance of privacy. For that, I was grateful.

"I'm okay, Noella, really," Lara said. I reached up and swept a piece of straggling hair and tucked it behind her ear.

We stared into one another's eyes for a long minute before I took both sides of Lara's face in my hands and brought our lips together.

It was gentle and sweet and the heat from Lara's mouth felt comforting, like home.

Pulling away slightly to look for where Riedyn went, I called out through the store.

"You can come back now, Commander," I said with a wry smile.

He walked out from in between the two bookcases at the back of the room. His clothes weren't fae made which meant only one thing. He was here on a mission.

That would be the only reason this faery would don those threads. Colorful and brash as they were. He must have picked them up from that vintage store down a few blocks over.

Lara went to the counter to grab another cup of coffee to calm her nerves. It was her safe space. I knew that. The fact that she needed it made my chest ache.

Watching her closely, she tried to nonchalantly pull the first aid kit out and discretely open a bottle of aspirin. I'd let her think she was protecting my feelings. She wouldn't want me to fuss over her pain, but I couldn't help the sensation that my magics wanted to hunt down Quinn and make her hurt too.

Clamping down on that notion, I internally fought the dark stir of the power inside. It was a constant struggle to not let my magics turn me dark.

Power corrupted even those with the best intentions. Draxus tried to teach me to be its master and not let it master me, but my fear of losing myself to it always put a hindrance in our training.

"What brings you to the city, Riedyn?" I said, trying to re-direct my focus elsewhere. "I noticed your new digs." Smirking, I couldn't help myself.

I had known the Commander for a few centuries. Remembering him as a fledgling fae was a treat. It helped remind me that we don't all start out as the villain or the hero.

Our nature may play its part, but we all get to make our own choices as to where life leads us.

Riedyn considered me for a moment, deciding if and what he would reveal. Queen Talisin would have her own agenda, that much I was sure of.

Her EU Commander would never say anything to jeopardize his Queen's plan but apparently, he'd determined that I was not a threat to his Majesty's goals.

"Well, I was following up as to where Quinn had disappeared to this morning," he said. "I had just come from the woods in Avalon

Park and caught her scent in this direction. When I was at the end of the block, I heard the commotion from the same direction that her scent was leading me in. I made swift haste to find the source."

"You were following Quinn?" That could only mean that his mission for the fae queen was something to do with Lucian. "Was there a reason that the Commander of Her Majesty's Elite Unit wouldn't be the one following Lucian?"

Riedyn paled slightly and I understood, in that moment, what he wasn't saying out loud. I wouldn't push him any farther on the subject.

Lara strode over and sat some cucumber sandwiches on the table with a pitcher of spring water and mint. She gave the Commander a dip of her chin.

"I thought these would be more natural to you than our usual Tuesday lunch." A flush reddened her cheeks as she spoke.

She was amazing. I gazed at her in awe. How had I gotten so lucky to have this thoughtful creature as my own?

"What's your usual Tuesday lunch?" he asked.

"Pizza with the works," I said with a grin.

Riedyn nodded his thanks. I laughed. I knew Riedyn wouldn't mind the pizza, but he just picked up one of the sandwiches and ate it without protest.

Out of all of the fae I'd ever dealt with, he was the most ridged, yet still laidback. He pulled it off seamlessly. The opposites of his personality weren't like a tug of war. They were more like paddling a canoe to keep it going straight rather than off to one side.

"What are your takes on this situation with Lucian?" I asked him. Even if he wouldn't give his Queen's agenda away, he might still have some insight he'd be willing to share that we could both benefit from.

"If we could stop him before he gets what he wants, my Queen wouldn't have to worry about the after effect so much." He rubbed a hand over his smooth jawline.

The small hoop earring hanging from one of his lobes glinted in the light coming from the shop windows. It sparked a repressed memory in my mind from when he was in his youth.

"The Fae Queen was sitting on her throne. The courtyard around me was lively. Revelers were dancing and making merry.

Riedyn was just a young teen, no cares, trouble free.

Draxus had brought me to formally meet the Queen of the Fae. I sat on the steps of the Dias leading up to the throne.

My father was deep in conversation with the Queen when he noticed that I wasn't paying attention to them.

He called me up to interact with Her Majesty when just moments before, my whole body had begun to lift and inch towards the revelers of its own accord.

"Your Grace, can you tell us the story of the portal to St. Augustine?" he said. "My daughter would so enjoy that tale."

From the look on his face, I could tell that he wanted me to pay close attention, but the Fae music was singing in my mind, in my blood.

"*Again, Draxus?*" she said with a wry smile. "*I think you just like hearing me talk.*"

My father smiled his crooked little smile. I knew he was playing on her vanity. It won out.

She turned her body towards me, and I tried really hard to concentrate.

"*As you know, child, the realms of Sidhterra and Lagomshire overlap. It's like a piece of tracing paper laid over a bold map.*" She smiled up at Draxus again to make sure he was as rapt with her story as he was before she had started.

"*Please, go on your Majesty,*" he said. Her wicked smile lit up her face at his flirtatious manner.

"*Well, there is another realm that does the same. If Sidhterra is on the tracing paper above the bold map, then St. Augustine is traced on the paper below it.*" She smiled wickedly as my mouth popped open.

"*Are you saying there's another world we could access?*" I asked timidly.

The Queen turned to Draxus and pursed her lips. She was known for playing a long game. Immortality became boring the longer you lived.

Draxus and I were immortals but not from her realm. The Queen was careful with her words and what she chose to reveal.

"*Your daughter is perceptive.*" She said this as an annoyance, not a compliment.

The Demigod cast a long warning look at me. I knew I needed to hold my tongue and just listen, but the question had just popped out.

"*She is an astute pupil. She will give you her full attention without interruption from here on,*" he said with a smooth smile that showed off the dimple on his left cheek.

I'd always known my father to be charismatic and handsome but with his perfect jawline and brilliant blue eyes, when he flashed that dimple, no one could resist him anything.

The Queen smirked in the wake of his coquetry. She swiveled back to face me once again.

"There is another realm. With the same basic layout as ours here in Sidhterra. And the same as the layout in your realm of Lagomshire," she said.

The Queen lived on the edge of mischief and cruelty. Draxus had told me to watch my words and my body language before we'd arrived.

The Queen would speak more with what she wasn't saying than with what she was choosing to reveal.

"The three realms are all very different. The Low realm of St Augustine is a place that has no exposed magics. They still exist but the Humans that live there have a way of denying anything they see. A small fraction of them are aware of otherly things but the majority go out of their way to explain away any magics that come to light."

She gave Draxus a knowing glance. He returned it with an encouraging wry smile.

"I've sent a few of my warriors to the Low realm a few times. They always returned in a state of subdued capacity. It would take weeks for them to feel like themselves again." Her finger tapped at her chin for a moment.

I could tell that she was considering if she should say anymore. Patiently, I waited.

"They always seemed older, more worn. Their immortality was leeched from them on their visits. It aged their features. Even after they'd returned to the land of Faery their abilities remained depleted for days." Her eyes were far away in remembering. "I forbid travel

to the Low realm after the last party returned in a diminished capacity."

Draxus selected his next words carefully, maintaining a casual air about them but no doubt he wanted me to listen intently for the Queens response.

"Your Majesty, if I may ask, where did your warriors stumble upon the Low realms entrance?" he said as he gazed into the Queens cold eyes.

She pursed her lips into a hard line. It was clear he had pushed too far.

"Forgive me. I was caught up in your captivating story telling. I meant no disrespect with the question." His words were elegant and beguiling and I couldn't help but stare in awe at my father's charms.

The Queen waved her arm dismissively. The revelers were beginning to succumb to the debauchery blooming from the dancing.

"Thank you for telling us such a charming story Your Majesty," I said. "I really enjoyed it."

"You're welcome, dear. I think it is grand to dream of far-off places. The reality of seeing them never matches expectations though." Her statement was a rebuff and a dismissal.

With a quick glance around the open courtyard, Draxus' eyes landed on bare skin and acts of debauchery that brought heat to my cheeks.

I was a grown, young woman, but he was still my father.

Ushering me out of the area, he addressed the queen once more.

"This was a nice visit. I hope we can do it again sometime," he said, bowing at the waist.

Flattery appeared to be Queen Talisin's weakness. She tipped her head back and gave him a small laugh that sounded like windchimes.

"And maybe next time you won't be here simply for information," she said with a knowing smirk.

Draxus feigned a blush and rose to link arms with me protectively.

Glancing back at the Queen and the revelers, I heard the first sounds of naked bodies slapping parts against each other.

My father led me out of the hall and towards the path that led to the portal. We didn't speak again until we were through it and back in Lagomshire.

"Do you know where the portal to the Low realm is?" I asked.

Raising his hand and running his fingers through his raven black hair, he looked around the woods.

"No. I have a feeling that it's going to be necessary to find it though. The prophecy is our charge, Noella. Having this knowledge could help in that regard." He walked a few steps and turned back to face me. "You know as well as I do that the ring Caylum holds isn't the biggest concern." He shook his head. "Even if he thinks keeping it on him is the safest option. That vampire he loves will be your brother's downfall one day. You mark my words."

"And the other two rings... how do we keep them safe?" My mind had raced quickly ahead at my father's words about my older half-brother. "This other realm that the Queen spoke of... it can't be better, can it?"

He waggled his eyebrows at me and smiled widely. I knew that look.

"I guess I'm going to have to find out." He began walking farther into the woods before he called over his shoulder again. "Searching these woods is going to take forever, but if I can feel my way towards it, maybe we'll have a shot of hiding one of the rings in the Low realm." His steps slowed and he turned to face me. "I think that hiding it in a

realm, where magics aren't looked for, will be our best bet at keeping this realm safe."

"That's the problem with prophecies though, isn't it?" I said. "They are so vague and basically, they are self-fulfilling. If no one knew about them or acted to prevent them from coming about, they would probably be avoided altogether."

Draxus raised an eyebrow at me. Pride and love shown in his blue eyes.

"Sometimes, you are so much like your mother it's astounding. I catch myself forgetting just how she could see and cut through all of the bullshit that mucks up the works."

I didn't like it when he talked about my biological mother. It often led to him overthinking and sent him down the rabbit hole of over drinking and overindulgence. It could be years before he climbed out it his stupors.

"Thanks, I guess," I said. "With that in mind, maybe you should feel around for spots that hold no stir, like broth instead of soup. It may even feel like a drain of your magiks if the Queen is to be believed."

"Fae can't lie, Noella. It's tied to their magics. Theirs is a natural sort of thing. And nature doesn't lie. It may meander around and pretend to be something else, but it doesn't lie."

His words were plain enough but I didn't know if he meant them in the way that I was thinking.

"Well, it could take months to find the portal to the Low realm. I'll leave you to it."

And with that, I shimmered away.

Realizing Lara had called my name a few times, I came out of my recollections and turned towards the Commander.

The question on my lips bursting to be asked. I hadn't thought about that day for quite a long time and now I couldn't stop thinking about it.

"Riedyn, do you know where the portal to St Augustine is?"

He looked at me wryly. A sheepish grin stretched from one side of his face to the other.

I returned the smile tenfold. I felt a plan coming together.

Chapter Fifty-Six

Zane

I had told Kali that I'd explain to her in detail everything when we got back to the apartment.

When the carriage pulled up to the building, I paid the driver, helped her out, and made to open the door.

Kali walked in silence, and I knew she was holding it all in until we were alone. The way her silence tugged at me to comfort her hadn't been something I was prepared for.

Keeping my hands folded in my lap the entire way here had been the only way to not reach for her and pull her close.

I unlocked the door and was only seconds across the threshold when she pivoted, leveling me with her full glare. I took an involuntary step back.

Gods... She looked like a true goddess.

Putting my hands up in surrender, I took a few steps into the apartment, shutting the door as I went.

Biding my time and gathering my thoughts wasn't something she was willing to be patient for apparently.

"So?" she demanded. "What is it you were discussing with Thelzion that he thought the need to have to say it loud enough for me to hear?"

I'd debated the extent of what to tell her all the way back home. If I told her everything and she didn't want to be tied to me, it would crush my immortal soul.

Immortals were permanent things and getting over shit wasn't in our nature. It could take centuries.

My uncle was a prime example of that. Still, all this time later, Draxus clung to the memories of Solene.

On the other hand, if I didn't tell her everything up front and she found out some other way, she'd never forgive me That wasn't something I could risk.

Option A it was.

"Well, I didn't really keep anything from you." She crossed her arms skeptically. "Honestly, it was Thelzion who made everything click into place. I didn't fully understand what was going on before we'd spoken. I did have my suspicions though."

She relaxed a bit, uncrossing her arms and slowly seated herself on the couch.

"Okay. That's not as bad as I was imagining," she said. She let out a breath she probably hadn't realized she'd been holding. My poor vixen.

Sitting down beside her on the sofa, I took her hand in mine.

She stared down at the gesture. The moment she looked back up, into my eyes, I felt like I was flying.

We were both leaning in towards each other. I could feel a swell of pride and hopefulness and possessiveness.

Being alive for well over four hundred years hadn't prepared me for this experience. It was unruly and primal.

I'd had many relationships with many different females over the centuries and loved quite a few of them.

This was so disparate. None of them compared a fraction to what this felt like.

"Remember when you kissed me back at the warehouse?" Pink rose to the top of her cheeks but I went on. "And remember on the beach? That draw we felt towards each other?"

Her face scrunched up, perplexed at where I was going with this. She was the most beautiful and adorable thing I'd ever seen. It was hard to get out the words.

"I felt something, Kali." I didn't know if I could keep going. The thought of her rejection was torture.

Laughing softly, a grin spread across her face from ear to ear. "I'm a good kisser."

"I felt like you jolted me with electricity. It was a zing right to my heart."

My lame explanation hung heavy in the air between us.

"Is that what that was? I thought that I was just out of practice," she said. Her lips curled up at the edges again.

Gods, how was I going to get through this?

"Do you understand what it means?" She shook her head, so I continued. "Thelzion listened with his gifts. He heard a double beat in my chest. It's what happens when souls are Mated. Are you familiar with the term?"

She stood, pulling her hand out of mine. Ouch... not the reaction I'd hoped for.

The worry lines on her forehead crinkled in annoyance.

"It means that I belong to you, and you belong to me." She said it like it was a punishment.

My heart ached for a moment. I gave it that, just a moment of hurt.

Choosing my next words wisely, I drew on my long life's experiences before replying. With pain lancing through my chest, I tied up the chasm there the best I could.

"It means that you belong *with* me, and I belong *with* you. We don't own each other, Kali. The fates aren't that cruel. They choose to make souls Mated as a gift. As a love that transcends time and the mortal coil," my words coming out in a plea for understanding the difference. "I won't make you choose me. I will always give you space to figure out what's best for you."

She looked at my face in earnest. Her eyes were bright, but her voice was heavy.

"I like you, Zane. I really do feel a pull towards you," she said. I waited for the blow I knew was coming. "I only left Lucian's control days ago."

"I would NEVER try to control you, Kalina!" It made me almost angry that she'd think I was capable of that.

Not angry at her but at Lucian. Remembering that she'd been sheltered and lied to her entire life.

Taking a deep breath, I quieted the hurt that had risen up at her words. I could never be angry with her.

I was raging against the injustice of it all. "I'm sorry. It just sucks, that's all. I never thought much about the Mated couples that I've met. I never thought it would ever happen to me." The side of my mouth turned up on one side. "Thelzion said as much. He said that he never thought it would happen to him either. He said that the pull he feels towards your sister is the best and the worst thing he's ever felt."

Twisting a strand of her hair around her finger, her eyes shined with moisture beneath her long lashes.

"I think we should continue as we have been. It's been fun getting to know each other, hasn't it?" she said, smiling that adorable smile of hers. "If it leads us to more, then so be it. I just don't want my choices taken away again so quickly."

I laughed and she stared me down. Gods, this vixen was everything I could have ever want, if I'd only thought to ask for it.

"What's that for?" Her demanding tone, all cute and adorably threatening, was the best sound in the realm.

"Well, that's exactly what I told Thelzion. I said that I didn't want your choices taken away from you after you just finally got to live a life of your own." My lips turned up again. "That's what we were discussing when Thelzion took that part out of my hands. That's what you and Brie overheard."

She watched me like I was the most interesting program on the moving box, and it made my heart beat its first thump since the chasm had opened up.

Her face was carefully smoothed out. I was sure that Lucian had taught her a good card playing face, but I could see right through it.

I could read her like a book practically from the moment we'd first kissed.

Her gaze didn't stray from mine, possibly seeing what the appeal of being Mated was?

Fighting it was her little rebellion.

What I saw on her face made me hopeful that one day she may come around.

"I hadn't put it all into place until I said it aloud to Thelzion. And even then I questioned if it could be true," I said, shaking my head. "Zi insisted it was the same sorts of things he and Briella went through to figure out they were Mates. And when he put it out there the way he did, I realized that I couldn't deny it."

Kalina walked over to where I was now standing against the kitchen island. She stood shoulder to shoulder with me even though she was about a head shorter than I was.

"I didn't say I don't want to be YOUR Mate. I said that I wasn't ready to be tied to anyone else's way of thinking yet." Knocking her shoulder playfully against mine, she gave me that dimpled smile that tore away the ice I'd built around my heart over the years. "It's not a diss on you. I just want to choose for myself."

Hmmm. I could live with that. If all she'd grant me were scraps for now, I'd stitch them together to make a quilt.

I smirked. I could be patient, but I could also work on doing things that would insure she would choose me.

That thought made my pulse race and my heart inflate like a slow rising bubble from under water. The pressure wasn't going to burst it, but once it broke the surface, the air would be free and abundant.

"Then I say, challenge accepted. I'm going to earn my way into your life and worm my way into your heart."

I winked at her and her returning grin busted through the last of my frosty reserves.

Chapter Fifty-Seven

Lucian

The mausoleum was in disarray. There were urns upturned, grave plaques cracked open, and coffins pulled from their resting places.

Still, I hadn't found the Reverto Akasha. I was sure that Draxus would have hidden it here with Caylum's bones and the rest of his deceased line.

I'd hoped to at least find a script to reveal where it was, even if it wasn't in this crypt.

It was dark except for the few lanterns I'd lit around the outer walls. A shimmer of light caught my eye in the corner of the room, but it was gone when I'd looked back.

The stale air was making me nauseated. It was consecrated and I'd been in here for a couple of hours now.

Finally giving up, I headed for the stone door entrance to the crypt.

It was difficult to locate the spot for the Fainne Todhchai to be placed and get the slab to slide open, but I found it after a bit of rummaging around in the dim light.

It opened a mere fraction as daylight squeezed its way in. The slab of stone slammed shut again just seconds later.

"I could keep you trapped in here for some time, Lucian," a male voice rang out all around me. "It would be fitting, don't you think?"

"Caylum?" my shock made my voice quaver. Beads of sweat began forming on my brow and a hollowness threatened to open up a hole in my chest.

The voice laughed. It was amused to catch me where I clearly wasn't supposed to be.

"Ah. Yes. You would think that, wouldn't you?" A figure stepped out of the shadows and made its way towards me. "You'd deserve that kind of retribution."

I should have known. Caylum was long dead. Killed by my own hand... yet for just a moment, I'd basked in the cadence of his memory.

"Draxus," my flat tone with distain. "I should have known."

"Did you think that I wouldn't have security measures in place here where my kin rests?" Draxus looked from me to the mess I'd created. "I should flay you where you stand, vampire!"

It wasn't bravery I felt in this moment. It was pure adrenaline. He could send me back to the underworld with little more than a few scraps pouring from his magics.

"If I was that easy to kill, you'd have done it years ago, Godling," My cruel smirk a mere mask to the turmoil roiling inside my gut.

Caylum had Draxus' eyes and sharp jawline. Seeing him in his father brought back an ache I'd thought I'd long put behind me.

"Who says that it would be meant to kill you? The pain of regrowing a whole body of skin can be excruciatingly painful, from what I hear."

The glean in his eyes told me Draxus relished in the thought but my remembrance of the last time I'd been tortured under the

Demigod's retribution still rang agonizingly painful in the fore-front of my mind.

"Should I tidy up before I go or will we be adding blood and gore to the mix first?"

Perhaps egging him on wasn't the best idea, but if I could distract him long enough, I could make my move.

"It would be wise of you to not provoke me today. I'm not in the best of moods. I give you fair warning." He'd said it as if he was giving me a chance to get out of this unscathed.

Trying to open the door again, it slammed shut just before I saw a shimmer in the corner again. I must have been off my game today.

Putting it together this time, I turned and walked over, standing just a few feet from Draxus.

I lunged at the Demigod before I could think it through too much.

Just as I suspected, I went straight through him.

"Nice try, Draxus. You're not even here." Walking back over to the door again and applying the ring to the opening keypad, I shoved with all of my might.

Falling through the small gap, the door slammed shut, inches from the back of my head. My hand scraped the side of a rock where I'd fallen, and the blood was the darkest red it could be before black.

It had always amused me to see what color blood different beings produced. Call it morbid curiosity, but I enjoyed bleeding people to see the diversity.

Pushing off of the ground to stand, I noticed the imprint of large feet around the mausoleum.

Someone was watching me, trailing me... and that did not make me happy.

They were too wide to be Riedyn's and too small to be Draxus'.

The fact that I'd been so distracted as to let someone that close made my blood boil.

A breeze drifted through the trees and with it, brought the scents of the forest... and something else.

It wasn't Dhalls, Gifters or Demon. Fae smelled like nature, so it wasn't a Faery.

I was perplexed greatly, but I needed to get back on track.

Shifting shifted the Fainne Todhchai to my pocket, I pulled out the remnant of paper that held a portion of the prophecy Caylum had let me glimpse all those years ago.

If I concentrated my senses hard enough, I could still get very faint whiffs of my former lover's scent.

Emotions swept through my thoughts like the buzzing of bees.

Letting a single tear roll down my cheek before stuffing the clothlike paper into my pocket, now was the time to push all of this aside. I had a goal to obtain.

Emotions always clouded judgement. Caylum was the only love I'd ever known. Missing him even now, centuries later.

It had taken me a long time to come to terms with what I'd felt. Guilt. I felt guilty. And I hated it. Hated him for it. Hated myself for ever feeling such a useless emotion.

It had taken me even longer to understand that guilt and regret were two different things.

Regret was something I wouldn't do again if I had the opportunity for a do over. I still would have had to eliminate Caylum to achieve my goal, my kingdom.

My guilt though, that was the price of snuffing out the only light I'd had in my dark existence. Now my essence was black as pitch.

Making myself a promise here and now, I would not think of Caylum again until I was the King of Demons on this plane.

If it was at all in my power, I'd find a way to talk to him one more time. To thank him for his gift and to say goodbye.

I owed him that much.

For now, I'd make preparations for my future kingdom.

I would rule the demons and Dhalls with an icy heart and no remorse.

Then... I would conquer the other realms.

Chapter Fifty-Eight

Bastian

Noella had sent Hayden and me on a side mission after she'd gotten a call from Lara while we were at the diner.

Lara's advice was for us to go to our grandmother's estate and prod her to tell us a story from our youth.

She wasn't certain of the details. Only the direction to guide us in. To ask Chironna the tale of us getting lost in the woods when our grandfather had to find and bring us home.

Hayden greeted our grandmother with a kiss to her forehead. I hung back shuffling my feet, eyes on the ground.

"Well, isn't this a surprise," she said. Her face lit up at the sight of Hayden and me together. She motioned me to come forward. "Come here. Let's get a good look at you."

With a heavy heart, I did as she asked. I hadn't been able to bring myself to visit the estate in years.

When my grandfather died, a piece of me died too. Coming back to the estate made me feel empty.

I'd never meant to abandon her, but I was rebellious and selfish, and my emptiness had led to even more criminal activity. And for that, I was too ashamed to face her before now.

Bending down and wrapping her in my arms, her scent brought tears to my eyes. Gardenias and mint. A wave of nostalgia nearly brought me to my knees.

It was home. I was finally home.

"Mamsy," I bowed my head after letting her go and stepping back to Hayden's side. "I'm so sorry it's been so long."

She looked from me to Hayden and back again. It was all I could do to not pick her up again and spin her in my arms.

I'd grown up. Gotten my shit together. And now I wanted nothing more than for my grandmother to be as proud of me as she'd always been of Hayden.

I'd never been jealous of my cousin, just envious. An envy that dug deep sometimes, but never resentful.

Hayden let out a long sigh and motioned for us to head into the conservatory.

"Shall we sit?" he said.

Our grandmother rung a small bell on the table next to her chair and a servant appeared a few moments later.

"Ahh, yes," she said when the girl entered the room. "Pleshia. I think we would like to have tea and something for lunch."

"Do you have any preferences, My Lady?" the girl said.

At first, I'd been taken aback by her. She was beautiful and lithe with a magnificently curvy frame. When she'd opened her mouth, her voice sang her words. A nightingale could only aspire to be so melodic.

"No dear. Whatever you make will be just fine." Grandmother's smile made it clear how thoroughly she adored her.

No one spoke as we waited for lunch to be brought back. The silence was awkward, but I got the sense that Mamsy wouldn't speak first, and Hayden was giving me time to find my legs.

Pleshia returned with a tray of finger sandwiches, fruits, cheeses, nuts and a pitcher of iced tea with mint leaves. The girl turned to leave with a small curtsy, but Mamsy grabbed her wrist as she passed.

"Please, stay and join us my dear," she said.

She spun to face her. If I thought that she would decline, I would have been wrong.

Pleshia leaned in and lowered her voice.

"My Lady, are you sure?" she said. "It is your first visit with your family in a long time."

"You are my family too, Pleshia. My grandsons should feel honored by the opportunity to dine with a young lady such as yourself. And you know full well I've asked you to call me by my name, dear." Mamsy's tone made it clear there was no room for discussion.

Getting to his feet, Hayden motioned for her to take the end of the sofa he had been sitting on and went to perch himself next to Mamsy.

"So, to what do I owe the honor of this visit? It must be rich if the two of you are together," she exclaimed with a touch of defensiveness.

Hayden reached over and took her hand and her lips pressed down into a tight line. I'd known she'd felt abandoned by me but what in the sevens had Hayden done to receive such a cold homecoming?

"We would like you to tell us the story of when we'd gotten lost in the woods and Grandfather had to come retrieve us," Hayden said.

A burst of laughter fell from her lips, like she'd been holding her breath but couldn't any longer. The sound made my heart sing. It drew me in, and I longed to hear Grandfather's booming chuckle.

"Is that really all you want?" she asked warily.

She exchanged a look with Pleshia and shook her head. Picking up her tea and taking a long sip, she set it back on the side table before she spoke.

"Honestly, we thought you might be here to take over my affairs." The wrinkles around her mouth pulled tight as she grinned.

At this revelation, Hayden's mouth hung open and his eyebrows reached his hairline in shock.

It was my turn to let out a bark of a laugh. Realization settled in on me.

"I can see why you may think something like that, Mamsy, but I am not that royal screw up I used to be." Clearly skeptical, she allowed me to continue anyway. "I met someone who helped me get my head out of my ass," I coughed at my own blatantness. "She helped give me purpose."

"Oh, and where is this person who helped bring focus to your life?" she said. "Will they be expecting to be in my will?"

Hayden spoke up to intervene on my behalf. Thank the gods for my cousin's levelheaded shoulders.

"He isn't romantically involved with her, Mamsy," Hayden interjected, and I gave her a wry smile. "She brought Bastian and I back together. That speaks volumes in and of itself."

Looking between us, the after glance she threw to Pleshia wasn't subtle. It was clear they were having their own silent conversation we weren't privy to.

After another pat to the hand in encouragement from Hayden, Mamsy let out a large sigh.

"Well, I'm glad to hear that you're growing up, Bastian." The light in her eyes dimmed just a bit. "I wish your grandfather could have seen you... what did you say?... Oh yeah, get your head out of your ass," she said with a smile.

Heat rose to the tops of my cheeks, but we all laughed at that, even Pleshia.

"So, you want to hear the story of how you and Hayden gave me and Abraham more grey hair and near heart attacks." Her lips curled up at the edges while the sparkle of memory shown in the corner of her eyes. "That's a great tale. Pleshia, you'll like this one," she said, like they'd shared many tales over the years.

Swiveling in my chair, I met the gaze of the young woman beside me. Again, I was struck dumb by her beauty.

She had a full face and the body to match. It was plump in all the right places with a little extra sand in the hourglass. Her ash blonde hair flowed down to her waist but her eyes... they were a brilliant grey verging on silver.

"You're Fae!" I shouted, jumping to my feet.

"I'm sorry. What?" Pleshia replied.

Hayden stood too. He walked over and took a protective step in front of our grandmother. I looked to Chironna for an explanation, but she just smiled.

I couldn't make sense of what was happening. Was she on a mission? The same as us maybe? How did she worm her way into Mamsy's life?

"Why are you here? Has the Queen sent you to spy?" I demanded.

"I really have no idea of what you're talking about," the girl said.

Mamsy pursed her lips. The frustration in her eyes simmered in the background of my own muddled thoughts.

"Can we have a few minutes please, Pleshia?" Her tone remained gentle with the girl. It unnerved me more than I'd like to admit.

"Of course, My Lady... Chironna." She left without haste and shut the conservatory doors.

Mamsy picked up her cup and sipped her tea again. She was completely unphased by either of mine or Hayden's trepidations.

"Why do you have a fae working for you?" My voice came out a little shaky but still had a ring of demand in it. "Did you know?"

"I think what my cousin is trying but failing to say," Hayden began, "is that he is concerned for your well-being."

Disbelief clouded my mind. Why wasn't she more alarmed?

She had a faery here in her house and making her food. She'd even called her family. Her well-being was more than a little in question.

"She isn't fae," Chironna said calmy. "At least, not full Fae, I don't think but I can't be sure. And she's given no indication that she would want it acknowledged anyway."

Both me and Hayden looked at our grandmother like she'd lost her faculties.

"Oh geesh. Will you two both sit down and take a breath?" Her tone was mild, but we understood it was a command. Out of respect, we sat back down before she continued. "It's the Deum Velum."

Hayden clapped a hand to his forehead, but I was still lost.

"The God's Veil, dear. She is a descendant of a fae somewhere in her line, but she can't see the Shadowrealm. Or maybe she is hiding from something. Or perhaps she was made to forget." She sipped her tea thoughtfully. "Whatever it is, it is none of our business."

The fact that the girl wasn't lying made me feel better, but I didn't understand why my grandmother would knowingly employ her.

If she was in hiding from other faeries, it could put Mamsy at risk. That wasn't something I'd be able to overlook.

"Do not make her feel uncomfortable when I call her back in. And, by the gods, don't you dare say any more about whatever asinine thing I'm sure you're going to go on about." She finished berating us and then rung the bell for Pleshia to return.

"My Lady… Chirry," she said hesitantly, but the playfulness made a true smile appear on Mamsy's face. It lit up the room, making my heart thud in its wake.

"Please join us again, my dear." She made it clear that there would be no argument.

Waving my hand, I motioned for Pleshia to sit back down next to me.

I had let my bad experience with one fae female mare my judgement for them all. The least I could do was give her a fair shot.

"My apologies. I spoke out of turn," I said. "I haven't seen my grandmother in a long time. I was looking for problems where there were none. Please forgive me."

Mamsy's wide eyes met Hayden's, and she smiled ear to ear. He nodded his affirmation at this grown-up gesture from me. The family fuck up.

It felt nice to be seen as a better man. Now I really did wish my grandfather could see me.

"Please, Mamsy," I said, flourishing of my hand. "Tell us the tale of how we nearly never made it home again."

Chapter Fifty-Nine

Quinn

Jax and Parker ran into me coming up the road around the corner from where they had left Fhail's shop.

I was winded and frazzled. My hair had fallen from its careful placement and hung wildly around my face.

Dried blood was crusted on the side of my cheek. Whatever cuts had been drawn were already healed.

"Fancy meeting you here," Jax said. "Is there a reason you're fleeing the area or are you just out for a jog?" The joke was humorless, but his concern was real.

"Very funny," I said. "I was trying to retrieve something for Lucian and decided to grab some lunch but was interrupted."

Parker bent down, picked up a rock and threw it skimming over the water. It whistled loudly before falling beneath the surface with a plop.

"Did you get what you were there for?" he asked.

My head cocked to the side. We didn't usually inquire about each other's missions.

Now that I was paying attention, Parker appeared agitated about something. His mouth was turned down in a grimace and the shadows under his eyes were darker than they normally were.

"No." My mouth became a hard line. "The Mixling witch tossed me out."

Jaxson's smile fell from his face and his hands fisted as they hung down to his sides.

I wasn't oblivious to his coveting. I just wasn't interested.

"Should we go back? We could help you," he said.

"With what power?" My words came out more truculent than I'd intended but I wasn't going to take them back. "You know damn well that she's more powerful than the three of us combined."

Parker said nothing. His eyes spoke to a place of defiance. I could tell that he wanted to argue but he kept silent. Jaxson had no such qualms.

"Lucian is already in a mood from losing Kali. Maybe it would be better if we tried to get whatever you were assigned to get, Quinn." He said it with conviction.

I knew he cared for me. Sometimes I thought it would be easier if I did want him back.

The fact that he was willing to take up the battle with the witch so that I didn't have to suffer Lucian's wrath was just another example of how cruel the fates were.

"I don't think that us getting our asses kicked would be of any great bearing on his mood," I said. "Besides, don't you two have somewhere to be?"

Parker finally turned to face us. Something weighed heavily on his mind. I could tell by the far off look in his eyes and his lack of smartass comments that it was nothing good.

"Maybe Quinn is right," he said. "Maybe we should go on with our own missions." His hand came up to scrub at his face and brush his fingers back through the stray strands of his hair. "Or maybe, we should stop doing whatever Lucian wants without question."

"Careful, Parker," Jax said with a raised eyebrow. "That sounds an awful lot like breaking ranks."

Looking between me and Jaxson, he shook his head. Frustration seeped off him in dark waves.

"Aren't you guys tired of all this? We do whatever he says. We're not supposed to talk to each other about any of our missions. And for fucks sake, we don't even know his end game." He put his hands in his front pockets and hung his head again.

Jax clapped him on his shoulder and gave a light squeeze. Whatever was going on with him, I felt it too.

Maybe it was because the veil had started pulling away already? I hadn't a clue if that were the case, but I had been feeling that same disobedient strain he'd spoken of.

"It's what we do, man. He's higher up the chain of command than we are." Giving an uneasy huff of a laugh, Jax continued, blinded to the dilemma. "At least he keeps us close. You've seen some of the poor bastards that he's in charge of. They never even have a chance to make more of themselves."

Here we go. If ever was the time to voice my concerns to the others, now was it.

"Maybe Parker is right," I interjected. Jax's face fell. "Hear me out. He's supposed to be in charge of their protection and yet he uses them and doesn't care if they die. And the Meathlu in his district are let run wild with their deviant ways. Lucian doesn't seem to care if the gods or the Underworld bosses notice shit." Bringing my hand to my chin, I thought for another moment. "Whatever he is up to, we are all expendable."

I knew that look. He couldn't believe what he was hearing. Or maybe he didn't want to face facts.

"Well, what if he's just trying to keep us safe with a bigger picture that we can't see?" Jaxson was nothing but loyal to his core

It didn't matter if we were right. He'd stick by Lucian simply because Lucian was higher than him in the chain of command.

"If it was about the safety of the demons in his charge, he wouldn't make it so that there were secrets with us, Jax." I argued. Parker nodded in agreement.

"You two are off your rockers," he said. "I don't know which of you to watch out for anymore."

I'd felt like he'd slapped me. Parker took his hands out of his pockets and faced Jaxson with a cold stare.

"If you aren't willing to think for yourself, you're always going to be under the thumb of someone who controls your destiny." Parker said this with the conviction of a mind made up.

Putting a hand on each one of their chests, I stood firmly between them. I couldn't let them come to blows here, in the middle of a street full of Dhalls. Lucian would have my ass for sure.

"Boys, we don't have to decide anything right now." Looking only at Jaxson, I tried to ensure that Parker and I wouldn't be flayed alive. "Look, I know you're conflicted, but if you run off and tell Lucian what we've just discussed, Parker and I will be dead by sun up. Is that what you really want?"

Jaxson's eyes went wide. Now it was me who could have slapped him with that statement.

"Oh, by the Sevens. Why did you have to go and put it like that?" He rolled his eyes and stepped back. "I wouldn't do that to you, Quinn," he said. "You either, Parker." Shaking his head, he put his hand over his heart. "You're a pain in the ass most of the time but I still consider you my brother in arms, dude."

Parkers mouth drew up on one side. His eyes had that mischievous gleam back in them.

"And here I thought you wouldn't care if I disappeared back to the Underworld," he said, voice heavily marred with fake anxiety.

The tightness that had building in my chest eased the tiniest amount.

We all had separate missions to complete and none of us had succeeded.

Now was the time to be united if there ever was one. Jaxson wasn't a stupid demon by any means. He needed a push from time to time. Parker and I would keep buzzing in his ear, but it would take time.

Time that none of us might have.

Chapter Sixty

Thelzion

Brie sat on the front porch drinking a cold glass of sweet tea and listening to the sounds of nature singing in the evening air. I stood in the doorway waiting for the sun to set behind the magnolia trees. The breeze was nearly non-existent.

"I like her," Brie said. "She is still child-like but her abilities are up to snuff." Joy lit her feature as her mouth tugged up at the corners.

Opening the screen door, I walked over to the other chair that was next to her and sat down. A genuine smile crept its way onto my face.

"What?" she said.

Her smile was a balm to my miserable soul. A thousand years together would never be enough.

"You're happy," I said. "It looks good on you. Lucian threatens life as we know it, but I am so grateful that his selfish ways preserved your sister. I'm glad to see you happy."

"You make it sound as if I'm always gloomy," she said with a small chuckle.

Maybe I wasn't getting this right. I'd give my left nut to see her face alit with joy every single day. Words weren't my forte but, for her, I spoke them without hesitation.

"You are always the brightest spot in my darkness, Briella. Your smile lights up the night."

That foreshadower's dream sat at the back of my mind. There was no way I could lose her. One way or another, I'd make certain she was safe... even if the world burned.

"I know our love is true but your sister, she is a family that is ready made and fills a void that I left when I took your father's life." For a demon, my heart was heavy with guilt over something that should have been second nature to me.

"Zi, you're my family. Having Kalina is great, but I don't even truly know her yet." She took another sip of her tea. "And if Hayden's Foreshadowing comes to pass, either she or I may not make it. Do I really want to get close to her if that's the case?"

Taking her hand in mine, I brought her knuckles up to brush my lips against them. So soft. So strong.

"Oh babygirl. If you only have a short while to get to know the person whom you shared a womb with, forgoing that precious time because of fearing the hurt that may follow..." shaking my head, I blew out the last of my own worries. "It would be worse if you didn't get to know her, Brie."

Her whole body leaned into my touch. Cupping her face as she smiled at me, her eyes glistened. A single tear escaping down her cheek.

I wiped it away with the graze of my knuckle. I lived and breathed for this woman.

Heat followed in the wake of my touch. A trail of red sparks danced across her skin.

When we were alone, she often forgot to rein in her gifts, letting them run carefree and wild.

It was another spot in my heart that screamed at me to tear the world to sunder if it so much as pulled a single tear from her eyes.

She reached up, grabbing my hand, and sucked the salty liquid from my finger. It did things to me that brought the beast in me to the surface.

A guttural snarl tore from the back of my throat and with it, the heat pooled between her legs. Her arousal scented the air thickly.

Standing quickly, I swept her up into my arms and kicked the screen door open.

It was the third door we'd had in the last six months. More than likely, it'd need replaced before long. My patience for the door was minimal, but she'd insisted we have one to let fresh air in in the evenings.

Seven hells, what I wouldn't do to keep this woman happy.

The race to the bedroom was short and the need to have her demanding passions met was increasing with each step.

Laying her on her back, staring at her in all her beauty made me ache deep inside.

"What do you want, Hellfire?" I knew what I wanted to do to her, but her desires would always be put before my own.

Over the years, I found that my deep bass voice brought her lust.

The swelling of her sensitive pearl would be nearly painful against the fabric restraining it if I didn't relieve her of her clothing quickly enough.

My hard cock twitched at the thought. The primal side of me hummed in my chest.

"I want you to say it, like a good girl." My demand was met with her hand on my hardening length.

That breathy demand of hers always sent my body into over-drive. When she unleashed it, I was done in before I knew to brace for the rush of heated desire.

"Fuck me, Zi! Fuck me like the bad girl I am!"

Before the words finished leaving her lips, my mouth was smashing against hers with bruising force.

My fangs unsheathed and bit down on her bottom lip. Sucking in the swollen lip between my teeth, blood still trickled down her chin.

The sight spurred on my inner demon. All sharp edges and ruthless want.

With a single finger, I wiped the smear and stuck it in her mouth to suck dry.

Her moan filled the small space of the room, and it made breathing difficult to hear the depravity fall from her lips so readily. The flush of heat through my body was unbearable.

She grabbed at her shirt to discard it, but I was quicker. With one hand I yanked hard, and the blouse ripped away, falling to the floor.

Wasting no time seizing her pants at her hips, I whisked them away as well. The only thing between her skin and mine was the skimpy bra and panties she wore.

"By the Damning Stars, Brie! I know I tell you all of the time but seriously, you really are so damn beautiful." I was humbled every time. A mere acolyte worshipping at an altar. "I'm going to make you scream my name as you explode. I hope you're ready to be devoured!" I growled.

Her breathless pants only fueled my desire. I loved the little moments where I was the one to steal her formidable warrior armor away. The moments she only gave to me.

Taking each one of her knees and spreading her legs wide, I tore away her panties in one swift motion. The sound of the threads tearing set her sweet spot dripping.

"Mmmmm... don't you look like a feast," I said, licking my lips.

One hand caressed her plump breasts still in her bra. The other hand ran over the folds of her pleasure center. My thumb gently swirled on her engorged clit.

Bringing the other hand up to her chest, I ripped the bra in two. Her erect nipples were so sensitive that I knew the sudden rush of air made them sting.

Inching up her body, my mouth covered one of her nipples. Using the tips of my teeth, I scraped the sides before my tongue made laps around it.

She groaned in ecstasy and her hips thrust upward towards my still caged length.

My Hellfire was nothing, if not a needy little thing. Her want nearly throwing me off my game as her gifts pushed her desires through the space between us.

"Ah ah ah, no no," I said, pushing her back down. "You don't get to play until I say so."

Sliding a hand down between her legs, I rested it just before her entrance, teasing the area all around but did not penetrate her wet opening.

Blowing hot breath across her chest as I sucked and nipped on her erect nipples sent flames of ecstasy washing through her body that lit up around her aura.

"Thelzion, please," she begged. "I'm coming undone here."

Now wasn't the time to give in. Brie liked a firm hand in the bedroom, and I was more than willing to take up that mantel.

"Not yet, you aren't. You're only anticipating what I'm going to do to you." My smile was wicked but there was no lie in my words.

Hovering at her entrance with my fingertips, I dipped two fingers in just to the first knuckle. With the fluttering back and forth between them, I knew the sensation was maddening to her.

I'd learned to play her body like a fiddle over the years. If bringing her pleasure was the reward, I'd study the art for a lifetime.

"By the Damning Stars!" she cried out. "Please, Thelzion!"

My lips left her breast, and the suddenness of the air would be practically painful. I knew her well enough to understand, not only the road map of her body, but of her mind.

My mouth came crashing down on hers for the briefest of seconds before my head quickly dipped between her legs.

Her hardened jewel was standing at attention. The heat drew my mouth straight to the honeypot with one long, languished lick. Then engulfed the swollen pleasure spot of her clit.

Licking all the way up and down between the folds of her lips, she dripped like a tree canopy after the rain.

I lapped at it with a possessiveness that had her aching even more.

Now that my tongue was fulfilling her outer needs, her demands became more longing to be filled from within.

I was the luckiest bastard to ever live. Her moans and gyrating hips brought another thump of my heart to a standstill. *Mine!*

Raising her ass off the bed and undulating against my mouth, she couldn't scratch that itch that had her body writhing. Only I could do that.

My hands pulled away from her wet folds and clamped down around her ankles.

"What a naughty girl you are," I growled.

She couldn't make her ass lay flat on the bed if she tried. I was driving her wild as my tongue made slow, long licks from her entrance to her nub and back down.

My head slipped away from her muff and with a sudden jolt, my fangs sunk deep into the crease at the top of her leg.

Blood mixed with her personal nectar as I smeared the two together and licked them off my fingers.

"You know what happens to naughty girls, Hellfire?" I said before nipping at her pearl again. "They end up in situations they can't control."

With a devious smirk, I stood back and took off my shirt.

At the sight of my bare, muscular chest, a shuttering breath ran through her.

As my hands went to the drawstring at the top of my pants, she sat up and reached over to help.

"I didn't give you permission to touch... yet!" My tone made her shutter again, but she laid back down with just a small whimper that was my undoing.

Slowly, I unleashed the woken monster from its prison of restraining fabric. The sight of me in my full glory made her mouth water.

She could see the pre-cum glistening at the tip of my large cock and wetted her lips.

That tongue. Hmmm. She wanted me. That fact never stopped being a shock.

Taking my time to torture little whimpers from her made me painfully hard. The air hurt, I was so damned ripe with desire.

"You want this, baby?" I said as I began shamelessly stroking my length. "Let me hear you beg."

As she started to rise off the mattress, I shoved her back down with a hand to the center of her chest.

"Oh no, you don't get to use your womanly wilds on me. Beg me from right where you are." As I said it, my pre-cum dripped onto her mound from stroking above her.

The light coming from the window was barely enough to see my prize for the magnificent beauty it was, but I made to claim it all the same.

"Please, Thelzion. I want to feel you inside me so fucking badly!" She was practically rabid.

The begging pleas sent a shiver to the demon within. A demand to take what was mine.

"Why didn't you just say so," I teased.

Without hesitation, two fingers shoved into her slick opening all the way to the knuckles of my fist.

Before she could even gasp, my mouth came crashing down on her mound once more.

She undulated her hips and drove herself into my mouth and fingers like someone possessed.

With each circle of her hips the climax built and built. She was almost there, ready to flood the house with her hot liquid.

Just as suddenly as the assault had begun, I withdrew.

"Nooooo," she screamed!

My poor girl. Did she really think it would be so easy. I was a demon. Not a saint.

"Did you want to cum my sweet?" I said with another wicked grin. "All you have to do is ask."

"Damn it, Zi. Why do you keep teasing me like this? I need it!" she said.

Her whimpers drove me mad. If I didn't give in soon, I'd need to tip over the edge myself.

"Then say it baby. What do you want from me?"

I was baiting her, and she'd make me pay for it later but right now, she couldn't even think straight.

"I want you to make me cum like the naughty girl that I am... please, Zi!" she cried out.

Finally! There it was. My good girl.

"That's all that I needed to hear."

As my cock slid in between her folds, thrusting deep into her throbbing core, she screamed my name.

The strokes were hard and passionate and left no room for gentleness.

She took me to the hilt again and again and still begged for more. The orgasm that was rising inside her felt like a Phoenix about to take flight that would burn us both to cinders.

My lips met hers and I moaned into her mouth with a slow thrust that was like dying.

Grabbing her shoulders, I pulled out, spun her to her stomach and yanked her onto her knees, quickly slamming my cock into her from behind.

The wetness of her pleasure was a sloppy pool that had the entire area drenched. With each thrust, new bouts of pleasure heightened throughout my whole body.

Brie's legs began to shake as her ecstasy exploded from head to toe. Her tunnel enveloped my tool in ripples of squeezing pleasure.

She screamed my name as my hands gripped her ass and my thumb slipped inside. A small whimper escaped her lips at the sudden intrusion.

"You dirty little girl. Take, take, take. That's it." My other hand grabbed the back of her hair like reigns. Pulling tightly, my cocked swelled. "You're doing so well, love."

Pounding over and again, the sight of her in my grip, filling her, it sent more than physical elation running through me. My heart was going to burst at the seams.

"Damning stars, you're so hot, Brie!" She moaned under my ministrations. Thrust after demanding thrust, I raced towards ecstasy. "Gods, I'm... I'm.. oh gods!.

I exploded, filling her to the brim with my seed. She tensed with motion and came again as the sound of her name snarled from deep in my throat.

We both fell over, spent.

Cradling her naked form from behind, I placed gentle kisses along her back and shoulder. Her hair fell softly over her breasts and my hot breath caressed her neck a moment before my fangs sunk pleasurably into the soft flesh.

"My name falling from your lips was not part of the bargain," she teased.

Drawing in a long pull of her blood and licking the wound to heal it, I started to sit up.

Her reflexes were faster. Spinning to look me in the eyes, she was suddenly on top, straddling my already growing erection.

Brie dragged my wrists in each hand and pinned them over my head. I let her.

She was a strong, capable demon. Being a few centuries older, I knew my strength to take her was more than formidable, but my Hellfire did enjoy playing her games.

Anything that she wanted, I wanted for her.

"And just what do you think you are doing, my love?" I asked.

If I allowed myself, I'd fall under her spell forever, never leaving our room. She had a willing slave, no matter what depravity she wanted to grant.

"My turn!" she said with a wicked grin.

Without further warning, she was having her way with me before I could reply.

Chapter Sixty-One

Riedyn

"Your Majesty," I said dipping my chin in leu of a real bow. "I have a report of what the EU has gathered thus far."

Queen Talisin pursed her lips. I could sense her thinking my laxed demeaner meant that I had been out of Sidhterra too long. Perhaps she was right.

"On with it, my dear," she said. Her mouth relaxed but her eyes remained sharply observant.

Never a particularly warm female, she had always been a force of fascinated awe for me as I grew into adulthood.

"Lieutenants Willow and Oaken were tailing Lucian's thirds. We met up at the same time when his second ran into them around the corner of their latest missions." I said.

"And what is the intel you obtained from their chance meeting," her voice was flat, but I knew her sharp mind had already jumped ahead several moves on the chessboard.

Revelers carried on around, oblivious to any dangers that might await them should Lucian's plans succeed during the Breaking of the Deum Velum. If the demons couldn't be contained quickly after the veil lifted, we were all screwed.

"It would seem that there is some dissent in their ranks. Lucian holds many secrets, and they appear to finally be questioning his motives."

She steepled her hands and placed them under her chin in thought. Her youthful appearance gave away nothing of her years.

"And what of Lucian, Commander?" she asked. "Do we have any information on whether or not he is close to achieving his goals?"

"Lieutenant Borias followed him to the demigod's family mausoleum. He used the Fainne Todhchai to enter. When he exited, Lt Borias says that he observed him in an agitated state. He never wavered in his searching. He left the crypt and headed back to the manor and remained there as Lt Borias came to give his report. That was two days ago." I finished giving her all that I knew but I felt it wasn't enough.

Guilt for not having followed him myself ate at me from the inside. If I could follow him and serve my queen properly, I would. For now, I'd have to trust in my unit members to take up the task.

"The foretold Breaking is less than three days away, Commander. Am I to understand that you have no more information than this to present?" Her lips were in such a tight line that they were practically nonexistent.

"My Queen, we can only provide the information as it's presented to us." I was failing her and my people. "How would you like me to proceed? Your orders were to not interfere, your Majesty."

Anger flashed in her face. It was there and gone in the blink of an eye, but I hadn't miss it.

"I know what my orders were, Commander," she said in a huff. "Perhaps the General would be a better choice to send with the Elite Unit? He has no conflicting loyalties." The corners of her mouth pulled up in a wicked smirk and the dark mischief of the Fae danced in her eyes.

"No, my Liege. I am more than capable of gathering the required intelligence." Hanging my head, I spoke quietly. "My loyalty is always yours. It pains me that I have made you question that."

The Queen pursed her thin lips once again. A puckish expression lit her face, and I knew she was enjoying watching me squirm.

My brother, General Ashwood, was not my enemy but a rivalry had always existed between us. One that she saw to with every opportunity she could find.

"Come now, Riedyn. I do not expect miracles," she said with ease. "I know how deceptive and secretive the Donnchadh is. Lucian may not be a true immortal, such as we are, but he has been around for a very long time." She drummed her fingers on her throne. "Too long, I dare say."

Skylar came bounding towards the throne but stopped at the edge of the dais when she saw me there.

I couldn't put my finger on what her face was trying to hide but there was definitely something amiss. My intuition was screaming at me.

Queen Talisin saw her favorite messenger hesitating and waved her up in an eager manner. The way she held this particular fickle fae in high regards confounded me.

Skylar hadn't been anyone of importance when Griane had gone missing. She'd been a lowly faery in a realm of nobody's.

The queen had been drawn to her out of pining after her only daughter. Why? I had no idea.

Skylar was self-serving and conniving to a degree that even other fae around the court steered clear of her for the most part.

The queen's interest in her was a subject of contention that my brother and I agreed on. That keeping an eye on Skylar was in the best interests of the court... even if we had to hide our observations from our queen to protect her.

"Ah, Skylar. What word has Draxus sent?" she asked.

My head snapped up. The queen was attempting to contact the demigod herself. Why wouldn't she let me in on that tidbit of information?

Being kept out of the loop was not the best way to run the EU in protection of the realm. Heat rose to the points of my ears.

"Your Majesty," I began to say but she silenced me with a wave of her hand.

"Proceed, my dear," she said to Skylar.

Dismay was clearly written on the messenger's face at my presence. Good. I relished in throwing the whisp faery for a loop.

She let her gaze fall to me for a moment before approaching the throne. the music had slowed to a trinkling beat of light cymbals as the musicians took a small break.

"My Queen," she said. Trepidation saturated her tone. It grated on my nerves to hear. "Draxus has not responded."

"Then why have you come back so soon?" Queen Talisin looked down her nose at the lithe faery before her.

With another glance in my direction, my gut instincts flared again.

Directing my next statement to the Queen, I spoke in a commanding tone.

"Your Majesty, it would appear that Skylar would like to speak with you alone. Shall I depart?" I gave the small female a pointed glare.

"No, you shan't, Commander. Whatever Skylar has to say must be important for her to leave her posted duty." The Queen raised her eyes to meet both of ours. "The EU will remain informed of the courts goings on."

I smiled at Queen Talisin and turned to fully look upon Skylar's face.

Knowing that she didn't want me privy to her intel, I'd thwarted her attempt to keep me in the dark.

The sides of my mouth drawn up in a slight smirk that the fae grimaced her discontent at.

She leaned back and rocked on her feet. Her hands wrung in front of her with excitable energy and she smoothed her face into a false nonchalantness.

"Draxus has not given his reply because he isn't currently in the realm," she said.

"Sidhterra? Or Lagomshire?" the Queen asked.

She rocked on her feet again. The information must be juicy for her to be so mischievously dubious.

"Neither, Your Majesty," Skylar glanced at me again. "He is in the forbidden realm of Saint Augustine."

The Queen's face lit up. Taking in her expression fortified and renewed my hope.

"My Queen," I said. "I, too, have information regarding that realm." I waited for her nod before continuing. "I didn't see of how it might be important before but in light of this new revelation, I think they may be connected."

If I was wrong, it would mean that she'd send my brother and his forces to do a job my team was more than capable of. If I was right, it still might mean that, only I'd be the one on her skewer.

"Well, are you going to bore me into submission or come out with it, Commander?" Her smile was as false as her waistline in her tight corset, but I went on.

"When I was following Lucian's second, I ran into the Mixling witch, Noella." The Queen's eyes lit up. She was starting to put the puzzle together that I didn't have all the pieces for. "She unlocked a memory from her past with her father. They were here in Sidhterra, with you, my Liege."

"And what was this recollection of hers, Commander Riedyn?" she asked as if she didn't truly care for the answer, but her wicked eyes gave away her desire to know the story.

I rubbed the back of my neck, then ran it through my unkempt hair.

"It was a memory of how you told a tale of the portal to the double veiled realm; St Augustine's magicsless human realm."

The queen clapped her hands together and gave a quick, high-pitched giggle. I had never seen her so exuberant.

"That's wonderful," she said. "There may be hope for Lagomshire yet. And with their hope, our wayward children have a true shot at safety."

I looked to Skylar and she to me. It was clear that the queen knew more than we did but neither of us was willing to point that out to her when she was in such high spirits.

Skylar curtsied with her little feather light skirt, and I dipped my chin in respect of her new revelation.

"What are the Elite Units orders, your Majesty?" If she was pleased, it meant we were on the right path. That had to be a good thing.

"For now, keep to Lucian and his lackies." She put a finger on her lip and tapped, thinking. "And if the Mixling witch needs assistance, give it but not in an obvious way. She and those she associates with may be our greatest hope to achieving our own desired outcome of this retched Breaking."

Bowing at the waist, I gave another nod of my head in understanding.

I was off of the dais and nearly to the first of the courtly revelers when she called to me over the crowd.

"Riedyn dear, do try not to let Lucian toy with your emotions. It doesn't bode well when a demon out matches a mischievous fae." Her smile beamed in an impish toothy grin.

"Yes, my Queen." The dig was a quick slap to my bruised pride.

Sweeping towards the exit once more, I locked my heart up tight and threw away the key.

Chapter Sixty-Two

Lucian

The manor was darker than normal. Kali's absence weighed on my mind. More than I'd like to let on.

I wasn't sure when I'd started to care for her, but I didn't like this feeling of loss.

She was supposed to be a means to an end, nothing more.

Caylum's declaration about the part a Conservatrix demon would play in the Breaking and the importance of her blood is what led me to take the infant instead of killing her.

The more control I had over the narrative, the better my shot of unleashing demons from the Underworld and becoming their King.

Before me sat two of the Meathlu in my dominion. I had charged them with keeping mayhem going on in my area while not drawing too much unwanted attention from the gods.

"Davis, Seaders," I said in a droll tone. "Which of you would like to explain your failings first?

Watching the fear build in their eyes was a pleasure in and of itself.

These degenerates may be lowly murders, rapists, and dregs of society but they were not yet demons.

The blood that ran through their veins was nearly the same as a Dhalls. And the smell of fear made their acrid blood that much sweeter.

Davis spoke first. His face kept a forced composure that was easy enough to decipher.

"Lucian," he said. "I can't speak for Seaders, but as for myself, my area is just too big. I can't keep track of all the asshats under my jurisdiction."

My smile grew wider. Taking a step closer to Davis as I spoke in a low cadence, it was a web and I the spider. I'd found it to be quite more unnerving than yelling over the years.

"The fact that you feel comfortable enough to call me by my first name suggests otherwise." Standing back again to admire the menacing way my demeanor set Davis's skin crawling gave me immense satisfaction.

Stepping over to stand in front of Seaders next. This Meathlu had always had more balls than most of my other charges.

The fact that Seaders still smelled like fear and sweat but showed no outward signs of distress unwittingly made me proud of him.

If he made it to full demon, he would be a force to be reckoned with.

Pity. I couldn't have that, now could I?

"I don't know what to tell you. I have my own misdeeds to contend with. These misfits that you've saddled me with run amuck at all hours of the day and night." His face kept up the bravado but a bead of sweat at his hairline gave away a lot more than the words falling from his mouth.

I sat on the corner of my large wood desk and put my hands in my lap. The casual demeanor I'd crafted visually put the two Meathlu slightly more at ease.

"Which of you should I kill for the failing numbers in my district?" I said perfunctorily.

They looked to one another and gave a small laugh. The joke hadn't been funny, but they wanted to please me.

"No joke to be laughed away." Dropping a leveled glare at them both, my eyes never leaving their faces. "I have a bigger goal in my sights and the fact that the gods and demonic upper levels may be looking more closely at my area just when I need their eyes averted threatens my agenda."

Seaders surprised me, jumping to his feet. It was uncharacteristic to how he'd been over the years.

Something more insidious was in the works with this one. Of that, I was sure.

He spoke rapidly of his deeds and how he was more valuable than Davis could ever hope to be.

Davis remained seated but didn't speak of Seaders short comings, only his own value.

"You can't be serious about this," Seaders demanded. "We fucked up one time and you want us to answer for the rest of the Meathlu's in your charge under us?"

I still sat, calmly resting my hands in my lap. Emotions caused missteps.

Inclining my head to Davis who was also still seated. Fear sat heavy in his skin, but he didn't rise the Seaders' bait.

The smell of their anxiety was intoxicating. I lived for the turmoil.

Seaders made one more attempt to save his own skin.

"Davis is harboring an exiled demon from your jurisdiction!" he shouted.

In the blink of an eye, I was off my desk and pounced.

My strong vampirical hand closed around the male's throat and yanked out his windpipe. Blood poured in rivulets down the front of his shirt.

Bending over him, I drank forcefully from his convulsing neck.

Once the blood stopped flowing and the body stopped twitching, I threw him to the floor with a loud thunk.

Davis stared at me in quiet disbelief.

I wiped at my mouth and tried to smooth out the wrinkles from my shirt. Taking both my hands, I wiped down the front of my pants as well.

"I do not tolerate people who can't be loyal to me or others in my charge. He would have been a problem down the road anyway," I answered simply to Davis's unasked question. Not that I needed to explain myself.

After a few minutes of silence, Davis finally found his voice.

"I won't let you down again, Boss. I swear it." With the profession barely out of his lips, the male slipped from the chair and out the door without another word.

I couldn't stop the wicked grin that spread across my face.

I handled my district problems, caused fear and mayhem, and had lunch all in one meeting.

If the rest of the day went as well, maybe I could locate the Akasha ring before the end of the night.

Chapter Sixty-Three

Chironna

"There is a place to the west of the Manxtas river that houses a variety of different magical beings," I started my tale in a hush of whispered nerves. "There is not just the entrance to one realm in that forest. There are two."

Looking from Bastian to Hayden, I then let my gaze fall upon Pleshia.

"There are many who can feel the Shadowrealm but not see it. And even more magical creatures than we can fathom actually exist."

The tea in my hand had gone cold. Forgetting to set it down, my mind had wandered off to be with my late husband.

"This is the story of how Grandfather found us as lost boys, isn't it, Mamsy?" Hayden asked.

I'd nearly startled with the reminder that they were all present. Waiting for me to continue.

"Of course it is, my dear. Why else would I be telling this story if it wasn't what you asked to hear?" I said with an impatient wave of my hand.

Hayden's bashful face softened my nerves.

"I'm sorry. Please go on," he said.

"You and your cousin had set out on one of your adventures. The forest beside this estate isn't to be trusted but you were both quite the couple of rapscallions back then."

I knew I was frowning but the twinkle I'd felt in my eyes would only reveal the depths of my remembered love for the little boys they had been.

"The day had gone by in a blur and evening was fast approaching. Neither of you made your way back to the estate by sundown. I was worried but your grandfather pleaded the case that if you weren't free to take on adventures and make your own mistakes, then how could you grow into self-sufficient young men."

If I would have trusted my gut that day, perhaps Abraham would still be with me.

He'd been right to want them to have adventures, but I shouldn't have caved so easily when my instincts had been screaming at me that something was amiss.

"By midnight, I was completely beside myself with panic. I begged him to go look for you both. He finally agreed to go about an hour later."

Everything from that night played over and over in my head for years after.

"Somewhere along the night, I had fallen asleep. When I awoke to the morning light coming over the trees of the forest, I knew something must be dreadfully wrong." My voice started to trail off.

Picking up the kettle of tea Pleshia brought out after lunch was through, I poured another glass. The boys sipped from their iced teas but hot tea after a meal helped with my digestion.

The sun had gone down fully and the clear sky outside of the conservatory windows made way for the bright stars and sliver of moonlight to begin peeking through.

"You boys and your grandfather came traipsing through the door around noon, covered in sweat and grass stains, completely exhausted." It was a difficult memory. "It wasn't as if you'd had any sleep but the tiredness that seeped through your bones, your grandfather's included, felt off. He gave me the briefest of run throughs as to the events that happened in retrieving you but soon after, retired to sleep for the remainder of the day."

My mind wandered again. I was thinking about Abraham. I missed him terribly.

The story wasn't over. I was too lost in recollection to continue.

Pleshia reached over and took my hand.

"My Lady," she said quietly. "Is there anything that I can fetch for you?"

Snapping back from the past, I felt older for it. Tired to the bone.

"When Abraham woke for dinner, you boys had already just about finished up. I thought that you were being deceptive when I had asked where you had ended up and neither of you could provide any details about your little adventure."

They'd been mischievous little brats. I loved them for their spunk. It added character.

"That was until I asked him all about how he found and rescued you. His memory evaded him. I watched him struggle to put any of the pieces together. He had been able to tell me more in the brief bits he'd divulged when he came in the door than he could now that more than a few hours had passed."

It had been a strange thing to watch. If he hadn't been so tired, I'd have thought he was pulling my legs like his grandsons.

"By the next day, he barely remembered going to retrieve you at all." I said, shaking my head. "Your Grandfather always liked to tell tales of his adventures. The fact that he had no story to tell, even though it had been a good one, was disconcerting. When I pushed him for details of where in the forest you boys had gotten lost, I watched him struggle to recall the events. He said it was like the knowledge was just on the edge of his memory but every time he reached for it, it moved farther away."

Pleshia patted my hand. Bastian leaned forward, not seeming to realize that he was doing so. When his hand nearly touched the skirt at Pleshia's leg, he sat back abruptly. Hayden cleared his throat and spoke up.

"Is there anything that you remember from when he first came in, Mamsy? Anything that could lead us to the spot in the forest that we'd gone in?"

I thought on it for a moment, contemplating if I should tell them anymore.

The fact that Abraham had been well before going and unwell after his return weighed on me.

The boys seemed fine, but my husband's health went downhill after that. He could never get enough rest. He'd told me that the magics in his bones felt drained. It made it hard for him to function for more than a few hours without taking naps.

Hayden tried again. Bastian chimed in too. They wanted this information for something, but I had no idea why.

"The place you seek can only bring harm," I said. "It's better left alone."

"Please Mamsy, this is important. The fate of Lagomshire could very well rest on us finding that portal," Hayden said.

"We wouldn't be asking if there was any other way to get what we needed," Bastian added.

Thinking it over for a few more minutes, my mind didn't want to see them as grown adults.

Bastian had always been up to mischief but Hayden, he was grounded and responsible. He would never lie to me. Especially about something this dangerous.

"All that he could tell me when you lot arrived back home was that he went into a portal after you boys. He'd found evidence of some of your belongings in a small area near a rock formation that look like a reflecting pond. That, in the center, was what appeared to be a foot of water but when he put his hand into it, it went much deeper but wasn't wet... he'd gone into it and came out in another realm."

I stopped for a sip of tea. Hayden, Bastian, and Pleshia all waited on bated breath for me to say more.

I had the distinct feeling that Pleshia knew something about the portal. Her eyes grew watery but never spilled.

"He couldn't tell me any details about the other realm, boys. All that he knew for certain was that there were nearly no magics in it. And worse than that, it drained the magics he had from his very being." My eyes drifted towards the windows. "He never fully recovered from that trip."

My grandsons processed that bit of information, but I left them to their own conclusions as to why their grandfather may have died earlier than any other gifter was known to.

Hayden was the first to speak it out loud. The devastation was written clearly on his face.

"Mamsy," he said taking my hand and hanging his head. "I'm so sorry. We were foolish kids and Grandfather paid the price."

"Yes, Mamsy," Bastian chimed in. He walked over, bent to his knees and took my hand. "We're very sorry. Why didn't you tell us he wasn't getting better back then?"

My lips and I was about to answer when the doorbell interrupted.

Pleshia excused herself and went to answer the door. After a moment, I began again.

"It wasn't my place to interfere with Abraham's wishes. He didn't want you boys to blame yourselves for a simple bit of childhood mischief gone awry. I only tell you now because I suspect that you're attempting a dangerous task, boys. I couldn't let you go unwarned."

My lips were once again pressed into a hard line when Pleshia returned with someone in tow.

"Chironna, you remember my sister?" She looked at Hayden and Bastian. "This is Baelyn."

Hayden was transfixed by the girl's beauty.

My sour face relaxed as I took in my grandson's admiration of the newcomer.

Bastian was the first to stand and introduce himself.

I let a small chuckle escape me as Hayden stood stupefied.

I'd suspected for a long while that Pleshia was some sort of faery. Seeing her sister again, I knew for certain.

Abraham and I had plenty of interacting's with the fae in our lifetime, but the boys never knew our friends to be anything other than simply our friends.

"Don't be rude, Hayden," my words taking on a knowing, playful energy. "Introduce yourself."

Leaning forward, I whispered in his ear. "Fae beauty is something special, huh?"

Gliding back in my chair, I winked and resumed drinking my tea.

His eyes went wide but I discretely brought my finger to my lips in a shushing manner.

Baelyn smiled at him, and I delighted in the way my grandson had become undone.

Chapter Sixty-Four

Kalina

Zane and I arrived at Lara's shop a little early. The group was supposed to gather there around 9:00am but I'd wanted to look around and do a bit of browsing.

The smell of herbs and incense filled the air. It was pleasant and enticing instead of overwhelming the way the places that Lucian had me going to get the magical things he needed over the years had been.

Lara was busying herself laying out a tray of pastries that she'd got from the bakery around the corner.

The scent of freshly ground and brewed coffee pervaded through the store.

Sighing deeply, it was the first time in my life I'd truly felt in charge of whatever I did next.

My days used to be planned and filled with barely time for anything but Lucian's wishes.

Relishing in the quiet of the early morning stillness, I ran my fingers over the spines of the books in one of the aisles. Zane was close by, but he gave me space to enjoy the moment.

If I were being honest with myself, I knew that the pull towards him was a perfectly balanced culmination of my wants and needs.

The universe only Mated those who would furnish the gaps in each other like marbles and sand in a glass.

It wasn't that I didn't find Zane attractive or charming.

On the contrary, I found him irresistible.

I was fighting an uphill battle with my own selfish need to have a choice in the matter.

Really, why wouldn't someone choose a person that was designed specifically for them?

He was thoughtful and ruggedly handsome. I noticed how he'd put my desires before his own. The kindness that he showed to everyone around him was attractive in a way I hadn't realize I'd craved.

I'd seen him be angry on my behalf and protective when I didn't even think he knew he was doing it.

Then there was that incident at the diner. When that snarl ripped through my own throat in a protective and possessive way of him, it shocked me, but I didn't hate it.

The tinkling bell above the door sounded. My sister and Thelzion entered the shop and Brie headed straight for the coffee.

Thelzion came quickly out of the morning light and into the shadows of the sitting area. Long minutes in the direct sunlight weren't a vampire's friend.

"Good morning," I said to him. "I see Brie isn't a chipper ball of sunshine in the early hours, huh?" Brie walked over, coffee in hand and grunted.

A giggle escaped before I could rein it in.

"She's fine once she's had her coffee," he said but there was a note of humor in his deep voice.

I was more of a hot tea person, but as I knew quite a few coffee drinkers, I understood her grumpiness without her first fix of the day.

"Are you two going to continue talking about me like I'm not standing right here?" Brie grumbled and then took a sip. Her face actually lit up. It shined with an almost golden aura.

Smiling, I was sure I could do that too. I'd never thought much about how the emotions of my empathic abilities took on a life of their own in unguarded moments.

I'd been taught to repress them. Now, the wonder at the possibilities bubbled up excitedly inside me.

"You glowed," I said. "Did you know that? Just now, when you had that first taste of coffee, you glowed."

"Did I?" Brie said with a grin.

The next laugh was a deep dulcet grumble from her mate. I'd never heard a vampire express true mirth before.

"She glows when other things she likes happen too," Thelzion interjected with a smirk.

Briella smacked his arm, and I blushed.

Zane came into the sitting area just then. He looked between my reddened cheeks, Thelzion's smirk, and Brie's sheepish grin.

I was certain that he didn't want to know the cause.

The bell tinkled again as Hayden, Bastian, Noella and someone I didn't know entered the shop.

He was tall and lean muscled. His face was tight and unsure as he walked behind them toward where we were all sitting.

Lara bounded forward and kissed Noella with an unabashed show of affection and Noella's arms came around her waist in a warm embrace.

I wasn't used to people all caring for one another. The manor had been filled with heartless trysts but no genuine affection.

Releasing her lover, Noella waved her hand and more chairs appeared around the circle of the coffee table.

We all took a seat, the tall stranger among us.

Zane sat next to me without a thought. It was natural and easy and made me feel... comforted.

Such a strange word for me. I'd never felt wanted or welcome anywhere. It was nice, yet my stomach skittered at the emotions I'd never experienced.

Noella brought the group to attention after a few minutes of idle conversation and refreshments. Her tone had a ring of authority to it that I hadn't noticed before.

"There are only two days left until the Breaking. Our time has gotten away from us," she said. "From the information that Hayden and Bastian obtained from their grandmother and new information that I, myself, recalled from many years ago, we think we may have an idea of where the Reverto Akasha might be hidden."

She motioned to the stranger sitting beside Lara.

I looked him over fully now that attention was directed his way. It hadn't seemed appropriate before to stare since no one bothered to introduce him.

Other than being tall and handsome, he had muscles that were hard along his arms and chest. His eyes were silvery grey and lurking beneath his ash brown hair were the points of his ears.

Bloody Sevens, he was a fae!

I'd never met one in person. At least, not that I knew of.

The fae usually used glamours when they came to Lagomshire. That's what Zane had told me during one of our suppers.

I would inundate him with questions, and he would answer every single one, the best that he could. His patience with me gave me a warm feeling whenever I'd thought about it.

This fae before me was the embodiment of the forest. How did I miss that before?

He even smelled faintly of petrichor.

Goosebumps raised over my skin. I'd been taught from a young age that the fae were tricksters and should I ever meet one, never make any bargains with them.

Lucian's voice still sat at the back of my mind most of the time, burrowing into my thoughts and how I perceived the things around me.

Unlearning behaviors was vastly more complicated than learning them.

"Commander Riedyn confirmed the information Chironna gave us. We now have a pretty good idea of where the portal to St Augustine is," Noella said.

"Why are we working with the fae?" Thelzion said with a raised eyebrow. Looking over to Riedyn, he said, "No offense." Turning back to Noella he continued. "Especially the Commander of the Queen's Elite Unit?"

He sat back, mind working double time. Brie patted his arm in comfort.

"Do you really think that I want to be working with you, vampire?" the Commander taunted.

It was the first time I'd heard him speak. His voice was like an echo of sound deep inside of a well. There was a hollowness to it, but the bass rang true.

"Her Majesty's goals align with this group's. She doesn't wish for Lucian to be successful. It would mean harm to her subjects in this realm."

"Thelzion," Noella said. "You want to be good. You need to trust people other than just Brie. You need to trust in our circle and what they bring to it."

Thelzion seethed for a few minutes as we all watched. I hadn't seen him harsh before. Lucian would often fly off the handle at the slightest thing. He was the only other Donnchadh I had for reference.

Growing more anxious by the minute, Zane reached over and squeezed my hand. He could sense my tension.

The way I was reacting to Thelzion was the same way I'd always reacted to Lucian. It was all I'd known; how volatile they could be.

With another squeeze of my hand, Zane leaned in closer. His reassuring presence helped. My tense muscles slowly relaxed.

Brie had let her mate find his legs without interfering. I'd half expected her to... I don't know. Cower? Yell at him to stop? Make some kind of demand of him?

She'd done none of that. She simply let him think through his actions while being a steady force at his side.

"You're right," Thelzion said. "My apologies. Please, continue." His words were sincere, and I didn't know what to do with that revelation.

Feeling a little more than out of depth with this lot, I sank back into my chair.

Lara brushed a piece of hair from Noella's face before she went on.

"The realm of St Augustine is a nearly no magics realm. Those there that can practice even the smallest amounts of magics are extremely powerful, but they don't even know their own potential because of the double veil on their realm." She paused for a moment and took a long sip of her coffee. "If they were in this realm, I believe that their power would nearly match that of a demigods... or at least that of a Mixling."

"By the Damning Stars! Are you serious?" Zane exclaimed.

Noella looked at her cousin and gave a stern nod. It was Zane who now slumped in his chair, and my turn to give his hand a squeeze.

Smiling over at me, he brought my hand to his lips, gently brushing a kiss on my knuckles.

"So, let me get this right." Bastian said. "In two days, when the Breaking occurs, their realm's veil will be lifted too. Won't that be disastrous? I mean, undampening powers of that magnitude can't be a good idea." He finished lamely, not knowing what else to say.

I couldn't blame him. The whole thought was mind boggling.

Lara's eyes glazed over for a mere few seconds, but she'd seen enough to speak on the matter. I'd never seen a seer *see* in person. Eerie was an understatement.

"Their realm will be in as much chaos as ours but only one of their two veils will be lifted. Those with abilities in that realm are more grounded and focused than we are. They've tolerated the magics drain their entire lives and learned to keep the Shadowrealm secret more closely. Most live by a code of balance. Light and dark magics." Her gaze was still far away. "They've tuned into the universe as a set of checks and balances. They may even be more adequately equipped to deal with the coming chaos than we are."

Brie spoke up this time. I paid more attention when my sister spoke.

I didn't know what it was about her, but I felt so connected instantly. Brie was almost like an appendage that I hadn't realized was missing. Like we were connected by an invisible thread.

We were very different people with different personalities and levels of skill but somehow, we still mirrored each other.

"Commander Riedyn, tell us of what you know about the St Augustine realm... please." She said leaning forward, coffee mug in hand, "And don't leave out any details that you might remember."

The fae warrior sat to the front of his chair. He wasn't threatening, but unease at the unknown ate at my confidence.

I fidgeted with a loose thread on my shirt. Brie looked over at me, bemused. Being self-conscious under her scrutiny, I stopped fidgeting.

"When the Queen first learned of the portal to the now Forbidden realm, it wasn't a grand revelation. There are many portals that cover this world. She was not sure why another portal would be so close to Sidhterra's access door but thought it must just be one of those anomalies that can occur with magics."

His voice was steady but the way he delivered the information was indifferent. Detached and uninterested.

My empathic abilities were picking up on his underlying anxiety. Looking subtly to Brie, she gave me the smallest of nods.

"Her Majesty sent a few of her lower guard to assess the area around the portal. They reported back to her that it was nothing like Lagomshire. That the area was full of advanced technologies and that they felt strange," he said.

"Strange how?" Hayden asked. "Did they lose their gifts while there?"

"The lower guard does not have much in the way of extra gifts. Only a few have an extra gift but of the seven who were sent, the two with abilities claimed that they were diminished." His voice was lower now. "All of them reported that they felt sickly. That their strength was depleted, and it felt like the magiks were stripped from their very bones."

Shaking his head, he let out a long, breathy whistle through his partially closed lips.

"The Queen decided to send another group and my brother, Ashwood, was Commander of the EU then. He insisted that her Majesty allow me to go with them. That it would be a good learning experience."

His eyes were looking directly at the table, but his focus was far away. I had the urge to reach over and comfort him, but I held myself back.

"We entered the portal and came out the side into a fort of some sort. Their automated carriages were far more advanced than ours, but they still had horses pulling non-automated carriages in the area."

Bastian and Hayden exchanged a look and Lara didn't miss it.

"What is it? Do you remember something from your time there?" she said.

Tension sat heavy around the group. The walls felt closer with every piece of new information.

"It's mostly fuzzy. The memories left us almost immediately when we returned with our grandfather... but both of us remember the horse drawn carriages and the fort," Bastian said.

"It wasn't until we talked with Mamsy that we learned about the magiks draining Grandfather." Hayden hung his head as he spoke. "She told us that he never fully recovered from the trip. His abilities diminished and he died earlier than normal healthy gifters generally do, like the life expectancy of a Dhall."

Riedyn looked at them and his eyes widened slightly. Noella was lost in thought. It was Thelzion's long exhale of breath that caught my notice.

He was a lot more astute than I'd given him credit for.

"It was weeks after we returned before we started to feel like ourselves again," the Commander said. "Queen Talisin declared that the Low realm of St Augustine portal was Forbidden and no one from her court was to cross into that realm again."

Zane steepled his hands under his chin. Noella and Thelzion shared the same look of quiet contemplation. It was Noella who spoke up, the authority ringing in her voice again.

"It would seem that the strong double veil in that realm strips the magics from you. gifters are made nearly mortal. Dhalls would most likely not live long," and she looked at Zane when she spoke next, "And only immortals would have a chance at a full recover over time." With a nod in his direction, he inclined his chin.

A suddenly bad feeling rocked through my whole body.

"So, Zane and I will go to the Low realm and retrieve the ring," Thelzion volunteered.

Noella took Lara's hand and kissed it. Lara's returning look was what I imagined my own mirrored. Trepidation and anxiety taut in every feature.

"I'm afraid that won't work," Noella said. "You're a demon and that realm's strong anti-magics is in closer proximity to the Underworld. It would test your will and push you to be a worse version of the demon that you were when you were born to this plane."

"Well, where is Draxus in all of this? I thought you said that he was going to help." Thelzion wasn't happy to be told he couldn't do something that he thought would protect Brie. That much was obvious.

"I haven't heard from him in over a week. The last thing he said to Bastian, and I was that he was going to see a man about a horse," she said. "If I am right, after what Commander Riedyn said and Bastian and Hayden's accounts of their trip to that realm, I believe he went to retrieve the ring but he hasn't made it back."

She gave her cousin a meaningful look. Zane took my hand now and kissed it.

I got the sense that he was about to do something dangerous and reckless and found myself wishing that he wouldn't.

It clicked in my mind that it must mean I was already falling for him and his charms.

My selfish want to be on my own for the first time was warring in an internal struggle against the fates.

"We have to go, Kali," he said. "Noella and I are Mixlings. We stand a better chance at a quicker recovery than anyone else in this group."

The group was all standing by now. I was conscious of everyone's gaze upon us but didn't care. My head and heart fought for control while the world tilted.

Standing slightly on my tiptoes, I gathered myself together. Placing a hand on either side of his face, I lightly brushed my lips against his.

The zing sparked my lips to heat but I locked down my gifts the best I could.

"I know." With more resolve than I felt, I gave him control of his own destiny the way he'd allowed me mine.

Brie's earlier display with Thelzion strengthened my heart. It was my mind that tugged hardest to keep him here with me.

"You make sure you come back to me in one piece." I smiled at the astonished look on his face. "You'll come back whole and well. I like your face too much for you not to."

Taking my finger and running it along the scar that stretched down the one side, Zane gave an involuntary shutter.

After a few seconds of awkward silence in the room, Thelzion cleared his throat.

"So, Noella and Zane will head to the portal," he said.

Commander Riedyn chimed in. "I will show them the way, but I cannot go against my Queen's orders."

Thelzion gave a dip of his chin in understanding. Riedyn could work with us on this, but he wasn't one of us. Our agendas matched up for now, but the queen's favor only went so far.

"Brie and I will see if we can somehow intercept Lucian and retrieve the Fainne Todhchai. Hecate did say that we would need it." He reached over and took Brie's hand.

"I have one of my EU tailing him," Riedyn said. "If you cross paths before I return, tell him CROWS FLY BACKWARDS AT NIGHT, to which he should reply THE SCORPION IS SMARTER. If he replies with ONLY WHEN THEIR YOUNG ARE in the NEST, you shouldn't approach."

The fact that Thelzion would take orders from anyone still astounded me. It would take some getting used to for me not to flinch every time I thought he would be angry.

"Why not?" Brie asked.

"It means that he doesn't trust that you didn't learn the passcode by force. If you hold back, he'll reassess," he said. "That will be your only opportunity to give it another shot."

Brie smiled widely. Thelzion, on the other hand, looked aggravated.

"And what should we say at that point? I don't want to shed blood with your unit, but we have a job to do and I won't let anyone hurt my mate," the vampire practically growled.

Thelzion's eyes met Brie's and the way they looked at each other made me feel dithery. I knew the skittering bees in my belly were the same when I thought about Zane putting himself in danger.

Riedyn chuckled. "Tell them that GENERAL ASHWOOD IS A DICK."

Thelzion raised an eyebrow and Brie did the same. Riedyn raised his hands and shoulders in a shrug.

"They know my feelings on my brother but most outside the EU think we're tight." He shook his head. "Put the emphasis on DICK."

Lara and Hayden hung back while the rest of our group headed towards the door. Hayden called out to his cousin.

"Where are you going, Bastian?"

There was defiance in Bastian's expression.

"I'm going with Noella to the portal," he said. Zane started to protest but Bastian raised a hand to cut him off. "Look, I know I can't enter that realm but maybe I can sense something. There might be something I can Deblock. I need to try at least."

I linked arms with his once I saw the look that Hayden and Bastian shared.

It was a dejected look I'd worn on my own face when I was with Lucian. Bastian deserved the opportunity to do what he thought was right.

Zane peered over at me, and I gave him a wry smile, but he said nothing.

"Everyone be safe. And we'll meet back here around 3am." Lara said it with the confidence of a known fact.

It gave us all hope, but I saw how her eyes dropped to her feet and her lips pressed into a line as she turned away from us.

The seer knew something she wasn't saying.

Something would go amiss.

Chapter Sixty-Five

Parker

"You're late," I said. "Is everything okay?" I added with mock concern.

Her fluttery wings snapped like the crack of a whip. She swooped in quickly and planted a hard kiss on my shocked lips.

Gently as I could, I pushed her back. I didn't mind kissing the faery but there was a time and a place and this certainly wasn't it.

I knew I was using her, and she was using me, but the fae were not the nicest once they knew you'd played them. This wasn't going to turn out well.

"Does the queen suspect your treachery?"

Her eyes crinkled and her nose scrunched up at the indignation.

"Queen Talisin doesn't look for things that she feels are out of them realm of possibility," Skylar said. "I am her favored messenger and therefore I'm in her blind spot."

The whisp faery buzzed a few feet off the floor, circling me, picking and kissing whenever she got close enough.

My patience was beginning to fray but keeping my cool was essential in nurturing her cooperation.

"If that's the case, then why were you late?"

Landing beside me, her bottom lip jutting out, tucking her wings in tight to her back. Only whisp fae had dragonfly like wings. They were an interesting obstacle to maneuver over when we fooled around.

"Commander Riedyn was there, giving a report on your boss and you lackies." The distain for the Commander was evident in her tone. "I had warned her not to trust in sending him before but like I said, she is blind to those in her inner circle."

Playing my part well, I wrapped my arm over her shoulder and pulled her closer to my side.

Planting a small kiss to her hair, she sighed. I knew how to pluck her strings. Pretty little thing, but not the sharpest fang in the mouth.

"I planted seeds in Jax and Quinn's minds a couple of days ago." She looked up at me like I'd told her water wasn't wet. "Jax wasn't having it, but Quinn seemed to almost align herself with our thinking right away. Lucian is a problem that needs to be taken care of."

Tinkling laughter fell from her lips. The irritated the shit out of me. Faeries were the worst.

"Honestly, I didn't think you would do it." Her cheeks became rosy when she smiled. "When I think about how vicious Lucian can be when he's enraged, it would just make sense that causing that kind of wrath would be a deterrent."

"Geesh, thanks for having faith in me."

Pretending my feelings were hurt, I strummed those strings a little harder. Faery or not, she was a female.

They tended to lead with their heart, rather than us males who lead with our dicks.

"Oh, don't be like that." Skylar put her long fingers under my chin and pulled my face to look at her. "I'm glad that you did it. I just wasn't sure if you would is all."

I pulled from her hand and turned my head, smirking with my back to her. I needed to lay it on thick.

This faery had a wicked core and if I didn't play my hand just right, she'd more than likely get me killed.

Suppressing a chuckle, I turned back to face her.

Her big eyes were a depthless sea of silver blue. The way that that bottom lip of hers stuck out pouting was kind of adorable. Lilac and moss scents dominated the mixture of woodsy smells that came off of her skin.

When I leaned in, she closed her eyes, anticipating a kiss.

Chuckling under my breath again, I took her chin between my forefinger and thumb, turned her head slightly to the side, and kissed her cheek.

Watching the little female fae get flustered was probably one of my most enjoyable ways to pass the time.

Skylar's eyes opened and her hand went to the spot where my lips just were.

"Tease," she pouted. Her fingers ran down my arm and grazed the front of my pants.

"Now who's teasing?" I smirked.

We'd played this game plenty. Never fully partaking in the carnal act of fucking.

"Oh, I'm not teasing. I'm ready to play."

Reaching over, I grabbed her around the waist and pulled her close.

Bending down to where I was sitting, exposing the bare flesh at the top of the scoop in her shirt, her lips were a breadths distance away from mine.

Slowly, I brushed a finger along the fullness of her small breasts where they were exposed. She shuttered instantly.

Leaning in and placing a kiss at the base of her neck, I whispered with hot breath, "Mmmm. I'm hungry."

She pulled back quickly. Shocked by my vampirical yearning for something more than sex, her mouth hung open.

"Parker... I can't. The queen will know and..." She fumbled for words. "I'm sorry. I just can't do that."

Dropping my head in my hands, I faked being upset and chuckled as quietly as I could manage.

She reached up and ran her fingers through my hair. Without removing my hands from my face, I relayed my disappointment.

"It's fine. I think I need to be alone for a while," I said. Poor, stupid girl.

Skylar danced on the spot for another moment but didn't protest. Her wings unfurled from her back, and she rushed forward, pressing a kiss on top of my head before taking flight.

Hovering next to me, her voice quiet but frustrated, "I'm sorry. I hope you still want to work and play together."

Schooling my features into a grimace, I raised my face to look at her.

"Of course. We have a common goal, Skylar." My smile was saccharine sweet. "I still desire you. I'll just have to set limits on my wants."

Her cheeks reddened. I almost snatched her out of the air and took her right then and there. This game was hard on my self-control.

She tried to give me a small grin in response, but it didn't quite meet her eyes.

With one last glance in my direction, she flew off.

My mood in her wake was unusually good.

I hadn't lied. I was hungry.

Maybe I'd head over to that old pawn shop for a follow up visit.

Fhail still owed me lunch.

Chapter Sixty-Six

Quinn

Jaxson and i walked along the edge of Maylum manors property where we were out of ear shot.

It was completely shaded by overgrown trees that had been around for over three centuries, but the grounds were well maintained.

Grass dominated the majority of the eight-acre lot. There were jasmine bushes and rows of lavender and moss hung from the trees like tenacles of the sea beasts.

"Lucian sure likes his flowers fragrant," Jax said casually.

I glanced sideways at the big, dark demon knowing he was trying to point out niceties in a subtle way.

The fact that he knew who Lucian was at his core and still wanted to defend his character told me that he wasn't ready to face the truths Parker and I had brought up the other day.

"I'm pretty sure he didn't plant them, Jaxson." My tone was playful but still held truth at its heart. It was time to offer an olive branch. "He does like to walk the gardens a few times a week though."

The shirt he was wearing clung to every bulging muscle he had.

I'd found myself, not for the first time, wishing I could find an attraction to him. The chemistry we had as friends was great but there was no spark. At least not on my end.

"Listen," he began shuffling his feet, kicking up the smell of fresh cut grass. "It's not that I don't have those same thoughts about Lucian. It's just, well, he's our boss."

When you live as long as I had, you pick up on a few things.

Like when a person, or in this case demon, was a soldier. Even if they've never been in any military or guard structured unit. The chain of command was important to them.

These were the types to follow orders, without question, because it gave meaning to their lives. Yes men had their place, but thinking was for the leaders.

I was Lucian's *unofficial* second because I could think on the spot. I didn't need to be told what to do next.

As my friend, it was hard to watch Jax struggle with any new concept that deviated from the chain. As a leader, it was usually a relished quality.

I was a demon first though. And demons looked at things as survival of the fittest.

Physical attributes only helped you so far in the game. It was a fit mind that won the prize. And Jax was just a pawn. I could see that now.

"I get it. Think about this though, Jax. Bosses are made on the bones of the last one." I glared at him until that sank in. "We're here to assist him but that doesn't mean that he is always right. You need to figure out where your loyalties lie... with Lucian, or with demonkind."

He stumbled in response. His hand came up hard and gripped my arm just above the curve of my elbow.

"Are you saying that Lucian isn't looking out for his own kind? That's treasonous talk there, Quinn," he said.

With a yank, my arm ripped from his grip in frustration.

"Maybe you should take that up with the higher ups. I'm sure Saevus would love to know what's going on in Lucian's territories or better yet, what he is planning."

Jax dropped his hand to his side like he'd been shocked by a high voltage wire and shook his head.

Now matter how I tried, I couldn't get into his thick skull that Lucian had no one's interest but his own at heart.

"If your torn between what's right and what you believe to be treason, there's always a question you can ask yourself." Leveling him with a cold stare, I knew it would set his teeth itching.

Awkward silence stretched out between us when he refused to give in.

Finally asking me after I refrained from saying anything else to egg him on, "Yeah, what's that?"

"Well, if Saevus was to ask you what you do for Lucian or what Lucian was up to, could you tell him without feeling the need to hide anything?"

For his part, he mulled it over, but I had the feeling he was still not fully grasping the whole of the situation.

"Saevus is Lucian's boss. He is higher up in the demon hierarchy. And if you're answer is that keeping Lucian's secrets are more important than following the chain of command, then you'll know which side of the tracks you're standing on."

Shaking his head, he gestured for us to resume our walk. The estate grounds truly were some of my favorite trails to meander.

He wasn't a dumb guy. He just needed some other way to focus his thoughts.

I'd give him that chance. Just this once.

Parker had already given his blood oath that we'd work for a better demonkind.

I hated blood oaths, but I didn't trust Parker farther than I could throw him.

At least with the blood oath, I knew that there'd be consequences if he fucked me over.

"I'll think on it." Jax didn't look back as he headed towards the manor.

He'd left me alone to finish the walk we'd started without another word.

If I went to Saevus now, Lucian might be tumbled, but Jaxson would know it was me.

If I snitched and Lucian didn't fall to the underworld, I'd be a dead demon walking.

Parker wasn't a great partner, but with the blood oath in place, at least I'd have a safety net.

A safety net with barbs and spikes but a safety net all the same.

Chapter Sixty-Seven

Lucian

"You can come out Borias," I lazily called back over my shoulder.

The fae warrior stepped out from behind a tree and into the path. He was broad shouldered but not in a bulky way. The muscles he'd honed were strong and spry.

"You're not going to win, Lucian." The Lieutenant said. "Balance is the demand of the universe. You are not demon enough to throw that off."

Casually strolling over to him, I stopped just a foot away. Looking him up and down once. Calculating. My finger tapping the side of my chin.

"It appears being in the queen's circle has given you more balls than you're worthy of." A wicked smile spread across my face. My mind made up.

"My balls are just as big as my bite. I assure you," Borias said with less confidence than he wore a moment ago. "You can't beat the ever growing odds against..."

I pounced on him before he could finish his sentence. My fangs sunk into Borias's neck like a hot knife in butter.

The fae reached up with both hands and yanked me off. Blood gushed down his neck.

With a quick sweep of my legs, the warrior fell to the ground.

Borias was quick but I was quicker. I straddled the Lieutenant as he fought the losing battle. He was no match for me once I'd gotten the upper hand.

Snapping his neck to the side, it broke. Borias stopped fighting, stopped moving.

He laid gasping as I placed my lips to the holes in his neck and sucked the still pumping life from the fallen warrior. I'd missed lunch and it didn't seem right to waste such a meal.

Faery blood was divine. It had magical properties that set me higher than a drifting leaf on the wind.

Feeding my fill, I sat up and wiped my face. The stupid git's blood ruined my favorite suit.

Borias looked up into my eyes as the last of his breath left his lungs.

"Your queen's blood shall feed my demons soon enough."

The fae's eyes widened with horror. Leaning in, I placed my lips to the shell of his ear.

"She was wise not to give me all that I wanted from her. Your kind may be bound by their word but...," I licked the side of his face. "I am a demon. And will soon be a king who will bow to no one."

Borias's heart beat its final drum. Pulling back, I reached down and ran my fingers through the dead male's hair.

Licking my thumb, I wiped the stray blood from his face and straightened his collar.

Death was no excuse to be untidy. The warrior deserved dignity from a life spent in servitude.

It wouldn't be long until Queen Talisin sent her EU to avenge the death of one of their own.

I could only hope to draw out General Ashwood rather than Commander Riedyn.

A sacrifice was coming, and I was still rather fond of my former lover.

It'd be a pity to end him before my reign began.

Chapter Sixty-Eight

Baelyn

Chironna gave Pleshia the day off so that she and I could go shopping in the downtown district of Lagomshire. It had been a while since we had a carefree day to hang out.

I missed my lazy days with my sister. We used to be inseparable but as we got older, life got in the way quite frequently.

Work took up most of our time. We shared an apartment but still hardly had time for hellos and goodbyes before we were out the door for another day.

"What was that look I caught from Chironna's grandson?" I teased her.

"I don't know what you are talking about," Pleshia grinned sarcastically.

Looping her arm through mine, I pushed the issue. She could be a little more than stand offish when it came to strangers, but she didn't seem to mind Bastian's gaze one bit.

"He was looking at you like he was mesmerized and a little scared." Pleshia's smile grew into a cat that caught the canary gesture.

As we turned the corner, a loud rumble worked its way from my stomach. The gnawing sensation grew with every step we took towards the smells of food coming from the city shops.

I let her steer me towards the diner. It wasn't quite lunch time, but it was past breakfast, and we needed to eat if we planned to walk all of the shops today.

"Well, what about how Hayden was looking at you?" Pleshia insisted. "He looked as if you had him enthralled under some sort of spell."

"Did he? I didn't think anything of it," I played coy. "Does he not always look like that?"

My pace quickened as we approached Kraigen's. I had a downright hankering for some good old diner style greasy food.

"I only met them today. And he didn't look at me like that." Her grin landed its mark. Heat rising to the apples of my cheeks. "His whole face changed the moment he saw you."

Entering the diner, we sat at a table near the window. The scent of grilled onions and fresh baked bread made my mouth water.

I'd eaten an apple when I'd woken up this morning, but that was hours ago now. My appetite lately had taken on a beastly life of its own.

Picking up a couple of menus, we silently perused our options. She must have been as hungry as I was because our conversation ceased the moment we came in the door.

A tall man with an apron and note pad came striding over to the table with utensils and condiments.

"What'll ya have?" he said curtly.

"Can we get a couple of iced teas while we decide?" Pleshia nodded her agreement.

The man rolled his eyes and walked away. Exchanging a look, we giggled. Being with my sister often brought on a fit of amusement at the slightest things.

"I think we should get some appetizers for the table and then order our meal afterwards," Pleshia said. "I bet he'd love that."

I hadn't thought to tease the waiter. Pleshia's mischievous side reared its head at the strangest times.

I'd learned to overlook it over the years, but sometimes I found myself wanting to indulge in the shenanigans with her.

"You are so bad. Let's do it." Setting my menu to the side, I motioned for him that we were ready.

"Yeah, so what do you want?" he said a bit gruffly.

Let the games begin. Time to fill my demanding belly.

"Smothered fries, mozzarella sticks, and some fried pickles." They all sounded like a perfect start.

Pleshia chimed in, adding, "Oh, and can we get some chips and salsa for the table?"

"No meals?" his look told me of his mood. It leaked out of him like a slow rolling fog.

"If we're hungry after this, we'll order more when we're through with these."

The more I smelled the foods coming out of the kitchen, the hungrier I was becoming. I could probably eat my shoe at this point with no problem.

Mumbling to himself as he walked away, he dropped his note pad and swore. The poor guy was definitely having a bad day.

I jumped up to retrieve it, handing it back to him before he was even finished bending down. My fingers grazing his hand as I did.

"I'm Baelyn." I turned and gestured towards the table. "And this is my sister, Pleshia. If there's anything we can do to help, just let us know."

The man first seemed taken aback. He then straightened up and took us both in.

Where he had been grumpy just moments ago, he appeared less stiff, more relaxed.

"I'm Kraigen. I own this joint." He wiped the back of his neck with the rag he had hung at his side. "It's been a rough morning. Busy. And then the delivery got cancelled. I'm sorry if I was a bit mean before."

I waved my hand in a no bother manner and touched the top of his arm.

"It's very understandable. Really. Just let us know if there's anything we can do." Dropping my hand back down to my side, I stepped back to our the table.

After Kraigen returned to the kitchen and was safely out of earshot, Pleshia shook her head.

"How do you do that?" I didn't know if she'd meant to ask it out loud, but I'd heard it all the same.

"Do what?"

Fidgeting with the sugar packets, the corners of her mouth turned up.

"Oh, come on. You have to know the effect you have on people when you touch them like that."

There was something *knowing* in her look, but I could tell she was frustrated with my lack of response.

I thought about it for a minute. I didn't have any good answer. It'd been like this since I was young.

Once, I'd asked one of my teachers what they thought, and it had seemed reasonable enough to settle my nerves on the subject.

So, that's what I told her. "Touching someone while talking to them is a simple psychology trick. It doesn't mean anything."

Picking up my tea and taking a sip, that first jolt of caffeine and sugar hit all the right places. Yummy.

"Yeah, okay. I'm sure we all have that same ability to get our way," Pleshia said rolling her eyes.

Rationally, I knew she'd been teasing me. Irrationally, it was something that I'd overthought about for long hours, and it bit into my mind with tiny pin pricks of jagged teeth to not know the answer.

"You're being silly. I think that sometimes people just need to feel a connection. Like, they need to feel heard and under-stood."

Pleshia took a long drink of her tea before responding. She glanced around to make sure no one was listening.

"Bastian said something before you arrived." Her dubious eyes spoke clearly of mischief now.

"Ooo... what did he say? Something about wanting to take you right there on his grandmother's coffee table?" I smirked. Take that, sis!

Pleshia laughed but then turned serious again. Quite unusual for her once her fiendish side came out to play.

"No silly. He said something about me being a..." She leaned in across the table, blocked her mouth from prying eyes, and whispered. "Faery."

If I didn't know any better, I'd think she was trying to tell me something without coming straight out with it.

I bit at my lower lip. Knowing my sister was serious, I didn't want to make her feel stupid but the fact that we were actually discussing the possibility of her being a faery was ludicrous.

"And what did you say?" I asked politely.

"I didn't get a chance to say anything. Chironna ushered me out of the room and when I came back, it was as if they'd had some discussion about it. Bastian apologized and changed the subject. Weird, right?"

It was oddly peculiar. I could see why she might need some reassurance.

"Actually, that is rather strange." I was going to tell her not to take too much stock in what the elderly lady said, but I'd never seen Pleshia so rattled.

Kraigen came out of the kitchen with our food and set it in the center of the table. He clapped his hands together and asked if there was anything else we needed?

"Would you like to join us for a little break?" I asked. He looked like he could use one. "We have plenty."

The diner owner's face lit up. It wasn't very busy at the moment. With a lull in customers, it was the perfect opportunity to pop a squat.

"Really? Thanks. I'd like that." He pulled out a chair and practically fell into it. "I've been on my feet all morning. Two of my staff called out. I've got their replacements coming in in an hour, but I am beat."

"Aww, I'm sorry to hear that," It wasn't a good time when you were tired *and* had no help.

Kraigen popped a mozzarella stick into his mouth. The intensity in his gaze made Pleshia shift in her seat, but I found it comforting. He looked contented for the first time since we'd arrived.

"You gals sure are nice. Not many people have kindness for strangers anymore." He took a deep breath. "I miss the days when you could pop a squat next to someone at the counter and become fast friends for an hour."

My eyes lifted to Pleshia. We'd had many memories of our mother doing just that.

Before she went missing, she was the light in any room. No one who met her could resist her charms.

It made my heart ache to think of it now. I knew my sister was probably feeling the same thing.

"It's a shame, isn't it?" I said jovially. "A stranger is just a friend you haven't met yet."

Kraigen popped another fry into his mouth before rising to his feet.

"Well, consider us friends, ladies." He tipped an imaginary cap. "Thank you for sharing a meal with this old timer."

He smiled widely before heading back to the kitchen. The middle-aged man was lonely. That much was clear.

It'd be nice to venture here more often and have a good meal with great company. Plus, the mozzarella sticks kicked ass! That was reason enough for me.

Pleshia and I finished up our midmorning lunch and went to the register to pay the bill.

"Baelyn, Pleshia. It was a pleasure to meet you both." Kraigen then took the check and marked it void. "I hope you'll come and see me again sometime soon."

"You didn't have to do that," Pleshia said. I could hear the truth in her tone.

She'd never been comfortable owing someone an unknown debt.

We'd been brought up making sure that no lose ends hung over our heads and my sister had been nothing, if not a stickler, for that particular rule.

"But thank you, Kraigen," I cut in. I wasn't one to look a gift horse in the mouth. "We'll make sure to swing 'round this way whenever we are in the neighborhood."

"You ladies have a nice day of shopping." With a beaming smile, he turned back to the order of the couple who'd walked in a few minutes ago.

Pleshia pursed her lips. I knew she enjoyed a free meal. She was just too stubborn for her own good.

With more money to spend on our shopping now, we left the cute little diner with full bellies and an even fuller heart.

Chapter Sixty-Nine

Zane

The sunny skies began to have small grey clouds gathering in the distance.

I knew that it was necessary to go through the portal and try to retrieve the Akasha ring that we needed and yet, my mind could think of nothing but Kali.

Noella and I would be suffering the aftereffects from being in that magicless world when we came back for who knew how long?

Not being at full strength would leave me feeling helpless to protect my mate. Claimed or not, she was still mine.

That thought alone had my footsteps faltering at the entrance to the forest.

The fresh scent of pine drifted to me on a warm breeze. The sounds of chirping birds and skittering critters in the underbrush were the only noises as we ventured further inside the canopy of trees.

Commander Riedyn walked swiftly, with intent and purpose. We all filed along in silence as the trees swallowed us up whole and the clouds ominously started to roll in. The darkness along the trail hinted at something sinister for the mission ahead.

"This does seem familiar," Bastian said as we walked deeper into the woods. "Not like I remember the look, but the feel is the same."

Noella stepped to his side. Lifting her hand and wiggling her fingers, her face became stoic. I felt it too. The draining essence.

"It feels crushing. Not pain exactly but..." he said. "Riedyn? How much farther?"

The Commander turned just a moment later and stopped.

The warrior's face tightened. "We're here."

He motioned to a pile of stones in which sat what looked like a small pool of water that none of us had noticed before.

Our small group approached them with caution, as if they would bite.

They were blended seamlessly into the forest landscape. If not for being in a near circle formation, nothing would have made them appear out of place.

The sounds of the forest died down all around us. Eerie was an understatement.

Getting closer to the rocks, we could make out some sort of writing carved into each one.

"It's Anexian Script, the script of the gods." Noella took off her glove and ran a finger over every character. "It's an activating spell but also a warning."

Bastian stepped in for a closer look, but Noella stopped him. If I was feeling the drain with my godly blood from here, he must be feeling it tenfold.

"It's too dangerous for a Gifter or a Dhall. The drain of magics isn't what I thought it would be," she said. "It feels more like a drain of life force."

Commander Riedyn had stopped some fifteen feet away and never attempted to come any closer.

The queen was very strict when it came to enforcing her laws, but I didn't think that was the reason the fae warrior didn't approach.

The wrongness of the portal was in the air all around and the closer I got to it, the less I wanted to go through it myself.

Noella's hand pushed against an invisible barrier. I couldn't see it but no doubt it was a powerful ward of some sort if she couldn't push through it.

"There's still some sort of block. I can't get through it," she said.

Frustration leaked from her tone. My cousin wasn't used to being thwarted by anything magical.

We needed to get through that thing. Kali's safety was my top concern, even if I knew it shouldn't be.

"Let me see what I can do." Bastian stayed where he was but closed his eyes, concentrating.

After a few minutes, lights shimmered all around the rocks. The air crackled and spit small sparks before settling down to a simple shimmering surface.

"It should be open now. Be safe," Bastian said to Noella. "We need you. Come back safe." The earnestness in his voice made us all take a deep collective breath.

Noella looked up to meet his eyes. Her lips thinned but curled up on the ends. Taking his hand, she gave it a quick squeeze.

I reached over and took her hand from him. We both gave him a small smile before stepping into the circle of rocks.

With our intertwined fingers, I stepped forward with my cousin into the portal.

A strange sensation whooshed through the air around us.

There was darkness and nothingness for what felt like an eternity but also a split second.

That strangeness pushed and pressed into us with force but not pain. It was what one would imagine a babe felt being forced out of the birth canal.

When the pressure receded and light filtered back into the world around us, our first glimpse into this realm was one of awe.

The beauty of the land, the smell of the water, the hustle and bustle of a city full of stone buildings and people going to and fro overwhelmed my senses.

The drain of magics was intense but we both lost ourselves to the wonders around us without realizing time was slipping by.

Water flowed passed the building we stood beside, a fort of some sort.

Strange ships propelled themselves without oars or magics.

Lion head statues guarded a bridge to the other bank a little ways away. As two pieces in the center split and lifted, I was struck dumb by the vast amount of automated horseless carriages coming to a standstill on either side of the bridge.

Noella's face was as awestruck as I imagined mine to be.

Amazing. This place didn't have magics to use freely and yet it still appeared more advanced than our own realm.

"Well, where should we start?" Noella asked, bringing me back to the present. "I can't feel anything here. The void of magics is bizarre."

"I guess we'll have to rely on what we know about your father." I said as I began walking the direction of the first pub. "Are you coming?"

Noella looked at me with a wry smile but fell in step as we ventured to the nearest watering hole.

It was time to find this magicless horse and take a ride.

Chapter Seventy

Thelzion

Brie and I approached Maylum Manor with caution.

There was only one light on from a window in the second story. The grounds were quiet. There weren't even the sounds of any night birds to be heard.

As we approached the front walkway, the sound of buzzing flies hit our sensitive ears. It was a loud cacophony of sound cutting through the silence of the night.

The smell was the next thing to hit both of our demon noses. Blood. Not human. Not demon... That left fae.

It was a scent that neither one of us were particularly familiar with. We didn't deal with the faery realm too often and until recently, we had never worked with any of them.

Fae blood had an earthy scent, with under notes of natural sweetness. Pine, honeysuckle, fragrant flowers maybe.

It almost hurt my nose. It was right on the border of delicious and disgusting.

We were almost to the front stairs when Brie pointed to the body. It was tossed to the side, crumpled in a bush.

Whoever it was had been discarded like a piece of litter. No thought for the life that had once filled that body. Just used and thrown away.

Taking a step towards the lifeless form, I needed to get a better look.

Turning the head to expose the wound, I could see that it had been a vampire bite, but the fae healed very quickly. It had to be a powerful vampire to drain the body dry before it could recover.

Brie came up behind me. Her presence was soothing in times when I wanted to rage. Now was one of those times.

"There's bruising along his neck on the other side," she said. Lifting her finger and pointing to the dark purple, the truth of it hit her. "He broke his neck and fed from him while he was dying."

I'd seen it already. I'd done it before in my past. Lucian was as efficient as ever.

She made a disgusted sound in the back of her throat while I turned the fae over to get a look at his face.

"If I'm correct, this is Borias. Commander Riedyn's second." Pointing, I showed her the tattoo of two swords crossed with wings on either side and vines intertwining around the center on his wrist. "He was definitely in the Elite Unit."

"If I didn't know better, I'd think Lucian was trying to draw out the queen's wrath," Brie said, shaking her head.

I had a feeling she was right, but it didn't sit well with me. This move would bring Queen Talisin's wrath for sure.

"Why would he want the queen's attention? It seems like a shit move." I was honestly perplexed. "He wouldn't make a mistake this huge. It has to be some kind of strategy."

"I agree. He left the body to find on purpose, but why?" she said.

The clockworks working behind those beautiful eyes of hers made my heart yearn to be a better male.

After a few minutes, nothing appeared to click into place. Annoyance at having no solution to the puzzle was written in the squinching of her nose. The crinkles around her eyes. The breathy sigh that slipped passed her guard.

Damning stars, I loved this woman more than life itself.

"You know we have to tell Riedyn when we meet up at Lara's. We can't keep this from him." I didn't want to tell him but, it'd be better hearing it from us than discovering it later, when we needed him to be the ruthless fae warrior he was.

"I just hope he can focus on the..." Brie stopped talking mid-sentence.

I immediately went into protective mode, scanning the perimeter for any danger that might have caught her eye.

"What? What is it?" My nerves were already frayed from that foreshadowers dream.

If anything, it made me want to throw Brie over my shoulder and hide her away in a remote cave until any and all dangers had passed.

Brushing passed me. Taking another look at the body. Then snapping her fingers in my face to pull me out of my crouch. She was all serious and sanctuary at the same time.

"Saying it that way. It kind of clicks a bit." She held up a finger so I wouldn't push while she tried to fit the pieces together. "He and Riedyn had been lovers in the past. That must be why the Commander sent Borias to tail Lucian rather than doing it himself... Riedyn must still be fighting the enthrallment of him." She looked to me with wide eyes. "Thelzion, do you think that maybe he wants him distracted?"

That made perfect sense. One less formidable warrior to worry about. That fit Lucian's method of operation.

"Could be, but why would he want to chance Queen Talisin sending her army and General Ashwood? That's the part that bothers me." I wiped my hands on the front of my pants. "There's something we're missing. I hope Noella and Zane aren't walking into something they're not prepared for."

I couldn't shake the feeling of doom that had been making its way through my system for the last few days.

The demigod hadn't returned. What were the odds that Zane and Noella would? "We need that ring, but Draxus went missing a week ago. We sent them to the same place."

"I'm sure they're fine. We need to trust them, Zi," she said. "Noella is his daughter. She is the best of what the shadowrealm has to offer. I have to believe that Hecate wouldn't put her on a path that'd lead her astray."

Our two best shots at taking down Lucian and closing the leak from the underworld weren't even in our realm right now. Maybe that had been part of his plan... but how?

Brie touched my face, cupping my chin. A look past between us. It didn't need words.

The gods were fickle creatures. Trusting them, even when their own blood was involved, was a fool's gamble.

"We need to find Riedyn so that he can tell the queen of Lucian's betrayal," she said.

"This is going to open up a whole new can of problems," I kissed her lips gently. "I agree though. I just hope it won't interfere with our retrieving the rings and stopping this insane idea of opening the demon realm to this one."

A stray strand of hair had fallen into her eyes. Brushing it behind her ear, I voiced my frustrations to the only person who saw me. Saw the demon and the male trying to be better.

"I understand that the fissure or breaking or whatever they want to call it needs to be allowed to happen. Cracking it wide open though, especially when the veil lifts off and the Dhalls can see everything?" I shook my head. "We just can't allow that. Lucian needs to be dealt with swiftly. Hopefully, the queen's agenda still aligns with our own long enough to keep this realm intact."

No demon or god would keep me from keeping Brie safe. Not while I still drew breath.

If saving the world was the price of that, I'd gladly pay it ten times over.

Chapter Seventy-One

Hayden

Evening was coming quick. I'd decided to go back to the diner and work from there.

Feeling useless sitting around worrying, I needed to be doing something more. Something active.

Kraigen approached the table looking tired but contented. There was a grin at the corners of his mouth.

I couldn't recall ever seeing the man in good spirits. It made my heart happy to see. The poor fellow must have met someone.

Before I could stop myself, the question popped out.

"What's with the grin?"

The older man tried to make his face a mask of his normal stoicism. He failed miserably.

"I don't know what you mean." The grin widened, stretching his cheeks, smoothing out the wrinkles along his chin.

"If I didn't know any better, I'd think you were almost... dare I say it... happy." Smiling up at him, I could see the warring of emotions going on behind Kraigen's eyes.

Uncharacteristically, he sat in the chair across from me. I couldn't recall another time where he'd been so relaxed and carefree. The man did nothing but work.

It felt like I'd achieved a reward for earning his company.

How long had I come to this diner, time after time, trying to get this man to be a bit happier? Or even just friendlier to the point of joking around with me?

And here he sat there, grin on his face, making an attempt at connection.

"It's just, well..." Kraigen couldn't find the right words. "I'm here. All the time. I take orders and fix food and see people all day..." he trailed off for a second.

Keeping my mouth shut, I gave him the time and space to figure out what he wanted to say.

"I don't know when life got away from me," he started again. "I never even realized how lonely I was."

The look on Kraigen's face was a mix of regret and resolution.

At my ripe old age of twenty-six, I'd been feeling lonely myself. I couldn't imagine being middle aged and never finding that special someone to cherish.

"There were these two girls who came in earlier. I was short with them after things had been going awry all morning. They didn't get upset or anything." He shook his head. "They just kept trying to interact with me... ya know, like I was a person and not just someone who was there to serve them."

He rubbed at the scruff on his chin, and I leaned forward. It wasn't that we'd never talked. It was only that we never said anything with substance. It was refreshing listening to him ramble on.

"That's really nice, man. I've been trying to get you to loosen up for a while, but you never seemed to notice." My journal laid to the side of my plate, forgotten in the moment.

Kraigen looked at me like he was really seeing me for the first time. His eyes crinkled in the corners.

"I like you... but I tend to keep people at arm's length, kid. I don't know why. These girls though, the one in particular, they wouldn't let up until I sat and had a meal with them." His face lit up again. "It was really nice. They said they'd be back more often to see me; that we were friends now. And I don't know why but I believe them."

He was quiet for a minute. I didn't know what made me ask but his happiness made me want to know more.

"So, do these girls have names?"

Kraigen stood and took the empty glass from the table.

"Pleshia and Baelyn. Cute little things. Though that Baelyn was something special."

I hadn't thought I could be any more shocked but somehow it didn't shock me at all.

"That's great, man. I hope you know that I can be your friend too, if you let me."

Wiping a spot off the table, Kraigen smiled. A real smile.

"Let's see how I feel about it tomorrow."

He had actually made a joke. That was progress if nothing else. I returned the smile from him in spades.

"I guess I'll have to hold my breath and hope for the best."

Chapter Seventy-Two

Zane

"Oh, look. Horses!" Noella squealed as we made our way out of the fort and onto the street. "These carriages are darling."

Following my cousin's lead, I crossed the road to get a better look at them.

There were a lot of people, and it was a bit overwhelming.

We stayed in line with the others walking along striped areas of paint that met each intersection.

There were large lights hung above the roads that had red, green, and yellow tinted glass but only one lit up at a time. They went off in an arranged order and their version of automated carriages followed a pattern of movement with them.

As we came closer to the horses, Noella twinkled a laugh. "I guess he wasn't kidding."

"What?" I had no idea what she was talking about.

"Draxus. I guess he wasn't kidding. He really was going to see a man about a horse." A smirk drew up at the corner of her mouth and mine followed when I caught up to what she'd been going on about.

Observing the shops and crowds around us, we made our way to the closest bar.

It was a nice establishment called the Tini Martini Bar. It had a great view of the water and horses. Plus, it had a pleasant atmosphere.

Noella scoffed, knowing right away that her father wouldn't be in there. It was open aired and not dingy at all.

"You're seeing this, right?" Noella said breathlessly. "All of these spirits?"

There were a lot of wandering souls zooming in and out of the unsuspecting people all around us. I'd never seen such a concentration of ghosts in one place before.

Walking a bit farther down the sidewalk, I stopped to peer in a glass front. It was empty except for the ghosts of the past.

"Do you think that there's a leak from the ghostly plane already?" I asked.

"There are an awful lot of them. All over, from the looks of it," she said. "This leak has to have been happening for centuries, Zane." The bleak expression on her face said everything I'd been thinking too.

We walked a few buildings down and stopped in Meehan's Irish Pub & Seafood House. It was more or less the same.

It did have an inside that was a little darker but still not the place a demigod like Draxus would hang out in.

We decided to go a few streets over and check around. Noella was taken in by the sites, but I was more focused.

My abilities felt dampened, but the gifts from the gods blood weren't something a Mixling could be fully be stripped of, even in a magics draining realm.

Glancing at each building, a sign on the next one caught my eye.

It had the picture of a horse with a bottle in its center. The Drunken Horse. It was a bar and restaurant.

I steered my cousin inside when she went passed it with a wandering gaze.

The smell of the food coming out of this place was incredible. It was nice enough and dark enough at the bar area, which was separated from the dining section.

We saddled up to a bar stool and took in the surroundings. Wine bottles, old looking furniture, and dark decor covered the walls in an artfully done way.

A bar keep came into the room from out of the main dining area and made his way around to the other side of the counter. His long hair tied back in a short braid, the male faced away from us towards the bottles and glasses on the shelf.

Noella began to speak up, but I laid a hand on her arm and whispered in her ear.

"He's magical. I can't tell what or if he even knows, but my sense is that he is more powerful than we can deal with at half power if things go badly."

A snicker fell from the male's lips.

"Whispering won't help," the bar keep said, startling us both. Turning to face us, he smiled broadly. "Hello Noella.

Chapter Seventy-Three

Quinn

My intuitive abilities started flaring. I drew the knife I'd hidden in my boot early today.

Parker came around the corner, teeth bared. I didn't have the strength of a vampire, but I was skilled with a blade.

He flung himself on me before I could utter a single word. The knife went flying, crashing into the opposite wall.

Lying flat on my back, I was pinned under his weight. He brought his fangs down to my neck. Two tiny pin pricks made a small amount of blood pool on the surface.

"You'd be dead, Quinn," he whispered in my ear. "I expect more from my alliance with you. My life could quite easily be in your hands one day."

Standing with vampire speed, he extended his hand to help me up. I'd thought about smacking it away, but he'd had a point.

Keeping myself constantly aware of my surroundings was crucial and now was not the time to become complacent.

"Thanks," I said. "I guess I had that coming."

He had just come in from somewhere outside. I could smell the night air and sweat that clung to him.

If I'd been paying closer attention when I'd come down the hall, he'd never have gotten the jump on me.

Even here in the manor, mindfulness was essential.

"Where are you coming from? It's barely night fall." My question caused him pause for the briefest moment.

The hesitation was on his face and gone quickly. Lying was his specialty. I'd learned that the hard way a long time ago.

"Lover's tryst," he said.

I tried and failed to hide a smirk. Parker was never the touchy feely kind but the image of him getting close enough to fuck someone was laughable to me.

He was good looking in a rugged sort of way. An asshole, definitely. Fucking made you vulnerable though. I just couldn't envision him without ropes or shackles involved.

I wasn't certain what kind of lover he'd be, given his aversion of others.

Dwelling much? Geesh. Get it together weirdo.

Falling back to our normal routine, I taunted him. "Really? And was it with an intelligent species?"

He looked affronted. Had I struck a nerve? Interesting.

"I'll have you know, I am a sexual dynamo," he said. There was actual charisma in his throaty voice.

I almost leaned in. Almost. Damning stars!

Not knowing what to say to that, I changed the subject.

"I talked to Jax. He still isn't sure which way he's leaning but…" I hesitated. Something felt weird, charged even. "I made it clear that if he was in line with Lucian, that I would surely take the brunt of his wrath."

"Smart. We know how he feels about you." Parker looked me up and down. "I have no idea why."

His eyes lingered on my chest longer than necessary, of course. "Real nice... Ass."

Walking a few steps down the hall towards the kitchen, he turned his head back.

"My ass isn't even my best feature." The corner of his mouth pulled up. "If you're truly lucky, maybe someday you'll find out."

My mouth popped open. I watched after him as he disappeared into the shadows.

Standing there dumbfounded, I couldn't shake the intrigue that welled up in the bottom of my stomach.

Had he really just hit on me? What in the sevens was going on with us?

All vampires had a compelling way about them, but I'd never really consider Parker in more than an asshole associate sort of way.

He had been the most arrogant and insufferable person I'd ever had to deal with on a regular basis.

He was good looking, for sure, but his personality always got in his own way.

Just that slight pause to ponder him in that way made me feel like a fool... but it didn't stop the stirrings of lust.

After few minutes, I realized that I was still standing there, alone, in the darkened hallway... thinking about Parker!

Shaking my head, I gathered my wits about me and headed out.

Chapter Seventy-Four

Lara

I hated that I had to send Noella to that magicless realm.

The day had been long, and the sense of worry weighed heavily on my mind.

I knew that Noella would recover quickly but it still felt wrong to have her go.

Making coffee was almost ritualistic. It had the same effect for me as burning sage.

Even if I didn't drink it, it smelled amazingly good when grinding and brewing. If I could, I'd climb inside the scent and lose myself there.

As the grinder worked it's magics, a book sitting askew on the shelf caught I eye.

It wasn't something that would ever be out of place unless a customer didn't put it back properly but there hadn't been anyone but me in the shop for the last few hours.

Pushing the book back into place, I noticed the coffee table had all of the magazines facing upside down.

"What the heck is going on?" I'd said it out loud, but I hadn't meant to.

A light wind brushed against the side of my face. The front door and windows were closed and the tinkling bell above the door didn't sound.

Glancing around to make sure I was still alone, I saw no one but couldn't shake the feeling that there was some presence there.

With racing thoughts, my nerves wouldn't settle. "Kindly show yourself," I called out. I had the oddest feeling that I wasn't alone.

A woosh of more air and an opaque figure hovered near the shelf that had been out of place.

Immediately recognizing the goddess, I stumbled for the words. "Oh, my... um, Goddess Hecate."

Dropping my eyes and bowing low, I made myself as small as possible.

"Rise dear child. My granddaughter's favored. You are worthy of my regard." Her voice was as eerily strange and heavenly as it had been the last time I'd heard it.

Hecate wasn't as solid as she had been during that first meeting. Her transparent appearance now was more of an echo.

I hadn't *seen* her coming in any vision, so I knew this had to be something that pertained to me directly.

"To what do I owe the honor, my Goddess?"

Surveying the room, the figure spun around in all directions. Certain we were indeed alone, she spoke.

"I am not permitted to interfere, but Noella is my darling, my favorite." She gave a coy smile with the knowledge that favorites were not to be voiced.

Smiling weakly, what else could I do? I was quite fond of Noella myself.

"Aion has shown those of us who helped create the loophole several versions of what could happen next. In all but one of them,

Noella gives in to the darkness of my line. Magics on that level is a gateway to letting the power own you."

My eyes grew wide at her implication. I knew just how much power Noella had.

Sometimes it even scared me a bit, but the thought of her being consumed by darkness was terrifying.

"My Goddess, what can I do?" I asked in earnest.

If there was anything I could do to help keep that from happening, I'd do it.

Gods, I'd just found her. I didn't want to lose her already.

"It will depend on what path each of those involved take. I am here to ask a favor of you, child."

The goddess paused while she waited for my answer. Her eyes glowed gold and energy rolled off her in waves.

Even if she was mostly translucent, the power seeping into the room had my skin tingling uncomfortably.

"Of course!" I said without giving it any thought.

If there was anything I could do to help keep Noella grounded, I would do it. Regardless of Hecate asking it of me or not.

"Do not take this lightly dear. It will be a difficult task. For a God or Goddess to ask a favor, they must tie themselves to one in return."

I turned this over in my mind for a few seconds. I hadn't a clue what a favor from a goddess might entail, but it was an intriguing offer.

What the Goddess was saying was that it might be the easy choice, or the most moral choice... or there may be other consequences because of the choice made.

The time would come when the fork in the future was upon me, and it wouldn't be wise not to think it through thoroughly.

The robust aroma of coffee wafted through the air, pulling me back from my mind's wanderings.

We were talking about Noella. If anything happened to her and I could have stopped it, I'd never forgive myself anyway.

"I accept. I will grant this favor in benefit of the greater good and my love." I wasn't sure my voice sounded as confident as my resolve, but Hecate beamed a radiant smile.

Roiling sparks simmered slightly around the area. The goddess would accidentally burn down my shop if she didn't leave soon.

Pushing my luck, I asked the only thing that mattered. "What's to happen, great Goddess? What am I to do? I can't *see* the outcome. I'm ashamed to say it but I'm frightened."

"When the time comes, you will know. It's a choice you will make to keep her safe. It may even prove to keep the others safe as well." Hecate began to fade away, but her voice still rang true. "When it is done, consider us bound. One favor for another. Thank you, Lara."

Ouch. A stinging sensation seared my arm, just inside the crook of my elbow.

Rolling up my sleeve, a tiny tattoo had appeared. It was a circle in the center of two quarter outward facing circles. The symbol of the Goddess herself.

It had a mild glow to it as the pain faded.

Tattoos had never been my thing, but the corners of my mouth peeled up as I admired the small piece of the Goddess' touch pressed upon my flesh.

Strange as it was, I really liked it. Not what it represented. Not that it was gods given. The ink itself.

Moving my arm this way and that, looking at it from different angles, it felt right.

Turned out, tattoos might have been my thing after all.

Chapter Seventy-Five

Lucian

I stood before three Meathlu. My instructions clear.

There were less than twenty-four hours until the Breaking and with only Caylum's ring, I needed the rest of Lagomshire distracted.

Mayhem must ensue and the only way I could do that was with the chaos violent crime sprees caused.

It was a necessary distraction. It would draw the eyes of the gods and the underworld hierarchy alike, but it had to be done.

These three were to instigate problems with the Meathlu in the area under my care without them realizing they were being coerced into unleashing their inner dark sides.

If I could get away with not implicating me in the process, it would serve my agenda if things didn't work out the way I'd planned.

The distraction needed to be big enough to cause upheaval, but not so big that the gods eyes would be drawn to the mayhem before the rings were brought together.

After that, they wouldn't interfere unless I allowed those under my new reign to run amuck the way they had before the banishment.

I'd rule with fear and an iron fist. There'd be no need for the gods to worry about my domain anymore.

These Meathlu didn't realize they were expendable. All the better for me.

I had bigger sights to focus on for my future kingdom.

If they died before getting a glimpse of it, so be it.

Caring was a weakness I'd cut from my heart when I severed Caylum's soul from this plane.

It was time to give purpose to the spot I'd created in his wake.

It was time to fill the void with darkness.

Chapter Seventy-Six

Zane

Noella shifted on the stool but didn't move to get off. I remained slightly in front of her.

I had never had a power that could help in a confrontation but that was why I'd trained hard to be ready for any fight.

Well, shit. That perfectly executed plan from the universe was fated well. A long game that ensured I'd be useful in a realm with suppressed magics.

The bar keep threw the rag over his shoulder and rocked back on his heels.

Threatening wasn't the vibe I'd gotten from him but the fact that he knew who Noella was just didn't sit right. Especially considering that we were in another realm.

"I'm pleased to finally meet you," the strange man said it to me like he met people from other realms all the time.

I couldn't get an accurate read on what he was.

His magics still worked here, but the drain coming off his body didn't seem rational. I wouldn't think anyone could survive what I saw.

If magics were like blood loss, he'd be bleeding out and replenishing all in the same instance.

The fact that this person was magical and radiated it as such, even in a realm that sucked the essence right from your bones, meant that he was extremely powerful.

With that in mind, I further angled my body in front of my cousin.

"How do you know me?" Apparently, Noella wasn't as thrown for a loop as I'd been.

"Come now. Don't you see the family resemblance?"

I'd barely registered his words before catching a movement in my peripheral vision.

Coming out of the shadows from around the corner was another magical being. The aura around the figure brighter than the barkeeps.

With my own magics stifled, I couldn't make out what he was either.

"Noella, Zane," the shadowed figure called out. A ray of light fell across his face as he entered the room.

My uncle came striding in like he hadn't been unaccounted for in the past week and a half, smiling from ear to ear.

Noella couldn't contain her relief and irritation with her father. It simmered blue and red around her magical aura while I was trying to get my bearings.

"I suppose you have no idea how close we are cutting it?" Her voice was shaking but still held bite. "Why are you still here? You should have been back days ago."

Draxus's face fell. It was like watching the air being let out of a balloon.

He turned to the bar keep. "How is it she looks so much like her mother and yet her grandmother's voice comes out of her mouth?"

The man smirked but his eyes warned the demigod not to push it. Odd that a being from this realm would understand what Draxus had meant at all.

"Our mother does have that way about her, doesn't she?" he said.

My head snapped to his face and then down at Draxus. A sheepish grin curled up the edges of his mouth.

"Noella, you remember your Uncle Ezolus, my brother?"

Noella gaped, open mouthed, at her father's declaration.

I didn't know what to make of it, or him. The fact that I couldn't smell any alcohol wafting off of Draxus was something new.

He wasn't drunk, so he must have known what he was saying.

"You're my uncle?" Noella studied his face and the aura of his magics flared, just a little bit as he stared back at her.

The realization occurred to her a second later and she shifted in her seat to look at me straight on.

Well, fuck. Wasn't this a piece of delicious cake served on a trash can lid?

"Hello, Dad."

The tension was thick in the air but Ezolus grinned ear to ear.

He shared a quick glance with Draxus, nodded, and then turned back in my direction.

"I'm guessing you have questions son," he said, absentmindedly wiping at the countertop. "Shall I start from the beginning?"

Chapter Seventy-Seven

Riedyn

I'd met up with Oaken and Willow at the edge of the forests trail that led to Sidhterra.

They gave their reports on Lucian's lackies, and I wasn't surprised at all by the deteriorating loyalty from his minions.

Fear can only keep people under control for so long. Lucian had never understood that.

The forest animals were unusually quiet. The veil had begun pulling back more and more over the last week. Animals could sense these sort of things. It wouldn't be long now.

We waited half an hour passed the time we were to meet for Borias to show up. It wasn't like any of the EU to be late, let alone that late.

Something was wrong.

"He should have been here by now," Willow said with equal irritability and worry.

"Yes. He should have." After a moment, I twisted on my heels, heading in the direction of town.

"Where are you going?" Oaken asked.

Call it a gut feeling. Call it a failed knowing of a former relationship. Something wasn't right.

"I feel something is amiss. I'm going to see what that something might be." I began walking again, briskly this time. "You two stay here and wait for my orders."

I was only halfway back to the main road when I ran across Thelzion and Briella on their way in.

Brie's head hung low, but sorrow shined in Thelzion's eyes.

My gut plummeted, already suspecting what would cause them to come search me out.

"Tell me!" I demanded. "It was Lucian, wasn't it?"

The two demons silently shared an unspoken conversation before Thelzion placed a hand on my shoulder.

"It was. And... it was brutal," he said, not holding back. "I'm sorry."

Shrugging out from under Thelzion's hand, I headed towards the road without looking back. Lucian would pay for this with his life.

Brie was faster. She stood blocking me a heartbeat later.

I'd heard that Conservatrix demons had speed that could rival that of a vampire, but I'd never witnessed it before.

"Riedyn, you need to inform the Queen." Understanding saturated her tone. "This is something that the Commander of the Elite Unit must do. Not the vengeance of a former lover."

Placing a hand on my arm, her empathic radiance surged in a wave of calm from her straight into me.

I didn't want to let her take my pain or my rage but rationally, I knew I needed her to.

I be no good fighting with my emotions running wild. It'd only serve to get me killed.

"You're right," Deftly. I moved away from her touch. "I must tell my troops and Queen Talisin. It may change our involvement in the coming events."

Thelzion offered a nod but didn't say anything. Understanding written in the features of his face.

If circumstances had been different over the years, we may have been friends.

The woods were dark and the walk solemn. The trees had slight movement, but the air didn't shift as it usually did. The forest was in mourning.

Knowing I sent Borias to do what I was unwilling to do myself splintered directly into my heart.

Willow and Oaken would be the first of many to see my shame and feel the pain of loss.

General Ashwood would be insufferable. My brother was a great general, but he had never had any familial empathy. He would only see my failure and berate me endlessly.

I deserved it. Borias was a great warrior. A fae who followed my command and met his end because I'd been a coward.

Lucian would pay for taking his life, but first, I needed to suffer the consequences of failing my team.

Chapter Seventy-Eight

Jaxson

Walking towards the shops in downtown, I thought about what Quinn had said.

Here I was, heading into another one of Lucian's schemes that I didn't have the full picture of, yet willing to rough up some poor defenseless person to get what the boss needed.

Inner conflict reared its head. Demon or not, the fact of the matter was Lucian never divulged enough information.

I knew that taking orders came with a no questions asked policy.

That didn't make it sit any better when Quinn and even Parker had started seeing fault with Lucian.

Now I had to wonder if I was doing the right thing in following blindly. My locked away darkness reared its head at the thought of chaos.

Reaching the shop I was told to go to; I'd opened the door without realizing it.

The chime of the tinkling bell sounded throughout the space. A woman with a kind face came from around the corner of a bookcase and smiled at me.

Yeah, I'd played the dick in Lucian's story many times and here I was again, a pawn in his schemes. Seven hells!

"Hello there. How can I help you?" she said.

It wasn't that I wanted to be mean but the need to send a message and doing Lucian's bidding rang through my head. I was a demon and needed to act the part.

Smiling at her, I reached one hand out and yank hard. The shelf closest to me came tumbling down with a loud crash.

Her hands flew to her mouth while I continued with my horrible grin.

"It looks like remodeling might be in order," I said. "Should I start with the next shelf?"

She dropped her hands from her face. I could see the resolve. The courage that more than likely wasn't in her repertoire.

Stepping forward, the sweet thing gave me a weak smile. "Yes. Thank you." Her hands shaking, she took a steadying breath. "That would be fine."

Tightening my eyes in wonder, this hadn't been what I'd expected.

Usually by this time the pleading would come, soon followed by the begging. Honestly, her attitude was refreshing.

That little niggling voice of chaos inside me stirred.

It wasn't often that it made its way to the surface. I kept it locked up tight behind wall after wall.

The last time I'd unleashed it, the havoc it wreaked was talked about in the demon communities for a century.

"Where's the book?" I said with a snarl.

"I don't know which book you're referring to." She gestured to all of the shelves and books that lined them. "You'll have to be more specific."

Cheeky little thing. An evil curl of my lips crept onto my dark face. The menacing beast inside raised its head in delight.

My steps towards her were deliberate and calculating. Intimidation had always been my specialty, but she stood her ground. "Interesting."

Inner Jax growled and broke through the first wall. He was dying to be uncaged.

I leaned into him slightly and it gave me pause. What the fuck?

With a shake of my head, I tried again to show her that I meant business without resorting to the horrors I knew myself capable of.

"I think you know which one I'm talking about. We can do this the hard way if you like." I toppled another shelf. "I just didn't think it'd be something you'd enjoy."

The woman took a step backwards and I mirrored the movement.

Her hands went to the side of the table behind her. Something caught my eye with the small gesture she made.

As she tried to nonchalantly arrange the papers on the table, I noticed an indentation at the edge to one side.

Roughly pushing her aside, she fell into one of the puff chairs that laid around us with a huff.

Running a finger over the notch a hidden compartment came into view. The inner demon purred.

An old cloth covered a rectangle I knew had to be the book. Excellent.

Slowly, I unwrapped it. Fingers grazing the cover, a hiss of pain escaped my lips.

That moment of distraction was my undoing. The inner chaos demon seized its opportunity and crashed through another wall.

It was so close to the surface now. My mind splintered for a breath. Cracks formed along the cage walls.

My hand flew out and wrapped around her neck. It wasn't something that I'd usually have done.

The fact that she hadn't warned me about the books' defenses pissed me off.

No... that wasn't right. It pissed *him* off.

Her hands clawed futilely at her throat. Constricting her breathing, I watched on, like a passenger in my own body.

As she went still, I dropped my hand like I'd been burned.

Checking for a pulse, I breathed a sigh of relief when it thumped lightly against my fingertips.

Lucian needed her alive and I'd almost fucked that up. He'd have had my head before I could finish telling him what I'd done.

My dark side was too close to breaking free.

It whispered in my ear, trying to gain my trust. Trying to be let loose.

I was tired. Not on a physical level but in a bone deep sort of way.

The others didn't know just how hard I had to work at keeping *him* in check.

The missions I had to do while having some semblance of decency and the arduous task of keeping my inner chaos demon locked firmly away was draining.

Being a length demon meant giving in to all of the evils that existed on this plane. I was tired of fighting my nature.

Bending over her unconscious form, I brushed the hair from her face. The finger marks bruising the delicate features of her throat would be there for days.

There was nothing I could do about that.

Wrapping the book back up in the cloth and securing it inside my jacket, I scooped her up into my arms and carried her towards the front door.

With a glance over my shoulder, I surveyed the shop. There was enough damage to send the message.

Doing more wouldn't serve any purpose other than mindless destruction. My inner demon purred in my ear. "Aww, come now. That's where the fun lies. Give into it."

Shaking my befuddled head, I replied out loud, "I am better than that." Closing my eyes, my cheek rested against the female's hair. "I am better than you."

The chaos inside me hissed but said no more.

I walked out the door into the night with the still form of a kind and gentle person weighted in my arms.

How could I be cruel and a better person at the same time?

I felt a smirk from within. It purred again, "You can't."

The crack walls in my mind gave a slowly. vibrating quake as the beast began to laugh.

Then the walls shattered completely.

Chapter Seventy-Nine

Lucian

Saevus appeared in the shadows of my office out of thin air.

Even after centuries of him doing it, I was always caught by surprise. My wards were the strongest known to this realm.

If I'd had any pet peeves at all, it would be being caught unaware. It was unsettling.

"To what do I owe the pleasure, my Liege?" Keeping my voice bored. My movements casual.

Saevus stepped into the low light coming from a lamp on the ornate desk in the study. His form menacing even in its stillness.

"The Breaking is tomorrow. I wanted to see what my faithful subject was doing with his time." The upper-level demon sounded bored as well.

I knew all too well, the act was a way to instill a false sense of security in one's inferiors. It was Saevus who'd taught it to me eons ago.

"Everything is as it always is. The Meathlu are causing just enough mayhem to keep them evil but not enough to draw the attention of the gods. The demons in my charge are performing well in their respective areas. And the humans are none the wiser."

Saevus strode over to the desk and swiped two fingers over its surface. The corner of his mouth drew up to meet the scar on one side of his ugly face.

He'd made a bit to overthrow his own boss a thousand years or so ago. It hadn't ended well for him.

"I suppose keeping a tidy house keeps you busy then?"

I raised an eyebrow but didn't reply. Upper-level demons tended not to have any sense of humor. My sarcasm would be lost on him.

"A tidy house and a tight ship go hand in hand."

He chuckled and the sound rubbed me the wrong way.

"Ah, I think that with all of your," he cleared his throat, "sophistication these last few decades, you've forgotten that chaos is where demons reign."

Thinking over my next words carefully, I stood and rounded the desk to be face to face with my boss. Reign had been a pointed word to use.

"Sophistication and civility are two very different things. I assure you."

He looked down a few inches to stare me directly in the eyes. It wasn't for the first time that I felt I was being measured by his power.

He was nearly seven feet tall, and it radiated from every pore. The annoyingly tall hell's spawn had been a thorn in my side since my essence came together to form a soulless demon.

Backing down was seen as weakness and I wouldn't give Saevus that satisfaction.

If all went as planned, I would be the king of demons on this plane soon and wouldn't have to contend with him for much longer.

"It would be nice to stir up some trouble tomorrow," he said.

I held my breath. Had he found out about my plan?

Saevus smirked, probably mistaking my vexed expression for incredulity. "The gods will be distracted. It would go unnoticed. Within reason, of course... maybe you should give your subjects a small amount of leeway for a short time? Let them have some fun."

As to not prolong this visit or draw unwanted suspicion, I didn't argue.

"I shall take that under advisement." Little did he know, I'd intended my Meathlu's to do a lot more than cause a little mayhem.

The poor bastard will be in heaps of trouble from his boss for at least another century because of my power grab.

If things didn't work out as planned, this meeting could give me the scapegoat I needed to stay off of higher-up's radar.

Even thinking about my goals not coming to fruition felt like a bad omen. I wasn't going to dwell on that possibility.

Appeasing him could work in my favor. "The mayhem would be the perfect reward for their continued efforts to be good little mischief makers."

Raising his hand and waving it in agreement, Saevus stepped back into the shadows. "Serve well, Lucian."

And with that, he was gone.

Serving well was the last thing that I would be doing in the future.

Being served by all of demon kind was what I had my sights on.

No more following the rules. It was time to make a new world.

Chapter Eighty

Draxus

The tension felt like a living thing in the room all of a sudden.

Looking between Zane, Noella, and Ezolus, I stepped to my nephew's side and placed a reassuring hand on his shoulder.

My brother did what needed to be done for the fate of the realms but faced with a father and son who'd never met, I knew I had done Zane a real injustice.

It was my fault he'd never gotten to know his father.

"Ezolus is the Keeper of the Reverto Akasha. He came to this realm to keep it safe after a meeting with Hecate and Aion." I shifted towards Noella. "You were nineteen when Ezolus took up the task of keeping the ring safe. It was after I took you to meet with the Fae Queen and we'd discovered this realm might hold possibilities. I'm surprised that you don't remember him."

Clapping Zane firmly on the back, I sat down and faced my brother. "Do you want to fill in the details here or should I?"

A bottle of brown liquor in hand, Ezolus poured three glasses and grabbed a bottle of water, handing it to me.

"I didn't want to do it, leave you and your mother, I mean," Ezolus said after downing the drink in one go. "Draxus and I fought over who'd be the Keeper."

His eyes were far away. The past had a funny way of burying you six foot deep when piss poor choices chased you into the shadows.

I cleared my throat. My brother hadn't deserved the pain and loneliness he'd been given with this burden. "Um, yeah... well, we decided that I'd stay in Lagomshire. Noella was only nineteen years old and I couldn't bring myself to leave her. She wouldn't be strong enough to endure the Fountain at that age and still retain her immortality."

"The Fountain?" she asked.

A slight nod from Ezolus and I continued. He was the Keeper. If he didn't want me to tell the story, I wouldn't.

"The Fountain of Youth. It's what keeps the magics in this realm low."

I shifted on the barstool, my posture suddenly feeling stiff. Opening the bottle of water, I took in half in one long pull before starting again.

"The humans that are in this realm believe that the Fountain of Youth here in St Augustine is a water source. One that has healing properties to combat aging. The truth is, it's an essence siphon. It makes their skin a touch smoother but sucks the magics and the life forces from every living being in this realm."

Noella's hand went to her mouth. Zane stared at me like I must have been telling some sort of terrible joke.

Ezolus took the glasses and washed them up with the rag he'd had over his shoulder, almost bored. I couldn't blame him.

He'd been the Keeper for centuries. The constant magics drain and replenishment as a demigod was horrible. I'd been here two weeks, and it felt like forever already.

"Why?" Noella struggled with words. "Why would that even be a thing?" she finally managed to say.

It was Ezolus who spoke up. "As harsh as it sounds, it's a necessity. The Ghostly plane is the only thing that separates this one from the Underworld. It takes a lot of force to keep the barrier intact."

My brilliant, beautiful daughter gasped. Realization shone through her bright eyes.

"Is that why we could see so many spirits wondering the streets here?" she said. "We couldn't understand why there'd be so many souls at unrest but that makes sense if there are cracks."

Ezolus' face darkened slightly. "I am only one Demigod. I can't keep everything in its place."

I patted her shoulder and glared at my brother.

"Oh, no. That's not what I meant," her voice cracked a little at the end. "I was just trying to understand."

Zane had been quiet through the discussion. He'd laid a hand on top of Noella's and turned to face his father.

"Why didn't you come for me? After you found out my mother was with child, why didn't you come for me?" he seethed.

Ezolus looked uncomfortable but he didn't drop his gaze.

I was sure Zane could see the lines on his face. The dull color of his skin. The way he looked haggard next to me.

He was my younger sibling, but his body didn't look it.

"I couldn't. If I left this plane after bringing the Reverto Akasha ring here, even briefly, the barrier I created would bust wide open. The Breaking was foretold but not to be allowed before its time."

Ezolus's eyes pleaded for some understanding from his son. I knew he'd loved Zane's mother.

It was one of the biggest reasons we'd fought over who would come here and who'd stay in Lagomshire.

In the end, we weren't given any choice.

Finally looking away, he lowered his voice to almost a whisper.

"I had only found out that your mother was with child hours before I was to leave Lagomshire. Everything had already been decided. The gods don't change their minds easily. It's the biggest regret of my long existence. That I wasn't there for you." His eyes held unfallen tears briming at their rim.

After a few minutes of awkward silence, he cleared his throat and straightened up.

"I'm sorry. I couldn't let the barrier break. If it did, then it would only be a matter of time before many spirits and eventually demons, made it into Lagomshire. I was entrusted to protect the ring. I thought that this was the best way to protect you and your mother and everyone else that I cared about."

He gave me a tiny nod and went to the back wall.

Tapping twice on one side, then flicking three times on the other, he placed his fingertips in the center.

Magics hummed. The brick shimmied its way from the wall and Ezolus reached inside.

When he brought his hand out, a small box inlaid with twining serpents, lay in his palm. The snakes wrapped around the box and each other in a never ending flurry of movement.

Setting the box on the bar, he waved his hand over it and said words of unlocking in the language of the gods.

The snakes unwound and disappeared altogether. Opening the lid slowly, it revealed a glowing, ancient looking ring.

Noella's eyes lit up. A shadow of darkness shimmered over her face making Zane and I shudder.

Reaching for her hand, I gave it a quick squeeze, bringing her back from wherever shadows touched her mind.

A bashful smile played at her lips as she reached a hand towards the ring.

Ezolus snapped the cover of the box shut and she jumped back.

"The ring isn't to be touched before its time of use!" he said.

Zane looked from his father to me. The corners of his mouth turned down as understanding crept in.

"This is why you haven't come back yet, isn't it?"

Swirling emotion stirred in his eyes... sorrow, hurt... guilt, maybe? Zane looked back to his father.

"You said that this realm sucks life essence. Does that mean that your life force has been at a constant drain for centuries?" Horror took the place of anger in his heart. I could feel it at its source.

Ezolus' mouth became a tight line. He gave a small nod of his head.

"So, when we take the ring back, you'll be able to come with us and heal, right?" He knew the answer before it was fully out of his mouth.

Squeezing his shoulder, I shook my head.

"When we leave," I lifted my chin to Zane and Noella. "Ezolus will stay."

Zane looked like his feet had been knocked out from under him.

He'd gone from anger with his father to abject horror at his situation.

If I was feeling an aching emptiness. The emptiness of loss and sudden grief Zane must have felt? I couldn't imagine.

Noella looked to Ezolus. "Why can't you just come back with us? You'd heal and we could use your help."

He just shook his head. The look was almost pitying.

"Once you all leave with the ring, I'll have to use all of my remaining power to seal the portal to Lagomshire from this side," he said. "It will take so much of my magics that I'll be nearly mortal at that point for quite some time." One corner of his mouth curled up.

"This isn't funny!" Zane slammed his fist on the bar. "Why are you smiling?" Fumes rolled off him in waves.

Ezolus looked at his son, nothing but pride in his eyes, stretching a smile across his entire face.

"I'm smiling because I never thought I'd get to meet you." He leaned forward. "I'm smiling because I'm proud of the man sitting before me. That he would take the chance to save Lagomshire knowing the odds." He put a massive hand over Zane's. "I'm smiling because it will be the greatest honor of my life to seal this world and the demons off to help save my son."

There was no argument that could be visited, no alternative to the outcome. He'd seal his fate along with the demons.

"But... you could die." Zane's voice was barely above a whisper. Tears brimmed his lower eyelids but didn't spill over.

"I could," Ezolus said. "And if I do, I will go down fighting... for you."

He took the glasses back out and poured three more drinks.

I drank my water stoically. Noella knew me well enough to see the guilt and anguish below the façade.

As the minutes ticked by, we sat in near silence.

Once our drinks were finished, we'd finally came to face the facts that the Breaking was in a mere few hours, and we had to get back.

We still needed the Fainne Todhchai that Lucian had stolen from Caylum's tomb.

Ezolus came from behind the bar and hugged Noella. She hugged him back as a single tear rolled down her cheek.

I clasped arms with my brother and pulled him in for an embrace. Clapping him on the back, I was grateful that I'd gotten to spend the last couple of weeks with him.

When he got to Zane, he stood awkwardly, not knowing how to interact with the son he'd never known.

It was Zane who broke the tension.

He wrapped his arms around Ezolus in a bear hug and Ezolus returned the gesture.

A light glow surrounded them. Noella and I could feel the love radiating from the energy.

They broke apart and Ezolus tapped his son's shoulder with his fist. His color had come back a little. Some of the lines in his face had diminished as well.

Picking up the ring box off the counter, we all headed to the door.

Ezolus spared one final glance at the place he'd called home for the last several centuries.

With a sigh, he closed the door behind us as we all walked off into the night.

Chapter Eighty-One

Hayden

"Hayden!" Someone was shouting and shaking my arm. "Hayden, what's wrong?"

My eyes began to focus, and unease took hold of my senses.

"You okay?" Kraigen said.

"What happened?" I asked.

Panic had crept into my voice.

"We were just talking, and it was like you'd fallen into a daydream, but you started shouting." Kraigen shook my head. "You scared the shit out of me, man."

I started to apologize when the recollection of the foreshadowing slapped me in the face.

"I have to go." My face was flush, and emotions were running amuck.

I'd never had a foreshadowing take me into a daydream state to get its point across.

I knew that powers grew over time, but this felt like a pull, not a growth.

"Where? What's happened?" The older man looked like he would protest but I shook his head, laid some money on the table, and side stepped the diner owner.

Calling over my shoulder, I said, "I have to go make sure Lara is safe. I just have a feeling..." I trailed off.

Kraigen gave a quick nod, and I was out the door.

I ran. Ran for all I was worth.

It unnerved me how vivid the sight of Lara being held captive by some big thug was.

Normally, my foreshadowing's only happened when I was asleep at night. And they were never this acute.

There was no fork, no choice. This was something entirely different.

The feeling in the pit of my stomach was hollow. I knew, even before I rounded the corner of the shop's street, I would be too late.

Coming to the door and yanking it open, the sight before me was just what I'd anticipated.

Shelves were knocked over. Objects smashed. The store was in total disarray.

There was no sign of Lara anywhere.

Hurrying to the spot she had shown me that she'd been keeping the book, it was open and empty.

She'd trusted I would keep every secret we had ever had between us.

We were never meant to be lovers, but she was my absolute best friend and now she was missing.

Something inside of me shattered as I dropped to my knees.

The vision of the person holding her unconscious body was crystal clear in my mind. He was one of Lucian's demons.

A scream of rage pulsed out and away from my body. The energy vibrated like a shock wave.

It was an hour before midnight. The pizzeria a few shops down was still open and a few of the other shops were just closing up for the night.

Maybe someone saw something. Maybe if I knew what direction they'd gone in, I could follow?

A swishing sound reached through my haze and into my ears as I got to my feet.

Two shadows appeared just outside the door. Picking up a dagger off the shelf to my right, I took an enraged step forward.

Then halted.

Brie and Thelzion entered the shop and just a few seconds later there was another shadowed figure... Kali.

They must have all vected here. I didn't know how or why but I was grateful.

"What happened here?" Thelzion looked as unhinged as I felt.

"What was that energy blast?" Kali asked.

Confused, I gestured to the surrounding chaos.

"Lara was taken! By one of Lucian's demons." I practically snarled out. I'd never felt this helpless before. Or this angry.

"Were you here?"

Of course, Thelzion would think that. Me, a mere gifter, was here and didn't do everything in my power to keep it from happening?

"NO!" I shouted, pissy as my voice would allow. "I Foresaw it and ran here as fast as I could from the diner... I was too late."

My head hung at the realization that I'd been given the *sight* and was still too late.

Gods, pathetically useless should have been stamped on my forehead.

"That still doesn't explain how we felt that energy blast that created the pull here." Kali said, shuffling her feet.

Brie walked over and wrapped her arms around me. Solace rolled off of her and into me.

Gently as I could, not to offend her, I pushed her away.

"I wasn't fast enough and now she's missing, Brie," I said. "I don't deserve your comfort."

"What do we know?" Thelzion was all business.

He had no time for emotions when there was a mission at hand. In this moment, I appreciated that immensely.

"I was at the diner chatting with Kraigen. I fell into some sort of daydream. When he shook me out of it, I knew that it was more vivid than anything I'd ever felt. I ran all the way here and found that the shop was a mess and Lara and the book were missing." I lowered my head in self-flagellation. "I dropped to my knees in rage and heartache and then felt a pulse of energy shoot out from my core... then you guys showed up."

Just as I finished, another shadow appeared at the door.

Bastian came bounding into the room and halted at the sight before him.

"What in the Seven Hells happened?" he exclaimed. "I was down the street at the pub having a drink before our meeting and BOOM! I was hit with some sort of urgent energy pull."

"You felt it? That far over?" Kali said. "And it pulled you here too?"

"Too? You guys had that same pull? No one around me did. I thought maybe I'd had too much to drink but I'd only finished a single pint."

Brie walked over to the Runed bowl and looked inside. Her mind worked quickly.

"I think that Hecate must have tied us together in this," she said. "And Hayden's Foreshadowing gift is close enough to Lara's Seer gift to send him the vision, since Lara can't get visions that pertain to herself."

Thelzion rubbed the scruff on his chin, thinking her words through.

"That makes sense." His voice was rough with concern. "It still doesn't explain how we were summoned here by Hayden's rage."

It was Bastian who chimed in. He'd often sat back and let others talk but more and more lately, his gift of Deblocking expanded.

It let him unlock things that were puzzling.

He felt it like a bunch of knotted shoestrings he'd once explained it to me. His mind worked them one at a time until the knots were all untangled.

"I think it does," he said. "If Hecate did indeed tie us together for this, then it stands to reason that we have an energetically magical bond."

"What, like Noella has magics and we're sharing it?" Kali asked curiously.

That was an interesting take, but it didn't feel quite right.

"No. I think it's from Hecate herself. She is the Goddess of Sorcery." His face scrunched up in concentration for another moment. "If I am correct, then the energy Hayden let out came from a place of love and anguish. And what is more chaotic than love? There's power in it that evil tends to overlook."

"I think you may be right." Thelzion glanced at Brie. "So, what do we do now? Zane and Noella haven't returned yet."

Kalina shifted her weight from one foot to the other. Brie reached over and took her hand.

"They're fine," she said. "I'm sure they'll be back any time now."

She looked at the clock on the wall and sighed. We still had three hours or so before the meeting was supposed to take place and only a handful of hours after that before the Breaking was to occur.

Thelzion's eyes went wide, like he just remembered something important and couldn't believe he'd forgotten it.

"Where's the ring?" he demanded. "I know Lara and the book are gone but did he get the Akasha Exolo too?"

Snapping out of my pain long enough for it to register the possibilities the other's had been discussing, I ran to a shelf in one of the cases that held different crystals and various metaphysical objects.

Pulling a crystal ball down and turning the stand over, I tapped in a code. A compartment popped opened revealing the cloth that contained the powerful ring.

A collective sigh of relief went around the room.

"It's still here," I said. "The bastard must not have known it was in the shop."

Relief washed through me. At least we weren't totally lost yet.

"Did the vision show you what the demon who took Lara looked like?" Brie asked tentatively.

"It did. He was tall. Muscular build. Dark complexion. And seemed to be at odds with himself."

I bounced from foot to foot. I couldn't dispel this useless energy.

"What do you mean?" Bastian hadn't said anything for a bit. "How?"

I thought long and hard about how to put it. In my head it was clear as day but voicing it wasn't as easy.

"I mean, it was as if he was fighting an internal war and in the end, he'd lost."

Thelzion swore. Brie hung her head and put a hand on Thelzion's wrist.

"It sounds like Jax. He's worked so hard over the last century and a half to keep his ruthless side in check," Thelzion said. "It sounds like he's lost the battle."

"And this is bad?" Kali asked.

Brie turned to her sister. Kali grew up with Jax coming in and out of the manor. She had worked with him on many missions for Lucian.

It must be hard for her right now, reconciling the two sides of herself.

The fact that Lucian raised her and his minions were her allies and then switching sides and working against them had to be hard.

"Jaxson was about as evil and vicious a demon as there ever was. He made a vow to himself, long before we were born, after a certain massacre, to lock that side of himself up tight. He'd been hit with a hex that caused him to feel all of the hopes and dreams of the people that he'd hurt." Brie paused and her mind seemed a million miles away.

Thelzion picked up were Briella left off. "Jax isn't a good demon. He's just been trying his hardest to outrun the curse. It wasn't meant to last this long but I think that he'd been doing the fake it until you make it thing for too long."

He then turned to face Brie. "If his other side has been unleashed, we're in for a lot more problems than we'd planned for."

"What do you mean?" she said.

"Jax is loyal to Lucian... not demonkind. Lucian. He tried to maintain his chain of command spiel for the sake of keeping his langth chaos side locked away and justify doing the vampires bidding." He shook his head. "If he's back... if Jax is really back, then we are up against a whole different beast. He's unhinged. Jaxson's true self is Lucian's greatest asset."

Kali didn't say anything for a few long minutes. Her normal, bubbly energy dimmed. She seemed as lost inside her head as the rest of us were.

The quiet around us was endless. The smell of the pizza and garlic coming from a few doors down wafted into the door of the shop.

Standing and facing the room at large, she headed toward the door.

"Where are you going?" Brie called out.

"I'm going to get us some cheesy goodness, " she said. "And then I'm coming back here and we're going to pick ourselves up off the floor and make a plan to kick these Gods Damned demons back to the seven circles!"

With a flip of her hair and a smile her lips, she was gone.

I admired her hope and her fortitude, even if I didn't feel it myself.

Bastian smiled at Brie. "Your sister is about the best thing to happen to this group since we all met."

Brie cracked a smile of her own. "She truly is."

Chapter Eighty-Two

Riedyn

Riedyn arrived at the court with his head hung low. The Queen was seated on the dais and the crowd around it was thick. Approaching the throne, he finally looked up to meet the Fae Queen's eyes. A quick glance to her left had him biting down the disdain that rose to the surface of his thoughts. His brother, General Ashwood, was in attendance and he had to deliver the news of Lt Borias' demise in front of him.

"Your Majesty," he said.

"Commander Riedyn. You're just in time to see your brother off to the outskirts of Sidhterra to make sure that our borders are secure." She tilted her head sideways after noting his head still hung in subjugation. "What is it, Commander? Why the solemness?"

"My Queen, Borias is dead."

She gasped like he'd slapped her. "By who's hand?" she demanded.

"From what I have gathered, Lucian's own."

General Ashwood stepped forward. His hulking size towered over Riedyn as he remained humbled before his Queen.

"You allowed one of your Elite Unit to die under your supervision?... Pathetic," the General tsked.

"My Queen, I take full responsibility for his demise. I should have followed Lucian myself but I was needed to be in better placement for the task you set me." Riedyn felt nothing but guilt and hatred inside him. For Lucian. For himself. "I should have known the treachery of the Donnchadh would prove lethal. I am to blame for this failing."

"You should be stripped of your command and beaten..." General Ashwood was silenced by Queen Talisin with a single finger raised to stop him from his tirade.

"Did you put into place the measures of the task that I'd assigned you, Commander?" she said.

"Yes, your Majesty. The others are following the..." he looked towards his brother. He didn't know how much of the EU's mission the Queen shared with the General so he didn't want to reveal anything prudent. "They are following down the rabbit hole."

The Queen nodded her understanding and Ashwood looked daggers at his brother. The General was in command of her army but Riedyn was the leader of the special unit that acted on a separate level. She looked over at the General and smiled.

"General Ashwood, thank you for your continued service. I hope the trail is mild and the journey tranquil." She waved her hand and he knew he was dismissed.

"Thank you, my Queen." The General turned on his heels and started towards the outer doors. Riedyn watched him go. Just before reaching the door, he cocked his head over his shoulder and sneered. Then he was gone.

"Commander Riedyn, I accept your responsibility for the demise of Lt Borias. You made a difficult call in the line of duty and he died honoring his Queen and his realm. He will have full honors bestowed upon his name and his family." Her tone may have sounded cold and distant but he knew her well enough to recognize the sadness inside.

"Thank you, your Majesty. And how shall we proceed with the cause? Shall there be retribution for the act?" Riedyn stared intently at her face, not breaking eye contact.

"The EU has remained a force to be reckoned with under your command. I would like it to remain that way." She thought for a moment before she continued. "We need to concentrate on the upcoming Breaking... help the others to do what needs to be done." She took a long sip of Faery wine from her glass. "Once we've secured our people after the Breaking, if there's anything left of the vampire king, then I want you to take his head." She smiled a rueful smirk and waved a hand at him in dismissal.

Commander Riedyn headed towards the outer opening of the court. He knew she meant it as a punishment for Lucian, but he also knew that it was her own, slightly cruel, way of punishing him too.

Chapter Eighty-Three

Quinn

The Breaking was less than a few hours from starting. The veil was a separate issue.

With its thinning, more Dhalls were able to see the shadowrealm creatures in their midst.

Chaos had been ongoing for hours now. Meathus ran amuck. Death, blood, and carnage covered the outlying areas as I'd made my way back to the manor.

Nothing too out of sorts had been happening within the city limits yet, but that would change quickly once the Breaking occurred and vast numbers of demons from the underworld made their way through the crack.

Lucian's feet made no sound as he approached the painting on the wall of the study. Lifting it to the side, he pressed his palm to the access pad. A quick scan later and the door swung open.

From my vantage point in the chair, I couldn't see inside of it, but I knew it was where he'd kept all of the most important things he cared about.

He turned to face me with a hard look planted firmly upon his stupidly beautiful face.

A predator in every sense of the word. His beauty was meant to draw you in, and his strength and teeth were weapons once they did.

"I'm glad to see that you've come to your senses, Quinn." He sat back down in the chair behind the desk and gazed at the Fainne Todhchai now in his hand.

The thin cloth between the ring and his flesh provided little protection from the gods made relic.

Small whiffs of smoke wafted in my direction from the burn of his skin, but he held onto the ring all the same.

"What?" I stuttered. "What do you mean?"

Nerves frayed, the hairs on the back of my neck stood on end.

"You can't possibly think that there's anything that goes on with those in my charge that escapes my attention, do you?"

His smirk was a taunt, and I had to be smart if I wanted to live past my next few breaths.

Choosing my next words with great care, I decided that lying would only make it worse.

Weaving a truth that centered around a lie would be my only shot, no matter how small.

"I'm sorry. I was confused," I practically tripped over my words. "I know you like your secrets, but chain of command dictates that I..."

He was in my face in less than a blink, spitting and red faced. So close I could feel it like a living thing, separate than Lucian himself.

"Chain of command dictates that I am your liege!" He so rarely lost control that it unnerved me in more ways than one. "I am the only one that matters on this plane of existence, or have you forgotten that?"

I thought quickly through the next few moves in my head.

If I pushed; I was dead.

If I agreed too quickly; I was dead.

If the wrong answer fell from my lips; I was dead.

"My apologies, Lucian," I said. "I didn't have the whole picture, but I should have trusted that you would know more of the situation than I did."

His breathing was still erratic. Heart beating faster in his neck than it should be, the redness in his face began to recede.

He stepped back just enough to straighten up and compose himself slightly.

"I would have thought that after all these years in my service, my leadership wouldn't be one that you'd feel needed to be justified," he said quietly.

Glancing at the set of his shoulders, I took in the weight of the ring still firmly in his grasps.

His eyes were downcast and sad. I'd never imagined such an emotion could come from this ruthless vampire.

Reaching out with my demon senses, I could feel the gravity of his aura and the pain that flowed in rivulets around it.

"You're right," I said. Lifting my hands in surrender. "I'm sorry. I wasn't thinking. Of course, you'd have reasons beyond what I can see." Rising to my feet, I stood before him, head bowed.

Lucian blew out a long breath that I hadn't realized he'd been holding. His heart rate returned to a normal level and the adrenaline that I'd smelled coursing through his veins burned off quickly.

"I can't have this much discord in my inner circle." He shook his head like he really believed we were supposed to be loyal to him, not his position. "You wounded me, Quinn. I thought we understood each other."

"You're right, Lucian. It was my mistake. It won't happen again." My fingers remained crossed behind my back.

It was old magics, an out clause. I just hoped it worked. The blood oath that I'd made with Parker was more binding than the half lie I gave to him.

He looked me over one more time. The wrinkles at the corners of his eyes softened a bit.

"The Breaking will be just the beginning. I need the Akasha rings to open the cracks wider and keep them open." He paused, deciding what more to reveal to me. "If all goes according to my plans, I will become the King of Demons on this plane." Intensely staring, he arched an eyebrow. "Do you understand what that will mean?"

Shaking my head, I felt the weight of his glare like a pile of stones.

"It means, that as my *official* second, you will be my closest advisor and trusted liaison." He smirked at the incredulity that spread across my face. "It means that I will trust you more than I am used to trusting anyone."

The thought of being someone he trusted was all that I'd wanted for well over a century.

Pride in my duties and the hierarchy of demonkind warred with my need to be validated by this heartless demon in front of me.

Shifting my weight from one foot to the other, I cocked my head to the side and made my decision.

I'd walked into this room with valiant and lofty goals of hiding my true intent of turning him over to Saevus. Now, I was climbing the ladder of the future.

I'd make sure that it was in the benefit of demonkind or else the blood oath would claim me.

"I have one question," I asked, hoping not to incur his wrath. "If by some chance we can't get the rings and open the floodgates from the Underworld, what will we do then?"

He didn't like to be questioned but at the same time, he'd wanted me to be his advisor.

That meant he'd have to learn to be more patient and forthcoming if I was meant to help him.

Lucian returned to the chair behind the desk. As he steepled his fingers and rested his chin upon them, I could tell that he was giving my words actual thought this time.

He wasn't placating me with the façade of his normal leadership role.

"If that happens, albeit the smallest of chance's," he said finally leaning forward to look me in the eyes. "Then the veil will be lifted. Chaos will still reign."

Gazing far off out the window for a few moments, he added, "There are always avenues to be exploited."

Pouring two glasses of demon mead from a decanter on the desk, he handed me one and took up the other.

"Those who don't know of the Shadowrealm will be scared. And you know how intoxicating fear can be." He lifted his glass for an in-air cheers and we both took a sip.

"So, we will still try to control all of them?" I asked.

"Quinn, my dear, there are those who belong to the Shadowrealm that don't even know what they are. With the veil lifted, and more demons pouring out of the Underworld than usual..." he let his eyes gleam with seeing something far away.

If my instincts were right, the benefits I'd reap would outweigh the risks.

Sighing a contented sound, he chuckled.

"The Dhalls will be begging the gifters for help. Some will let fear turn to hate. And hate can always be cultivated. And us... we'll be ripping apart their new reality." He lifted his glass once again and downed the rest of its contents.

"Then, here's to whatever future we may have... My King!"

Chapter Eighty-Four

Noella

Zane and Ezolus walked behind Draxus and I on the way back to the portal.

I could sense my father's diminishment from being there only less than two weeks. I couldn't imagine the centuries of drain that Ezolus had endured.

The feeling of my magics just below the surface was constant but it was like a layer of solid stone lay between them and my reach. An awful feeling, not painful but just at that edge of hurting.

"How do those with magics in this realm endure this torture?" I asked, turning to my uncle.

"Very few can do more than low magics in this realm. They are connected to the lands and elements closely here."

I walked a few more steps before turning again. Crafty, that one.

"That still didn't answer my question though."

Ezolus chuckled. "I guess it didn't." He stopped walking and took off his socks and shoes. Zane and I stared at him like he was crazy.

Digging his toes into the ground, he reached over and placed a hand on one of the tall trees to the side of the path.

"They practice grounding. The land has a heartbeat, for those who are willing to listen." He began putting his shoes back on. "It helps them attune to the magiks in the air and takes the edge off of the essence drain. They have also discovered that different natural crystals have various properties that help for different things."

He pulled some stones out of his pocket. I recognized a few of them... tigers eye, amethyst, quartz.

"We have those too, but I didn't realize they would work here."

Zane took the tigers eye from his father's hand and turned it over a few times. "What does this one help with?" he asked.

"That one's main aid comes in the form of grounding and protection." Ezolus reached over and took it back. "It has helped me greatly when I can't get away to ground to the land properly."

He put all of the crystals back into his pocket and patted them, like it was some sort of unconscious ritual.

We approached the portal, noticing the dulling of the colors around its immediate area right away this time.

"What happens after we leave?" Zane's voice cracked at the end. "It's only a few hours until the Breaking begins."

Ezolus put his hand on his sons shoulder. The air felt like it thickened.

"I have a magical friend who will help me do all that I can to maintain the breach from this side. It will be up to you guys on that side to keep those rings from the wrong hands. The prophecy was vague."

Draxus rolled his eyes. "They always are," he said to his brother. "Those aunts and uncles of ours just love crypticness."

"Is that even a word?" Ezolus smiled over at him.

Laughing, they both sighed in that same familial way.

"I'm a demigod. It's a word if I say it is." Draxus returned the smile.

Zane's nervous energy had his hands shaking. "If we can make this right… if we stop the prophecy's full brunt you can come…"

"I can't son." Ezolus cut him off. "Even if the Breaking only lifts the veil and the fissure to the Underworld doesn't bust open completely, I can't unseal the portal. I have built a life here with people that I care about. I have to stay here and fight for a future that the people of this land can maintain."

He laid a hand on the side of Zane's face before he continued and Zane reached up to hold it there.

"These witches will be more powerful than they ever have but they'll still need my help keeping the demons and spirits in check. I won't have any spare magics to unseal it, Zane. I'm sorry."

With tears brimming his eyes again for the second time in an hour, Zane reached over and pulled his father in for a heartfelt embrace.

After patting each other on the back a few times, they stepped away, but Ezolus left his hand clamped on his son's shoulder.

"I will hold the Underworld at bay for as long as I can. You should have enough time to use the rings and seal the barrier."

I hadn't thought passed us going back into the portal. My hope had gone up and down for the last few hours.

"What can we expect if we do?" I asked from next to the water and rock formation.

"If all goes well, when the Breaking is complete, the rings should keep the rift to a minimum." He looked over at his brother and then back to me, and finally to Zane. "That being said, the veil will be lifted and the shadowrealm will be visible to the humans…

Dhalls is what you call them in your realm. You'll also have a lot of people who never knew they had magics scrambling for meaning."

My eyebrows shot to my hairline. "What do you mean by that?"

Draxus stepped forward to face me and Ezolus dropped his hand from Zane's arm.

"It means that the veil did more than keep Dhalls from seeing what's in the shadows." Draxus stare was far away but he kept his voice level. "There are a lot of people who have had problems fitting in for a reason. They're going to suddenly realize that they are part of a realm that they'd had no idea existed."

Zane cleared his throat. "We'll help them. I mean, I know I'd want to understand what in the Sevens was going on if it were me."

"Of course we will," I replied. "First things first. We need to secure the rift. I can already *feel* the Breaking's beginning... little fissures. It's making me itchy."

Taking a hold of the tree branch to the side of the stone portal, I held out my hand to my father and squeezed it.

Draxus hesitated for a moment, turning back to his brother.

"There's no way to ever repay you for this burden you've taken on. I will make sure our mother gives you the honor that must be bestowed upon you and your line!" he said with more exuberance than I'd imagined he'd had in him.

Without another word, he stepped through the portal.

"It's your turn son," Ezolus thumped his fist against Zane's arm in a gesture of pride.

"I'm glad that I got to meet you... Dad." Pushing past the embarrassment of using the word, it'd be the first and last time that he had the chance to address him as such with true feeling.

A knot formed in my throat as the tears now brimming in Ezolus' eyes rolled down his cheeks.

"I love you, Zane. I wish we'd had more time." His words were clear and yet mumbled at the same time. "Go, son. Let me keep you safe."

Zane walked the last few feet to the portal and took my hand.

Turning one last time to see Ezolus beginning the magics to seal it closed, I waved a small, sad farewell to my uncle.

Then just like that, the portal sealed behind us.

And with it, Zane's father was gone forever.

Chapter Eighty-Five

Kalina

Walking back to the shop with the food, I caught a figure out of the corner of my eye.

Two girls had just exited the pizzeria before me, weighed down with shopping bags. They walked past the front window of Pandora's Box.

As they passed the store, the silhouetted figure coming from the shadow of the woods was watching them, not me.

Shuffling the food to one hand, I retrieved the dagger sheathed in bracer.

After the girls were a few shops down the block, the figure emerged from the tree line as light from a street post brought his face into full relief.

"By the Damning Stars, you gave me a fright," I said.

Riedyn cocked his brow, looking down at the food I was carrying.

Reaching over, he helped take half the burden without jostling anything amiss. The grace of the fae was well known, but damn. Crazy graceful was an understatement.

"You know Kalina," he said. "If Lucian wanted you dead, you'd probably already have been attacked before now."

I hadn't been thinking in that direction, but now that he'd said it, it irked me that I hadn't.

"I guess you're right." A moment or two passed and we still stood a few feet from the door. "Why were you watching those girls?"

At first, I thought he wouldn't answer. Now, I got the sense he was choosing his words carefully.

"I thought that I recognized the one... it was like a glamour was shimmering away from her true features." He stopped talking, lost in thought. "The other girl looked familiar. Not the same but similar to someone that I used to know. And the bizarre part was that their ears were pointed, fae like."

Thinking about it for a second, air rushed from my lungs in huff.

"Riedyn, do you think the veil is lifting already?"

"I felt the beginnings of the realm Breaking open about twenty minutes ago, so it's a real possibility. The veil has been thinning for some time now. The fae are connected to nature. We feel it more astutely when we are in this realm."

Opening the door for me, we both stepped inside and were greeted by Bastian running up to take a pizza from my hands.

"I didn't realize how starving I was until that smell hit," he said with a smirk. Bastian seemed to be overly dramatic when it came to food.

Hayden laughed at his cousin. Sauntering over, he helped me and Riedyn with the rest of the food bags.

"Geesh, Kali," he said. "What all did you get?"

"I got some pizza and subs. Garlic knots and wings." I laid everything on the table in the sitting area. "Oh, and some cannoli's and sodas. I figured this is the last time we'll be able to pack in some energy before we go up against Lucian and his brood. Might as well make the most of it."

Hayden chuckled again. Magics took a lot of energy and apparently gifters needed even more than demons did if Bastian was anything to go by.

My hope was that Thelzion had his fill of blood beforehand. This food wasn't his type of nourishment.

Brie and I were able to eat real food but did need to consume blood every month to keep our demon strength up.

"Noella and Zane should be back any time now," Brie tacked on. "We need to save them some."

Bastian looked at her with guilty eyes as he popped a fourth garlic knot into his mouth.

We all laughed at the expression on his face, but the laughter died in our throats when Riedyn asked about Lara.

No one wanted to speak up first. Thelzion set down his meatball sub and looked the Commander in the eye.

"She was taken. We think it was Jax, on Lucian's orders of course." Taking a long swig of soda, he added, "We're going to get her back. The biggest problem will be telling Noella..."

"Telling Noella what?" Coming through the door with her cousin and father, she faltered after glancing around at her friends. "Where's Lara?"

She already knew without anyone voicing it.

The room started to shake. The shelves that were already teetering toppled over. The shops air was heavy and then non-existent.

The control of her darker magics bubbled to the surface with enough force to blast everything and everyone across the room.

Draxus came up behind her, wrapping both arms around hers to force them to her sides. He called her name over and over again to no avail.

"Sleep" he commanded.

She instantly drooped and dozed in his arms.

I'd never witnessed a demigod before. Draxus's power was legendary throughout the realm but seeing it firsthand? I was glad I'd switched sides.

He looked to the others. "Do we still have the other ring?"

Hayden got to his feet, rubbing his head where he'd collided with a shelf. Stepping forward to hand it to the demigod, he stopped when Draxus shook his head.

"Keep it safe. I have the other one. We don't want to bring them together until it's time." Laying Noella's sleeping form on the chair, he turned to head towards the door.

"Where are you going?" Bastian demanded. Glancing at Noella, he struggled to control himself. "She needs you!"

"I'm going to go find the Gregarius. Without it, we won't be able to combine the rings." He glanced over at Zane and then to Thelzion. "I will check with the Custosres."

We all looked at him, puzzled. I was glad I wasn't the only one who didn't have a clue what he was talking about.

"The Keeper of the Buxis. It's the object that the rings will need to be puzzled into. It was entrusted to his care many centuries ago. I'll meet you all by my family's crypt around dawn."

"That's less than a few hours away," Thelzion let his skepticism bleed into his tone.

Draxus was out of patience. He wasn't angry. I could feel that much... but there was anxiety coming off him with waves of sorrow.

"We're out of time. I can feel the veil lifting more with each passing minute. With the realm cracked open, our time is about up. The Breaking has begun to pull the rift apart."

Stepping forward, Hayden nodded. "We'll be there. Just make sure you have that Gregarius thing."

With a dip of his head and one last glance to his daughter, Draxus was out the door.

Chapter Eighty-Six

Parker

Feeling the hairs on the back of my neck stand on end, the shadows gathered darker under the trees to my left.

"Saevus," I said, bowing slightly.

"It's good to see your demon senses are still in tuned. The other upper-level demons have noticed their subjects have diminished the longer they are on this plane." Saevus stepped out of the shadows and into the moonlight scattering through the trees.

"What can I do for you? There must be a reason you've come to see a low level, such as myself." I wasn't sure I really wanted to know but not knowing was probably worse.

He waved his hand to the path in front of us and began to walk. His dark robe billowed in the light breeze around the property. Reluctantly, I shuffled along to catch up.

"Lucian is becoming a problem. We suspect that he is attempting things above his station." Steepling his hands in front of his chest, he turned to look me in the eyes. That gift of his for seeing intentions could be inconvenient at the best of times. "What would it take for you to be our inside spy?"

Taking a carefully measured breath, I pretended to think about it. If I answered too fast, Saevus wouldn't trust that I truly meant to do his bidding. If I answered too slowly, he would doubt my conviction.

"Why have you come to me and not Jax or Quinn?"

A huff of a laugh escaped from under the hood of the robe.

"This is precisely why you were our choice. You don't mix words and have the fortitude to push through with a task." He said nothing more. We continued to walk the path in silence.

After what I thought of as a sufficient amount of time, I touched the sleeve of Saevus' robe to stop our progression. An old trick for the mind to associate familiarity with feeling at ease.

"What am I to be looking for? What is it that Lucian is suspected of exactly?"

"The veil has begun to thin. The Breaking is only hours away." He waved his hand in front of us and an image appeared. "We believe he'll use the Breaking to crack the rift open farther than it is meant to open and keep it that way."

Seven hells! He was on top of Lucian's plans already.

I'd wanted to give him the information as my leverage, but he'd already known what the bastard was planning.

Time to change tactics.

"And why would that be a bad thing? I mean, more demons on this plane would be a good way to spread discord, right?" Shaking my head, I still needed to play the part.

"If too many demons enter this plane again, it would draw the full attention of the gods. And what do you think will happen to our food source?" Turning his head, his hood fell away from his face.

I'd never gotten used to that gnarly scar. The red line always looked infected. It may have been. The punishment he'd received for trying to usurp his station was a good reminder for me to play the next few moves carefully.

"Control of the demons wouldn't be effective. They *Are* demons, after all." We walked a bit farther up the pathway. "We believe Lucian wants to rule here. He does well with the demons in his jurisdiction but the majority of those in his command are mere Meathlu. He doesn't grasp what it would mean to have full demons unleashed here."

Really contemplating this for a moment, this time it was no act. I hadn't thought of it the way Saevus described.

What would that mean for my position? And what would full demons do if they ran out of Dhalls to torment and their blood to drink?

If Lucian did make it to Kinghood, and he found out that I was conspiring against him, I was fucked.

Then again, if Lucian didn't make it as a king, still lived, and found out I'd played a role in keeping him from his ultimate goal, I was fucked.

The safest thing to do would be to remain loyal to Lucian until he could be dealt with. Saevus couldn't guarantee my safety from the Underworld but that left me with the dilemma of deceiving an upper-level demon and surviving the aftermath.

The blood oath with Quinn for the betterment of demonkind meant that she would be in the know of my disloyalty.

All in all, I was fucked.

I had plans in the works in Sidhterra. I had plans in the works here in Lagomshire. None of my plans mattered if I died before they'd come to fruition.

"I'll keep my ears open. I can't promise that I'll figure anything out. You know how secretive Lucian is, even between his trusted followers."

My best option was still playing every piece on the board. From every angle.

"I understand that this puts you in quite a predicament but think through the consequences of Lucian's success." Saevus drifted towards the shadows of the tree line once again. "You would make a good Donnchadh. Food for thought."

With that, he disappeared back to the Underworld.

As a vampire, I was the only one in the manor that could be elevated to Lucian's level. To become a Donnchadh, I'd be given more power from the source of demonkind.

Did I want to be in charge of the others? I'd never considered it before. It was more work to put in but the power boost that came with it was definitely a perk.

I'd started down this path with Skylar. I'd involved Quinn. I'd tried to sway Jaxson. And now Saevus had offered me exactly what he'd thought I wanted.

After my talk with Skylar, my hunch about the Queen's daughter, Griane, was another rabbit hole I wanted to explore.

If I was right, she'd never went missing. She'd hidden, had a child, and lived here in Lagomshire.

If Lucian wanted my loyalty in exchange for me having only small responsibilities, I'd give it to him... for now.

Playing my part as demon asshole would leave me time to work towards my own agenda.

Commander Riedyn didn't seem as tormented as he could be. I liked pushing him to his limits. It gave me warm, fuzzy feelings inside.

A broad smile spread wide across my face.

With my mind made up, it was time to let my demon side out to play.

Chapter Eighty-Seven

Quinn

Jax pushed the door to the study open when he heard Lucian and I finish our conversation.

"Lucian," he said with a dip of his chin. "I have a present for you."

From around the corner of the door, he picked up a still, unconscious form. He walked into the room and laid her down on the chaise and stepped away.

I recognized the shop keeper. Lara stirred but didn't wake. The bruising around her neck left me to wonder if she was breathing at all.

"Jax, what did you do?" Looking from him to Lara and then back to Lucian, I caught the corner of Lucian's lip curl up.

All of his attention was on Jax. A wicked smile curled into a full-blown beam at the burly demon's lips as well.

"Jaxs?" I asked tentatively.

He was different. I'd never seen him so cold and... demonic.

I'd been with Lucian for over a hundred seventy years but Jax, he'd been with him for more than three centuries.

Rumors whispered from lesser demons said he had changed after an event a few years before I'd joined Lucian, but never did I imagine he could be... *This.*

"Welcome back, Jaxson." Lucian said. "It's been a long time, old friend."

The length demon smiled, all pearly white teeth that contrasted against his dark skin tone. Seven circles, sinister didn't even scrap the surface of that look.

"Quinn... I've been eager to meet you firsthand." He licked his lips and rubbed his hands in front of him like a fly.

"You've known me for over a century, you ass! What are you talking about?" I demanded.

My skin crawled with thousands of maggots the longer his lingering glare remained along my body.

Lucian came from around the back of the desk and looked down at Lara. A single finger on his large hand stroked the side of her face. He brushed a stray hair behind her ear.

I hated how he could be so thoughtful one minute and pure evil the next.

It had been the main reason I'd felt drawn to him for the past century.

Reminding myself that he was no good, not for anyone, I sighed discontentedly.

"Quinn, I'd like to introduce you to the real Jax." He smiled broader than I ever recalled him doing in our long history together.

Turning back to Jax, he asked, "Is your other side fully subdued?"

Bloody hells, this wasn't the male I'd come to call a friend at all. Evil oozed from his every pore.

"He's still fighting the arrangement, but I've locked him up tight." He gave a huff and gritted his teeth.

My Jax was still fighting. It was written in the tiny wrinkles around his eyes.

"Jaxson?" Lucian looked concerned.

"It's alright. He's loud, screaming at me all the time." He smirked widely. "It just helps to fuel my rage."

I wondered if that was what my Jax had been fighting secretly against for all the years he'd put on a brave face?

"Good." Lucian clapped him on the back. "It must have been horrible not being able to access your own rage all those years."

Jaxson grunted his agreement, and I had to look away from the intensity of his stare.

My eyes fell on Lara again. The blood that crusted her forehead had stopped the bleeding, but her appearance wasn't going to do us any favors once Noella got her eyes on her.

"Why don't I take and get her cleaned up?" I said. Lucian gave me a suspicious glance. "It will do us no good if the Mixling witch loses control when she sees her lover a mess like this."

"This is why I keep you close, Quinn. Always thinking ahead." He grinned his approval. "Get her cleaned up but do not let her talk. A gag over her mouth will prove a nice look to the threat without letting her give away any seer insights to her friends once the time comes."

Throwing Lara over my shoulder like a sack of potatoes, I headed towards the door. Demon strength counted for something.

I wasn't gentle about it, but I made sure not to jostle her more than necessary.

Jax was casting lustful looks my way as I exited the room. He'd watched me before., but this new Jax... I'd have to watch my back.

As I exited, I heard him say something lewd to Lucian and a shiver went down my spine. Lucian knew my body well. I could only hope I wouldn't be the topic of their conversations for the next however many years.

He'd always flirted with me, and Parker always teased him about wanting me. Now, I wondered how much of this new Jax was going to try to push that flirtation further?

Another shiver went down my spine. Life was about to become perniciously interesting.

Chapter Eighty-Eight

Baelyn

Pleshia and I had stayed out all day. It was something we hadn't done in a very long time.

Our automated carriage was one of the last ones in the parking lot.

With arms full of packages, our bellies were full of pizza.

The glow coming from the overhead streetlamp cast dancing flames of light into the shadows.

Bending down to retrieve the key from my purse, I set my parcels on the ground. They toppled over and I spent several minutes picking them all back up again.

Shopping was great, but hauling our found treasures back to our place was proving a pain in the ass.

When I stood up, my sister was wide eyed with what looked to be panic. It instantly gave me the skitterbugs.

Spinning around to see what alarmed her, no one was around. The lot was empty except for the two of us. I couldn't sense any threat.

"What's wrong?" I demanded. "Is something out there?"

Pleshia shook her head, but her eyes remained troubled and unblinking.

"It's nothing," she said. "I'm just tired."

I could fully understand that. I should have worn different shoes. The blisters I'd have come morning would be a bitch to work with this week.

Opening the doors, I shoved all of the bags inside. The back seat couldn't hold any more if our lives depended on it.

Once everything was secured, my gaze landed on Pleshia. My own mouth popped open in stunned shock.

"What's going on with your ears?" I started to go to the other side of the carriage but at the first step, my body felt strange, different. I swayed slightly at the weirdness.

"We should get home," Pleshia said. "We're both tired and I think that that, combined with that glass of wine, must be messing with us."

I did feel like I was altered but it didn't feel the way I normally felt after a few drinks. A simple glass of wine wasn't enough to usually even make me tipsy, but I couldn't shake the feeling that something was amiss.

"Sounds like a plan." Getting in the automated carriage and adjusting my seat, I caught a glance of myself in the side mirror.

My hand flew up to my ears. They landed on the tips. Pointed tips. What in the Damning Stars was going on?

Pleshia was chewing on her bottom lip the way she did when she was anxious. It hadn't been a trick of the light earlier. My sister's ears were even more pointed than mine.

Seeing my reaction, Pleshia reached up to touch her own ears. We couldn't both be hallucinating the same thing, could we?

A shimmer of light swam in and out of focus over Pleshia's face. What in the seven circles was in those drinks?

It was nearly one in the morning. Exhaustion sat heavy in my bones.

Turning to look in the mirror again, my face appeared a bit longer than usual. My lips looked pinker and fuller. My cheeks had a slight rosy glow.

My initial reaction was that I looked pretty. Dare I say beautiful even? That wasn't how I usually viewed myself.

I'd never worn make up. My features weren't anything special on any given day.

This look though, it was stunning. What was happening?

Pleshia wasn't freaking out. Why wasn't she freaking out?

My sister's now beautiful full figure and face should have had her going mad with questions like me, but she was maddingly calm.

Pleshia had always been beautiful, but I had to admit, this new version of her was flawless, if but a little robust.

We must have ingested something we shouldn't have. It was the only explanation... Except... why wasn't Pleshia more concerned?

"I have a lot to explain," her voice dropped to nearly a whisper. Looking up from the floorboards, her eyes locked with mine. Tears streamed down her cheeks. "Let's go home so we can talk."

"Start talking now!" Waiting wasn't my specialty.

My ears twitched and I could hear... everything.

The night birds chirping in the trees. The water from the river skimming over the rocks a few blocks away. The chairs scraping the floor as they were being turned up onto tables of the closing pizzeria we'd just come from.

I could even hear Pleshia's heart beating faster than it should.

With reddening cheeks and a timid look upon her face, she whispered across the space between us.

"We're Faeries. And I'm not really your sister."

Well shit!

Chapter Eighty-Nine

Riedyn

Oaken and Willow came into the shop shortly after Draxus left.

It surprised me to see them so soon after they'd returned Borias' body back to Sidhterra. I'd have understood if they needed more time.

"The Queen has informed us of your mission," Oaken said.

Willow chimed in, "We're here to make sure that bastard fails!"

Grateful as I was to have them here, but I also felt guilty about Borias' death. It should have been me that followed Lucian.

"Stop." Willow cut my thoughts off midstream. "Borias died in service to Sidhterra and the Queen. You do not get to tarnish his memory by belittling his choice to do his part."

She touched the tattoo on my arm. A subtle reminder that we were a unit.

"It will be my honor to have your assistance. And we *will* make that bastard pay one day," I said. "Today though, we have a specific mission."

Thelzion fill them in all of the details. We sat in a contemplative silence, sometimes asking minor questions, while waiting for the time to go and for Noella to wake.

It had been hours. I'd begun to worry when she started whimpering in her sleep.

As Noella stirred, Brie stood to block the others from view. It'd make sense that she didn't want her to be overwhelmed. It was why Draxus had to put her under in the first place.

Zane made to get up, but Kali lightly rebuffed him with a gentle brush of her hand.

He glanced down at her, and she shook her head ever so slightly, giving him a weak smile.

He sat back down nonchalantly putting himself in a more direct path to block her from his cousin. It was cute when she raised an eyebrow but didn't say anything about it.

I'd had fond memories of Kali as a small child. She wouldn't remember me because of how a Trixie's young mind worked.

Lucian and I got into some of our biggest tiffs during her youngest years.

As a couple, I wanted to raise her like any normal child. Carefree and adventurous. He wanted to control her attitude and responses to every little thing.

He and I split up the first time when she was only twelve. We'd gotten back together several times over the years, but he never let me near her again.

The Mixling witch sat up and you could see it all come flooding back to her. I braced for whatever came next.

She'd realized that Lara was missing, and the shop was a mess. Her father had stifled her magics and knocked her out to keep it contained.

Brie glanced at the clock above the door. The hour was late... or early, depending on how you looked at it.

The feeling of the lifting veil had the magics sitting heavily upon the air.

Lucian had Lara and we were running out of time, but Noella was not in the right head space to move forward yet.

"What are we waiting for?" she asked the room. "We need to go!"

Briella placed a hand on Noella's head. "How are you feeling?"

Noella swatted her away and got to her feet. "Does it matter? Lara needs us and we need to stop Lucian."

Thelzion tried to say something, but Noella cut him off.

"I don't want to hear it, Thelzion. I want to be acting, not sitting around here."

He stood to the side of Brie and tried again. "Draxus said that we need the Gregarius to combine the rings. He went to retrieve it."

Noella was making her way to the door. That feeling of helplessness in a situation was one that Lucian had perfected over the years.

"I'm going now! I know we need to stop Lucian, but I have to save Lara." Her voice was strained.

Brie and Kali winced, feeling the roiling emotions coming off of her. Both of them grimacing in response

"It's only a little over an hour until dawn now. I say we go." Bastian came to stand beside Noella.

For a gifter, the guy had balls. I'd give him that much.

"Alright, let's go," Thelzion looked around the room to all of us. "Keep your wits about you. And don't make any moves until we can get a full picture of the situation."

I caught the glance he threw Zane's way. With a small nod, he passed his gaze from Brie to Kali and back to Zane.

A silent conversation between the two. With the foreshadower telling them of one of the twin's deaths, my guess was that they'd see to it both females lived... no matter the cost.

Hayden passed us all and held the door open. He'd been wanting to go find Lara since I'd come in the shop hours ago.

The ten of us filed out into the predawn night.

With one last look to each other, we headed in different direction to meet up at the same place.

Our salvation or our doom.

Chapter Ninety

Draxus

Opening the door to the Keepers shop, the room was in disarray. The shelves were knocked over. Artifact laid cluttered and broken on the floor.

The I smelled it... blood.

Walking farther into the pawn shop, a wheezing sound coming from the back room.

I pushed passed the mess next and made my wat to the counter. Fhail laying on the floor, covered in cuts, bruises, and his own blood.

Rushing to his side and dropping down, I lifted his head into his lap. My magics could do many things but healing a body as thoroughly broken as his wasn't one of them.

"What happened, old friend?" I said softly.

Gently as I could manage, I wiped the blood from Fhail's mouth and cleaned the smudges off his thick glasses.

A garbled gasp escaped his lips. The poor fellow wasn't long for this world.

"I guess Lucian's minion, Parker, didn't believe that I knew nothing." He sputtered and coughed up more blood. "I know why you're here."

"I'm sorry to have to ask but it is vital, and time isn't on our side." I said, brushing the hair from the Keepers face.

He'd always been a kind soul. In all of my many long years, Fhail had never wanted anything more than a cup of tea and good reading material. Simple wants from a simple male.

"I know. It's time," he said through bubbles of blood. "The circus carousel beside the books there." He pointed just beyond the cash register.

"The circus carousel?" I asked skeptically.

Fhail smiled through his pain. "No one ever looks at the cheesy items. I promise, it still works." He coughed up more blood. "The bottom comes off. Turn it upside down and you'll see the slots for the rings."

Laying Fhail's head gently to the floor, I made my way over to the carousel.

Turning it upside down and removing the bottom easily, sure enough, the slots were visible. A winding mechanism was still attached to the bottom.

"Is this how we activate it?" I called over. No reply came.

I walked back over to my old friend. His eyes were open, and a smile curled the edges of his lips, but he was gone.

With his task complete, he had left this world knowing that those in charge of the Prophecy would now have what they needed.

"Rest well, old friend."

Picking up the Gregarius and headed out into the coming dawn, my heart ached for his absence.

It was always the softest souls that paid the price in blood in the realm. I hated the gods for that.

Sending up a silent prayer to my dead son for his forgiveness, it was time to fulfill my destiny.

Chapter Ninety-One

Riedyn

The sun had begun to rise, and light filtered through the trees on the other side of the river.

I'd happened to glance over my shoulder towards the parking lot at the end of the line of stores several hundred feet away as we walked.

My fae hearing picked up on the sound of two females arguing. The same two from hours ago? I wasn't sure.

I couldn't make out the details of their faces from this distance, but I could swear there was the shimmer of a failing glamour on the one I'd thought I'd recognized earlier.

The briny smell coming off the Manxtas River was stronger than normal, dulling my ability to catch their scent.

Anxiety rippled in waves through my system knowing we would be confronting Lucian soon. More distractions weren't what I needed right now.

Willow leaned over and whispered in Oaken's ear. The Lieutenant gave her a curt nod.

He fell back to my side. The swagger he usually exuded wasn't there.

"Permission to speak frankly?" he said. It was my turn to give him a quick, sharp nod. "We can handle this if you need to excuse yourself."

The two females drove away before I found the words that ate me up from the inside.

"It's my responsibility. Not yours. And not Willow's." The words came out more forcefully than I meant them, but they were true all the same.

"Borias wasn't your fault. And your history with Lucian may cloud your..."

I cut him off with a stern look. Going into this situation with my head all in tangles wasn't going to help us.

Thinking through my next words carefully, I chose the only ones that mattered.

"Lucian is not the man he portrayed himself to be during our time together. I understand your concerns, Lieutenant, but I will do the Queen's bidding and then avenge Borias without hesitation."

Breathing harder than normal, my conviction bolstered my resolve once I said it out loud.

Brie looked back at us and gave me a sad smile.

I knew that she and Kali could feel everything that I was feeling.

Kali had been more a part of my life than she realized. I couldn't reconcile the little girl creating mischief around the manor with the full grown conservatrix ready to go up against her father.

I'd caught her looking back at us too. Her grin lit up the night. If she could find her smile after a lifetime with Lucian, I could find mine someday. That was the hope I'd cling to.

We would separate here soon enough but we were all walking into the lion's den once we met back up at the mausoleum. Call it a gut instinct but I had a strange feeling not all of us would walk out of the den intact.

Willow brushed her shoulder against mine but didn't say anything.

Of all of the fae who knew how crappy my life's dramas had been, this female had never shied away from standing strong by my side.

I'd never said it, in so many words, but she'd been my best friend for many years now.

It's why I'd pushed her so hard to get into the EU after the Queen suggested it. I was happy to be her friend, not just her Commander.

Brie and Thelzion had gone through the woods. Zane and Kali split off and went over the side of the buildings down the road. Bastian, Hayden and Noella had already split away from our group when they'd reached the parking area.

Now that Willow, Oaken, and I approached the outer grounds, we halted our conversations.

With a nod at the others coming in from three different sides, it was good to see no one had been attacked.

We'd thought Lucian might send a few of his charges to stop us before we could reach him. Thankfully, that wasn't the case. Though it was odd.

Stopping in front of the gate, we all chattered idly as we entered the bounds of the cemetery.

The silence that followed filled the air with a heavy tension that settled on my chest and stole my breath as easily as the wet, humid forest after a midsummer shower.

Walking farther in through the winding paths leading to the mausoleum, the trees thickened in density and less light filtered through.

We'd approached the crypt in the last of nights cover as dawn threatened on the horizon. A purple haze gave light to the area around Caylum's grave.

Quinn and Parker stepped onto the path from out of the tree line. Hayden gasped but I wasn't surprised at their stealth. They'd always been quiet, deadly shits.

"Well, isn't this just a motley crew of misfits?" Quinn tilted her head in Zane's direction and Kali growled.

Parker's arrogant head shook side to side. He let out a low whistle.

"I think this doesn't count as a crew. It's more like a hodge podge of rejects." An evil smirk donned his face as he took a step forward.

Asshole through and through. I'd never liked the bastard.

Thelzion put himself between the two demons and the rest of us. He was a Donnchadh, same as Lucian. That was something I'd often forgot.

Powerful and dark, Thelzion wasn't morally good, but he wasn't exactly evil either. Finding his mate had tamed him in a way.

The crack of a branch had me spinning in the direction to the left of the crypt. I sensed it was him before anyone else.

"Thelzion," said the figure coming out from behind a bush. "It's been a long time."

Lucian took a step towards our group and Thelzion growled.

"Ah, Kali." Lucian crooned. His eyebrows rose as her scent hit him full on. "You aren't Kali."

Brie walked to her sister's side and nodded to Zane.

He kept his stance wide. Protective. Kali stepped out from behind him and his features grew more tense.

"Hello, Lucian," she said.

To everyone's surprise, he didn't appear shaken. Just unhappy.

"I see," he said. "Well played, Thelzion."

Chapter Ninety-Two

Baelyn

The ride home was in awkward silence.

I hadn't dared open my mouth to ask any more questions or anything else until we were back home behind closed doors.

I'd stewed for the better part of an hour, still knowing nearly nothing. Pleshia had promised me answers but only once we were home.

Opening her mouth to speak as soon as the door closed but I'd lifted one finger to let her know that I wasn't ready to hear it yet.

All in one sentence, my world crumbled around damned pointed ears.

Walking into the kitchen, my mind poured a glass of juice that I didn't want. After taking a sip, I'd realized just how much that wasn't going to cut it and added vodka to the glass.

Downing the first glass, I poured another before taking a seat on our couch. With calming breaths, in through the mouth, out through the nose, I gathered my resolve.

With an intense glare, I gave my "sister" a once over and then waved a hand for Pleshia to get on with it.

The curvaceous fae sat on the edge of the coffee table, laid a hand on my leg, and sobbed. A choked breath bubbled up from her chest.

"First, let me start by telling you how much I love you and that your protection is all that I've ever cared about. I tried to broach the subject at the diner but..."

Leveling her with a cool glare, it faltered. Her love for me had shown through the depths of her eyes. She may not be my sister, but I was confident that our connection was true.

Pleshia swallowed back her emotions and continued.

"We are fae... faeries, Baelyn. Lagomshire is our home, but this isn't our realm."

Playing with a loose thread on the bottom of my shirt, I took another sip of my drink. It was all too surreal.

I wasn't ready to talk yet, so Pleshia went on.

"We are from a realm called Sidhterra. There is a portal that brought us here before you were born."

Setting my drink on the table and looking Pleshia in the eye, I finally found the courage to ask the question that had been eating at me since she'd dropped this bomb in my lap.

"If you're not my sister... then who are you?"

Pleshia's head fell into her hands, and she wept. I gave her time to collect herself but didn't reach out to comfort her.

My thoughts ranged from cousin to bodyguard to kidnapper. I couldn't fathom being a faery much less that the sister I'd grown up with wasn't my sibling at all.

After a few moments, the sobs slowed. If I'd thought I'd been ready for the answer, I'd have been so far past wrong, it would have made a turn at the moon and headed straight for the sun.

"I am your mother, Baelyn."

I stood so fast that my head spun. Her words made no sense.

We were nearly the same age. We'd grown up together. None of this could be real.

"You can't be! Our mother disappeared only a few years ago, Pleshia! Why are you saying these things?!" I demanded. "You and I are around the same age. It's not even possible."

Finishing with a huff, I folded my arms, not knowing what else more to say.

Pleshia reached out to touch my shoulder and I shrugged her off. Unshed tears rimmed my eyes.

The air crackled around us, and I froze in astonishment. She appeared a handful of years older than she had only seconds ago.

"I'm sorry," Pleshia said hanging her head. "I did what I had to do to keep you safe. To keep you from having to live a life that was predetermined before you were even conceived... I glamoured myself to look around your age throughout your youth and we grew as sisters but more importantly, as friends. Fae don't age like those of this realm."

"What does that mean, glamoured?" I asked. "What, you used magics on me?"

My mind shied away from her new look. If any of this was real, I needed all of the answers I could get.

"No. I used magics on myself. I am an immortal. I don't age like the beings here. The magics made anyone who looked at me see the same thing you saw... A toddler, then a small girl. A teenager, and before now, a young woman."

She adjusted the hair around her pointed ears. Her face was still roundish, but her chin and jawline were more angular now.

"So, who was the woman we called Mom, Pleshia? Who was the woman we both grieved after she went missing?" A thickness filled my voice with my unshed tears.

The woman in front of me suddenly looked older. Not because of her appearance. It was a feeling. An older person's account coming through her features.

Gods, I couldn't put my thoughts in order in my own head.

"I came from the portal pregnant. After a few nights on the streets, I met a very kind woman. Her name was Pleshia." A sorrowful look passed over her eyes. "We became friends, and she took me in after I revealed to her that I was with child. You and I were tended to by her affectionately. She had always wanted a child but couldn't conceive and after her husband had died, she stopped trying to find happiness in the world. She was kind but had no friends. No family."

I'd loved my mother dearly. To find out she'd lied to me my whole life? Not to mention that my real mother had lied to me as well? I'd need a head doctor for decades after all of this.

"So, what, you two just cooked up a plan to have her be my mom? Were you going to just leave me after having me?" My breathing became ragged, but I refused to cry.

"No honey. I would never have left you. Ever!" Pleshia took my hands, and this time, I let her. "After I had you, I realized the danger that I was putting on her. I did a little magics and it convinced her that her name was Shea and that I was her toddler, and you were her baby."

Okay, that was kind of nice of her. The woman had wanted children... but my "sister" was willing to let me be Shea's baby.

I thought through her words. "Danger? From what?"

Pursing her lips, she closed her eyes tightly. Anxiety came in the way of angry, quick breaths.

After gathering herself back together, with a long exhale, she continued.

"Not from what, but from who... your grandmother and some of our kind." Pleshia looked into my eyes and her silver rims swirled. "We aren't just Fae. We are royalty. Your grandmother is Queen Talisin. Leader of the Summer Court Fae. She believed that mortals were beneath us and that the bloodlines should not be mixed."

My mouth popped open in shock. She had to be pulling my leg.

"I am Griane, daughter of the Queen, Princess and heir to the throne. I had been pre-arranged to marry from birth, but I fell in love with your father after coming here on a trip many years ago."

Whoa! Back the horse up. Was this why my ears weren't as pointy as hers?

"So, my father is a mortal?"

I still couldn't wrap my mind around the fact that I was a fae. That my "sister" was actually my mother. Throw in the fact that she was a princess, and now this? It was a lot to take in.

"Not exactly. He was a gifter," she said. She held her hand up in protest when I started to ask more. "The simplest explanation is, a gifter is a person of this realm, Lagomshire, that has some form of magics."

I didn't know what to make of any of this. Thinking back on what she'd just said, something clicked.

"Was a gifter? He's dead?" I asked.

How should I feel about that? I'd never known a father before now. It wasn't a concept to me, but it felt wrong not to be saddened by his loss.

I was numb in every way. Too much information about too many things.

"He died getting us safely back to this realm. It was his final act of love for us." Her eyes filled again with tears. A faraway look sat heavy upon her face.

"Was it my grandmother? Did she kill him?" I didn't know if I could handle the answer, but I had to have the truth anyway.

Wet streaks flowed freely down Griane's face.

I couldn't very well call her Pleshia any longer, not with it being the name of the woman who'd raised me. And I certainly wasn't ready to call her mom.

"In a roundabout way... It was the arranged marriage and the distain for mortals my mother had that brought it about from our people." Her hands were in tight fists at her side. "They believed that I was a traitor to our kind. That Mason's love for me was a ploy to take up a spot on the throne. He'd never cared for any of that. He just loved me for me, and I loved him."

I sat in silence, trying to process the whole of everything I'd been told.

My thoughts wandered to what the land of faery might look like. Pondering the idea of being raised by Griane and my father here, or there even.

"I'm not happy about all of the deception, Griane," I said.

The twitch of my mother's ears and the slight upward curve of her mouth at the use of her given name amused me.

"It's going to take some time to get used to the way things really are, and I just can't see you as my mother. We've been sisters for all of my life. And friends."

Shaking my head, that's what hurt the most.

"You're just going to have to give me time to process... And eventually, I am going to go to Sidhterra and meet the rest of my kind, Queen Talisin included."

Griane began to protest but the stern look I leveled her with had her thinking better of it.

Putting my hands on my hips and glancing at the long mirror on the living room wall, I studied the way my body now looked.

"You're also going to have to show me how to style my hair with these things," I said, pointing to my ears that now stuck out through my hairline.

Griane laughed but nodded.

I took in the beautiful angles of my own face. It was still me, only my beauty was at the forefront and there were no flaws that I could decipher easily.

Looking over at Griane, I realized just how beautiful she was too.

"Are all the fae pretty?"

Another chuckle escaped Griane's lips. She stood and crossed the short distance to draw my hair behind my ears.

"Painfully so... Your father was a very handsome man, but I found that the minor flaws in his appearance were what attracted me to him the most."

She pointed to a small beauty mark on the side of my cheek. It was a small flaw, but it held weight.

It would serve as a reminder to me from now on of my father's contribution to my being.

Taking Griane's hand, I lead her back to the sofa.

"Tell me all about my father."

Chapter Ninety-Three

Lara

"You could all save yourselves a lot of problems if you just hand over the ring," Lucian said with a coy grin.

"That's never gonna happen," said Thelzion taking a step towards him.

Lucian tsked condescendingly.

His hand came up and Jax stepped from the shadows so that they could all see his blade firmly planted against my throat.

Noella let out a small gasp. Even though she wasn't fully recovered from the trip to the Low realm, her hand began to shimmer with crackling energy and dark shadows.

My beautiful witch would lose herself if I didn't do something to stop her. Hecate said as much.

"Let her go... Now!" Noella exclaimed with a primal roar.

Jax tightened his grip on my shoulder and the blade bit into my neck. A small moan of pain slipped past my lips.

Noella's breathing became heated and heavy. Her power grew in intensity with each intake of air to her lungs. The movement of her chest made my heart pound loudly in my own ears.

A purple mist that hung in the area began to lift but I couldn't see clearly out of my left eye.

Sparks of light mixed with swirling shadows gathered at her hands and travelled up her arms.

Zane glared at Jax. Kali took a step forward and he grabbed her arm, holding her back.

"Thelzion," Zane yelled. "There's a double image in him. I can see one being restrained behind a forcefield of some kind."

"Jax?" Kali tried to reach for him but Zane held her back.

His grip on my shoulder became painful. Blood leaked from the press of his blade down between my breasts.

"The Jaxson you know is locked away tight." Lucian grinned wickedly. "This Jax is a true monster."

His smile spoke of appreciation for this version of the demon. Lucian was a foul scourge on Lagomshire that needed to be eradicated.

I'd never been a violent person, but I hoped for all I was worth that when this was all over, he'd lie dead in a pit somewhere.

"You're the monster, Lucian!" Kali seethed. Her heart was full of rage that burned a bright red for us all to see as she stared at her former father figure.

The red waves of energy began to coil around her.

"Easy, Kalina," Bastian said. "He wants us riled up so that we aren't in control of our abilities."

Briella cocked her head and the red waves around her sister turned blue. She'd dosed her with calming emotions.

Lucian's smile faltered. Briella was sharper than he'd thought apparently. He hadn't anticipated this chess piece on the board.

Kali took a breath, rolling her shoulders, and unclenching her fists.

Noella's eyes never left my face. The very air was swimming with the anger coming off of her. I wanted to go to her. To comfort her so badly, I'd forgotten Jax's knife was at my throat.

Bastian looked at Jaxson closely. Cocking his head to the side and squinting in concentration, he focused solely on the demon. I could feel a pull and sway under his skin as his free arm encircled my waist to keep me in place.

Quinn realized what Bastian was trying to do and lunged at him, but Zane pounced on her.

She ripped her claws at the ends of her fingers through his shirt, tearing his flesh and drawing blood from his chest, but he pinned her beneath his muscular arm.

Parker dashed over to break his hold and Kali let out a snarl before diving into the mayhem.

"Give me the ring, Noella." Lucian looked to her and then to Jax.

He gave a little nod and Jax twisted my arm. A resounding crack rang throughout the cemetery.

I screamed. I couldn't help it. The pain was intense.

Tears ran down my cheeks and more of blood dripped from the spot the knife pressed into my neck.

Jaxson leaned in from atop the steps of Caylum's tomb, looking Noella in the eyes the whole time, and licked the blood from my throat. He continued with his tongue all the way to my ear.

A whimper escaped me before I could reign it in.

One look at Noella and I knew that every sound from me would push my lover towards the dark side of the magics.

Clamping my lips in a tight line, I vowed to myself not to make another sound. Why couldn't the bastards have left that damned gag on?

Hayden ran at Jaxson but tripped over the rocks and debris that Noella's power was floating all around us all.

A whooshing noise sounded to the side of the crypt's shadows.

Draxus strolled into view holding some kind of... carousel?

Lucian's eyes widened but he quickly recovered his composure.

"Cutting it close, aren't you?" Thelzion hollered to Draxus.

His mouth was turned down and his eyes were red, ringed with more unshed tears.

"Fhail is dead," he said.

His gazed turned to steel as he looked at Lucian.

"You killed my son. You killed my friend." He made a sweeping motion towards Noella. "You have my daughter on the verge of darkness."

Lucian smiled but it didn't reach his eyes. His voice was hollow when he spoke.

"I am a demon, not a saint... but I *will* be a King."

Riedyn and his two Fae companion's dove at him before he'd finished his boast.

Using his vampiric speed, he dodged their advance and was in front of Kali before she knew that he'd moved.

Grabbing her by the wrist, he yanked her forward. Leaning in, he quickly whispered, "I truly am sorry, my pet. I didn't want you bled this way."

Catching her by the throat, his claws sliced through the soft flesh of her neck. Her hand flew to cover the wound as she gasped and struggled for air as blood spewed everywhere.

Brie gasped. Zane lunged for his mate, grabbing her before she hit the ground.

Briella's hair stood on end and her hands came out from her sides, energy coursing through them.

Noella was frozen, her gaze was steadied on my face, unseeing anything else around her. Her power was a swirl of chaos, crackling electricity and shadows.

Tree limbs fell where the energy touched. Whooshing shadows swept the grounds and knock all of us around, to and fro, pushing at enemies and allies alike.

With the escalation of the situation, Hayden stood and took the ring from his pocket. He unwrapped it from the protective cloth.

"This is what you want?" he said to Lucian. "Let Lara go and you can have it." He held it out in front of him but kept his grip on it tightly.

What was he doing? That hadn't been part of the plan.

Thelzion was frozen. He stood protectively in front of Brie and was torn between ripping Lucian apart and keeping Brie from harm.

Her sister laid gasping for air and bleeding profusely as Zane kept pressure over the wound in her neck.

Willow rushed to where Kali laid in Zane's arms. She tried to get him to move his hand but he growled at her.

Oaken came to her other side. He grabbed Zane from behind to restrain him, but he was losing the battle and Kali was bleeding out.

Riedyn stepped to his other side and the both of them finally got him to release his hold on her long enough for the female fae to wedge herself between them.

Willow bent down quickly and placed her hand over the wound. A green glow spread from under her fingers. Her face strained with the effort of healing the Trixie.

Hayden looked from Briella to Noella. The dark shadows gathering around Noella filled her eyes. She was lost to the rage. To the darkness.

Brie's face was tear stained but hope had her heated energy simmering just under her skin. Both of them were powerful enough to rip us all from this realm if they would lose control.

Finally snapping out of his protective stupor, Thelzion realized what Hayden was about to do a moment before he did it.

He reached up, touched Brie's lips to his, and whispered "I love you." She looked up at him confused. Her eyes widened.

Bastian yelled. "I got him," and the old Jax escaped just long enough for him to loosen his grip on my throat. "Shit, his other side's strong! It's fighting my hold."

The knife fell to the ground, and I collapsed in a heap at his feet, my arm twisted in an unnatural angle.

Hayden threw the ring to Lucian in that same moment.

Time didn't slow. It stood still.

Thelzion vected in front of the Donnchadh. He caught the ring and threw it to Draxus.

The touch of the Gods forged metal burnt him the second it touched his skin. He turned, midair, meeting Brie's eyes. "I love you, Hellfire."

He smiled at her just as his body disintegrated from his hand up to his head and into ashes, no one quite registering what happened yet.

Briella screamed! Her entire body convulsed. Heat from her body built and radiated wave after wave of volatile energy.

Draxus caught the ring and placed it with its sister ring in the Gregarius.

Lucian still had the Fainne Todhchai but it wasn't needed to close the barrier, only to keep it from closing.

A wave of blue light blasted from the Gregarius and washed over the entire land.

The veil was completely lifted. Many demons had poured out of the fissure and into the realm but the barrier to the Underworld was now sealed.

With one last look to his daughter as she tried to get herself under control, and one long lasting look at the demon he hated with the depths of the Seven Hells, Draxus disappeared into the shadows to take the newly forged key safely away.

Gathering my strength, I crawled to Noella. Darkness roiled off her as she struggled not to lose herself to the shadow magics.

I pushed myself up and wrapped my arms around the center of her waist.

"Noella," I said, barely above a whisper. My throat ached from the abuse I'd suffered under Jax's hold. "Noella!" I said a little more forcefully.

Noella's breathing was erratic, her body trembling. She was trying her best to fight her way back but the pull of the shadows was strong.

Pulling myself onto my tip toes, I placed a solid kiss to her lips, not letting the turbulent air whipping the sides of my face raw deter me from bringing Noella back from the edge.

Briella's energy waves weren't helping. Her pain and sorrow and sadness bled through the space in horrible lashes of heat and debris. Splinters of branches and twigs stung my skin from every angle.

Noella's shadows pulled and nipped at my arms, my neck, my face. Still, I wouldn't give up.

Pain from my broken arm had tears streaming down my cheeks but I was not ever going to give her up to the darkness.

I moved my hands through Noella's hair and drew my breath in. My tongue forced the witch's lips to part and heat flooded my body instantly.

Noella snapped her eyes shut and took a shuttering breath. My lungs ached as the heated energy started receding. Her lips were soft, and her body pressed against mine as her mind caught up to the fact that I was alive.

A light glow began to chase the dark shadows away. I felt her senses returning to her and her mind catching up with the scene in front of her.

Parker and Quinn went flying as Noella swung her hand out in a wide arc.

Parker and Quinn flew into the side of the mausoleum. Jax stumbled backwards but remained on his feet. Lucian's eyes darkened. He backed up a step.

I knew he hated to lose but also knew that he'd pushed my witch too far. She was more than ready to end him and, more than likely, could do so easily.

"The veil has been lifted. It may not have worked out how I wanted but, all in all, I'll take what vantage I can. Loads of demons passed that break in the barrier before Daddy dearest got it closed." Lucian pretended to tip his hat and bow his head. "We will be seeing each other again very soon, my dear."

He nodded to Quinn, Parker and Jax. They all vected away without another word.

The air was thick and hot as Brie's anguish at losing Thelzion left her body in waves. If we couldn't console her soon, we'd all succumb to her pain.

Noella let go of me with a pat to the arm and weak smile.

She dropped down to where Willow was still struggling to heal Kali and laid her hand on top of Willow's. White light joined the green and the skin began to knit itself together more quickly until it was finally closed up.

Brie's state was getting worse by the minute. The wind and heat coming off of her body were increasing and melting everything around her.

Kali sat up with a gasp and Zane broke free of the hold Riedyn and Oaken had on him. He pulled her into his arms and sobbed in relief. Her eyes met his and her sickly grin tugged at my heart.

She tried to stand and he held her tightly, not letting her move an inch.

"I have to go to her," she whispered. Her raw throat burned with the emotions we all felt.

Zane pulled her to a standing position but looked reluctant to let her move away from him.

She smiled up at him and pushed her way through the energy field coming off of Brie's body. It was hot and thick, and practically a forcefield but she pushed through.

Making it to stand in front of her sister, she couldn't speak so well, so she simply hugged her.

Brie thrashed and screamed and thrashed some more but Kali hung on.

Finally, the screams turned into sobs and the sobs turned into trembles and tears.

We could all see how the emotions left Kali's already hurting body raw and bare as she tried to take some of Briella's pain and force comfort onto her. She let her sister collapse in her arms and stroked her head, brushing her fingers through her hair.

Zane came forward and hugged Brie too. Then each of the rest of us gathered around to do the same.

The empaths could feel all of the sorrow, but they would also feel pride coming from us. Resilience. Relief.

Thelzion gave his life for the greater good. He'd earned a place among the heavens. That wasn't an easy feat for a demon. It provided some sense of solace... just not for Brie.

We stayed there for hours. After Briella cried herself to sleep in her sisters' arms, Zane suggested they bring her back to the apartment to stay with them.

Kali nodded. All of us feeling a sigh of relief that the worst was behind us.

I was ready to go home to heal and spend the rest of the day curled up next to Noella.

It was a small consolation for losing our friend, but we had stopped the Breaking from being much worse and thwarted Lucian's goal at the same time.

Now that the veil was gone, we'd have a lot of new consequences to deal with.

That was tomorrow's problem.

For now, we'd won ourselves another day.

Chapter Ninety-Four

Baelyn

It's been over four months since the Breaking. That's what the people of Lagomshire have come to call the event that changed their existence.

The scientists were so intent with testing their experiments for what they wanted to see, they'd never thought about the possible outcome if their experiments didn't go as planned.

The fact that they had no idea how the gods veil worked or that it existed at all, for that matter, had little bearing on their egos.

A fizzle and glow of energy went out once, completely around the world, changing it forever.

When the world changed, it was overwhelming.

Once the frequency shifted, the clarity of the situation was apparent.

Some had great gifts that had been dampened by the veil that was now lifted.

Gifts of sight. Gifts of great empathy. Gifts of problem solving and calculations, amongst other things.

There were also those who were figuring out that, what lived formerly hidden in the shadows, were truly real.

Everyone could now see things of fairytales, folklore, and myth.

I was adjusting to the idea of being part fae rather well.

It had taken me by surprise how great my hearing was now that the constant ringing in my ears had stopped.

My touch often brought about what I wanted from others. Griane had been right about that. It wasn't just the psychology of touching when you spoke.

I could see the other worldly things and the magics. It was strange to suddenly realize that magics were real and that you were part of a realm that you had never known existed.

My apartment was in the heart of a town with one of the most pivotal Nexus. It only added to the eye-opening revelations surrounding me.

I lived there with my sister and only recently found out that she wasn't my sister at all. She was my mother.

I was a freaking Fae Princess like her. It had all been a lot to take in. It took me all these months to start accepting the fact that I wasn't mortal.

Walking around the shops in downtown before the Breaking was one of my favorite things to do on her days off.

I'd would often feel more connected and at home there than most places I'd traveled.

The smell of the garlic and fresh baked bread coming from the shops and the briny scent of the water from the river always put me in such a pleasant state of mind.

Me and my sister, because my refused to call her mother... Griane, made friends with the diner owner, Kraigen before the Breaking.

I loved to sit at the diner, sipping coffee, watching the people shuffling to and fro on the street.

Catching glimpses of things that I thought couldn't be possible before, I knew now that they were actually there.

The gods veil had been lifted. I could see everything. All of the shadow realm was revealed to those who belonged a part of it.

I'd had my first encounter with one of the hateful mortals, who didn't appreciate those who were different from them, about three weeks after the Breaking.

I was at The Shadow Pub, a local bar that I liked to stop at occasionally after work for a drink or two.

My newly pointed ears were hidden under my hair to keep the mortals from gawking.

It was still taking me some time to get used to my new features and the look that Griane sported now that the veil had lifted.

"Where did I put my keys?" I'd asked quietly to myself.

I looked around for a moment and sat back down. Mild frustration itched in my mind and in my fingertips.

No sooner than I'd thought about where my keys could have gotten to, they'd shockingly flew from under a bar stool a couple of seats down and into my hand.

"Ugh", an older man spat. "You're one of those shadow folk, aren't you?!"

Loathing on his face and hostility in his tone had me turning to leave quickly.

The man stood up and strolled over, blocking my path.

"Your Kind make me sick," he said, spitting at my feet. Gross.

I took a step back from the towering figure, but I didn't make any retort. Drunken men didn't respond to reasoning anyway.

From my other side, I could feel the eyes of the patrons lingering on the scene. The bartender, with whom I was friendly, happened to be out back getting another keg or I would have asked him to walk me out.

Attempting to walk around the man again, he stepped back into my path.

Was I going to have to resort to violence just to be able to leave? My fingers itched as I thought about it.

"Babe, are you heading back to the house?" asked a young man coming up beside me.

"What?" I responded stupidly. He was clearly trying to de-escalate my situation.

He wasn't my typical type of handsome but with dark hair and blue eyes that seemed to have a golden haze over them, he was still quite the looker.

More than that, I'd felt like I'd recognized him. I just couldn't place from where.

"We need bread and milk. I have some cash in my car if you want to stop and get some on your way home," he said with a wink that the man couldn't see. "I'll walk you out."

Without even a backwards glance at the drunk man, this familiar stranger took my hand and led me out of the bar.

And I'd let him.

When we'd gotten to my car, he gave me a wry smile.

"Hello, Baelyn."

His face was warm and friendly, and I looked at him with fresh eyes.

A cheery grin shown the dimple on his cheek.

With another wink, I could see what I'd missed before.

I did know this charmer after all.

"Hayden?"

Chapter Ninety-Five

Epilogue

Noella

Lara was tidying up the store when I'd come in with some fresh pastries from the shop around the corner.

Putting them on the counter, I went to the puff chairs in the seating area and plopped down with an exaggerated sigh.

It was my little way of getting Lara's attention when she was in full shop keeper mode.

The sound of the drip, drip, drip from the coffee maker playing on my moody act was a nice addition.

After a few minutes more, Lara retrieved us both a cup of coffee and a couple of pastries before coming to sit next to me.

"Okay, El," she said. "What's with the put upon frown?" A grin pulled at the corner of her delicate mouth.

Arching an eyebrow, I pouted.

"Am I that morose, Sweetpea?" I'd have to work on that. I didn't mean to come off all *put upon.*

The tinkling sound of Lara's laugh brightened my mood considerably. I still had woeful things on my mind but the fact that Lara was safe, alive, and mine made me feel beyond grateful.

"You are who you are, Love." Lara reached out and placed her hand on mine, leaning in for a kiss.

I leaned in too. The moment our lips touched, soft and wet, we both release a pleased sigh.

Leaning back and taking a sip of my hot coffee, I was caught up in thoughts from over the last few months.

The loss of Thelzion, the lifting of the veil, the turmoil of conflict with the mortals who were opposed to magical beings.

It had been exhausting. More than a lot to deal with, some of it was life and death to a few poor new gifters who'd crossed paths with hateful dhalls.

The fact that mine and Lara's relationship had progressed and flourished through all of it made my heart a bit lighter, though shadows still tended to creep in from time to time.

"I ran into one of those magics hating Dhalls in the bakery," I told her after a few more bites of her croissant. "He was blah, blah, blahhing to anyone who stood near him. Such unenlightened dribble."

"We need a name for that kind of Dhall," Lara said. She tapped her finger against the bottom of her lip, lost in thought.

"How about... losers?" I said.

Lara huffed a laugh but kept thinking.

"Maybe we should start calling them Bods."

I looked at her to her, confirming she was serious, and then busted out laughing.

"You think that we should call the deplorable Dhalls the Fae slang word for Dicks?" By the gods, I didn't deserve this wonderful creature.

"I really think we should," Lara said.

It had merit. They were the worst kind of un-evolving being.

"Then we'll spread the word to all of our magics wielding friends. Any Dhall who is hateful towards our type will be known as a Bod!" I said.

We giggled until we were laughed out. When the quiet reigned again, I returned to my previously morose state.

"I heard from Zane today," It wasn't good news he'd had for me. "Kali told him that Brie is hunting every single night." My head hung lower. "She wants to enact revenge on Lucian but hasn't come up with anything to attempt yet."

"So, Kali is still living with her? Zane must be going crazy at the snail pace their relationship is taking."

Zane and Kali's non-relationship wasn't the biggest problem right now. Though it did little to help the situation.

"If you can call it that. He told me Brie is hardly ever there. And when she is, the dark hollowness that radiates from her is nearly unbearable." Thinking of my cousin, I smirked. "Zane is an immortal, but he is definitely not as patient as he should be. He's giving Kalina time to sort it out but in private, he's barely holding himself together."

I took another deep sip of my coffee. The rich aroma soothed my disquieted mind.

"Personally, I'm glad that Brie has Kali there, even if she's hardly home. I can't imagine what it's like for her to even come back to the house that she and Thelzion had shared without him there."

I knew that Lara felt horrible over it all. She'd blamed herself for getting taken.

Hayden had been willing to throw away the world to keep her alive and I couldn't bring myself to hate him for that.

Thelzion gave his life away to keep the world safe for Briella and the rest of us.

Lara wasn't upset with him anymore. She was having a hard time dealing with it all. With all of the pain and loss.

The last time Lara had seen him, Bastian was dragging him out of the shop as she and Hayden were yelling back and forth at each other.

She hadn't spoken to him since and I knew it was hurting her preciously soft heart.

"I wish there was something that we could do for her." There was something my little seer wasn't saying.

Lara sat with her hands folded in her lap. A mischievous grin lit up her eyes as she smiled.

"What?" I asked. "Why the big grin?"

"I may have a crazy idea," she shrugged. "I think it's worth a try though."

We shared a look, but Lara pressed her lips into a hard line and said no more.

I understood that she didn't want to give anyone false hope. Lara had filled me in on what had happened while I had been in the Low Realm.

The Goddess owed her a favor, but I wondered what Hecate's divine limits might be if my lover asked for a life...

Queen Talisin

"Your Majesty," Riedyn said as he approached the throne. "I have confirmed my suspicions." He bowed his head and offered her the enchanted leaf he possessed.

"You're one hundred percent sure that this half fae is my granddaughter?" I asked.

As much as I longed for hope, hope was the one thing I couldn't allow to cloud my heart or my resolve.

"Yes, my Queen. She is Griane's child." He backed away from the dais and rose to his full height.

My eyes stared nowhere but straight ahead. I refused to let the tears fall as they brimmed my lower lids.

"And what of my daughter? Does she live?" My voice low and hollow in my own ears. The ache in my chest made my heart beat painfully against the cage of my ribs.

Commander Riedyn lowered his head and spoke to his feet. "She lives, your Majesty."

I swallowed the sadness that had been building inside the chasm her absence had caused.

Clenching my fists and drawing blood from my palms with her nails, the hurt was replaced by anger.

"Bring her to me."

Riedyn looked up from his feet and took in the scowl on my face.

"As you wish, my Queen."

I hope you enjoyed Book 1 of the Veil & Shadow Series. Stay tuned for Book 2; The Bleeding... Coming Soon.

ANEXIAN SCRIPT
A B C D E F G H
I J K L M N O P
Q R S T U V
W X Y Z

Acknowledgements

I want to say thank you to my husband, Tim. Without his love and support I would be lost. He goes above and beyond whenever I need anything. His light gave me a safe space to blossom.

Thank you to my mom, Sandra Kay, for reading my writing and not backing down whenever I needed the push to keep going forward, especially with edits that seemed never ending.

Thank you to Laura, Ashley, Keay, Kayla. They gave me direction and motivation to get on the right tracks. And I want to give a shout out to my friends, Kristina, Beth, Lisa, LeAnn & Angel who had to listen to my meandering tangents of thoughts during the whole process.

And I know they can't read this, but I want to give big love and smooches to my dogs. They were my constant companions while I was writing. I'd forget to eat or drink or do many numerous other adulting things but they would sense if I needed a break and make me take one.

About the Author
Anexa O. Saphire

I was born in Maryland and love steamed crabs. I moved to Florida for a few decades but have moved back to Maryland recently. I love to write, create art, read, and sing. I've become extremely introverted as I have gotten older, but I do still love going out for an occasional night of karaoke. My hubby and I live a simple, quiet life with our furbabies. Life becomes simpler once you let yourself dream and let go of whatever holds you down.